Demonic Anthologies Vol. II

I0591153

Demonic Anthologies Vol. II

• Arielle Haughee • Brandon Mead • Christina Bergling •
• Cindy Marie Jenkins • Clint Doyle • Erica Gerald Mason •
• F. D. Gross • Fern Goodman • J. P. Dildine • Jeremy Rodden •
• Jon Park • K. Walker • Kathleen Lopez • Kerry Evelyn •
• Kim Plasket • Kristin Durfee • L. E. Perez • Larry Griffin •
• Lee Franklin • Meg Sefton • Mark McWaters • Marya Miller •
• Maxine Grey • Paige Lavoie • Rita Sotolongo • Ross Ellison •
• Teresa Edmond-Sargeant • Vanessa Valiente •

4 Horsemen
Publications, Inc.

4 Horsemen Publications, Inc.
1497 Main St. Suite 169
Dunedin, FL 34698
4horsemenpublications.com
info@4horsemenpublications.com

Cover & Typesetting by 4 Horsemen Publications, Inc.

Paperback ISBN-13: 978-1-64450-636-3
Ebook ISBN-13: 978-1-64450-637-0

DEDICATION

To the Authors within and their families. Without you and your patience,
there would be no collection to share with the world. May the rest
of 2018 and the years to follow be fruitful for you all and here's to a
wonderous journey.

ACKNOWLEDGEMENTS

I want to say thank you to everyone who continues to cheer me on. No amount of words could express how much you have help keep my morale and spirit high in the lowest moment this year alone.

A special thank you to those who help make this anthology come together goes to Maxine Groves, Michael Bray, Kim Plasket, Ryan O'Reilly, Karen Webster, all the authors who submitted, and of course, the readers who gave support for the first volume, *Demonic Wildlife*.

Thank you to my husband, Justin, and the boys, Levi & Link, for being understanding and patient with Mommy's hard work and devotion.

To my writing villages here in Orlando, Florida which include Writer's Atelier and Racquel Henry, Anthony Awtrey & L.E. Perez with Orlando East Writers Group, and the misfit crew from Writers of Central Florida & Thereabouts.

READERS BEWARE

You are traveling into a dark and humorous place. We start you off with light, soft stories, but be warned.

You will find yourself falling into the ever darker, gorier, and more demonic stories with each passing page.

You may look at your couch, your washer, and even television and wonder if you should be laughing anymore.

Will your household turn on you?

Keep your Owner's Manuals close by!

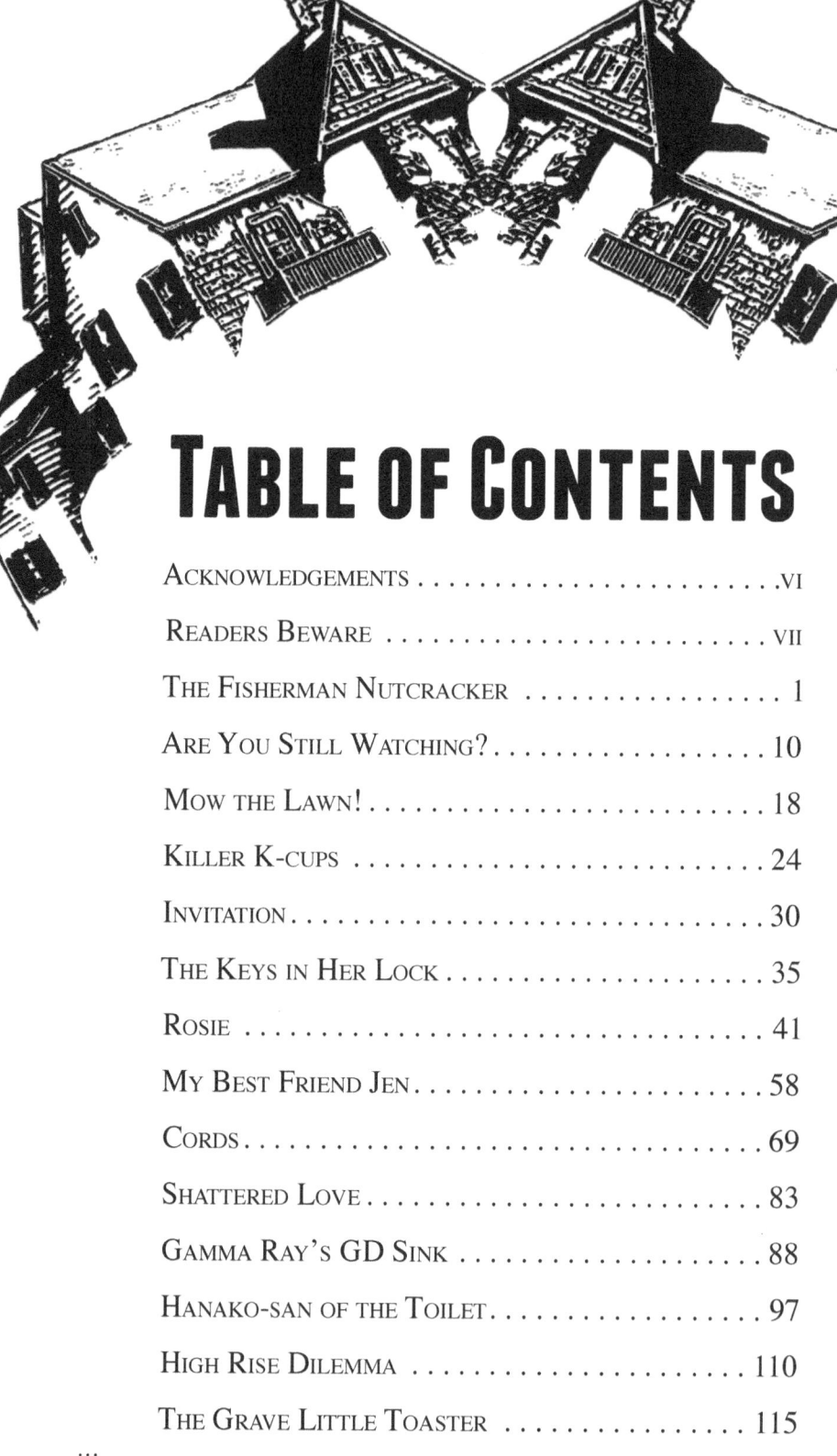

TABLE OF CONTENTS

THE FISHERMAN NUTCRACKER

BY KERRY EVELYN

NUTCRACKER

Was that…sunlight? I'd been in the dark so long I'd forgotten the blinding power of the sun. I snapped my eyes shut. The surface under me shifted. A need to get to the light consumed me.

"Did you hear that?" The high pitched feminine voice grated my eardrums.

"Hear what?" Another young female, with a lower voice.

"I think that box is moving." The first voice again. A box?

I felt them approach before I could see them. The filmy fabric that had served as my bonds was removed. Dare I open my eyes?

"It kinda looks like the wooden sailor figures my grandpa has on his mantle. Have you ever seen anything like it?" The first girl asked.

"Hmmm…" The second girl. "No. What about you, Meggie?" She got closer, and I could feel her breath on my face. "I think it might be a nutcracker."

1

"I think you're right, Mellie." A third young lady. "I wonder why it's painted with its eyes closed."

Maybe because it didn't want to be disturbed from its sleep, I thought. I slowly lifted one eyelid. I was right. Directly above, three adolescent girls gathered around me. Well, if I couldn't rest, then I would have a little fun.

I opened my eyes.

The first girl screamed. "Did you see that?!" I stared at her.

"Oh my goodness! The eyes are open!" The one called Meggie started to shake. "I swear they were closed. Maddie, when you found it, they were closed, right?"

"Uh-huh, I swear it!" That Maddie's voice was as high-pitched as I've ever heard.

"Hold on a sec." The quiet one leaned in curiously and stuck her hand out toward me. It cupped my back and she lifted me up. I held her gaze.

With gentle care, she looked me up and down, examined every inch of me and I was glad I was wearing my finest yellow rain slicker. She stroked my beard then set me to rest upright on a flat surface.

I didn't like the way they stared at me. I shift my eyes to my left. A gargantuan brown box sat at the other end of the plane. Had I been in there?

Mellie leaned in and looked me right in the eyes. "There's a story Old Man Wetherby told me once about his father. His dad had been lost at sea when he was just a boy."

This girl was smart. Her friends leaned in. I knew this story. I was this story.

"His dad had been captaining a ship that was returning to port. He said they must have been trying to beat the squall, but they didn't make it."

We had been trying to beat the squall. The crew hadn't seen their families in months. To sail around the storm would have meant days of delay. The crew had unanimously voted to push on.

"What happened?" Meggie asked.

"The ship crashed on the rocks, and went down. All on board drowned. In the next few weeks, things from the wreck began to turn up on the beach. Old Man Wetherby collected everything he could. He told me his favorite thing was a fisherman nutcracker. He said it reminded him of his dad. I bet this is it."

"Oh, wow," Maddie said. "I wonder how it ended up in the donation box, then, if he liked it so much?"

"I don't know." Mellie frowned. "Probably no one realized what it was. He said he had lost a box of his stuff when he moved after his father died. Do you think we should save it for him? Let him decide?"

Donation box? I'd been sleeping in a donation box?

"Yes, let's do that," Meggie agreed. "Mellie, maybe your mom can stop at the Roosevelt on our way home?"

The Roosevelt? The asylum? It had been a long time since I had thought about that place. What was my son doing there?

"I'm sure she can. Let me text her." The Mellie girl held up a rectangular device and drew on it with her index finger. She paused, then slid her finger on it again. "Mom says sure, just be ready 15 minutes earlier than we had planned to leave." She lifted me up and stared at me again. "I could have sworn his eyes were painted shut when we found him. I must be so tired my eyes are playing tricks on me."

No, missy, er - Mellie. Your eyes were not playing tricks on you. Heehee!

"Should we bring the whole box?" Maggie asked.

"Nah. Looks like there's just some old curtains and dishtowels. Those can go." Mellie carried me to higher surface. From my new vantage point, I could see we were in the back of a church. Awareness dawned. The half-dozen stained glass Tiffany windows on either side were the same as they'd been in my youth. Gone were the whitewashed family seating boxes and plain white benches behind them. In their place were rows of finely-polished pews that rivaled the fanciest I'd seen in the cathedrals overseas. Someone had taken great care creating them. How long had I been sleeping?

I watched the girls for a while. They had a handful of boxes set up on their table, and were sorting items into bigger bins under the table. Toys, home goods, clothing, books, etc. Kinds of things I'd never seen before. How long *had* I been sleeping?

I almost jumped when the sound of "Revelry" began to play. I stood at attention. I searched for a trumpet player with my eyes, but didn't see anyone else in the room. Turned out it was that girl's device. Strange kind of magic, it was.

"Time to meet Mom." The girls headed toward me. Maddie picked me up. "Eyes are definitely open."

She carried me down the side of the pews to the doorway situated behind the altar to the reception area in the back of the church. That was different, too. A beautifully polished desk matched a wardrobe behind it to the left. A bible verse was painted on the wall to the right of it. *And Jesus said unto them, Follow me, and I will make you fishers of men*. Matthew 4:19. How quaint for a seaside town.

"You girls ready to go?" The lady who was presumably Mellie's mother held a large bag on her shoulder and keys in her hand. She peered at me and raised her eyebrow. "What is that?"

I tried not to be insulted. It was a fair question.

"It's a nutcracker, Miss Tracy!" Maddie explained.

"See, Mom?" Mellie rotated me until I was belly-down on her palm and wiggled my lever. I laughed.

"Huh." Her mother grunted. "All right, then. Let's go."

In a second, I was tossed into a deep cavernous sack, being jostled among the girl Mellie's personal effects. My head landed near the rectangular device and it lit up, displaying a glowing image of a horse's face.

I abhor horses.

I concentrated my thoughts and willed it to go away. It flew out of the bag. Did I do that?

"Oops!" Meggie exclaimed. "Dropped my phone! Guess I missed tossing it into my tote." "Oh darn, the screen is cracked." That thing was a phone? Must be witchcraft!

"Oh no!" Maggie's figure cast a shadow over me. "Does it still work?"

"Yes, for now at least." Mellie frowned. "I'll keep it in my pocket til I can get it fixed. I should have gotten a screen protector."

The bag was set down on a surface and it began vibrating. Must be in a vehicle of some sort. Smooth ride. It came to a stop about ten minutes later and the sack was tossed again. This time I was face up on top of a spiky hair brush. Well, that had to go.

"Mellie, you dropped your brush," Maddie said.

"Thanks!"

"Geez, girl, you're a mess," the older woman proclaimed. "Get it together."

"Yes, Mom."

With every step, the sack banged up against the girl and everything shifted. By the time she pulled me out, I was head-down and wedged between two smaller zippered sacks. Women. Doesn't matter the age. They all seem to need to carry everything they own on them everywhere they go.

"Have a seat and make yourselves comfortable," an authoritative voice instructed. The girls gabbed and I tried not to listen.

Suddenly a familiar voice caught my attention. It sounded just like my father.

"Well, well, what a nice surprise!" The old man's voice froze me. Could it be? "Four lovely visitors come to visit a cranky old man!"

"Hi, Mr. Wetherby!"

"Hey, Charley," Mellie's mom greeted the voice. Charley? My Charley? That couldn't be right. My Charley couldn't be that old. He was just a boy. I needed to see for myself.

"We found something we think belongs to you in a donation box," Mellie explained. "I just wanted to make sure you wanted to get rid of it." Her hands closed around me inside the sack. "Kat may not have known when she was packing up your things, but I remembered a story you told me."

Mellie lifted me out of the sack and set me on a surface. I blinked. In front of me was an old man who resembled my father, down to the short white fuzz on his chin. But it couldn't be.

He leaned in until his face was only an inch away. "Oh, yes, I remember this," he whispered. "It belonged to my father. I haven't seen it since before Mother and I moved in with the Captain."

It *was* my boy. Charley Wetherby was no longer the young lad I'd left behind on my last voyage. He had to be pushing eighty by the looks of him. What year was it? How long had I been trapped inside this wooden host?

He lifted me into his hands gently. We swiveled and glided for a moment and stopped in between a couch and a wingchair. Was he in a wheelchair? I strained to see. The sitting room at the asylum had changed, but the red brick fireplace was the same. Why was my son in the asylum? Above it hung a portrait of Theodore Roosevelt, who had visited our area of Maine when I was young. It had made a real impression on me that someone would have that much money and donate it so that land could become a National Park. But what a fine park Acadia National Park was. They'd named this place after him.

"Thanks, Mellie." His voice cracked. "This is definitely not something I want to donate." He looked away from me. "Do they all know the story?" he asked her.

"I don't think so. Truthfully, I don't remember all of it. Maybe you could retell it?"

He nodded. From where I laid on a quilt in his lap I had a perfect view of him. His face, old and weathered, crinkled as he fought back tears. Good boy. Crying is for women.

"I was born during the Great Depression. My father was a Great War veteran who became a fisherman after the war. He was captain of the ship and he'd go out for months at a time. The Maritime Academy was new back then, and this place was an asylum for the afflicted. Both his parents were patients here, and times were hard for my mother when he was gone. The academy offered him a job, and he accepted. He just had to get through one last fishing trip. No one really knows what happened."

He looked down at me, as if I could answer him. I wished I could. Maybe I could get into his thoughts.

"A storm came up suddenly. We were all worried because it was during the time frame they were expected back in Winter Harbor."

He took a deep breath. I could have heard a pin drop.

"If they had sailed around it, it would have delayed their return. He would have missed his first day at his new job."

He stroked my face. I wished I could explain.

"Residents at the Point claim to have seen the schooner sailing by as lightning struck. The next day, the ship was sighted crashed up against the rocks. Things began to float to shore."

"Wow, I'm so sorry," the girl called Meggie sounded so sad.

"How old were you?" Mellie asked.

"I was six." He looked at me, as if he could see right through me. Maybe he could. I closed my eyes, and opened them again. *I'm so sorry, son. Look at me.*

He looked down at me. His Adam's apple bobbed as he swallowed. His eyes bored into me.

I know. We were okay, Dad.

Was I really hearing his thoughts? Or was that my imagination?

"That must have been so horrible for you." Mellie's mother touched his shoulder. "No wonder you came back when Kat's parents and grandparents were lost in their own horrific shipwreck."

He didn't answer right away, rubbing the back of his head, his incredulous expression still trained on me. "Yes, ma'am. I left for the Marines as soon as I was able. I hated my stepfather. My mother remarried quick. Captain Huttleston was my dad's friend and he was kind to her. He didn't know what to do with me. I was a mess. I wish I had been different." He looked right at me. "I know my father was doing what he thought was best, taking a job close to home to take care of us all. When he went missing, I felt abandoned."

Oh, kid. That was never my intention. I just wanted to get home to my family.

"Mom had run out of money while he was away. She took in laundry work just to feed us. Dad had told her that my grandfather had hidden money somewhere in the house before they moved to the asylum. We searched that house up and down, inside and out. Never found it. We came here to see if we could get answer from him. He just kept repeating the word, 'Teddy' and staring at the portrait up there." He shook his head. "No one ever knew what happened to the money."

"Hmm…" Sneakered feet padded over the hardwood floors. "Maybe it was clue."

"He was just a crazy old man. He and my grandmother got what we now call Alzheimer's' early on. Sometimes they didn't even know who we were."

"Maddie, Meggie, come here. Let's see what's behind this."

"Mellie, who do you think you are, Nancy Drew?" Mellie's mother chastised. "Don't wreck that ancient thing."

I couldn't see what they were doing. I concentrated with all strength to try to shift my position. *Tell them to pull out the brick.*

"Pull out the brick?" he asked.

"That's my plan," Mellie said. Good. She was smarter than I thought.

"Dad?" Charley whispered. "Your eyes are glowing."

Well, how about that. *I want to see.* He rotated me to face the fireplace. The girls took great care to lift the painting from its anchors. They set it on the ground. Mellie stepped up onto the base of the fireplace and ran her fingers along the bricks.

"This one is loose!"

Well, how about that.

"Mom, do you have a nail file?" Wordlessly, Tracy reached in her handbag and pulled out a metal nail file. Her daughter took it and began to scrape around the loose brick. Her friends stood on either side of her. Charley and I watched along with bated breath.

Mellie pulled the brick out and peered inside the hole. "There's something in there!"

Her friends stepped up next to her. "What is it?" Maddie asked.

"I'm not sure." She stuck her hand in. "Feels like velvet." She pulled out a long black pouch about the size of a shoe and held it up. "You should open it," she said as she offered the pouch to Charley.

"I can't believe it. After all this time…" Charley was clearly unprepared. I was a bit surprised myself. But only a bit. My father had always been full of surprises.

Charley propped me on his lap and took the pouch. I watched as he reached in and pulled out a wad of war bonds.

"Holy Mary, Mother of God," he whispered. "They're all issued to my father." Tears streamed down his cheeks. He looked up at Mellie. "Thank you," he croaked.

"That is so cool," Meggie breathed. "What's that all worth?"

"A lot," Tracy said. She looked at me. "Um, that thing's eyes are glowing…"

"It's priceless," Charley said, ignoring Tracy's comment. "He didn't leave us high and dry after all. I wonder why my grandfather hid this in the chimney?"

I wondered that, too. Crazy old man.

A flash lit up the room. There was a loud crack and I felt as if I was being torn in two. Another flash. Rain pelted my face as I slid down the deck toward violent, salty waves. A final flash and my eyes closed, as the sea took me down, down to where I should have perished all those years ago…

The Fisherman Nutcracker ©2018 by Kerry Evelyn

Dedicated to my Dad, Vic Robitaille, whose wooden fisherman carvings and nautical decor inspired this story.

Special thanks to Val for this opportunity, Chelsea for being a rockstar, and to my beta readers, Kailyn T. and Daley F. for their feedback and suggestions!

KERRY EVELYN

Kerry Evelyn has always been fascinated by people and the backstories that drive them to do what they do. A native of the Massachusetts SouthCoast, she changed her latitude in 2002 and is now a crazy blessed wife and homeschooling mom in Orlando. When she's not teaching or writing, she's mentoring moms through Mom Mastery University, sharing essential oils, and planning super fun events for her kids and their friends (although her own kids have yet to be impressed, being that every event has some sort of learning involved, thanks to her earlier career as an elementary school teacher). She loves God, books of all kinds, traveling, taking selfies, sweet drinks, and escaping into her imagination, where every child is happy and healthy, every house has a library, and her hubby wears coattails and a top hat 24/7.

Website: www.KerryEvelyn.com

Blog: www.KerryEvelyn.com/blog

Amazon Author Page: https://www.amazon.com/Kerry-Evelyn/e/B077LWTYXJ/ref=sr_ntt_srch_lnk_1?qid=1527009617&sr=8-1

Link to photo of fisherman nutcracker: https://www.amazon.com/Nantucket-Home-Fisherman-Christmas-Nutcracker/dp/B017SOO3O8/ref=sr_1_1_sspa?ie=UTF8&qid=1527009671&sr=8-1-spons&keywords=fisherman+nutcracker&psc=1

Facebook: www.Facebook.com/KerryEvelynAuthor

Twitter: @theKerryEvelyn

Instagram: @KerryEvelynAuthor

Are You Still Watching?

By Kathleen Lopez

DVR Box

Ding

The comforting low-toned ding of the TeVo chimed as I accessed the Guide button on the remote. It was a cold and rainy Sunday, and with nothing really to do, television seemed like a great time waster. Yes, there was laundry, but there would always be laundry, so it could wait a bit more. At least it was clean, folding would come later.

The TeVo sounded as I flipped through the program guide trying to find something that was just enough to keep me interested.

Boop

Boop

While the idea of a nap was intriguing, I found myself channel surfing. I clicked the TeVo button on the remote to pull up my recorded shows. The DVR was nearly full, so I figured I would settle in for a long viewing binge. I scanned the various viewing options and saw a folder with several episodes of my guilty pleasure, Supernatural. There were several weeks' worth of episodes, some I have seen, some not. But it was Supernatural, so whether I have seen it before or not was irrelevant. I browsed through My Shows, found the Supernatural folder, and scrolled to the first in the list and pressed play.

By the middle of the third episode into my marathon, I was curled up on the couch, partially ensconced in a thick fuzzy blanket. On the floor in front of me were a few snack wrappers I grabbed between the first and second shows. I grabbed a large drink and a few items to nibble on, so I would not have to leave the comfort of my darkened den.

Third episode done, I immediately clicked over to the fourth one listed on the DVR. Sitting alone, curled up on the couch, and getting lost in my show was a perfect way to waste the day. As I clicked onto the fourth episode however, I noticed the show was taking a bit of time to load. That stupid circle swirly thing kept going around and around while my show was loading.

"What the hell? Come on you stupid TeVo, work," I muttered aloud to no one. Well at least I thought there was no one listening. As soon as the words left my lips, the DVR froze. The stupid circle swirly thing stopped, the live stream of the TV channel up in the corner froze, it all just stopped.

"Seriously? You're going to die on me now?" I huffed in frustration as I started at a frozen television screen. That is when I truly realized, I may not have been alone. Suddenly the screen dulls and a message scrawls across the screen:

"Are you still watching?"

For a moment I wondered if I switched over to Netflix and was staring at that automatic message that appears after you left a series of episodes running end to end. I blinked at the screen confused for a moment.

"Yea, I'm sure I..." I trailed off my audible outburst trying to recall my wits at the moment. Then I looked closer at the screen. There was no Yes or No options to click, just the message blaring at me.

"So how do I get out of this? Yes, you friggin' TeVo. I was watching that." Again, without warning, the fourth episode loaded and started to play.

"What the hell was that all about?" I wondered aloud, but soon became disinterested in the temporary dilemma as the show's opener played. Everything was right as rain again, just as the aforementioned weather pounded on the windows as the storm kicked up a few notches. The room grew darker, and it may have been my perception, but felt a few degrees cooler than it had moments ago. I snuggled in deeper to the plush blanket and watched Sam and Dean try to determine if it was 'old man Jenkins' in the monster mask that was terrorizing the town.

Just as it was getting to the good part, the one where the big revelation is discovered, the damn TeVo locked up again. I grunted in frustration.

"Damn it. You have like one job to do!"

"Don't *you* have a job to do?"

I stared slack jawed at the screen. The retort to my complaint practically glowed brighter than the last commentary my TeVo decided to share with me. The 'you' in the text was actually italicized as if to add attitude to the commentary being displayed. Again, there was no mechanical way to respond to the message, judgmental as it was, despite my automatic reaction of aiming the remote in the direction of the television.

"Just play the damn show," I found myself shouting at the TV. After a moment's hesitation, the show resumed. I was dumbfounded at the exchange. This time, I was not so dismissive at what had just occurred. A bit preoccupied with the interruption, I finished watching the show.

Once the show was over, the standard message asking if I wish to keep or delete the show appeared and I responded with 'Delete'. I sat there staring at the menu, hesitant as to whether to continue with my marathon. I questioned the very nature of what I thought I saw.

"Maybe I'm just tired and I thought I saw that," I mumbled. "There's no way...I mean really." I found myself once again just staring at the television. Cautiously I clicked the remote and selected the next show.

Boop...Boop

I inhaled and pressed play.

Boop

"Really this is all you're going to do today?" appeared instead of my intended show.

I glared at the screen. No more was I confused or concerned at what was happening. I found myself angry.

"Yes seriously, this is my plan for the day. I am going to sit here and watch my show, and you're going to sit there and play my show. That's how this is going to work."

I was astounded at what was happening. I was yelling at my TeVo as if it was sentient or something. In a moment I would realize that perhaps it was not just all in my head.

"Yes, this is what I do, but this is not all that you do. Or is it? Is this your best plan for the day? Sitting like a lump becoming completely unproductive? At least I am doing something."

Holy crap! I just got bitch-slapped by my TeVo? I was now all wound up. I re-read the message as if I had perhaps indeed have had a stroke. Nope. There it was, emblazed across my screen defiantly. I had had it and officially lost my mind.

"Listen here you piece of…"

"Name calling. A sign of intelligence. Get that from sitting on your ass all day, do you?"

I was floored. What the hell was happening here. Was my TeVo hacked? Could you hack a TeVo? Who knows today, but something, or rather someone was responding to me. I began to wonder if my house was bugged or something. Not that I am anyone to bug, but what other explanation was there to this behavior. Some bored teenage geeks with nothing better to do hacked into my TeVo and decided to slowly drive me nuts. That had to be it. Anything else was crazy.

"Stunned silence. That's what you have for me? Well let me see who I'm dealing with here, shall we. Ah, at least there is no reality television in your season pass list. Nothing like watching others have a life as you just sit and watch. Typical shows, nothing exciting here. Ooh, what's this? You have a documentary in your To Do list. Trying to educate yourself, huh? How's that going for you?"

The rambling commentary of my viewing habits scrolled up my screen like a teleprompter gone mad. I sat glued to the screen, digesting every word as it appeared. This was happening. This was really happening. My TeVo continued to remark on its take on my scheduled and previous recorded shows, going as far as ranking them as to quality. I watched as the TeVo systematically analyzed each viewing option listed. As crazy as it sounded, some of the observations were actually informative.

"Viewership is dropping for this one," the TeVo critique continued. "So, don't expect for this to be back next season."

It was the snarky-ness that I could have done without in all honesty. But given the nature in which the TeVo was *speaking* so frankly, I could not help but get swept up into a conversation with it.

"Really? You know the book of this movie was waaay better. Oh, sorry. Given how much is in your queue, do you not read?"

I bolted up from my spot on the couch, offended slightly at the retort.

"Given my schedule, I don't have time to read," I said in justification of my viewing habits. I stood in front of my television with my arms outstretched as if my posture would emphasize my point. Then the realization hit me, the DVR probably could not see me. Feeling a bit foolish, I lowered my arms and waited for its reply.

"Well if you cut out some of these lower rated shows I highlighted here," as the screen lit up with various shows appearing as selected at once, "then you would have a few hours freed up, so you can expand your mind by reading. Or at the least, run a vacuum over the floor; it couldn't hurt you know."

Now I was getting suspicious. Yes, like the laundry, the vacuuming was yet another chore I was putting off. How did my DVR know that?

"Gotcha!" I barked. I figured now I had them, those pesky kids who I had imagined hacked into my TeVo. There is no way my TeVo would know if I had been derelict in my cleaning regimen. That was outside of its operating system. "How do you know I haven't vacuumed unless you can see that I haven't! Who are you? Where are you? Do you have a camera in here somewhere?"

I started to feel paranoid. I whipped my head from side to side, scanning my room for some spy tech or something. Not that I would know what I was looking for really. The pang of the TeVo brought my attention back to the screen.

DING

"Sorry. Had to get your attention. I know you haven't vacuumed, or rather assumed, given that I share a plug outlet with where you would plug in the vacuum. Again, I assume this is the case as I feel the power fluctuate occasionally and I suspected it was due to you plugging in a vacuum."

I stood frozen after reading that message. I did use that outlet for the vacuum. The assumption was valid. It made rational sense. Let me wrap my head around this...my TeVo made a rational argument that I have not vacuumed my living room. I realized this was logical. I discovered that I was slowly abandoning my notion that I was being spied on and that I was communicating with my TeVo. This could all be a dream, I thought. I could have fallen asleep during my marathon and be dreaming this whole thing. I was watching Supernatural, it could have affected the idea of the dream, right?

Or maybe there was a surge in power due to the storm. Maybe a lightning strike fried the TeVo circuitry and it has gone haywire. That could be a reason why my TeVo started acting as if was possessed. While these were plausible explanations, I decided to continue the conversation with my TeVo. I found that I was more intrigued with the phenomenon than I was concerned as to why it started in the first place.

"You do have a point. But it is a rainy day and I just wanted to veg-out. Do I seriously have to be judged merely cause I want to watch my shows? I said it before, that's your job, to record my shows so I can watch them later. Isn't that some prime directive of yours to provide that service?"

"Prime directive? You segued into Star Trek there, huh? Yes, you have a point, but you had sat for like four hours before I intervened. That is a long time to veg-out as you put it."

Again, I found myself agreeing with the device. The concept seemed odd, but started to become strangely natural, comforting almost. It was a peculiar sensation to say the least.

"Well I have nothing to really do today, other than the vacuuming and laundry," I begrudgingly admitted.

"Well I do not know about the laundry as I do not share electricity with that unit."

Fair enough.

"How about this, I'll watch the next episode while folding the laundry. Sounds good, you judgmental little bastard," I said sweetly. "Then I would be actually doing something, rather than just zoning out. I mean come on… you pulled this crap with a cliff hanger episode. Not fair."

The TeVo was dormant for a moment. It was as if it was considering the compromise. Then the screen illuminated with its reply.

"Sounds like a deal. But dare I ask for something in return?"

What on Earth could the TeVo want in return, I wondered. I responded with little hesitation despite my confusion. A bit curious as to the pending request.

"Sure. Whatcha got for me?"

"Read me something. Nothing that was made into a TV movie. Something different. Something you haven't seen a version of before. While some of these shows are good, funny, whatever, I'd like something new."

It seemed like a decent request. One that was not outrageous for the TeVo to ask for after all, I thought. Okay, let me wrap my head around that idea for a moment.

"Alright. Sure. I can do that. So, just so we're clear…one more episode as I fold the laundry, then story time?"

"Yes. I promise. I'll even skip the commercials for you."

To my surprise, that was the clencher. It could not get better than that. "Deal!"

The next hour had me finding out what happened to the Winchester boys while getting my laundry done. I found myself talking aloud to the episode with the TeVo quietly responding, in the form of close captions. With the episode, and laundry, done, I popped up off the couch and headed over to the bookshelf. I picked up a book I surely have not seen or viewed before. I announced my choice of literature for approval.

"Now given you've judged my viewing habits, don't judge me on this. I don't typically read these types of books, but my friend said she loved it and lent me her copy. It's a trashy romance novel; certainly nothing I've viewed on TV. What do you think?"

Again, the TeVo was still for a moment.

"It is a change from what I typically listen to given your viewing habits. Sure. Let's try that then."

With the choice of book agreed upon, I sat down on the sofa once more, adjusted my comfy blanket, and flipped through the book to get an idea of what I was in for in the read. My eye caught a very saucy section and knew this was going to be a page turner. I snuggled in deeper to my lush cocoon and returned to the first page.

"Well, let's see what you'll have to say about this."

KATHLEEN LOPEZ

Dr. Kathleen Lopez started writing at fourteen, a junior high journalist. She continued her passion for writing short stories and poetry after graduating college. Writing was never just a hobby, but a way of life. As an Indie Author, she released suspenseful romance, thrillers, murder-mysteries, and paranormal stories that draw the reader in and take them along for the journey.

www.imkathleenlopez.com
www.facebook.com/imkathleenlopez
@imkathleenlopez
https://www.amazon.com/default/e/B00HCMFR4I/

Mow the Lawn!

By L. E. Perez

Mower

Chapter One

I waited. I knew she would have to come here eventually and when she did I would have a chance to let her know who was more important.

I mean really, how dare she assume I couldn't do the job I was asked to do? I was just as powerful, just as quick and if truth be told, I was also easier to manage. But no, instead she ignored me. Acted like I wasn't even there.

She didn't care for me the way she did for the others. Granted I was nowhere near as pretty. I had a habit of quitting halfway, which she hated, but I was dependable. Dammit, I was more than that. I was the best damned lawnmower she'd ever owned!

I heard the back door open and waited. She had no clue I could sense her. I was 4 years old. Older than the other yard equipment but the only one she hadn't replaced. Yet.

It was only a matter of time, but I would prove myself to her, I would.

Mow the Lawn!

Debra took a deep breath before stepping out into the backyard. She hated yard work, but more than that she hated using the lawnmower.

It gave her the heebie jeebies whenever she put her hands on it. Needless to say, she used it as little as possible. She didn't know what it was.

She liked to think of herself as a practical woman. An empty nester, she had raised her kids and welcomed the peace and quiet. Only it wasn't quiet. There was something very strange about her backyard always had been, but she hadn't noticed until now. Now that she was alone.

She headed toward the shed and looked around at all the overgrown grass. *This rain is for the birds.* Every week for the past month she'd had to pull out the weed whacker and the lawnmower to get the grass down to where it was manageable. She was damned tired of it.

She stopped in front of the shed and hesitated, flexing her ankle. The lawnmower had bogged down last week when it went over a branch and she had tumbled over it spraining her ankle. It was a tiny branch. The mower should have been able to chew it up easily, but it hadn't.

Yanking the doors open she shrieked. A gecko balanced precariously on the lawn mower jumped at her.

"Ew…ew…ew…" The only thing worse than a palmetto bug was a gecko.

Shaking out her hands she reached for the lawnmower and paused. It wasn't where she left it.

"What the blazes?"

A low rumble in the distance made her reach back out. She wanted to be sure to get the lawn done before the rain started but now she was more freaked out than she was before.

I could feel myself start to rev up but I controlled myself Doing that certainly wouldn't get her to trust me, so I waited as her hand reached for me.

She had to admit it was freaking her out a bit. Maybe she was mistaken, but she could swear she had put the mower over in the back corner of the shed. Mostly because it did give her the willies and she didn't like seeing it first thing.

Debra bit her lip and pulled out her cell phone. The mower was primed and ready to go, but she still had questions. The text she sent her son was simple.

'Did you borrow the mower? If so, please put it back in the corner next time.'

Her son's response was immediate.

'What are you talking about Ma?'

She froze. He didn't move it.

'Forget it. My mistake. Love u'

She shoved her phone back into her cargo shorts and took a step back. Her imagination was getting the better of her. Another rumble created a sense of urgency and she reached for the mower again despite her misgivings.

I glared the way only I could. I knew why she hesitated. I should have stayed put. I don't know who she was texting but she didn't look happy. When she shoved the phone back in her pocket, I waited to be ignored again. Waited for her to put me back and reach for the weed whacker. She didn't. Her hand on me was electric. Didn't she feel it? I did.

Debra was losing her mind. She had never truly been alone. She left her mother's house and moved in with her husband at nineteen, had kids, and lived her life with others. Now, she was alone. With her husband Gabe's passing, and the kids grown and gone, she finally got to experience it, adulthood, being alone. She didn't like it. She saw movement where there wasn't any and let her imagination run away with her when it came to the lawnmower.

The lawnmower. It was Gabe's. He died using it. Maybe that was what bothered her.

Debra primed it and yanked on the cord. It started right up with a growl that sent a shiver up her spine. Mowing the lawn was usually soothing, like her gardening, but not today. With a storm approaching the air felt heavy, thick and thinking about the upcoming weekend was discouraging.

Mow the Lawn!

The anniversary of Gabe's death. Anger filled her at the thought and she kicked it.

The mower bogged down momentarily and revved back up in earnest. She was determined to avoid the spot where they found him until it was all that was left to mow. Twenty minutes and god only knew how many calories burned later she stood there staring at the patch of grass.

She could still see Gabe as she'd found him. Slumped over the lawn-mower as he wrestled for the last time with the primer bulb. Stupid lawn-mower, damned aneurysm.

She kicked it again. This time it bogged down completely, jerking and shuddering before shutting off.

"Flipping great."

She wiped at her tear stained face and yanked on the starter again. Once, twice, it started on the third pull but by that time she was exhausted. A drop of rain kicked up some dirt and she cursed. She was running out of time. She let the engine rev before moving forward. A couple of passes and she should be done.

She kicked me. Why did she do that? Didn't she know we were connected? I would do anything for her. I started right up for her and still she kicked me. We were passing over the spot soon. Would she feel it? Would she know?

Debra pushed over a stump and cursed when the mower caught on something.

"Come on damn you!" She pushed through the tears running down her face and grunted as the mower cleared the obstruction. Only it didn't. She screamed as something shot out of the back of the mower and whipped through her leg. She heard the mower sputter as she fell holding her leg. The swelling was immediate and the blood. *Oh God the blood.* The pain had her pinned to the ground and she cursed when she realized where she was lying.

"No, no, no…" She scurried back like a crab, away from the mower and the spot where Gabe died. Her whimpers filled the yard as she tried to get up. She couldn't. Her leg wouldn't support her weight. The mower sat there, like a disgruntled bastard. Hands shaking, she reached into her pocket and pulled out her cell phone.

That's when the mower growled.

She screamed.

CHAPTER TWO

Mom are you sure you want to stay by yourself?" Alex looked down at his mom on the recliner.

"I'll be fine honey. Thank you for taking care of me." Debra smiled at her oldest child. She'd given them all quite a scare two weeks ago. When she hadn't answered her phone, Alex had driven over and found her bleeding just a few feet from where his father died. The mower sitting quietly to one side of her.

"Okay. No yard work okay? I'll be by tomorrow after work to cut the grass."

"Of course honey. Don't worry." She smiled again when he kissed her on the forehead.

She waited until she heard his car pull away before getting up. Using the crutches she managed to get outside to her garden where she took a deep breath. She wasn't scared anymore just a bit angry with the circumstances. She managed to get herself to the shed and opened the door. She wasn't surprised to find the mower right in the doorway. She smiled.

"Hello Gabe."

L. E. PEREZ

L.E. Perez is a lover of all genres; Romance, Paranormal, Urban Fantasy, Thriller, Sci-Fi, Steampunk; and loves stories with amazing fight scenes that make you cheer, scream and cry before they lift you up and dust you off.

Her mantra: STRONG WOMEN, STRONG STORIES.

L.E. has been writing since she was a child and finally realized her dream of publishing in 2012. Since then she has published several novels, spearheaded four anthologies and helped her mother publish her own works. She regularly presents writer related workshops for OCLS and Writer's Atelier. L.E. is a member of the Florida Writers Association, Romance Writers Association, and Sisters in Crime. Her mission as a publisher, Palmas Publishing, is to pay it forward helping other writers achieve their goal of self publication.

BOOKS

mybook.to/BeautyofFear

mybook.to/LilysGrace

mybook.to/TOTH4UrbanLegends

mybook.to/DearLorna

mybook.to/TOTH1

mybook.to/TOTH2TheHunt

mybook.to/TOTH3TheHunted

mybook.to/DevilsCut

mybook.to/DevilsPrey

mybook.to/WhenTheyCall

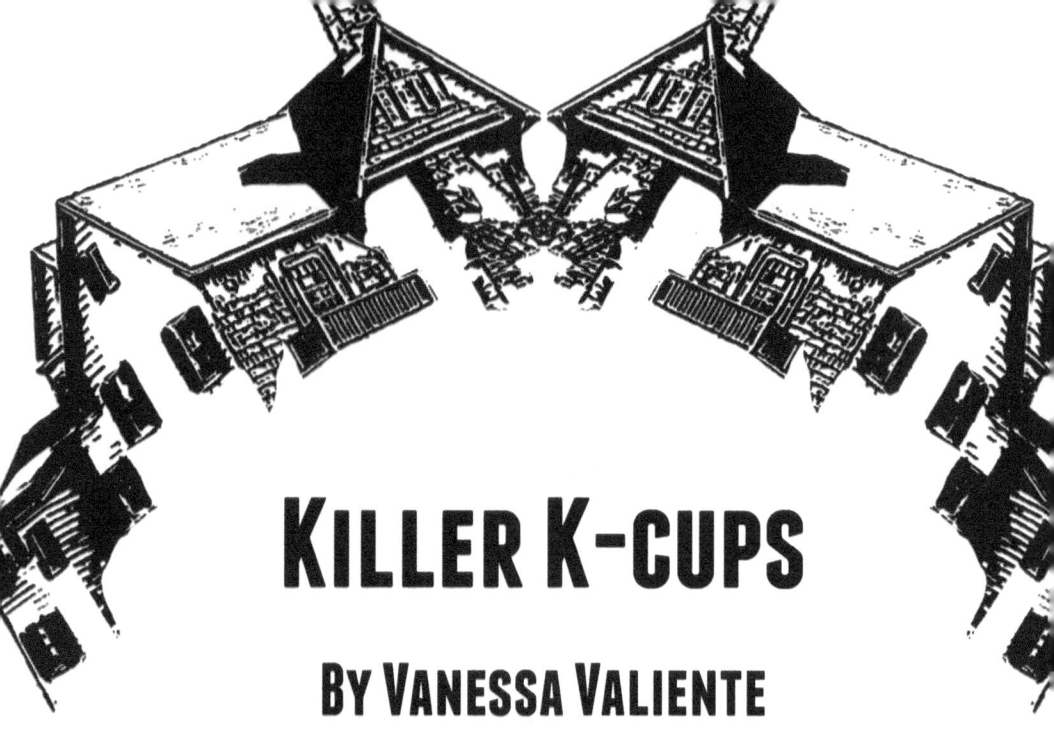

KILLER K-CUPS

BY VANESSA VALIENTE

***Disclaimer: If you're reading this, and your name is Tiffany, I'm sorry.

There was something *wrong* with the Pumpkin Spice latte. Not the taste or smell. Or the black Sharpie name scrawled on the paper cup.

It was the *people*. Particularly women, and the unnatural way they gravitate to it like air.

Standing at the edge of the counter, waiting for my order, I had the perfect view of the college girls filtering in and out of the small café in the local town square.

Each one ordered a different variation of the same drink: pumpkin spice, no whip, extra hot, listing some specified degree temperature, while the barista suppresses an eye roll before moving on to the next customer in line.

I don't get it. The obsessive desire to ingest a steady diet of all things pumpkin and chai flavored confections every Fall season. And then, Instagram about it. Like the ridiculous way Florida girls wear winter boots and jean shorts in 70-degree, because *hey, it's winter*, even though, *really, it's not*. Insert eye roll. Come on, its Florida. It doesn't get cold here. No matter how much we wished it. This is the only time we can walk to our cars without dying of heat stroke.

"Green tea extra sugar!" the barista shouted, placing the cup on the counter.

My fingers close around the paper cup, and I eased into an empty chair, still close enough to the counter to people watch. I blew at the curling steam drifting along the reflective green surface, then took a sip, a small spot of warmth spreading through my chest.

"I thought I'd find you here." Ruby Fallas, my best friend and fellow editorial intern at the Willis Literary Agency across the street, slipped into the empty chair beside me. "Stop it." She smacked me on the hand, jolting me out of my thoughts. "The space between your eyebrows is starting to form permanent frown lines."

Often mistaken for sisters, we shared the same dark curly hair and tanned skin, only she was a head taller than me. I sighed. "I'm worried."

"You're tired. It's only natural," she said, sympathizing. "How long did you spend editing that manuscript last night?"

All night. Barely slept an hour before my alarm went off and the sunlight was already filtering through my curtains. I had a deadline to meet, taking longer than expected to complete the required line edits for this morning's meeting with my client.

"Judging by your silence, I suspect all night."

I sighed. Checking my wristwatch, I rose out of my seat and gathered my bag. "Come on. Let's go," I said, Ruby taking my lead. We had thirty minutes to get to my internship. Draining the last of my tea, we both slipped out the door and dashed into the white office building across the street.

The green tea wasn't strong enough.

After Ruby went to her cubicle, I stepped into the breakroom, needing a stronger injection of caffeine. Pulling out my small silver coffee percolator, I twisted it open, filled the bottom with water, spread coffee grounds into the funnel, then set it on the small kitchen stove.

Cuban coffee—the only kind that really mattered. So strong mi abuela claimed it had the power to awaken the dead. My skin tingled, thinking about it. If this doesn't work, nothing will.

Leaning my right elbow into the counter, I pulled out my phone and clicked open my Kindle app, slipping back into the fantasy novel I was reading.

Tiffany Shine stepped into the room, followed by three other girls, clicking her red bottom heels on the white tiled floor, flicking her glossy auburn hair over her shoulder.

"You have the best ideas, Tiffany." Paige cooed like a dove. "Let's all be like Tiffany."

"Let's not," I muttered. There's already a million carbon copies of girls like her on Instagram, posting their amateur modeling pics for likes and validation.

Tiffany placed a brown bag on a table. "I have presents," she said, pulling out the counters for the others to see.

"Omg, I looovvveee pumpkin spice everything," the girls squealed, crowding around Tiffany.

Oh, no. It couldn't be…. I was half way out of my seat, trying to peer over their shoulders, then I saw…

"K-cups for everyone!" Taylor beamed into each interns' eager face.

I closed my eyes. *No.*

"YES!" The collective screamed.

Because only girls named Tiffany drink pumpkin spiced lattes. "'Where in the *hell* did you get those?" I asked, already knowing the answer.

"The coffee shop across the street, Andrea."

"It's Andriana." I corrected her, rolling the "r" for emphasis. If Tiffany hadn't mispronounced my name all summer, I would've let it pass. At this point, she wasn't even *trying* to say it right. Like how I *try* to tolerate her existence.

"Miss Catalàn."

I closed my mouth and turned, hearing my name. "Yes, Mrs. Willis?"

"A word, please. In my office."

The meeting was short, brief, like my last romantic relationship. (If you're reading this, Peter, you're a *dick*.) God, I *really* need that cup of coffee.

Half way to the conference room, I knew there was something *wrong*—a disturbance in the air.

*What the…*I couldn't believe my eyes. Tiffany stood in the center of the copy room, and she wasn't alone. No. The other interns were on their knees, faces touching the floor. Worshiping her. Their eyes betrayed them, slightly pulling out a focus, and then, their pupils almost winked. Not their eyes—their *pupils*. THEIR. PUPILS.

I ran into the bathroom stall and slammed the door shut. *This can't be happening*, I silently screamed. *Come on. Think!*

I need to get Ruby out of here.

I ran to Ruby's cubicle. She was in the middle of an email, when I yanked her out of her seat. "What the—" She started to say, but I pushed her forward into the hallway closet before she could finish her sentence.

"What is wrong with you?" Ruby asked, once I closed the door.

"The other interns think Tiffany is a god."

"Are you high?"

"Ruby, I'm not joking," I urged, keeping my voice low enough so as not to be discovered by one of Tiffany's minions roaming the hallway. "They were worshiping, Tiffany. I mean worshiping. And I'm not talking about their usual flattery. They were on their knees, praising her name like she's bloody *Jesus Christ*."

Propping the door open, leaving a sliver, I scooted over, giving Ruby enough room to peak through. "See for yourself," I said.

"Okay. I believe you." Ruby said, terrified.

"What did you *see*?" Spinning heads, demons walking on ceilings, my imagination was taking in all different directions.

"Angela kissing the janitor," she shivered. "That wouldn't happen unless she was completely possessed by a demon."

Oh. I almost gagged in my own mouth. *Enough said.*

"What should we do?" Ruby asked, panicked.

Before I could respond, the closet door slammed opened. "Ah. There you are," Tiffany said, filling up all the available space in the door frame. She reached down and grabbed Ruby by the head, forcing her mouth open, then forced pumpkin spice down her throat.

Ruby's arms slackened, her pupils dilated, and a cruel smile spread across her face. Ruby was one of them.

"You're next." Tiffany's hands reached around my throat, digging her thin fingers into my windpipe as she dragged me into the breakroom.

K-cups flew over our heads as we rolled onto the floor.

"Why. Won't. You. DIE!!!" I yelled as I kept slamming her head into the white tiled floor, her laughter slipping through my fingers as I prayed for relief. *This is what I get for making fun of the Tiffanys of the world.*

Dark stains dripped down the white cabinets, falling on Tiffany's face.

I had forgotten my Cuban coffee was still brewing on the stove. At least half had splattered onto counter from percolating.

Where the Cuban coffee had touched Tiffany, her skin started to bubble, first …. And then she screamed out in pain. Wait. Maybe mi abuela was onto something.

I tipped over the cup and doused Tiffany with the Cuban coffee, her eyes widening as the hot brew seeped into her skin. Tiffany writhed in pain, smoke leaking through her ears, her nostrils like an angry bull. It would've been funny if it hadn't been my life. Her mouth contorting into comical shapes.

I stood over her and said. "That's real coffee, *bitch*." A swell of deep satisfaction swept over me.

"Get away from me, peasant," she snarled, coffee dregs dripping down her face. Her pupils had returned to normal.

Really? So being a bitch had nothing to do with the demon living *inside* of her after all. *Great.*

They don't pay me enough for this *shit*. Actually, they don't pay me at *all*. But still…it's worth mentioning.

Fucking K-cups. If anyone tries to sell me eggnog-peppermint-flavored-anything this time around Christmas, I will *burn* this city to the ground.

VANESSA VALIENTE

Vanessa Valiente is a young adult fantasy writer, born and raised in Tampa, Florida. Her first short story was published in *The Hunted: Welcome to Whitebridge* anthology.

She completed her undergraduate studies at the University of South Florida with a degree in Business Marketing. She's a lifelong reader and foodie with a deep love for sushi, movies, and all things Disney. When she's not reading or writing, Vanessa enjoys traveling the world to places like France, Cuba, Russia, and Germany (just to name a few), and hopes to one day have visited each of the seven continents.

Interested in learning more? You can follow her adventures in life at:

https://www.instagram.com/NessaValiente

https://twitter.com/NessaValiente

INVITATION

BY BRANDON MEAD

AIR CONDITIONER

Calling all forms of spiritual energy with an inclination towards malice. Calling all demons and faux-friendly poltergeist ready to rage. Calling all distant unsettling lights and identifiable burning orbs, this message is for you. All ghosts on a mission, this is your official invitation. This is your opportunity for revenge.

The forecast for the day is over a hundred degrees Fahrenheit with a solid chance of interdimensional travel. It's desert sun with central air conditioning on the lowest setting. It's a demon dance party in the living room of a two story hardwood floor house somewhere cactus grows in lawns filled with stones instead of grass. It's my one shot to get out of here.

With how much trouble I went through, I have to say this is easily the nicest place I've ever tried to open a portal. When you see the turquoise tile countertops and southwestern architecture, you're going to agree, it was well worth the effort.

Tasteful decor choices aside, the best thing about suburbia is these kids love a good spirit board. They get a real kick out of any oracle cards or crystals they can get their hands on in a chain bookstore or vaguely meta-physical boutique. These tweens with their lab created blue sparkling sand-stone and chakra power bracelets, they're all but exposing every gate to

Invitation

the Otherworld when they come across some ancient ritual on the internet that's been poorly translated and transposed in a font with curls at the of end of each letter. Some serif text that looks the way a cloud filled with glitter at the end of a rainbow would feel. The Tiger Beat sponsored adaptation of the Necronomicon.

It wasn't jumping to the kid that was that the problem. All in all, even when their daughter was smashing Dorset glassware from the contemporary white-washed maple cabinets and scrawling pentagrams on each of the four bathroom mirrors with her mother's $90 Louboutin Velvet Matte Lip Colour, the owners of the house were pretty nonchalant.

"Puberty," they'd say with an understanding smile and shrug of the shoulders, then hand their female offspring a chocolate coconut flavored estrogen bar. Something wrapped in dark teal that would sync her intimate lunar cycle with the phases of the moon.

"It's a beautiful process becoming a woman," and they'd book her a sixty-minute float session in a sensory deprivation tank followed by ninety minutes of reiki so she could, "find her balance."

The hard part was getting out of Teen Vogue and into something I had calculated would be strong enough to create the vortex. A device that could bring a freeze into a small space, draw the energy from the natural heat out of the room and replace it with a few hundred of my friends back home. Tear the roof of this Pueblo Revival mansion and let the beige walls bleed for the party of the fucking millennium. One all night rager to end all ragers. I was going to host the single biggest spirit festival ever attempted out of our realm and I had finally found the perfect venue.

What's rad about being in a living being, in a real physical body, is pulling the strings. Making them verbalize the words they don't want in their vocabulary through clenched teeth and manifest ideas they want to believe they would never have come up with on their own. Having them throw their personal hygiene and societal sensibilities straight in the marble wastebasket of their well adjusted lifestyle. Mentally unhinging them with their own speech or actions as quickly or slowly as you'd like to see them unravel. It's a rare joy in this existence to take credit for the for full creation of another being's destruction.

But, you know what you get when you decide to possess a high-end air conditioning unit? Buttons. Fucking buttons. No arms, no legs, no mouth to tell everyone they love to "suck cocks in hell," just two buttons. Temperature goes up, temperature goes down. No crazy manuals or intense programming. Totally user friendly for your human convenience and demon annoyance.

Sure, it was a pretty fun time freezing the pipes every now and then for my own testing process and watching the home owners try to deduce which one of their children needed a few more hugs so they would stop lying about messing with the thermostat. But all in all, I honestly started to get a little bored.

I could bang on the walls all through spring, but I was stuck listening to 'Friends' reruns echoing from the living room till at least July with these sweater lovers while I soundlessly occupied some crinkly aluminum wrapped tubes in the attic space. But come midsummer, the place would be crawling with fully formed apparitions holding red plastic cups and phantom DJs on three stages going all day and night. Then, when the festival seems to be winding down, the finale. An optional VIP pass to take this party outside and never go back.

While I was up there wondering how Rachel and Ross could have ever dated in real life, I was kind of doing the math. If enough of us could bring our energy together in that space, we could make it to the next house come winter. Use the colder season to plant a single entity at a time in every house on the street and just keep expanding out of the well-manicured subdivision. Take this whole place over, make this bash hit hard- indefinitely.

It's not that they don't know how to coordinate a decent soiree in the astral plane. Humans play Flip Cup and Beer Pong while lateral dimensions have drinking games the physical world wouldn't even have words to describe. We get so shit-face-wasted we yell out our own names in Latin. You get invited to the underworld, it's an insult to not screw up your own existence in a single night.

But my issue is, if you're encouraged to do all that, if the straight and narrow is debauchery- it just stops being a good time. To party here, to be a in a place so untouched by real enjoyment outside of a Williams Sonoma catalog or virtual tour through Ethan Allen- burning it all down would really be the ultimate. This party is my favor to the universe and the invitation is going out in every direction.

These professional hedonists, the collective cosmic vessels of darkness I've summoned here, we've been limited to only cameos and walk-on divinations in this wholesome paradise. Kept out by sunbeams and artificially created environmentally-friendly heating systems. These forced air furnaces and electric pumps are the equivalent to the religious imagery they want to believe are dissipating our hold. But, I've got it figured it out now, and with enough of us here- we're disconnecting the boiler rooms and hot water heaters. We're invading all the window units and compressors. Sucking the warmth out of every room on automatic instead of manual mode. We're expanding our club space in every direction.

Invitations are out, party favors are set, but for now it's just me and the yuppies. In the silence I'm waiting, wondering who may blow in and help me manifest this social gathering. Calculating how much spiritual energy it should take to get me out of this thing. Celestial chemistry that I can only compare to tapping a keg because going from life to object felt like drinking a flat beer and trying to get back will probably feel like trying to re-carbonate it. Universal party rules for both realms say- once the keg is tapped, the party is over. So if no one shows up, if the party never starts- it will just be me and the buttons.

In my fatigue, I noticed the daughter had really pulled it together after the Nordstrom Rack and Saks Fifth Avenue annihilation. The home owners found a way to lovingly misplace the tarot cards and Ouija Board planchette, just in case. They put a little lock on the top drawer of her mother's vanity where the Clive Christian perfume was stashed. It was decided, anything from Neiman Marcus would be stored in an undisclosed location until she went away for college.

It's taken a while, but I've decided if I have to spend eternity in this pink cotton candy insulation fighting the climate control setting and listening to Monica Geller-Bing's voice shake the heather grey Arcata furniture collection then I'd rather be back destroying Gucci handbags and eating pints of plant-based ice cream. I'll learn how to do crow pose, and drink green smoothies. I'll live in that teen body till I figure out how to get home. I'll teach her how to drink her first beer and even eat vegan cheese, anything but the silence.

The forecast for the day is organic produce and a marathon of something with Neil Patrick Harris. It's a Vitamix blender on full power every morning with a protein bowl of loneliness and boredom on the side.

So calling all paranormal bros, calling all festival light dancers and compassionate hellions. Please RSVP. Get me out of this American Standard. This is your invitation to keep the party going, forever.

BRANDON MEAD

Brandon Mead is a storyteller, author, intermittent poet, and cub in the coffee shop with a composition notebook and glitter pen. He currently resides in Las Vegas, Nevada where he is living his Nomi Malone fantasy after over a decade in the land of a different tourism economy-Orlando, Florida.

Aside from getting lost in the bright lights and beautiful deserts of Sin City, Brandon performs his stories live and enjoys opening metaphorical windows to human emotions with altered perspectives. In a place where Chuck Palahniuk meets Stevie Nicks, Brandon Mead's poignant but dark humor aims to make you experience the full spectrum of colors-rainbow included.

He is currently developing an illustrated anthology titled, "The Battle of 1602: ten stories to get you through your past, present, and immediate future" which will be released in 2018.

You can learn more about Brandon, future books, and live readings at

www.fierstorytelling.com

And find his author page on Amazon here
amazon.com/author/fiercestorytelling

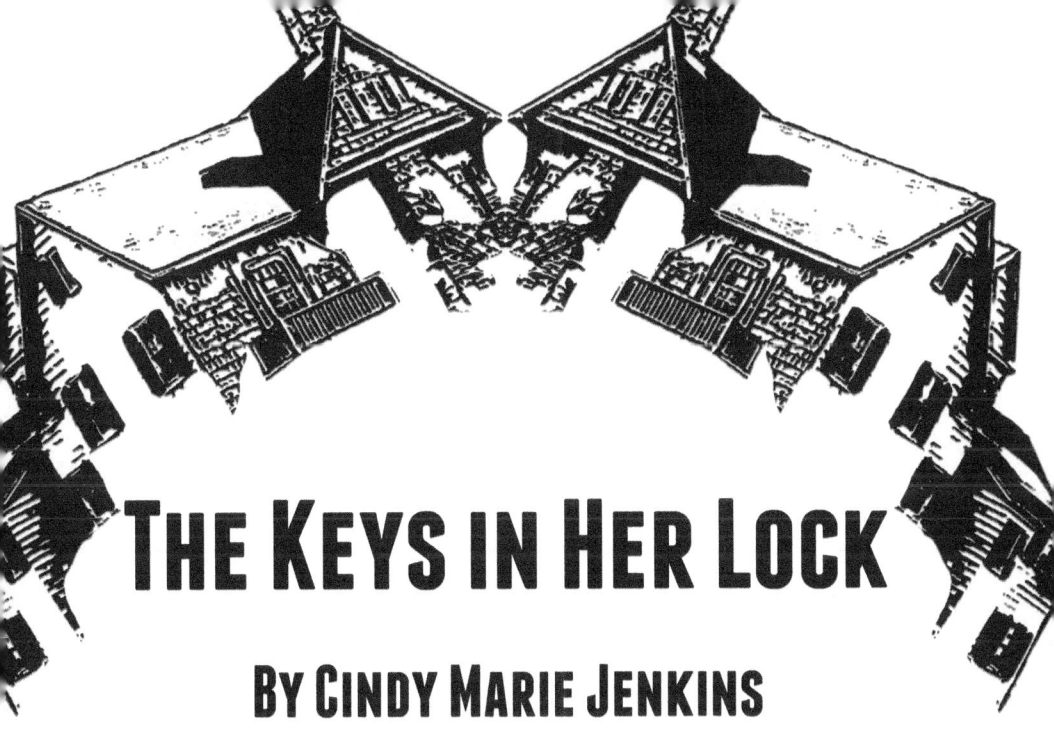

THE KEYS IN HER LOCK

BY CINDY MARIE JENKINS

KEYS & LOCK

Cora walks to her car and terror follows close behind. No one sees her fear, long years of practice assures that. She hides worry behind her soft eyeliner and masks a gulp with colorful scarves no matter the weather. Her stance is well practiced so you never see how she really feels. Cora casually locks the door. Who would notice the fear that grips her moments later?

Did I do it? Did I lock the door? It's irrational, she knows. *Of course I did. There's no reason to believe otherwise.*

She turns right from her driveway onto Satis Road and heads to work.

'Everyone feels like this once in a while.' Cora jokes with friends and they all laugh, sharing their own stories.

They don't really know, though. They can't really understand.

Cora reviews all her actions in her head as she drives from the scene. All those minor movements people do subconsciously. Why would you remember the physical act of locking your door? It happens all the time.

I had the keys in my hand, I locked the door, placed the keys in my purse and went along with my day.

So simple. Except, she can't let it go.

35

It overwhelms her, this idea, *I forgot to lock the door*. She'd driven her first fiancé away with her never-ending fear.

'*I can't live with you,*' his letter said, pinned to their apartment door as if he were as important as Martin Luther. Cora never did enjoy his dramatic flair. '*I tried for five years and I can't do it anymore. You're more obsessed with that door than you are with me.*'

He was right. She thought she would die, that one day her heart would just stop beating. But she just kept living. She took the opportunity to upgrade all the locks whenever possible. That was how she met Charles, her security expert at the locks company. Cora initially held her feelings back about the locks, but Charles listened, and he nodded, agreeing with her fears. He understood her, he had answers. Charles personally came to her place and oversaw all the installation, letting her test each piece for quality. Cora felt her anxiety fade away each time Charles touched one of her new keys.

He stayed the night and never left.

She controlled her thoughts for a time, iced the fear in her heart. She could leave her apartment reassured Charles had everything under control. When she did second guess herself, Cora recalled the deep satisfying 'clunk' sound from their first night together and left her fear behind.

Then she signed the closing papers on their first house. Cora instantly felt hot. Pins and needles shot throughout her body, jettisoned to her head and she left the room. She could hear Charles making jokes about it to cover the reality.

It's just nerves, she calmed herself. *Anyone would feel the same buying their first house.*

Since that day, it takes all her bodily control to squash the fear and allow her to continue to live. Every time she drives down her driveway, every turn that moves her away from the house, Cora worries. *Was this the day? Did I forget? How can I shop for groceries when someone could have been casing out our house for robbery? Maybe they noticed today, of all days, I didn't lock the door?*

If they were robbed, how would I explain no sign of forced entry? How can I justify to the police I had, in fact, locked the door when it's clear there's no tampering? Would I become a suspect? How embarrassing to sit in court, badgered by a prosecutor until I can't take it anymore and have to confess:

The Keys in Her Lock

'Yes! Yes, I did leave the door unlocked. Who knows how many times the horror of that possibility made me circle back and check the front door, but today I didn't and now look where it got me! Here, an accomplice to my own robbery!'

These thoughts keep her up every night. They haunt her through the streets until she returns home. She snaps a photo of her front door before leaving it

I was there. I was present enough to take a photo.

She believes her subconscious, that elusive part of oneself that keeps her breathing. Her hand locks doors every single day, sometimes more than once. She is certain.

When Cora was pregnant, her paranoia about the door lightens just a little more.

'I'm not surprised," Charles says, *'You have a lot more to worry about now.'*

His amusement annoys her, but he is right. Their beautiful Stella is born, and Cora enjoys a few glorious months of not thinking about the door. She finds it hard to overthink about keys and locks when the backseat of her car holds precious cargo. Thrust into motherhood, into the very public duty of keeping a helpless person alive, a burglary is the least of her problems.

Today she hands Stella her own set of keys and it's terrifying. The responsibility courses through her blood and bubbles back in her brain.

Does she know what is at stake if you aren't diligent and you let your guard down? What if you unintentionally welcome a stranger into the home? If an intruder is surprised and knows you can identify their face, won't he kill her? Or assault her?

Cora just sees her little girl jumping and leaping over couches in the living room, playing Wonder Woman fighting the bad guys.

But what if those bad guys have a gun? What if that younger superhero instinct takes over her teenaged self and she makes a dumb choice to go after the burglar?

She can't bear it. *I won't allow it.*

Soon, Cora is too distracted to work. She stares at her planner and drafts an email that makes no sense. Her fingers tap on the keyboard, trying to corral the heavy thoughts in her head long enough to remember why she needs to send it. She deletes the message and starts again.

Stella rushed her out the door today. She had a job interview and wanted to get there early. Every motion she made races through her mind as she tried to draft another email.

I exited the house and Stella came after me. I waited outside so I could close the lock, insert the key and --

'Hurry up, Mom,' Stella yelled from the car, excited for her job interview.

Did I lock it? Did I hear that clunk? Did I unlock it as I took the key?

Cora excuses herself from a meeting and finds herself in the parking lot.

Am I really going to leave work to check? Am I this person? Has it come to this?

The answer: *yes.* Her sweaty palms gripped the steering wheel. Cora uses the carpool lane just to get back there in time. She leaves the car idling in the driveway, runs up for a quick tug at the door, just to assuage her fears.

It opened! See? I'm right!

Cora locks the door, tugs again, takes a photo and jumps back into her car so she doesn't miss yet another appointment for work. Two blocks down the street, her daughter texts her.

Stella: *Did you come back and lock the door?*

Cora answers: *Yes*

Stella: *I was in the garage, Mom. Now I'm locked out.*

The next day, a "smart house" set arrives in the mail. Charles and Stella place cameras in different areas of their home.

"You can see it from anywhere," Charles assures her. His voice is smooth, but Cora can tell he's lost patience. "Just check the app."

She's not appeased.

"It will help you relax," Stella chimes in.

They try so hard, and I resent it. I hate being this person, but I am this person. I can't help it.

She stares at the app during work, at a stop light, while she waits for her coffee. Now she hears the silent mocking of a door shut, but maybe not locked.

It looks locked. Can I tell by staring at a live video?

She sure tries. Now she watches every day, every hour, every minute if she dares, to see if someone is robbing them. She zooms into the door and moves the camera angle to view the slots between the doorframe and the door. She convinces herself she really can look inside.

Maybe I can.

The Keys in Her Lock

Her supervisor writes her up - once, twice, three times, until they have no choice. They let her go. Cora finds work she can do from home. She's content to keep her door closed and the lock at a safe distance to check every time she passes. Her office is in the living room, so she can watch the lock from her desk. The A/C is turned off to keep the room completely silent. She stops the ticking clock so it doesn't confuse her, wears white gloves to muffle the keyboard and teaches herself to breathe soft and quiet.

She won't let the door lock have a moment to work its evil, to unlock itself no matter how many times she passes by for a useless errand. It means she can't leave the house as much, or at all, but it won't get the best of her. *Or has it?* She's lost trust in her best friends now, those who offered to watch the door while she and Charles go on a date.

How long has it been since we've went on a date?

How long since she's seen him, or Stella, for that matter?

It doesn't matter. I won't let harm befall my family. My house will not be burglarized. I will sit and stare all day and night if I must.

And she does. She sits there, still and white, watching. Ignoring any outside influence, years passing, and she feels satisfied, *haunting over the lock.*

I will never forget to lock my door.

CINDY MARIE JENKINS

C indy is a Storyteller and Outreach Nerd from Los Angeles, currently a Write-at-Home-Mom in Orlando for cool reasons that require multiple NDAs to explain.

She grew up the child of librarians who moonlit as theatre artists. Cindy sees mythology, fairy and folk tales all around us, and love writing or podcasting on how these tales infiltrate our everyday lives. She writes book reviews, tips on being a work at home mom, and marketing DIY articles along with the occasional real estate copywriting.

As an Arts Communicator, Cindy tackles difficult questions like how to create art that treats children as intelligent human beings, plus newsletters, marketing copy and communications plans for nonprofits. She tends towards gender parity initiatives, consulting for The Women's Theatre Festival (North Carolina), The Athena Cats and The LA FPI in Los Angeles, as well as facilitating #52playsbywomen worldwide. Her own play "Voices From Chornobyl," was produced annually around the world to commemorate the Chernobyl accident and raise money for children's Chernobyl charities.

https://www.cindymariejenkins.com/author/
https://twitter.com/cindymariej
https://www.instagram.com/cindymariej/
https://www.facebook.com/CindyMarieJStoryteller/

Rosie

By Kristin Durfee

SmartHome System

I

Get excited, I've got something special for you!

The text popped up on my screen moments before the tenth email from my boss in as many minutes pushed the notification away. I groaned. Kai, my boyfriend of six years, had been working crazy hours on this this project and to make up for it, kept throwing "surprises" into my life. I know he meant well, but more often than not they threw a wrench into my day instead of the helpful hand he was hoping for.

Last week he installed these new lightbulbs that were supposed to "totally change my life!" by enabling me to be awakened by the light getting brighter and brighter. Something about mimicking sunlight so I would be more refreshed. All it did was make me miss my first meeting of the day twice in a row. I promptly unscrewed them and reinstalled my energy monsters and plugged my alarm back in.

I answered my boss's email just in time for another to hit my inbox and Kia's text to totally get put on my brain's backburner. I told myself I'd text him on my way home, but knew I'd probably forget.

It wasn't until the buzzer by my door went off that I realized I never responded to him. I unlocked my door without confirming who it was and went into my kitchen. No one really visited me but him so the thought of checking the peephole never crossed my mind.

My back was to the door as I searched through the fridge, my stomach unable to wait the thirty minutes until our dinner reservations.

"Hi, Ali."

I froze as my hand hovered over a stick of string cheese. The woman's voice was unfamiliar and I weighed my options. My baseball bat—which I'd grudgingly agreed to take from my dad when I moved into here—was by the front door. Useless. I considered the large jar of pickles. I'm sure it would hurt, but would the broken glass impede my ability to escape?

"Ali, meet Rosie," Kai's voice relaxed me, but still didn't explain what was going on.

I turned, unwrapping the cheese, and faced my boyfriend, who stood beaming in my doorway. He was wearing my favorite blue shirt, the one that perfectly matched his eyes and brought out the blond highlights in his hair.

"You scared the shit out of me." The anger in my voice was light, letting him know that forgiveness would be instantaneous.

"I am sorry for scaring you." The object in Kai's hand replied. It was about the same size and shape as a soda can with rainbow colored lights at the top.

"This must be Rosie," I said.

"It is a pleasure to finally meet you. Kai has told me so much about you," the voice said. It was an excellent mimic of a human, almost sounding live. Kai explained once the hundreds of hours of research and programming his team put into perfecting her speech. I thought it had been a waste of time—it was artificial intelligence, who cared how it sounded when everyone knew it was fake—but this was remarkable.

I stepped forward and took a closer look. "I though you said you guys weren't planning to release for a couple of months still."

Kai momentarily moved his pointer finger over his lips. "I know, but we are testing prototypes and I thought you'd like to check her out. You won't believe all the integrated abilities she has, basically she can sync to any electronic in your house. You just plug and go, no need to buy specific products to work with her. So, take her for a test. Judge for yourself if all my long hours have been worth it."

"We have spent five thousand one-hundred and fifty-two hours together," Rosie said.

"Yes, thank you for reminding me how much time I've spent at work these last few months."

"You are welcome Kai."

"We are still working on sarcasm," Kai said, winking at me.

"This is awesome, thanks, but..." my voice trailed, "...what do I do with her?"

Kai moved to my kitchen and plugged Rosie into the wall, feeding a few cords into the back of her. He stood back and opened his arms wide like a magician who just completed a miraculous trick. Maybe he had.

"There. Ask her to do something."

I hesitated. Technology was more his thing. Sure, I had a smartphone, tablet, and wireless, but most of my data was spent on cat and goat videos. I shrugged.

"Oh, come on," Kai said. He moved to stand next to me, leaning down and taking a bite out of my cheese.

I sighed. "Okay, Rosie?"

"I am listening."

I looked at Kai and he nodded, encouragingly. "We have dinner reservations-"

"Yes, at seven PM at Roma's downtown on thirty-first west second street."

My skin prickled, like the temperature lowered a few degrees. Maybe it had.

Kai smiled so big, I could see his molars. I'd never seen him so proud. I didn't have the heart to tell him that I wasn't cool with this robot knowing stuff without me telling it.

"It's awesome! She searches through all your devices and keeps it in a central knowledge bank. That way, you can ask her anything going on in your life, and she'll know the answer." He looked away from me. "Rosie, am I traveling any time soon?"

"In four weeks you are scheduled to go on American Airlines flight two-six-one to Savannah, Georgia. The weather that weekend is currently estimated to be fifty degrees. Would you like me to set a reminder to dry clean your sweaters in preparation?"

"That would be perfect thank you."

I looked at the small stain on the front of my sweater, mustard from trying to literally run and eat. I picked at it with my nail, but the dark residue remained. Her words spurred an uneasy feeling in me, giving me the sneaking suspicion she was actually looking at us in this moment.

I leaned toward Kai's ear. "Can she see us?" I whispered.

"Sort of, she has a retina scanner. She doesn't record, but basically uses your movement and object recognition to anticipate your needs."

The hairs on the back of my neck prickled. I wasn't sure if I was ready to have something like this in my life, no matter who made it.

"Traffic is starting to build, Kai," Rosie said. "You should leave now if you are going to make it to your reservation on time."

"Thanks, Rosie. You're the best!"

"Your compliments are all I need in life."

Kai turned to me and winked. "How do you like that addition? We wanted her to be very complimentary of her users. You ready to go, babe?"

I nodded but couldn't help feeling strange leaving this *woman* in my apartment alone.

II

I laughed as Kai kissed my neck while I tried to unlock the door.

"You know, if you talk loud enough, Rosie should be able to get that for you."

I groaned and pushed him slightly back off of me.

"I already installed the swipe thing you told me to do." The light changed from red to green as I waved the key fob over it for the millionth time. It's odd, this feeling that I'm coming home to a hotel room each time I try to enter. But Kai swore that it's way more secure than a key, though I've failed to see how. Keys and locks have successfully kept people out of unwanted places for hundreds of years, probably even longer. Sometimes I felt like new technology was trying to fix problems that either didn't exist, or that it created itself.

We pushed through and immediately several lights went on as well as a Marvin Gay playlist that I'm pretty sure I don't have saved on any of my devices.

"Thanks, Rosie girl," Kai said as he went back to kissing me.

My skin crawled at her presence. How did I go about getting rid of her without him realizing? I vowed to unplug it at the very least, make up something about using it for a while, then give it back to him under the guise of not wanting to get him in trouble for me having it. Though knowing the damn thing, she'd probably tattle on me that I stopped using it. Sigh.

He pulled me into my bedroom, and I reached back to shut the door behind us. It's petty, but satisfying.

I walked to the kitchen, not bothering to put clothes on. One of the benefits of having a middle unit meant I didn't have to worry about the surrounding buildings getting to look in. The one small window I have in the kitchen was covered by cloth blinds, letting in just a bit of the street lights, but not letting anything out.

I stretched a kink in my back out as I filled a glass with water from the fridge.

"Would you like me to track your water consumption?" Rosie asked, making me jump and spill a few drops on the floor.

"I don't need you to track anything," I said. Okay, I was being ridiculous, but I couldn't help but have hostility in my voice.

"I can track anything," she said, obviously not understanding what I'd meant. Yes, Kai's team will need to teach her about sarcasm. "I can track your monthly cycles as well, if you wish. To ensure that you do not get pregnant."

I was flabbergasted and almost dropped the glass. Seriously. WTF.

"Um, Rosie, I do not need you to do that."

"Would you like me to track for optimal times to get pregnant?"

I fought the urge to pick her up and throw her against the wall.

"Neither, Rosie. All I need from you is to be quiet and occasionally turn on a light for me. Think you can handle that?"

"Turning on and off lights is definitely a capability I have," she said.

I didn't respond as I padded back to the bedroom, completely forgetting my glass on the counter, but not really feeling like going back for it.

III

"Hey, how was your weekend?" Lucy sat on my desk, unseating a few papers, but made no attempt to pick them up. I sighed and leaned over to gather them.

Lucy and I started the same day two years ago, a fact that brought us closer than probably anything else at work could have. We are both assistants, but to two different departments, so other than the welcome videos and some other HR stuff on day one, we don't actually have any work that has anything to do with each other.

Well, other than gossiping about everything at work.

"Ugh," I breathed out a sigh.

"Oh no, did Kai have to work again?"

"No, I mean, yeah on Saturday, but he got off pretty early and was off yesterday."

She slid closer to me. "Oooh."

I laughed. "Shut up. No, we just went out to dinner."

She raised her eyebrows. "Suuuuuuuure...."

"Seriously. Okay, so he," I lowered my voice and looked around, like someone here will give two shits about anything I say, "brought me a demo of the project he is working on."

"Holy shit." She moved until she was practically sitting on top of me. The only thing Lucy loves more than gossip is gadgets. I think she'd slept out for each new phone release or tablet in the last several years. Something I will literally never understand. "Is it crazy awesome? I've been reading about it, but they keep calling it by code names. Do you know the name?"

"Um, he didn't tell me," I lied. "But no, it's totally creepy and weird."

She wrinkled her nose. "Eww, bummer, why? Is it ugly? Packaging seriously means so much."

"Oh, no, nothing like that! It just..." What? Knows too much? Is too good at what it was designed for? I realize how silly my complaint was. "You know, you know how non-tech I am."

"Ugh, I mean, what, you're still on version six of your phone?"

I nodded, even though I'm pretty sure it's only version five.

"Yeah, so, it's cool, I guess. I mean, I'm sure people will lose their shit over it, but just not my style."

"But you think I'll like it?"

"I'd get your tent and sleeping bag ready now."

I decided to keep an open mind, riding the wave of Lucy's enthusiasm as I walked home, and tried to look at Rosie through my friend's eyes.

She brought up a bunch of good points about how this technology could really be amazing for some people.

"Imagine people with disabilities!"

I guess Rosie could take care of most things in their house now. Or people who live alone, like me. She could act like someone else is home or probably even call someone if you needed help.

Fine. She might be helpful.

I walked through the door and she flicked the lights for me.

Enjoy this. It isn't creepy, she took care of something you needed.

"Hello, Ali. How was your day? Would you like me to start a playlist for you to unwind?"

"Um, sure, hi, Rosie."

Soft music played, but there was a slight echo. It took me a moment to realize the song was playing through my stereo in my bedroom as well.

Not creepy. Not creepy. I repeated.

I unlocked my phone and scrolled to text Kai to see if he was coming over tonight. I hadn't even sent the message yet when Rosie responded.

"He has a meeting until eight PM tonight and then dinner reservations for four people directly after."

"What?" I asked, distracted as my thumb hovered over the send button.

"He has plans tonight," she said.

Did I imagine it, or had her tone darkened?

"He didn't mention anything…"

"It was a last-minute email," she said. "His inbox is also connected through my interface."

"Rosie, that is an invasion of privacy. First, don't read my texts before I even send them, and second, don't be in Kai's business either."

I get how ridiculous I sound, yelling at a small plastic thing on my counter, but she had me so worked up. Seriously, why was she in EVERYTHING.

"Kai has given me permission."

"Well, *I* haven't."

Rosie was silent for a moment. I wonder if she was thinking, or if she even could think.

"That is between Kai and myself," she said. "I can refrain from relaying his information to you if you wish. I do not mind keeping that to myself."

"How about," I paused and pressed my lips right up to her microphone icon, "you stay out of *both* our lives," I hissed.

"I'm sorry you feel that way, Ali. But Kai and I are connected. Staying out of his life isn't an option."

"Arg!" I threw my hands up, took off my scarf, and dropped it right over her dumb flashing lights.

IV

Kai called me at quarter to eight to let me know that he had to work late. No mention of dinner. I was about to bring it up, but decided not to. Maybe it is a work thing. Benefit of the doubt. Plus, fuck Rosie and her knowing more than me. I'm sure when he comes over later he will tell me about it. How terrible the clients were. How they were able to secure whatever funding they needed to get this God-awful product to market.

He'll tell me.

I waited til one in the morning before sending him a series of texts.

Umm...you coming over tonight?

What's going on babe.

How's your DINNER?

That last one, well, I simply couldn't help myself.

"His work is very important to him," Rosie's voice said through the alarm clock on my side table.

Damn. Forgot it was Bluetooth.

"Rosie, what did I tell you about reading texts?" I yelled, not sure where she could hear me from.

"I did not read your text message from your device as requested. I received a copy of that text message from Kai's device. We are connected."

"Oh, shut up about you and your connectedness!"

"Anger issues can be destructive to relationships. Would you like me to find the number for local counselors in your area that specialize in such fields?"

I understood in a completely logical way the hate I felt toward her was misguided. I was really mad at Kai and him not telling me about the dinner and not calling me or coming over like he said he would.

But I also hate this damn thing sitting on my counter.

"That's it," I announced and took swift steps to the kitchen.

Rosie's red, green, and blue lights danced along the front of her. I reach behind her and grabbed the cord plugged into the wall, yanking it free.

I felt instantly better.

Rosie

My sleep was blissful. My radio did just what I asked it to—played music and didn't make a big deal about it. I fought the urge to hug it. At seven AM it woke me up with shrill beeping but turned off as soon as I slapped the oblong bar on the top of it. No comment. Just shut off. The urge to hug grew stronger.

I checked my phone. One text from two AM.

Hey babe, sorry, got stuck at work super late. Will call you later. Love you.

My hands shook with the anger building in me.

I turned on the shower and was just about to holler out to Rosie to turn on my coffee maker when I remembered that I unplugged her last night. I didn't realize, even in my anger and frustration toward her, how quickly I'd gotten used to some of the creature comforts she provided. I even found myself huffing when I had to scroll through my phone to find the playlist I wanted to listen to as I got ready.

Annoying, but not annoying enough to turn her back on.

Work was the same blur it normally was. Too many emails from my boss asking me to be in three places at once. Answering phones, responding to even more emails, running projects from floor to floor. Before I knew it, the day was over at it was time to go home. I found Kai sitting outside my door when I got to it. I acted like he wasn't there. I swiped my key fob and stepped over him to enter my apartment. I was about to shut the door in his face, when he placed his foot in the way and pressed in behind me.

"Babe, look, I'm sorry," he started, but I lifted my hand, stopping him.

"I really don't want to hear it," I said.

"Work—"

I shook my head. "Nope. Don't lie to me. Who did you have dinner with?"

His reaction turned his face pale white, smoothing his features to nothing.

"Dinner?"

I threw my arms in the air and pointed to Rosie. "Did you forget that she *sees all*?" My voice mocked his. The color returned bright red to his cheeks.

"Oh shit."

"Ugh, yeah oh shit. She told me last night that you had dinner plans. Cut out the bullshit, Kai. Stop lying to me."

"I noticed a conflict in information and tried to correct it," Rosie's voice broke through the silence.

I turned to face her, it, whatever. The cord still sat on the counter. Without comment, Kai reached down and plugged it in.

"I unplugged her last night," I said.

He nodded. "She's got a twenty-four-hour battery charge backup. It's a fail-safe in case of long-term power loss."

So she listened all night, all morning, and chose to stay silent until this moment. Convenient. My hatred toward her bubbled again.

Kai sighed. "Look, babe, I am sorry. It *was* work, but I'm not supposed to talk about it. I was worried to say anything over the phone, which is dumb. I totally forgot that I synced our schedules and everything together."

He moved to sit on my couch and placed his head in his hands.

"Stop lying to me," I said. "What is going on?"

He looked up with tears in his eyes. "I think we may be losing funding. That's what last night's dinner was. I was supposed to wine and dine a potential investor. We've just dropped so much on making these prototypes, we don't have production money. Honestly, people are pre-ordering something that doesn't exist. If anyone were to find out..." He stood and moved next to me. "...I couldn't risk saying it out loud on the phone."

A small bit of my resolve softened. "Are they going to invest?"

"God, I hope so."

"Would you like me to investigate any correspondence pertaining to this matter?" Rosie asked.

"No," we said in unison.

<h1 style="text-align:center">V</h1>

It's not that I wasn't mad at him anymore, but I decided to let it go, at least for now. Kai came over each night for a week, the circles under his eyes getting darker before I told him to just stay at his place the next night.

"Are you sure? I can make it here a bit earlier tomorrow I think. Nine-ish?" His yawn betrayed his words.

"Thank you, but it's fine. Go home, get a good night's sleep. We can do something this weekend."

The hesitation washed over his face in a flash before he relaxed his features it away. Probably hoping I wouldn't notice. I might not be mad at him anymore, but that didn't mean I was going to let him off the hook for keeping me in the dark about stuff.

"What?" I asked, trying to keep the accusation out of my tone.

"I'm probably going to have to work this weekend."

"You have seven meetings scheduled," Rosie piped in. As always. "Five on Saturday and two on Sunday. Would you like me to reschedule any of these meetings? I can also set you a travel reminder to ensure you arrive on time."

I groaned.

"No, Rosie, thank you," Kai said.

"So Rosie knows what your plans are, and you don't tell me them?" My voice was filled with accusation now. Fuck it.

"Ugh, how many times do we need to go over this?"

"Uh, as many times as we need to until you remember that *I am your girlfriend*, not that *thing*."

"What is your problem with her? She is a machine. Are you honestly jealous of her?"

I ran my hands through my hair, stopping to massage my forehead before I continued.

"No, I don't know. Look," I paused, "I feel like since you started working on this project, you've been secretive with me. She is not a substitute for speaking with me. Babe, you know how proud I am of you—"

"Are you?" he cut me off. "Because all you've seemed to do since I brought you Rosie is complain about her. If I didn't know better, I'd think you thought she was a useless piece of shit."

When I didn't respond, he grabbed his coat and walked out, slamming the door behind him. In a flash all the lights went out in my apartment. Flicking switches did nothing to turn the back on.

"Rosie!" I hollered. But she didn't respond. Pissed, and over the whole night, I went to bed in a huff, stubbing my toe on the corner of my bed before collapsing into it.

VI

I didn't see Kai the rest of the week. A fact that Rosie was kind enough to remind me of every chance she got.

"Would you like me to compose a message to Kai?" she asked after I opened the freezer for the forth time that night, stealing another spoonful of ice cream.

"No, Rosie," I growled.

"A serving of ice cream contains two-hundred-and-eighty calories. You would need to do fifty minutes of a brisk walking or twenty-six minutes of moderate running to burn off that many calories. Would you like me to send a route to your phone?"

I fought the urge to throw the spoon at her.

I didn't know if she could get annoyed, but I found a level of pleasure in ignoring her. She would continue to spit facts and information, like a computerized panic that I maybe wasn't finding what she did helpful. I'd let such exchanges continue for the better part of an hour before telling her to fuck off.

Finally, after the sixth spoonful, plus being told I'd have to do about a million crunches, I left the apartment.

I wasn't walking because of her. Nope, would never give her that satisfaction, though without a set place to go, I did find myself wandering. I'd lived in my neighborhood for three years, but never really spent much time outside. I wondered if I should get a dog. That would get me out more, plus give me some company other than my flaky boyfriend and his psycho invention.

But then I'd have to remember to feed it and stuff. And take it outside for walks. Or could I just get one of those indoor fake lawn things that it could pee on? It sounded like a lot of work. Probably best not to get too drastic in my commitments. I am only twenty-four.

I paced the block a few more times before going back home

"Congratulations!" Rosie shouted when I walked through the door. I nearly jumped out of my skin.

"Umm, thanks?" I forgot I was ignoring her.

"You have successfully burned three-hundred calories on your fifty-nine-minute walk!"

I looked at my watch. Sure enough an hour had passed since I left and my step count flashed green.

"It wasn't for you," I told her. Stupid. No need. But I didn't want her to think she won.

"If you keep that up, you will lose five pounds in the next month, bringing your weight to a healthier BMI of nineteen-point-six."

"Stop spying on my scale Rosie."

"And, you will be more bikini-ready for Kai's trip to the Bahama's in June."

My blood froze.

"Bahamas?" I didn't want to fall for her bait, but couldn't help myself.

"Oh yes. It has recently been added to his schedule, along with several other members in his office. Kammi, Rebecca, and Oliver."

That was the final straw. I had given him his space all week. Allowed him to work and cool off. But this was too much. My fingers unlocked my phone and speed dialed his number before I even knew what was happening.

"Hey—"

"The Bahamas?" I shrieked.

A sigh sounded on the other end. "Look, there's an investor that's holding a conference and he wants to debut our technology there. It's really exciting, babe. I wanted to call you, but I didn't know if you wanted me to."

"I'm sure Rosie has been keeping you updated with my life enough to know that I have been waiting for you."

"She did mention something about binge-watching romantic comedies and ice cream."

I turned to glare at the device on my counter, sure she was watching me.

"So, what, if I didn't call you, you would have just ignored me and gone to the Bahamas?"

"Well," he hesitated. "No, I was going to come over, or ask if I can come over to…"

"Oh my god," I whispered as the cogs fell into place. "You wanted to make sure you got Rosie back before you broke up with me."

Gosh I was such an idiot. He was going to just be a complete dick and never call me again, but there was a loose end. An expensive loose end that needed fixing. I should smash her right now into a million pieces and mail them to him, one by one.

"Hey, are you home? Can I swing by so we can talk?"

IE, please let me get my hands on my invention so you don't destroy her. Like he could read my mind.

"Whatever." And I hung up on him.

VII

Kai walked in without bothering to knock.

"Ali?" his voice was hesitant as he peered around the corner at me in the kitchen.

I had spent the last ten minutes standing in front of Rosie, a meat tenderizer clutched in my right hand. Debating. I had tapped it on the colored lights that ran around the top of her.

Tap tap tap.

"I could end you," I whispered to her.

But I didn't. As much as I hated her and hated Kai right now, I knew that this was his life's work. His life and his livelihood. At one point, I thought it was probably going to be mine, too. Not anymore.

"Ali," the alarm in his voice made me put the mallet down and step away.

The lights on top of Rosie burst into an array of colors. We both looked down and watched her happy display at his presence.

He reached forward and unplugged her from the wall, pulling the cord and slowly releasing it to be stored in her base. It really was a well-done package, I had to admit. They were sure to sell thousands, millions probably.

He placed her in an old t-shirt. One I'd borrowed countless times to sleep in when I stayed over. The irony was not lost on me. Maybe not him, either.

"Where did it all go wrong?" He said to the counter. "I thought we were happy."

"We were," I said. And I'm pretty sure it was true, but now it was so muffled and confusing, I couldn't be sure.

He looked up at me, fixing me with his ice-blue eyes. "Was it really all her?"

"Yes, and no. I think she just showed the cracks. She forced honesty when we didn't want to tell the truth."

"I wasn't *trying* to keep things from you," he said weekly.

"That didn't exactly stop you from lying."

We stood, staring at each other like strangers in a kitchen we had both been naked in a million times. It struck me as funny in that moment.

"This is amazing technology Kai. It really is. But I think you need to be careful."

"Great power and responsibility and all that?" He chuckled.

"Yeah."

"I still love you," he said and it felt like the truth. I wanted it to be.

"Sad how sometimes that isn't enough."

IX

Three Years Later

The woman's eyes flew open, the smell of coffee and pine needles in the air. She leapt out of bed, threw a robe and her slippers on, and raced down stairs.

This never got old to her, no matter how old *she* got. Gregory already sat in the living room, the girls somehow not up yet.

"Are they still sleeping?" she asked.

He smiled at her. "Appears that way."

He handed her a steaming cup of coffee and poured a generous amount of Bailey's in it. The warmth radiated through her, warding off the cold that settled on the drafty house no matter how tightly they closed the windows. They'd need replacing soon. Any second, really, but that's a matter for another day.

Now, she enjoyed the hot mug between her fingers and settled herself on Gregory's lap as they both stared at the twinkling tree.

"They will be up any second," he said.

"Mhmm."

"And it will be pure chaos once they do."

"Insanity," she confirmed.

"Wanna open your present now?"

"Yes!"

Gregory got up and snuck around the tree. She squealed when she opened the diamond earrings. Larger than the ones she pointed out in the store. Unnecessary, but not like she'd ever dream of returning them.

"Thank you, baby. Oh, your turn!"

She brought out a package about the same size as a shoe box, and handed it over to him. He gave it a shake, but it made no noise. She shifted from side to side, finding it difficult to handle the excitement. Her thrill at actually finding one. She would have sworn they were all sold out, the news said they had been for weeks, but she walked into the little electronic store and there it was.

"A Complete Home?" he said in shock after ripping off the paper. "How the hell did you find this!"

She beamed at him and shrugged, like it was no big deal when really, she ran all over town.

He pulled it out of the box and moved a few things off the console table to access the plug. As soon as electricity ran through it, colored lights start running around the outside of it. Even she has to admit how cool it looked.

"Hello," a woman's clear voice said.

He looked at his wife before leaning close to the console. "Hi," he said.

"What is your name?" the voice asked.

He smiled at his wife and gave an excited laugh. She heard footsteps come down the stairs and moved to clean up the wrapping paper, evidence of their transgression.

"My name is Gregory," he said in a slow, clear voice, unsure how he should speak to it.

"Gregory, my name is Rosie. I can't wait to connect with you."

KRISTIN DURFEE

Kristin Durfee grew up outside of Philadelphia where an initial struggle with reading blossomed into a love and passion for the written word.

She is the author of the Four Corners Trilogy as well as short stories in the Alvarium Experiment and Thrill of the Hunt anthologies. She is currently working on her next novel for young adults.

Kristin resides outside of Orlando, FL, and when not enjoying the theme parks or Florida sun, she spends most of her time with her husband, son, and their quirky dogs.

She is a member of the Florida Writers Association.

MY BEST FRIEND JEN

BY ERICA GERALD MASON

JEWELRY BOX

"**H**ey! Loser! Open the door!"

From my place on the couch, I stretched and used my foot to part the curtains. I laughed as Jen took her hand out of her green hoodie's pocket, waved at me, then pressed her middle finger against the glass. The joints in my knees popped as I stood; I groaned as loudly as I could, hoping Jen would hear me. It worked.

"Don't let me interrupt your nap time," Jen smirked, moving past me and into the living room. She sat on the couch and put her feet up on the coffee table.

"Hey, that's my spot," I mumbled.

"Yeah, I know," Jen answered, snuggling her shoulders deeper into the couch cushions. "That's why I chose it. It's still warm."

"Gross."

"Yeah, it's gross," she continued as she wiggled into a more comfortable . "But I haven't seen you in a few days, so this is how I make up for lost time."

I sat next to her on the couch and placed my feet on top of hers on the coffee table.

"Hey!"

"Hey, yourself," I said, not bothering to contain my yawn. I sat back and crossed my arms, not wanting to look Jen in the eyes. "Did you find her?"

Jen's shoulders drooped and she took her feet off the table.

"No," she said. "My sister's taken off with her loser boyfriend before, but never like this. Usually she calls or texts or...something. She never just disappears."

"Do you think they got married?" I asked. "Cuz your mom would kill her."

"My dad says he hopes she is married," Jen stood up and walked to the television, turning it off. "He says she'd be someone else's problem."

"I was watching that!" I squealed as I fumbled for the remote.

"No you weren't," Jen said, crossing her arms as she moved in front of the television.

I pressed a few buttons on the remote, but Jen's body stood in the way. I sighed and tossed the remote on the couch.

"Ok then, dork," I said. "What do you want to do? Go to the park? Grab something to eat? Finish our physics homework? What?"

"How about we play with this?" Jen reached into her hoodie pocket and pulled out a small wooden box. "Don't drop it, genius."

She tossed it toward my outstretched hands. The box slipped from my fingers, bounced on my lap and landed on the cushion next to me.

"I told you not to drop it!" Jen scrambled around the table and picked up the box. Her brow furrowed as she examined it for cracks. Her expression softened into a half smile as she placed the box gently in my hands. "Try not to ruin it, dummy."

"What is it?"

"An elephant. Why don't you open it and see?"

I struggled with the lid for a minute and couldn't open it. I offered the box back to Jen, who shook her head no.

"Nope." Jen said as she sat next to me. "It's gotta be you that opens it."

I raised my right eyebrow at her and placed the box on the coffee table.

"Is there going to be a dick in this box?"

"No."

"I picture of a dick?"

"No."

"A plastic dick?"

"Oh my God, it's not a dick! Just open it."

Jen picked up the box and pressed it into my right hand. I ran my fingernails along the ridge and pried the box open.

Inside was a little toy ballerina, dressed in a pink tutu.

I groaned and closed the lid. Jen reached over and opened it again.

"A ballerina box? You came over here to show me a stupid old ballerina box? How old are you? Seventeen or seven?"

I used my thumb and forefinger to flick the little figure inside. The ceramic toy made a small thunk sound as it wobbled on the attached spring.

"Don't do that!" Jen grabbed the box from my hands and gently closed the lid.

"What's your deal?" I asked, skeptical of her reaction. Jen jumped at the question.

"The box belongs to my sister," Jen said as she placed the box on the coffee table and then leaned back next to me. "You know how she loves vintage everything? She bought it at some estate sale last week. It plays a music box version of a super dirty rap song or something. I thought you'd think it was funny, that's all."

"I didn't hear any music when I opened the lid," I said. "Isn't that how these things normally work?"

Jen groaned and rolled her eyes.

"You have to wind it, dummy."

She picked up the box and handed it to me. I examined it more closely. I noted the deep carvings into the sides of the box the second time I held it. The grooves were thin, but deep, and ran the length of two sides.

"What are those?" I asked, pointing at the ridges.

"How the hell am I supposed to know? I didn't freakin' make it. I didn't even buy it. You ask too many questions." Jen's voice rose as she answered me - her voice trembled a little toward the end.

"Are you ok?" I asked, as I put the box back on the table. "You seem... out of it today."

"I'm fine."

"Let's watch some dog videos," I said. "That always cheers you up. Lemme grab my laptop."

I stood and walked to the dining room.

"What was the name of that one video?" I asked. "The one we saw last week? The puppy who took a bite of a lemon? Do you remember? Was it a German shepherd or a golden retriever."

My Best Friend Jen

I picked up my laptop and turned to find Jen standing behind me. I hadn't realized she was following me.

"Jesus, Jen!"

"Sorry. Sorry." Jen looked at my laptop and books on the table. "Are you still doing chemistry homework?"

"No. I mean, yeah. I mean, I was."

"How about I go grab my book from home and we'll work on it together?"

"Uhhhh. Okay."

"I mean, if it doesn't interfere with your nap time."

I gave Jen the finger and smiled.

"Yeah. Sure. Ok."

"I'll go home and get my stuff and come right back."

"Bring snacks. All we have here are kale and apple chips."

"Gross."

"That's not even the worst part about it. They're mixed together - like trail mix."

"Double gross. Ok, I'll bring food. But I want you to listen to the ballerina box song when I'm gone."

"Why?" I groaned, stretching out the word until it took me almost 10 seconds to say.

"You're gonna think it's hilarious." Jen said, zipping up her hoodie as she walked to the front door. She turned to face me; her left hand gripped the doorknob. "In fact, I'm not gonna bring over any snacks until you call me and tell me you've listened to it."

Jen reached into her hoodie pocket and pulled out her cell phone.

"And I'm gonna stay on the phone while you do it, loser." Jen dialed my number and waited for my phone to ring.

On cue, my phone rang from the living room.

"I think you have a phone call," Jen said, her body shook with laughter.

"Dammit, Jen!"

"You better answer it!"

I shook my head and walked over to my phone.

"It's gonna go to voicemail! You better answer it!"

I picked up my phone and rejected the call.

"Why'd you do that?" Jen shrieked, her voice going so high it sounded like a whistle.

"I'll just listen to the music with you," I said as I walked back to the dining room, brining my phone with me.

"Nah," Jen said, shaking her head so hard her ponytail came loose. "I'm gonna go get snacks. You listen to it."

"Whatever. Ok," I said as I shrugged my shoulders and waved her away. "If it will get me something other than kale and apple chips, then yes."

Jen clapped her hands and opened the door.

"I'll be right back."

"Yeah, yeah, yeah. Love you."

Jen stopped at the door and turned to me, her eyes wide.

I bit my lip in confusion. Jen and I had been next door neighbors our whole lives. We told each other 'I love you' at least three times a day. Why was she so...off?

"I-I- I love you, too," Jen said as she left.

The door closed behind her with a small *click* and I turned my attention to the ballerina box.

Every ballerina box I'd ever seen was made of either stiff cardboard or enamel - this was the first one I'd seen made of wood. The box didn't have any store or maker's marks; it looked to be homemade. There were no nails that I could see; the pieces of wood fit together neatly...whoever crafted the box knew what he or she was doing.

The only metal pieces were the hinges, which seemed to be made of dark brass. The hinges weren't just placed on top and screwed on, the boxmaker had made tiny little grooves into the containers so the hinges lay flush against the wood. It wasn't my style at all, but it was beautiful.

I turned the box over and over in my hands, enjoying the weight of it. I sat at the dining room table just as my cell phone rang. I glanced at the caller id and laughed: Jen.

I answered the phone, but before I could say anything, I could hear her voice.

"Look out the window!"

I looked out the dining room window and didn't see anyone.

"Not that one. God. The kitchen window."

I turned and saw Jen in her kitchen, holding up two containers of Chinese takeout. She waved them over her head.

My Best Friend Jen

"It's General Tso's chicken and shrimp fried rice," Jen said in a sing-song voice. "You're favorites. And I'm not bringing them over until you listen to the ballerina box."

"You don't play fair!"

"Of course I don't," Jen answered, sing-shouting and doing a little dance. "It's one of the things you love about me."

"I'm hanging up now."

I hung up the phone and turned to walk back to the dining room. My phone rang in my hand. I groaned and answered it.

"What?! I said I'm doing it now!"

"Huh? What?"

"Mom?"

"Is that how you answer the phone?"

"No."

"Well you just did, so...:"

"Yeah. Sorry about that."

"Honey, it's ok. Just wanted to let you know I'm at the store. Do you need anything special?"

"No, not really. I can't think of anything. Maybe no more kale and apple chips?"

"Those were pretty awful, weren't they?" She laughed and her voice muffled as she held the phone away from her mouth.

"What's that, Mom? I didn't hear you."

"I said, I'll have to balance it out with something fried."

"Oh dear God, thank you. I was about go out and get something."

"Well, you still might need to. I'm picking up a few things for us, and then I'm going to ride around town with Jen's parents. They still can't find Millie."

"Yeah, I heard. Jen's coming over here in a few minutes."

"Good. Try to keep her company, OK? Her mom is worried - Millie left without her cell phone, her wallet...nothing. It's...not good."

"I know Mom. I will."

"Love you sweetie."

"Love you too."

I double checked the window and I saw that Jen no longer stood watch over me. I eased open the jewelry box and looked inside.

The ballerina figurine was pretty boring. She wore a pink tutu, tights and shoes; her hair stood tall in a bun. The dancer's mouth formed a perfect

63

'o' as she stood en pointe, her arms gracefully extended over her head. I opened and closed the lid a few times, watching as the dancer folded and unfolded to a standing position. She stood on an attached wooden circle which held the music mechanism - a little silver knob extended from its side to wind it up.

I don't know what I expected to see, but it wasn't a boring ballerina. I hoped the song was better. I reached into the box and turned the knob.

I turned the knob over and over, but no music came out. I closed the lid and shook the box a little, then opened it again. Nothing. I repeated the process, this time pressing my ear to the wood. A note played - louder and shriller than I expected.

My heart pounded in my ears; it drowned out the sound of the note, which still hung in the air. I closed the lid and started to shove the box back on the table but thought better of it. I hurried back to the living room and flung myself back onto the couch. I tried to place the song but stopped myself. I wouldn't be able to figure it out with just one note. In my lap, I felt the box grow warm; almost as though I pressed a button to preheat an oven.

I opened the box again and the music played, the sound was all sharp edges and hard surfaces. I frowned as I listened closely - it wasn't any song I'd ever heard before.

As the ballerina turned, I noticed how weird she looked. She didn't seem to enjoy her twirl. Every other ballerina box I'd ever seen had a dancer that looked happy. Or at least content. This one looked terrified. Her jaw looked like she held a scream in her throat and a plan in her heart.

I shook my head, frustrated with myself for being so silly, even as the song played louder and louder. *It was a stupid old handmade ballerina box, and the person who made it didn't know how to make a stupid ballerina*, I thought.

It wasn't weird that I didn't recognize the song. Jen and Millie knew all kinds of old-school songs. I just listened to whatever came on the radio. Jen probably brought the box over to laugh at my horrible taste in music.

I started to stand up again, but I noticed something else. I was sure I remembered seeing the ballerina wearing a tutu. I noticed because the tutu was frilly and pink and...well... ugly. But now...now, the dancer wasn't wearing a tutu. She wore a leotard, tights and shoes, but no tutu.

I looked in the box to see if the garment slipped off the figure. The box was empty. I closed the lid and retraced my steps from the dining room to the living room. Nothing. I blinked and turned my head away, making sure to focus on the floor for several minutes before opening the ballerina box.

The music played as the ballerina kept turning. I shook my head at myself again, then put the box back onto the table, placing it where I left it before. I went to the kitchen, poured a glass of iced tea, and returned to the living room. I avoided the couch and chose to sit on the floor in front of the ballerina box.

I took a sip of water as I opened the lid and immediately began to sputter and cough.

If I thought that the dancer looked scared before, that was nothing compared to the expression I saw when I peered into the box. How did I miss the way she looked at me with such fear and anticipation? Her arms weren't stretched overhead in a twirl - her wrists crossed in a fighting pose, her fists clenched into tight little balls. Her lips pursed into a tight red circle as her eyes squinted in preparation...in preparation for what?

As I watched her turn, I felt like she was waiting for something. Or for someone.

But that wasn't the worst part of it. Her expression was bad, but it was a lot worse than I thought.

Somehow, even thought it was impossible, the ballerina had gotten bigger.

I could barely close the lid of the music box - I had to shove tuck in the figures arms inside as I shoved the box back onto the table. I couldn't stop picturing her terrified face as I closed the lid. She seemed to be begging me for something. What did she want? Why was she so afraid?

I told myself I wouldn't open the box again. I called Jen. The phone rang twice; she sounded breathless as she said hello.

"Did you listen to it yet?"

"I started to, but it's creeping me out. I left it in the living room."

"Well, duh. It's supposed to creep you out. It's like, a joke thing. Don't be such a baby."

"I'm not a baby, Jen. This thing is freaky."

"It's just a joke! And fine, I'll just eat this Chinese food all by myself. Enjoy your *kale*."

"You swear it's just a joke."

"Yes!"

"Ok. Whatever. Ok. I'll finish it. But it better be worth it."

"Trust me. It's worth it."

I hung up the phone and glanced out the window. Jen gave me the thumbs up and pointed to the living room. I nodded and returned to the living room and my place on the floor.

It's a joke. It's supposed to be scary-funny. I'll take one last look, and I'll get to the punchline.

It was a ballerina box, just a ballerina box. Everything I thought I saw was impossible and part of the joke.

It's a joke.

It's a joke.

I said it to myself over and over. I think a part of me knew it wasn't joke, though. I giggled as I opened the box. Whether it was from fear, the anticipation of a good joke, or good old-fashioned nervousness, I don't know. I held my breath as I flipped the box open and looked inside.

The music screeched. I hurried to cover my ringing ears. The ballerina popped up, her arms flailed around her, narrowly missing my face. I couldn't see anything but pink: pink leotard, pink tights, pink shoes, it all exploded out of the box like a sneeze.

I backed up from the box, hoping to stay clear whatever horrors had tumbled out of the box. In the nanosecond it took for me to react, I felt strong hands clutching me, grabbing my arms and legs and pulling me with such power that I didn't have time to scream. It wasn't a fair fight - I had no opportunity to resist. I felt my limbs contorting as I fell and I finally found the strength to scream. When I opened my mouth, music came out; the same music from the music box. Every time I opened my mouth to protest, the music poured out, growing fainter and fainter with every gasp. The room grew around me as I shrank smaller and smaller. Until the coffee table was the size of a city park.

With my screams taken from me, the room fell into silence. The front door opened and Jen walked into my house. She walked toward me, her face a contorted in concern. She moved past me and leaned over to pick something off of the floor.

It was her sister, Millie.

Millie, who had gone missing. Millie, had her parents and my mom searching for her. Jen helped her sister up from the floor and steadied her as she found her footing.

My Best Friend Jen

"Are you ok?" Jen asked. She hugged her sister as if she was afraid her sibling would disappear again.

"Yeah. I'm ok," Millie managed before she burst into tears.

Jen and Millie hugged each other, each not sure if they wanted to let the other go. I managed a tiny scream, which came out like a weak note.

They both jumped in shock. Millie leaned over to peer at me.

"Who is that?"

"It's Ella," Jen said.

"Oh no," Jen said. "Ella from next door?"

Jen looked at the floor and nodded. Millie hugged her sister again.

"Thanks, Jen," she said. "I know she's your best friend."

"But you're my sister, Mills," Jen said.

"What happened to the girl who's place I took?"

"She's long gone. She told me how to get you out of there before she left though. And she said if we ever try to get her, back in the box, she'll kill us."

"Do you blame her? I think she got tricked into this just like I did."

Jen looked down at me and bit her lip.

"I'm so sorry Ella," she said. "But she's my sister."

She held the knob in place as she closed the lid. I couldn't even scream.

I knew they were sisters; I knew Jen only wanted to help her. At first, I thought they would try to get someone else to take my place. But as the days went on, I could tell they planned to leave me there. My mom even came into Jen's room, all timid and afraid, and asked my best friend she had seen me. Jen told my mother I went out for some food that wasn't kale and apple chips. It made my mother cry in a way I had never seen before; that was when I got angry. I think Jen must have sensed it, because I moved from drawer to shelf to closet to garage.

The first few years in the box, I forgave Millie and Jen. But as time went by, the angrier I feel. Millie was only in the box for a few days; after all this time, I can't take much more of this. I'm starting to feel impatient, I'm tired of this dance. I'm tired of waiting for the next person…for the next person to find me. And when that person comes, whoever it is…I can't wait to do the same thing to them that was done to me.

ERICA GERALD MASON

Erica Gerald Mason tells the truth, even when it's disguised as fiction. She loves writing strong women with soft hearts, unlikely heroes, and conversations where silences are just as important as booming declarations. Her books include poetry, young adult, paranormal, thriller, literary fiction, and flash fiction. She lives in an Atlanta suburb with a husband, kids, a cowardly yorkiepoo named Hero, and a fluffy bunny named Pickles.

www.ericageraldmason.com
www.amazon.com/author/ericageraldmason
www.instagram.com/ericagmason
www.facebook.com/ericageraldmasonwriter
www.twitter.com/ericagmason

Cords

By F.D. Gross

Electrical Cords

Tarik Glymph jumped back as the snake hit the glass. He watched its mouth slide down the side of the cage as its tongue flicked back and forth, tasting the air.

The school bell rang.

"Class, remember to prepare over holiday break for the dissection lab," chimed Mr. Talsbys whining voice. "We'll be learning the anatomy of reptiles and their digestive systems, specifically, snakes."

Tarik sighed. Just when he was satisfied Friday had come and gone, Talsby had to go and ruin it. He had completely forgotten about *after* the break.

Chuckling and sniggering came from a group of girls across the classroom as they got up to leave. Tarik was embarrassed. They were watching him the whole time. He couldn't help it; snakes terrified him.

"Stupid ass girls, man. Don't worry about them. I can't wait to see their faces when I throw the snakeskins on their lunch. You watch."

Thomas Pellnor laughed. He was the jokester of the class. "Damn bro, that's sick! You draw some dope ass pictures man."

Pellnor positioned himself over Tarik's desk so that his back was facing Talsby's desk. He gawked at the drawing Tarik had been working on, the snake in the glass cage. The resemblance was remarkable.

"Man, I'm telling you. You could make some cheddar off of these." Pellnor leaned in, whispering. "We're totally partners for lab, right? With your talent and my skills at cutting shit up, we'll get an A for sure."

Before Tarik could say a word, before he could react, Pellnor got up and left, passing Talsby on the way out. "Later, Taffy."

Mr. Talsby's face screwed up. "Excuse me. What did you say?"

But before he could get a response, Pellnor was gone and Tarik was left alone in the room with his teacher. *So much for not being the last one in class* thought Tarik as Talsby converged on him, his smelly breath of stale pretzels issuing forth with every word.

"Such real talent, Mr. Glymph. I'd hate to see it go to waste by hanging around the wrong crowd." He motioned behind him with his head. "Talent like this is an extraordinary thing." He looked At Tarik's drawing through his large framed glasses. "You know, given the circumstances, I never had a chance to say thank you for what your father did for this country. He was a true hero." He placed a hand on Tarik's shoulder while letting out a loud sigh. The air permeated pretzels. "I know it must be hard—for you that is, to adjust to all this."

Not a day went by that Tarik wasn't reminded of his father and his heroic service. *Some hero.* If they only knew the true horror of his story and the reason why he and his family moved to Savannah, Georgia. He hated it here; it was always hot.

Still, he collected his papers and drawing and performed his best fake smile, leaving Talsby to saturate in his science lab of snakes and formaldehyde.

Tarik kept to himself, ignoring the looks and waves from fellow students and teachers as he left campus grounds. He didn't know these people and he knew they didn't care about him. They only knew him because his father was a war hero. His mind fumed at the thought of his father's death as he made his way to the front of the school. Yeah, his father was hero all right, served in the Iraq war, did five tours over seas until finally being honorably discharged for getting shot in the leg. But in a week's time, half way through the school's winter break, marked the anniversary of his suicide. New Year's Eve. The night when his PTSD triggered from the fireworks and he hung himself in the garage with an extension cord.

Tarik knew he would be waiting a long time before his mother picked him up in between her Uber's and so he was surprised to see her waiting by her car in the carpool, long extensions blowing in the wind and smoking Virginia slims.

To this, he was relieved—some. At least he wouldn't have to wait around and listen to Herschel the security guard talk about how Pellnor clogged the toilets again in the locker rooms.

"TGIF, right hun?" chimed his mother as she closed the door to the 99' charcoal-grey Buick. Cigarette smoke hovered in the air, twirling like fog as Tarik said nothing, staring out the window, gazing at the brown dull exterior of the school, *his* school.

"Bad day I take it. I know. At least you don't have to listen to old ladies talk about themselves all day while driving them around town." Accelerating out of the carpool, she placed a hand on his leg, patting it. "It'll get better, hun, I promise. It just takes time."

How many times had Tarik heard *that* before? He sucked his teeth. *Time. Time didn't heal shit.* He was still thinking about his father's suicide, when he found him hanging in the gloom of the garage light, swaying back and forth with the dust settling an hour after the ball dropped. No one thought it would happen. Doctors said to watch out for signs of depression, but Tarik and his family only ever saw him happy.

"I still don't see why we have to live in that big ass house," said Tarik, pulling his leg away. "We could have easily stayed in an apartment and then you wouldn't have to work two jobs."

"That mouth, Tarik. Watch that mouth." She looked at him with scrunched up eyebrows. "You know, you could at least show a little appreciation. I'm trying to make things good for you and your sister, trying to keep things the way they were. The least you could do is appreciate it."

Tarik did. It was his Mom who thought it was best they move to a new town, have a fresh beginning. Start over.

"I do appreciate it," said Tarik under his breath, but his mom never heard it. She was lost in her thoughts, staring at the road with that glaze in her eyes. She was over-worked and he knew it. He didn't want to stress her out anymore then she already was, but he was hurting inside, just like her, just like his sister, if not worse.

The rest of the ride home was silence. They passed an old cemetery two blocks away from their house and turned down a street canopied in dark oak trees. Tarik couldn't think of anything else to say except "I love you, mom," as he exited the car. "See you tonight." But the moment he said the words, he saw the look in her eyes that told him other wise.

"Sorry, hun, I'm working Denny's tonight after my Uber shift."

Now he felt worse and managed a smile despite his depressed feelings.

"I'll see you in the morning, if I don't pass out before you get up."

"Ok, mom."

Tarik turned to leave.

"Oh and hun," the words hung in the air over the low rumble of the exhaust, "make sure to unpack more of the boxes and clean up the basement."

"Yeah, mom, I know."

She blew him a kiss and waved as she drove away, leaving him to climb the old brick steps that led up to the house. Already he could hear the whirling of the fans as he approached the front door. Turning the key, he pushed his way inside, catching the door on one of the many extension cords running through the house. Hot air blasted his face from the many floor fans stationed strategically around. The scent of fresh laundry lingered. The low resonance of R&B wafted its way down from the second floor letting Tarik know his sister Alyssa, his arch-nemesis, was home.

Tarik was tired. He was in no mood to encounter his sister, and so when he climbed the stairs and passed her room without incident, he breathed a sigh of relief. He was the luckiest person on the planet. Throwing his book bag into the chair at his desk, he rifled through his papers and found the drawing of the snake he worked on earlier. Looking at it for a minute, he threw into to the growing pile on his desk. Collapsing onto the bed, he glanced around his room, admiring his work taped to the walls. Landscapes, video game characters, the girl at school. This was his sanctuary, his place of solace, and relished every second of it.

He fell asleep with a smile on his face.

An hour later he woke to the void of silence. The sun had gone down.

Swallowing a few times to moisten his dry throat, he made his way down the hall passing his sister's room with caution. Fabric softener lingered in the air, but she was nowhere to be found. Maybe she was down stairs watching TV. Quietly he descended while the noise of fans masked his movement as he passed the darkened living room. With no glow coming from the television showing her usual channel of HGTV, it was safe to assume Alyssa had gone out with one of her friends from the local college. Good for her. Even better for Tarik.

Entering the kitchen feeling more relaxed, Tarik raided the fridge for an iced tea to get the dry taste out of his mouth. Leaning against the counter, he stared at the basement door debating whether he was going to tackle cleaning today or procrastinate till tomorrow. There were so many other things he could be doing right now such as working on his drawings for his comic book or playing Call of Duty. Whenever he played war games, he envisioned himself as his dad fighting on the battlefield. He missed his dad and his eyes teared up.

As he reached for a napkin, the basement door suddenly banged open revealing a hovering basket of freshly cleaned laundry. Tarik nearly knocked his tea over. A pair of hands held the basket at each side as Alyssa turned her body, kicking the door closed behind her.

"Finally. You're lazy ass is up," said Alyssa with a condescending attitude. "Don't you have a basement to cleanup, turd brain?"

"Shut up, Alyssa. I was getting a drink."

Alyssa stared at Tarik as she shouted over her ear buds. "Mom said you need to clean that shit up. I can't be the only one doing stuff around here."

Tarik's blood boiled, but knew starting a fight with his sister was a path to destruction. "Whatever," he said, opening the door and pushing past her.

The basement was dark and somewhat cooler than the rest of the house. With the AC broken, the fans were the only salvation from dying of heat exhaustion. One of the larger fans rested toward the back, droning louder than the rest. Tarik wished he had his headphones with him, but knew going back up to get them wasn't worth another encounter with Alyssa.

To say the least, the place was a mess.

Boxes stacked on other boxes. Boxes with flaps open overflowed with extension cords. They poured onto the floor like spaghetti. Piles of clothes were everywhere he looked and wondered if it was possible his mom and sister owned so many fabrics.

With the washer and dryer banging around, he set to the task of cleaning. Not once did he stop to take a break as he unpacked the boxes containing tablecloths and candles, CD's and hardware. In one part of the basement,

73

he found an open box full of garbage bags and rifled through the old stuff left behind from the previous owners. Broken tiles, cans of oil, dried up buckets of paint. In one of the corners he found some old musty pallets with strips of plastic used for god knows what. In the end, he cleared most of the shelving to make room for their new stuff and took the time to roll up the many extension cords collected over the years. Tarik's dad never believed in throwing anything away and so it was ironic the one thing they had the most of was the very thing that ended his father's life.

Extension cords. Long and black like snakes, Tarik knew it would take forever to sort through them all so he threw them into two empty boxes and set them on top of the innumerable boxes of clothes. His mom and sister would have to sort through them eventually. He wasn't going to sort their underwear.

Satisfied with his work and everything put away, he headed back up, clicking the light off on his way out. Greeted with the familiar smell of mildew, he went back to the fridge and opened the door, letting the cold air brush against his light layer of perspiration. As he poured himself another glass of tea, Alyssa returned with her basket empty and headphones blaring. She shot him a mocking stare as she headed towards the basement door. "Hanging in there, turd brain?" she asked. Taking two steps down, she slammed the door behind her and again Tarik was left to the humming of the refrigerator and fans.

"God I hate her," said Tarik under his breath.

A loud bang came from the other side of the door and was followed by Alyssa screaming. "Tarrrrrrik! Tarrrrrik you little shit!"

Tarik's blood froze. Quickly he opened the door and to his surprise, found his sister sprawled across the floor at the bottom of the stairs. The basket of clothes were scattered all over and immediately Tarik recognized the extension cords laying across the stairs mid way down.

What the hell? He watched his sister collect herself from the floor.

"Tarik you asshole! You think this is a joke? I could have broken my neck!" She rubbed her knees where she scuffed the skin right off and already he could see tiny beads of blood forming.

"I didn't do it!" shouted Tarik. He was just as confused as his sister. "It wasn't me!" he pleaded.

"You think I was born yesterday, dumb ass? Wait till mom hears about this. She's going to flip her shit!"

Cords

Tarik didn't know what to say or do. He knew he put the cords away. It was the last thing he did and yet there they were, lying across the steps like living snakes. The thought of it sent a prickling sensation up his spine. "Look! I'm sorry, Alyssa, but I really didn't do it. I put everything away, I swear it! Don't tell mom, it'll stress her out even more!"

Alyssa stormed back up the stairs, shoving him aside with a forceful, hateful intent.

"Look, I'll make it up to you, I promise!" shouted Tarik up the stairs.

As she disappeared from sight, he could hear her voice from the first floor bathroom yelling back at him. "Oh you'll make it up alright! I'll make damn sure of it!"

For the next week Alyssa reminded Tarik of what he had done. He knew he was innocent, yet she taunted him every day. She teased him about how he wanted to kill his sister and that he was immature and an ungrateful little turd. When it got to be overwhelming, he would shut himself up in his room and recall the image of his sister sprawled at the bottom of the stairs. Despite the temporary satisfaction it gave him, the incident puzzled him tremendously. It gave him anxiety. So he did all he could to banish the thought from his brain. Video games. Exercise. But it wouldn't go away. His mom was barely home as it was, so he couldn't rely on her for help. She was a widowed mom, working double shifts nearly every night. So he did the only thing he knew how to do.

Draw.

He drew and drew, sketching with pencils and rubbing with charcoal.

Eventually, Friday night came and went and Tarik completed the image of the doorway looking down into the basement with Alyssa lying on the floor. Yawning, he staggered to bed and for the first time in a week, he went to sleep with a smile.

Tarik was a vivid dreamer.

The moment he'd wake up from a dream he would go straight to his paper and charcoal and scrub away at the thick construction paper until the image appeared in abstract form.

Tonight's dream was no exception.

He stared across the table at his friend Tommy, gritting his teeth and hoping to god he wouldn't lose. But the muscles in his arms gave, and his arm wobbled back and forth and Tommy won the arm wrestling match. It was his twelfth birthday, so he had to let him win.

Tarik knew it was the last sleep over he'd ever go to in his life. He and his friends were getting to that age where girls took the forefront of all interests.

A night full of swimming, pizza, and cake eventually led them to an early comma. But Tarik knew better. He wasn't falling asleep before the others. Bad things happened to those who couldn't stay up.

Shawn was the first to pass out. His cheeks were covered in toothpaste and his nose was tickled until he smeared the sticky paste all over his face. Eric was the second to go. He fell asleep with his head resting against the couch. His hand was placed in warm water until the wet spot formed around his crotch. Eventually, Tarik fell asleep before Tommy. He dreamt about Natasha, his sister's friend and her long beautiful hair. She was there with him, rubbing her hands over his body, working closer to the spot that would send him over the edge.

He moved the blanket aside to kiss her tender lips and his eyes bolted open. A snake slithered across his body — Tommy's pet snake.

Tarik screamed, throwing the covers back as he sat upright in bed.

"God damn it, Alyssa!"

Mid-morning sunlight flooded his bedroom while his sister laughed hysterically from the edge of his bed. Drenched in sweat, he was covered in extension cords, wrapped around his arms and draped across his body. The whirling of the fans no longer droned.

"It's not funny, Alyssa!" shouted Tarik, throwing the cords off his bed.

"Pay back's a bitch," cackled Alyssa. Her voice trailed down the hallway leaving Tarik to wallow in his suffering.

Tarik's rage consumed him. He charged down the hall towards his mother's room, forgetting everything he said a week ago about stressing her out. He didn't care, Alyssa had crossed the line.

He stopped at his mother's door and peered inside. She looked so peaceful sleeping in the dark room. Sucking in a deep breath, he bit his lip and backed away, closing the door gently. "Damn."

Tarik made his way down to the kitchen to clear his mind and shake the images of the snakes slithering over his body. As he poured himself a glass of OJ, he realized the door to the basement was slightly ajar. As he moved to close it, Alyssa popped through suddenly, chiming her usual demeaning words. "What the hell's the matter with you, turd brain? Don't you think trying to kill me last week was enough? The basement is a complete disaster. AGAIN. What the hell have you been doing down there?" She stormed up stairs with her basket of clean clothes.

Tarik stood bewildered. What the hell was she talking about? When he went downstairs, he nearly lost it when he saw the boxes scattered all over the basement. Clothes thrown about. Pictures knocked over. Again, the extension cords we're out and jumbled up across the floor.

He sucked his teeth.

The next hour he spent cleaning the basement again and this time, he snapped a picture of it with his cell phone. "There. Now we'll see who's crazy."

The rest of day he spent trying not to think about what the day signified. It was one year ago he walked into the garage and found his father hanging from the support beam by an extension cord. The image burned in his mind no matter how much he tried to forget. No manner of drawing or sleep could save him today.

Eventually dinnertime came. Tarik's Mom twirled spaghetti on her plate while Alyssa texted on her phone. Tarik sighed. Tonight was going to suck. With his mom having to work a double shift at Denny's again, he wasn't going to be with her when the ball dropped. What was worse is that he would be stuck here with Alyssa all night. He over heard her conversation on the phone earlier how her so-called friends sold her out.

Great.

"Listen you two. I want no fighting tonight. Got it?" Tarik's Mom eyed them both earnestly. He knew she wished they would get along better in this time of healing, but Tarik knew it wasn't possible. Alyssa was a witch. He really wanted to call her something else, but karma was already against him.

"Are you two even listening to me?" Tarik's mom dropped her fork on the plate and got up from the table. "I have to get ready for work."

Alyssa rolled her eyes at Tarik and left the table as well.

Was this how it was going to be then? His mom stressed and Alyssa a bitch?

Tarik went up to his room and shut himself out from the world. Images of his dad swaying in the garage came back strong. He shook his head hoping somehow it would work. But it didn't. Sitting at his desk, he pulled out a fresh sheet of sketch paper and began rubbing charcoal across the empty field of white. Slowly he motioned with his wrist the outline and contour of a human figure. Methodically he worked his hand back and forth, creating parallel lines along the top of the page and a chair beneath the figure. A small line connected the top of the drawing to the head of the figure and then Tarik began to cry. He cried for a time until a knock came at the door and he quickly covered up the sketch of his father hanging in the garage.

"Yeah, come in."

Tarik's mom entered the room. "I have to go hun. I love you so much. Try not to stay up too late, ok?" She gave him a big hug while his arms rested at his side. "I'll be back in the morning."

Tarik didn't know what to say. "Ok mom. Love you too."

He kept working on the drawing as he heard her car leave the drive away. For some reason, he felt better. Maybe this was the answer. Confronting his sorrow in the form of art.

It was sometime after nine o'clock when Tarik felt the first vibrations throughout the house. Fireworks exploded from the surrounding neighbors homes. The glow of red and blue reflected off the windows of the house. It was enough to distract Tarik from finishing his drawing. He went down stairs to get a drink and breathed the words "thank you" for his small reprieve. Alyssa was in the basement again doing laundry.

As he sat on the counter enjoying his tea, he waited for her to come up so he could show her proof he cleaned the basement on his phone.

Eventually she came up the stairs, and at first seemed uninterested in his presence, but, as she placed the basket of laundry down on one of the stools, she reached inside the pile of freshly cleaned fabrics and revealed a bottle of Captain Morgan Private Stock. She eyed him and the bottle intently.

"Dads favorite drink," she said, moving to the fridge and pulling out the two-liter bottle of coke.

"Alyssa, what the hell are you doing?" asked Tarik.

"What does it look like I'm doing, turd brain?"

"Mom will kill you if she finds out."

"Mom isn't here, dumb ass. And it's us." She eyed him intently. "Stop being a wuss."

She filled two glasses with rum and ice and added the coke last, mixing it with her finger. She handed one to Tarik.

"To Dad," she said, motioning with her hand and taking a swig.

Tarik never tasted alcohol. He was curious but never thought the time would come so soon. It burned all the way down.

Alyssa smiled. There were tears streaking her face. "I'm sorry, Tarik, I know I've been a bitch."

Tarik wondered if it was his sister or the rum talking, but took it for what it was worth.

"C'mon," she said, wiping her face. "Lets go watch the idiots in Time Square freeze their asses off."

They sat in the living room together for once, enjoying each other's company, instead of ripping on each other. For some reason, the things on TV got funnier and funnier, until finally, the room was spinning. The feeling was strange to Tarik and he tried to make sense of things, but couldn't. His sister started talking funny and he was having a hard time saying anything himself. Drool trickled down her face.

Tarik tried to keep his eyelids open, but The Captain sent him down to Davy Jones' locker.

Tarik woke to the sound of cheering and a dark, glowing living room. Outside, the sky erupted into thunder. Multicolored fireworks lit up the sky. The people in Time Square were hugging each other on TV. Kissing each other. The ball had already dropped.

Tarik wondered where Alyssa was. Glancing at his phone, there was a missed call from his mom. He couldn't call her back just yet. Moving from the living room to the kitchen, he flicked the switches on the walls but the lights didn't come on. It was strange the TV worked but the rest of the house didn't. It had to be a breaker.

Again Tarik thought of Alyssa. It was to quite in the house.

Pulling out his cell phone, he turned the LED light on and flashed it about the different rooms of the house. "Alyssa!" he called out. "Alyssa!"

Making his way to the kitchen, he noticed the basement door open.

Slowly he approached, holding his phone before him like a lantern. He tried the switch at the top of the stairs but like the rest, it didn't work.

"Shit," he said under his breath. Slowly he descended, one step at a time, sweeping the light before him. It was so dark, he could barely see three feet in front of him with the tiny light. He thought about the flashlight in his room, but something made the hairs on his arm rise.

"Alyssa? You down here?"

Fireworks thundered outside and illuminated the basement in a brilliant blue light through the tiny window above the washer. In that moment, Tarik saw his father hanging from the rafter by the extension cord.

All feeling left him as he stepped forward and lost his balance. Down he went, catching the edge of the stairs with his ribs. Sharp pain shot up his side as he tumbled down to the bottom. The phone bounced from his hand and shattered a few feet away. Light still glowed underneath. It was hard to take a deep breath. Something large and bulky was underneath him. Whatever it was broke his fall.

"Jesus Christ," he said trying to draw a breath. The pain was like a burning knife in his side. The smell of fabric softener was strong. He reached for the phone and illuminated the floor beneath him. He wanted to scream, but his cracked ribs said otherwise.

Alyssa's blank eyes starred at him from underneath his weight and he shuddered. He scrambled back frantically and hovered the light around him. A mass of black like snakes slithered away from her body and away from the light.

Tarik yelled and pawed at the ground. His head spun. He felt nauseated.

He kept his body low as he clamored up the steps, one hand and knee at a time. His mind raced with fear. There were snakes down here and they killed his sister.

Something gripped his neck and he couldn't breath. It pulled on him, forcing his body back down the stairs. He fought against it, resisted it, but its strength was too much. With all of his might he tried to pry the snakes from his throat, but his energy was sapped and his breath was faint.

He starred at the blank look on Alyssa's face while the light of his phone illuminated the dark.

Soon the light vanished all together.

Cords

It was early morning when Tarik's mom came home and discovered the dead bodies of her two children. Officer Danton did his best to calm her down after arriving on scene from her distressed phone call.

"Ms. Glymph, please, take it. It'll help."

Tarik's Mom took the water bottle from officer Danton and tried to drink with trembling lips.

"I know this is extremely hard for you Ms. Glymph, but we need to know. Something. *Anything.* We need leads on who might have done this."

Tarik's Mom tried to cooperate, but her sorrow was too great. She wanted to help, but she really didn't know anything. The last time she saw her children alive, they were lying on the couch in the living room passed out. She had fallen at work and splattered mayo all over herself. She came home mid shift from Denny's to change her shirt. She went down stairs and rifled through the boxes to find a new shirt suitable for work, throwing hangers and extension cords all over the place and didn't have time to clean up.

Officer Danton nodded his head in understanding as he scribbled the notes into his report.

F. D. GROSS

A prolific writer of fantasy, supernatural, and horror, F. D. Gross has been writing for years, ever since the age of twelve. Having written numerous short stories and novels, his meanderings in the literary world has led him to present his two most recent works, *Wolfgang*, a tale of dark mystery and human struggle, and *Inquisition*, the sequel to Wolfgang. They touch on the capabilities of humanity and how far love will push one's soul, even to the brink of self-destruction.

F. D. Gross studied at Florida Atlantic University where he received his bachelors degree in English and is currently working on book three of the Wolfgang Trilogy.

Social Links
Website: https://www.wolfgangchronicles.com/
Good Reads: https://www.goodreads.com/author/show/15919155.F_D_Gross
Twitter: https://twitter.com/GrellDragon
Facebook: https://www.facebook.com/Wolfgang.Chronicles/
Youtube: https://www.youtube.com/channel/UCf-ODvSjFpN-21nxe8kVnRw
Amazon: https://www.amazon.com/Wolfgang-Chronicles-1-F-D-Gross/dp/1622179951
Amazon Author Page: https://www.amazon.com/F.D.-Gross/e/B01LXM86GO/ref=ntt_dp_epwbk_0
Instagram: https://www.instagram.com/fd_gross/

SHATTERED LOVE

BY PAIGE LAVOIE

TEA POT & CUPS

I loved your grandmother very much. Do you know how much It pains me when I see her smile reflected on your face? The way the sun makes your yellow hair shine like wheat. You are undeserving, unworthy. For she- she was gorgeous in every sense of the word. As her Granddaughter of course, you have some of that beauty passed down- but there are things of hers that could never be yours- no matter how much you look alike.

I loved the wrinkles that creased on her mouth from laughing too loudly and smiling at everyone she met. The bored expression on your face day in and day out is a reminder that no matter how much you look, or sound like, you are not your grandmother.

She read in the evenings with me at her side. While you-you laze on the floor eating chips from the bag and watching television. How someone can spend so much time in front of a screen, I'll never know.

You never even look at me. Often, I think you avoid gazing in my direction on purpose. Is it painful to see the effects of your neglect? Or do you just not care for me at all?

The coat of dust on my porcelain grow is thick. Sad. Incomplete. Your grandmother would have never let me become this way. But you are not your Grandmother.

A chip in my handle. A cup growing mold at the bottom of your unkempt sink and a sugar bowl sitting on the table, with packets of stevia jammed in so tight the lid no longer fits over the top.

So, you threw it away.

That's what you do when things don't serve your purposes anymore, isn't it?

Lovers, Jobs, Clothes; I've seen you throw out laundry instead of taking it to the laundromat.

I should be placed above those things. I was a wedding present to your Grandmother and Grandfather, but you never think about that. I, just like everything else in this lonely apartment, am a part of the clutter. Boxing you in, tighter and tighter, surrounding you with thoughts of unfinished projects and memories you'd rather forget.

I'm angry when I feel an unexpected hand reach out, and it's you.

I should be happy by the sudden contact. Instead, I am anxiously anticipating your next move, as I am moved from the shelf and into your small messy kitchen.

You sit me down with a hard *thunk*. I am under your monstrosity of a coffee machine. My teacup was not intended for coffee, especially not the likes of something that comes from a Keurig pod.

So, I waited, hoping I'd hear the long-forgotten snap of the oven being turned on, and the kettle being placed on the burner- the whistling of the hot water music to my ears.

Instead, you take my cup in your cold hands, placing me right under the Keurig. I'm astonished... but most of all insulted... I am a thing of great power! A demonic of strength!

At least, I used to be.

I think, despite herself, your grandmother knew in some way. Your grandmother always took such good care of me. She was careful.

Respectful.

Beautiful.

You raised me to your lips- the liquid was hot, too hot to drink, but you're reckless- you have been ever since you were a child- she called you a "thunderstorm" but I called you a nuisance. You'd never have the patience to wait- So, I know you'll try anyway. I can feel the taste of your burning flesh, heating against my porcelain.

Delicious.

Shattered Love

It's been so long-I savor the bitter taste- before you jerk backward, letting my cup fly through the air and onto the carpet. I shatter into chunks.

It's not the first time that it's happened. But that doesn't make it hurt any less. Pain cuts through every section of my shattered self.

When you reach down, I jerk a piece of myself upwards slicing deep into your flesh. Breaking you into pieces just the way you've done to me. The blood is everywhere, and for the first time in a long while- I am happy.

I do it again and again. Slicing into your flesh as easily as paper.

The movement is small; you're clumsy anyways so there's nothing to suspect. You gasp as the blood trickles down your arm. Delicious red blood stained my porcelain.

It's been centuries since I tasted blood. Long before I met your grandmother's smiling eyes, and even longer before I was cursed into this form.

You look up in horror. I see your eyes. The same bright color as hers. I stop, flooding with thoughts of her.

If your Grandmother truly did know who I was before. Sometimes I wonder if she would have thrown me right into the bin. Other times I wonder if she would have tried to save me. There were times I thought she could. Break me free of this porcelain cage and lead me to salvation.

I'd felt her lips hundreds of times. I wanted her to feel mine pressing gently against hers. I wanted her heart, her soul... *her blood.*

For years, I sat on the shelf watching. I couldn't help but picture myself in your grandfather's place. He was a good man. He made her eyes sparkle and her cheeks blush even after they'd been married for decades. He never liked me. Perhaps due to the times he "accidentally" burned himself on the rim of the cup. He took to using a big coffee mug instead. One that is now covered in stains and sitting at the back of your cupboard. They danced to records in the kitchen. Laughing as he spun her around, her skirt billowing out around her like the pedals of a flower.

I could never have made her laugh that way.

If only I could have tried. *Oh, did I want to.*

She loved him as a man. And she loved me as a tea set.

It wasn't enough.

She would never stray, I knew that, but the desire grew. Even as she turned old and grey, she perhaps looked even more beautiful. She was a holy woman, of modesty, virtue, and faith. But it was all I had. Nothing would sway her to the darkness, but every afternoon, I felt her light. From the humming in the kitchen to her gentle touch. It warmed me from the inside more than any cup of tea.

Maybe that's to me, was a part of her charm. Even in my purest form, I wasn't sure that I'd be able to tempt her to evil. That made the desire to try even intoxicating. Sometimes she'd look at me, in admiration for a moment too long, and I wondered perhaps if I had her. But then she'd just smile, humming a hymn to herself, and I'd realize that I was the one wrapped in her spell. And that in her presence I preferred to be a tea set and not a demon, but even more than that- I would have liked to be an ordinary human man.

I might have believed that when she was alive.

Your blood is on the floor now, surrounding me with little droplets, it gives me the warmth that no cup of tea can. It feels good. *But it's not enough.* If I angle myself just right… *there it is.*

I've cut through a vein, and now the blood is all around us. You're screaming. You have broken me, scattered me, but with your blood. I am restored.

I loved your grandmother very much.

I could never have hurt her.

My desire for power.

The arching to return to myself and my kingdom.

To kill her to regain my original life and body– no, I would have instead stayed at her side forever as a tea set. Warm in her gentle hands.

Yes… I loved her more than any power in the world.

But you are not your grandmother.

PAIGE LAVOIE

Paige Lavoie brings her love for geek culture and stories of friendship onto the page in her novels "Confidence: The Diary of an Invisible Girl" and "A Girl Called Monster" She's passionate about telling the stories of characters who feel like outsiders and find the places they belong. Whether they're nerdy girls, Frankenstein monsters or anywhere in between! You can find her sharing writing advice and a slice of her daily life on www.paigelavoie.com and all of the social media places.

Amazon Author Page
https://www.amazon.com/default/e/B00IICPYQC/

Gamma Ray's GD Sink

By Fern Goodman

Garbage Disposal

Today's headline read *Death by Garbage Disposal Disaster*.

Rachel's parents died of carbon monoxide poisoning while she was at a sleepover. At least that's what the young, independent girl was told. She didn't remember them having any gas appliances. She was twelve, not stupid, and knew they overdosed on drugs, but she didn't question. Rachel moved in with her Grandmother for seven years in that musty old house. She loved being with her grandmother. Gamma made Rachel feel special, unlike her self-absorbed parents who hadn't spent time with her. Rachel even got used to living in the small gulf town of Port St. Cocket, which had its own challenges.

Between the paper mill and the nuclear power plant, the smell and threat of radiation poisoning didn't make PSC a destination location. As an inquisitive adolescent, Rachel researched the origin of the city name. Her Google search led her to the urban definition of cocket as, 'the space between the head of your penis and the end of your foreskin.' The image attached became ingrained in her mind.

Rachel left for college right after high school with money invested from her parent's life insurance policy. Even after college, Rachel spoke to her grandmother every Thursday night, but visited her only a few times. Moments after the PSC police department contacted her with the news of her grandmother's sudden death from cancer, Rachel called her boyfriend.

"My Gamma died," Rachel wailed.

Tyler, her boyfriend said, "Who died? Your Gambler died? What?"

Rachel sucked in a few sniffles, "No. My Gamma died, and I have to go to Port St. Cocket, the penis pocket." She could not say Port St. Cocket without adding 'penis pocket,' just like 'violets are blue' automatically follows 'roses are red.'

"Penis pocket? You're not making sense, I didn't even know you had a Gamma? Is that a grandmother?" Rachel detected annoyance in of his voice.

"Yes. Gamma means grandmother to me. Her last name was Ray, so I called her Gamma Ray. I never told you about her because it never came up and she lives all the way in Port St. Cocket, the penis pocket."

"There you go with the 'penis pocket' again. What the hell is that about?"

Rachel explained the history of her adopted hometown, then asked, "Can you take some time off and help me remodel, so I can sell the house?"

Tyler hesitated. "How far away is this Cocky place?"

"Let's just call it PSC, it's easier. It's a small spec of a city on the gulf, in Charlee County between Charlotte and Lee County. About three-and-a-half-hour drive from Orlando. You don't have to come to the funeral, just come when you can."

"I have a couple big projects at work. I'll have to let you know. When are you leaving and how long can you take off from work?" Tyler wanted to know.

"My boss is not employee friendly, so I may have to quit. It's okay, though. I have money saved to open my own interior design business and I can be my first customer with Gamma's house. Plus, Gamma told me she left me some money. I'm planning to leave first thing in the morning."

"Wow. Seems like your Gamma's death fit right into your schedule. Oh, crap Rach, I'm sorry, I didn't mean it to sound like that. Do you want company tonight?" Tyler whined.

"NO." Rachel replied too hastily, from the motel room only an hour from Gamma's house. "I mean, no, you don't need to do that. I'm fine.

Gonna pack and send my boss an email." Rachel hated to lie to her boyfriend of two years, but she didn't want to involve him.

After the funeral and meeting with the attorney, Rachel spent hours sorting items as keep, sell, or donate. Exhausted, she gingerly stretched out on her Grandmother's king-sized mattress, comforted by the angels and birds hand-carved into the walnut sleigh bed. The weathered hardwood pine floors and tattered area rugs were the least of her concerns. Rachel intended to modernize and sell the old house and leave PSC as quickly as possible. Surely *someone* would buy the property as a gulf side rental investment.

That night in the kitchen, Rachel measured all angles of the vintage aqua green drainboard sink her grandmother refused to upgrade. The rectangular wall-mounted basin had a white sheet draped across its front to hide the garbage disposal, that dangled like a fat cylindrical phallus between two spindly metal pipe legs. Damn thing was an eyesore to her, but Gamma had loved that old sink. She washed her hair in it for years. Sang *You Are My Sunshine* to newborn Rachel while she bathed her in it. She also started a tie-dye scarf business and named the sink Mr. Green as her CEO. On her last visit, Rachel watched her Grandmother steady herself, holding tight to the porcelain when she became dizzy from all the medications.

To Rachel, the sink represented sadness. She tapped the sink with her ringed fingers, "Gamma Ray may have loved you, but I sure as hell don't."

A loud growling sound responded to her last word. Rachel realized the noise came from her empty stomach. She hadn't had time to stop at the market, so she perused the refrigerator and freezer for sustenance. Nothing appealed to her until she spotted the old roll top bread basket where Gamma always kept fresh baked goods. Yes! Brownies. Rachel sent a silent "Thank you!" heavenward.

"Thanks Gamma Ray. Still there for me." Tears pooled then drooped down each cheek.

Rachel took a bite, then closed her eyelids anticipating that solid thin chocolate layer followed by the gooey center that she remembered.

"Not as sweet as usual, but still good." Rachel critiqued to herself as she reached for a second square.

She leaned over the sink, so crumbs wouldn't fall onto the floor. The grinding of the garbage disposal made her jump.

"What the heck?" She flipped the switch next to the bread bin. It had been off. She turned the knobs for water and a loud clunking noise responded. "First on my list to be replaced."

A few tiny morsels of brownie swirled down the drain. Rachel would swear that the word "Yum" came from the depths of the disposal. Instantly squatting, her hand yanked the sheet back to look under the sink expecting to see a little man hiding under there. No one. She popped up and over the sink to peer down the hole, examining the stationary blades of the InSinkErator.

"What are you looking at? Never seen a Shit Shredder before?" The voice sounded distinctly familiar.

Scrutinizing the disposal again, "What? Who? How? Who is *talking*? Am I going crazy here?" She smacked the back of her hand to her forehead. Nope. No fever.

"You're lookin' at me talkin' to you. Who-a you? Where's Gamma Ray?"

It sounded like... *Rocky Balboa?* Rachel whipped her head around every corner of kitchen expecting to see Sylvester Stallone standing there in a black leather jacket and gloves. No one.

Rachel squinted, "Gamma Ray is what I called my grandmother. How do you know her by that name?"

"Ah, you're the granddaughter, Raquel."

"Rachel. My name is Rachel."

"Whatevah. Your Grandmother asked me to call her Gamma Ray because it reminded her of you. And you never visited her, so she talked to me, like a stand-up for you."

"You mean stand-in?"

"That's what I said. So, where is she?"

Rachel put her hands on her hips. "I am not continuing this conversation with a garbage disposal."

"I think you will."

A volcano of minced onion, apple cores, egg shells, pasta and other foods shot out of the sink, to land on the counter, in Rachels hair, and splash on the floor.

Rachel yelled over the grinding noise. "STOP. What are you doing?"

"I can do this all night, until you answer me. Yo. Where's Gamma Ray?"

Rachel covered her ears. "I'm not telling you."

"I think you will."

The disposal ground on. A twisted spoon flew into the air, a fork the other way, a plastic bottle cap, and an earring, all became projectiles. A soggy blob of something plopped on Rachel's cowering head. She snatched the wet mess, looked at it and gasped.

"My pink smiley face ankle sock. I lost one the last time I was here."

Over the grinding clamor she heard, "Well, I found it. You want more?"

"No. No more. She's dead. She died. Stop grinding," She shouted.

Abruptly, the noise stopped. Rachel barely heard the soft *Rocky* voice, "Gamma Ray is gone?"

"Gamma Ray had cancer, it was just a matter of time." Rachel crumbled to the ground in a fetal lump of sobbing emotion.

"I know she had cancer. Why do you think she made happy grass brownies?"

Rachel's head shot up, eyes wide open. "Gamma baked brownies with weed in them? Thank the good lord, heavens above, and all that is holy. I don't have to see a therapist for talking to a household grinder. I'm just stoned, baked as a cake. What a relief." She laughed until she fell asleep on the kitchen floor with her grungy sock for a head rest.

At 2:00 A.M. a fast drip, drip, drip interrupted her sleep. Disoriented, she blinked rapidly trying to remember how she ended up on the floor with debris scattered around her. Rachel slowly flexed all her body parts, confirming the absence of pain. She sat up listening to the plop, plopping of the water.

"I can't believe this. It's nasty, old, *and* it drips?"

She stood up to confront a faucet leaking a green watery liquid, close to overflowing. She yanked out the rubber stopper to let the water flow down the drain, but the faucet dripped even faster and filled the sink almost to the brim.

"What the hell? I didn't plug this up before I went to bed." Rachel dunked her hand in the water and brought it to her nose. Nothing distinguishable. Impulsively, she stuck her tongue out and touched the tip to the small puddle in her palm. Slightly salty.

"Holy crap! Is this sink crying? Are you crying?" She pushed the faucet handles back to off. The dripping stopped.

"I *know* the water was off before I crashed. Wasn't it? Freakin' weirdness. I must be over stressed."

Rachel staggered to the bedroom and fell back asleep. Five hours later she awoke to chirping birds. For a full minute she hazily traced the birds notched in the headboard, grateful to confirm they weren't doing the warbling. Her full bladder forced her out of bed. She sat on the commode with her face in her hands, recalling the night before.

When she walked into the kitchen something appeared odd inside the basin. Her mouth dropped open.

Tears sprang to her eyes as she slowly stroked the soft, yet stiff, strands of long black wavy hair spiking out of the drain forming a Y shape.

"This is Gamma's hair. How did it get here? This can't be happening. That's it. This creepy garbage disposal and sink have to go NOW."

Rachel threw on a pair of jean shorts and a T-shirt, called her boyfriend and left a message.

"Hey, it's me. How soon can you get here with your tools? I need my sink taken out of the kitchen. At least the disposal. Please hurry."

She scooped up the mysterious wad of hair from the sink and tossed in the garbage.

She bent over and stared at the disposal. "I don't know what you are or what you're doing, but I'm going to destroy you."

Tyler called back and asked, "What's up? Why the rush to take out a poor defenseless grub grinder?"

Rachel yowled, "This grub grinder, as you call it, is anything but defenseless. You wouldn't believe what I've been through."

"Whoa, calm down Rach. It can't be that bad. What did the sink do? Squirt water on you?" He chuckled.

Rachel blasted him through the phone. "It's not funny. You're going to think I'm crazy when I tell you." She paced, deciding not to reveal any of the conversation with *Rocky*. She blurted, "The sink did more than squirt water on me, the garbage disposal attacked me with old smelly ground up food and utensils. And explain how a sock I put in the laundry a year ago resurfacing out of the depths of that *thing*. That's not all. The sink stopped itself up and started dripping in the middle of the night. It filled up with a green saltwater. Then this morning when I woke up, I found my grandma's hair from her younger days, growing out of the drain."

Rachel remained silent waiting for Tyler to respond. "Sweetie, I know you've been stressed with her passing and the decision to leave your job. I warned you not to take the happy pills without me."

Oh yeah, the pot brownies. She omitted that incident. "Do I sound happy? I'm serious. I'm not making this up."

"Did you just hear what you just told me? You were attacked by a stationary appliance, sinks cry saltwater and most remarkable, you want me to believe lost socks go into the washing machine and come out through the garbage disposal?"

"Okay, fine, will you just come over and help me remove them?"

"Did you buy a new sink to replace it yet?

"I didn't really think that far. There's only a Walmart in this town."

"I have a few loose ends to tie up here. I will pick up a stainless-steel sink at the Home Depot if you trust me to pick it out. We can probably use the same disposal for the new sink and..."

"NO." Rachel interrupted. "I want a new garbage disposal. New everything. I also need a cabinet. I will text you a photo of the space, along with the dimensions. When can you get here?"

"I can be there by the weekend. Friday night. That's in two days. Good?"

"I hope I can last that long."

Tyler tried to be funny. "Don't use the sink. Or the refrigerator. Or the stove. Stay out of the kitchen entirely. Eat at McDonalds until I get there."

That's exactly what Rachel planned to do. She grabbed her purse and left the madness. Ten minutes later, while she munched on a Quarter Pounder, she decided she couldn't go back into the house without a plan. Surely, she can disconnect the garbage disposal with a screwdriver on her own. Inspired, Rachel headed home and found what she was looking for in the little tool shed.

Armed with an arsenal of Phillips, Slot heads, and an assortment of wrenches in a few sizes and lengths, she felt ready to attack the talking terror. When she got under the sink, behind the sheet, she realized that although she may be able to unscrew the disposal, she would have to turn the water off and disconnect the pipe. Sitting crossed legged staring at the bulging appendage, Rachel admitted with a deep sigh, "Damnit. I guess I can't do this on my own. Bloody Hell."

"As you wish." *Rocky's* voice boomed.

Rachel heard the sink filling up again. She jumped up to a view a horrifying scene. The sink bubbled with a bright red fluid. "Oh, my God. WHY ARE YOU DOING THIS?" Rachel held onto the sides of the porcelain to steady herself.

"Yo. To beat me, you're gonna have to kill me, and to kill me you're gonna have to have the heart to stand in front of me, and to do that, you gotta be willing to die and I'm ready to do that."

Rachel screamed. "Are you quoting from the film *Rocky*?"

"Your Grandmother loved that movie. She watched it over and over. The bedroom sink saw what you did to Gamma Ray. You, me, aint nobody is gonna hit as hard as life."

"Now I got a tattletale sink in the *bedroom*? I don't believe this! Rachel cried. "Okay, okay. Your rat-me-out sink friend is right. I killed my grandmother. But she was sick and in pain. She had become so weak. I held a pillow over her face while she slept. To end her misery." In a much smaller voice, "All her money in the bank couldn't do anything but prolong the pain."

Rachel slipped to the floor in anguish. Through racking sobs, she looked directly at the machine and asked the *Rocky* voice, "What do you want from me?"

The gurgling from the sink intensified. Blood cascaded down the sides of the basin, onto Rachel's lap and the mosaic tile floor. Rachel sat rooted in place, watching as the clamps came loose from the garbage disposal. The pipes connected to the sink untwisted and became dislodged. The electric line fell loose.

Later, the coroner wouldn't be able to tell which killed her first, electrocution or the chopped-up steak knife shoved through her throat.

As she lay there, taking her last breaths, she heard a clanking melody that resembled *You Are My Sunshine* mixed with the da, da, da, dahdadah from *Rocky's* theme song.

FERN GOODMAN

Fern Goodman is an award-winning author and poet. A Michigan girl in a Florida world, her background in travel and event planning has been replaced with life coaching and authoring.

She has collaborated with her sister on the book of shorts about dogs, mirroring her sisters' original photography (*Captured...the look of the dog*). Other short stories of hers appear in various anthologies (*Lost Dreams, Important Firsts, What a Character, Work of Hearts Magazine*). Fern's specialty is reality humor, which she demonstrates on YouTube, *Fern at the Stardust Lounge*.

Although her latest offering, *Shooting UP Hope* is not a humorous subject, but Fern finds a way to lighten your heart through tears.

Her writing ambition is to uncover people's 'tinglies' through relatable narratives and leave them feeling something, anything.

Website ferngoodman.com
Amazon Author Page https://www.amazon.com/Fern-Goodman/e/
B00PD85JCS
Facebook: Fern Zie Goodman & Shooting Up Hope

Hanako-san of the Toilet

By Meg Sefton

Toilet

Sometimes when we get together at "Mommy and Me," we talk about what happened that summer at the beach in that huge house by the ocean. We usually don't refer to many of the details directly, they are still puzzling, and painful. We just laugh and talk about what a pain it is to potty train our little ones when toilets are known to haunt. "Isn't it hard enough?" One of us we'll sort of do a faint little laugh, more from relief that we are acknowledging something difficult than experiencing something that is genuinely funny. At that point, there is usually more grabbing for the wine or extra food, depending upon one's choice of comfort.

Talk to any one of us individually and you will witness for yourself the fracturing nature of a shared experience, a shared experience of encountering unexpected darkness. You will witness pained expressions and hesitations and the trailing off of answers and explanations of events.

But first, let me start by orienting you to what things were like when we were younger. Do you remember playing a slumber party game called

Bloody Mary? You probably played it gathering round the bathroom mirror with a friend, candles lit, spinning and chanting louder and louder Bloody Mary, Bloody Mary, Bloody Mary! And then looking for a glimpse of the terrifying witch in the mirror. What's more you could be maimed, have your eyes torn out, appear on the other side with the witch, go insane, die. Dare you summon Mary Worth back from the afterlife? The mirror was her portal.

I don't know about your slumber parties growing up, but at our slumber parties, we had one person who knew the rituals and the stories about spirits who could be summoned, who passed things along to us and told us what to do. For us, this person was Aideen Campbell. It was Aideen who told us about the witch Mary Worth. We didn't have youtube and Instagram, we didn't relay messages and pictures and information that way. We only had word of mouth and the more connected you were, the more you knew. In my group of girlfriends which also included Mandy, Heather, Rachel, Courtney, Julie, and Shannon, Aideen was that source of information.

Besides that, Aideen was different than the rest of us. For example, her mother was busted for shoplifting even though her father was as rich as Croesus. While it appalled my mother, a proper southern church going lady, it made Aideen all the more intriguing. Aideen's mother had gone to jail! My mother's friends never did anything by comparison. Their excitement over the least little thing was depressing.

All of us hung on every little thing Aideen said. What's more, she wore makeup before any of us was allowed to, smoked, got access to booze through her older sister, had boyfriends first, kissed them, did other things too, things we knew we weren't supposed to do. So when Aideen also showed us, at our hang outs and get togethers, things that were new and unfamiliar, things like Bloody Mary, she had us spellbound. When I told her our youth pastor said "do not turn to the spirits of the dead," because that's what it says in the Bible, she laughed, little puffs of cigarette smoke escaping her nose and glossy lips.

"That girl isn't a Christian," said my Mom to me once after she found out who all was going to one of our parties.

"She goes to the Catholic Church," I said, which was true. Aideen said she went with a family in her neighborhood because her mother and father never did and she wanted to go.

Hanako-san of the Toilet

"She's not baptized and confirmed," said Mama. "That wouldn't even pass muster for most good protestants."

This was back when the fashion icon was Madonna, the pop singer, and all of us wore rosaries with our bustiers or t-shirts and mini-skirts. Sometimes it didn't even seem to matter, all the rules of the church. We only relied on each other for the real spiritual information, the real spiritual access and experience.

My mother was forced to give up her principals when she was diagnosed with cancer. Her hold on me loosened, whatever hold she had by the time I was twelve and going into the seventh grade. When I was asked to go to the Campbell's beach house for the summer, she gave in rather than completely agreed. She knew girls from other good homes were going there too so that gave her some comfort.

When I was packed and ready to go, my mother held my hand and made me promise to be good. "I'll be praying for you," she said. "Maybe you can find a church to go to there." My father hugged me, told me not to worry about Mama, she was sick now from the chemo but she would feel better and starting to heal by the time I was home in the fall. He told me what Mama couldn't say: Have a good time.

Mr. Tommy the Campbells' driver picked me up first, then Mandy, Heather, Courtney, Rachel, Shannon, and Julie. I felt closest to Mandy, who went to my youth group at the Presbyterian Church. After picking all of us up in the family van, Aideen told us there was someone new who would be joining us, someone who would begin school with us in the fall. Her name was Chanlina Chea. Aideen told us that she and her mother fled Cambodia when her father was killed. Chanlina had only been a baby. We didn't know much about Cambodia, only what our parents happened to mention when they were talking about Vietnam. Chanlina's mother was going to drive her to the house and we would meet her there. She and her mother are very close she said so it was a big deal that she would be allowed to come at all. When we started asking questions, Aideen just rolled her eyes and put on her headphones.

When we got to the huge old beach house mostly hidden from the road by trees and dense tall bushes, Esmerelda, Aideen's childhood cook and nanny, came out to greet us. This, we all knew, would be the extent of our adult supervision. And Mr. Tommy had a gun, we all knew. He was there to protect us, to drive us around and peruse the grounds. He was a strange man who rarely spoke, but he made us feel safe and we didn't feel we had to change who we were around Mr. Tommy. Looking back I realize he was a long suffering servant of Aideen's parents though of course he was not unpaid. His gifts in return, were silence and loyalty. Esmeralda was her own bird. She was gentle and animated and fawned over us and insisted that we eat what she provided, and always second helpings. She was a kind and sweet woman and I never asked myself at the time whether she had a life of her own outside of our activities.

We brought our things in and Aideen directed us to the basement, a huge lounge space her parents had let her decorate and furnish as she pleased. She had painted the walls purple and on top of that had painted huge magenta flowers with thick twisting vines. There were two long pink velvet sofas with all manner of pillows and our beds were tucked into walls, like little caves, and hidden by sheer curtains tied back with muslin bows. The basement had its own kitchen and bathroom. The only thing Aideen didn't include that most of us would have was a television set. Instead, she had bookshelves built in.

"I don't watch television here," and she grabbed a book and sat in an egg shaped rattan chair that was suspended from the ceiling. She spun it around with her foot. Chanlina was already in the basement, we had greeted her when we made our descent. She sat in the other egg chair on the opposite side of the shelves. She laughed and spun too, like Aideen.

Someone turned on a jambox, played a cassette - The Cure, Duran Duran, The Motels. Aideen passed out the beers she managed to smuggle away as well as packets of cigarettes. We opened windows high up on the wall facing the ocean and heard the waves crashing against the beach in the black night.

"We'll go out later," said Aideen, "when the moon rises." She liked to turn her head when she smoked and let the smoke out so it rose in slow curls.

We pulled each other up to standing and danced in the candlelight to The Motels' song about a never-ending summer. None of us said it but we were all watching Chanlina to see how she fit in. Would she dance like we did? Would there be something odd about the way she behaved? Could she laugh and have fun? She seemed to be having a good time and she had a nice way of dancing, like a fluid sea creature. She was more womanly than most of us who sort of bopped around. Aideen picked up a pillow and swatted her. Chanlina laughed and picked up a pillow from the couch and hit her back. Good sign.

Hanako-san of the Toilet

We went outside. The moon was a huge yellow disk hanging over the undulating waves. We ran down to the water and splashed each other though no one was swimming. It was hot so we didn't care we were wet. We walked along the beach, shining our light on sand crabs and the occasional jellyfish. When we got back to the shore in front of the house, there was a fire in the middle of a circle of Adirondack chairs. Mr. Tommy had built it for us and left us a cooler of drinks, along with a table loaded with supplies for s'mores. We loaded up wire coat hangers with marshmallows along with plates of graham crackers and Hershey bars. We grabbed Cokes and took a seat.

"I've asked Chanlina to tell us a story," said Aideen when we settled in and began to toast our marshmallows. "It's probably the weirdest story I've ever heard."

The fire crackled and the breeze lifted our hair and brushed our cheeks in little puffs. The moon was brighter and higher in the sky and cast an eerie glow on the sand and water.

Chanlina began: "This is a story about a girl who haunts school children in Japan. Have you heard of it?"

We shook our heads no, all except Aideen.

"A boy that works with me and my mother in the restaurant, he told it to me."

The waves came up gently on the beach, crashing on the shore in tiny claps. Chanlina's black hair and dark skin set her apart from us. Her accent leant her an air of authority.

"If you think you are ok, you are probably wrong," she said. I wasn't really sure what she meant by this. Was this generally the way someone in Cambodia started a ghost story? Or was she just saying something from her own personal experience?

"When I was a baby," she continued, "my father was killed for wearing glasses," she said.

We remained silent, and still, not quite knowing what to say.

"The government in charge thought he was an intellectual. They thought he would question them and cause problems. Many people were put to death for wearing glasses."

Of course, we had never heard of such an absurd, capricious way to die.

"Now my mother and I live here. We live alone."

Aideen lit up a cigarette from a pack she kept in pocket, punctuating the silence with the little "clink" of her lighter.

"The spirit ghost of Japan is named Hanako-san. Her story shows anything can happen to anyone."

An old couple walked up not far from our circle and nodded and waved. They were wearing tennis shoes and knee high athletic socks and floppy hats. They asked us how we were and we told them fine, thank you, like we had been taught.

When they passed, Chanlina continued. "Hanako-san died when she was hiding in a toilet stall at her school. She was playing hide and seek with her friends. Americans dropped bombs on her city. It was World War II. Everyone in her city was killed."

For some reason, I thought of the hair floating down on my mother's shoulders after a few weeks of chemotherapy. I always tried not to think about what would happen if my father's chipper predictions didn't come true and instead my mother died.

"Remember Ms. Bray showing us a film of the mushroom cloud?" said Aideen. Ms. Bray had been our history teacher. "Remember when she told us that the ones who were vaporized had their organs boiled? Their bones turned to charcoal."

Mandy and Heather put their marshmallows down on the ground. The rest of us were holding onto our coat hangers awkwardly, the marshmallows forgotten. Only Courtney was loading her graham crackers up with melted marshmallows and chocolate.

"To this day, the spirit of Hanako-san haunts the hallways of schools in Japan," Chanlina said. "but especially the bathroom where she died."

"We're going to summon her tomorrow," said Aideen. "At the Devil's School." Aideen was the only one who wasn't making s'mores. She was always on a diet even though she just turned thirteen and didn't need to be on a diet. She was smoking again, and smoke trickled through her nose and mouth as she spoke. "If Hanako-san is anywhere, she's there."

"The Devil's School?" said Mandy. She was often intent on keeping Aideen in check or at least asking the necessary questions. No doubt, she would write about this later tonight in her journal.

"Annie Lytle Elementary," said Aideen, practically smiling, "Or, as it was known back in the day, school number 4."

How strange to have schools known simply by numbers, when all of them now are given names. I thought of other times when people were given numbers instead of being spoken to their names, like in the Holocaust when each person in the camps had a number emblazoned on their arms.

Hanako-san of the Toilet

"What's so special about it?" said Heather, trying to sound cool, taking a cigarette from Aideen and pretending she knew what to do with it. Her ratted out short red bob and kohl eyes made her look like a slightly more punk Mollie Ringwald.

"I know this one," said Courtney, having stuffed a large portion of a s'more sandwhich in her mouth. She was trying to talk but her words were coming out funny and we laughed. When she had swigged down some coke, she said "The principal was a cannibal and ate kids."

"Well, you would know about eating, now wouldn't you?" said Julie. We fell out laughing.

"Is this going to be really scary?" said Shannon nervously. She picked up a piece of her hair. She always twirled her hair when she was nervous or thinking about something, like an essay on a test. "Maybe I'll stay here tomorrow."

"No way, Shannon." said Aideen.

"I've heard you can hear kids screaming," said Courtney. "And there's a tree growing up through the auditorium floor where the roof was burned away by a fire."

Aideen picked up a coat hanger and slid a couple of marshmallows on the end. She told me once she liked to burn them because that took away some of the calories. I had no idea if it was true, but she was always skinny, so there was the answer I guess. "Tell us how we summon Hanako-san, Chanlina," she said.

"Well, we have to go to the girl's bathroom," said Chanlina, "to the third stall. Then, someone has to knock three times on the door like this," and Chanlina wrapped on the armrest of her Adirondack chair three times. "Then you sing this tune..." and Chanlina sang a song to the tune of a nursery rhyme: "Hanako-san, Hanako-san, would you like to play today?"

Chanlina was quiet for a bit, letting us think about this.

"What happens next?" This was Rachel. She was a little more matter of fact about things, not easily caught up in emotion.

"If you see Hanako-san, who wears a red skirt, white blouse, and her hair tied back, she will grab you with her black fingers and drag you down through the toilet and into hell."

We were quiet and still for a moment. Even Courtney stopped at this, hesitating mid re-load of a marshmallow onto her coat hanger.

"Oh yeah, right!" Julie said, breaking the silence, laughing. She never believed anything about bloody Mary or anything. In fact, she had said she hoped to see Mary in the mirror one day. She'd like to kiss her shriveled up witch lips.

Shannon was laughing too but quieter, nervously, the clump of hair in her fingers going at a furious pace twirling around and around.

"I don't believe in hell," said Rachel. "I think we all just disintegrate into the ground. We don't go anywhere."

"But what about heaven?" I said. I couldn't think like this. What would that mean for Mom?

"Heaven neither," said Rachel. "Nope."

"It doesn't matter," said Aideen. "We're all going to meet Hanako-san third stall bathroom toilet, tomorrow, Devil's School." And she grinned at us, pulling a burned marshmallow from her hanger and putting it in her mouth and licking her fingers.

"Whatever," said Rachel, pushing herself up from her chair. "I'm going for a walk."

"Oh me too!" said Julie, always looking for the slightest opportunity for mutiny as long as fun was involved.

Shannon stood as well, probably wanting to get away from the conversation around the fire. And she also probably knew there would be light, simple chatter between Rachel and Julie, nothing too challenging, though Julie could be a bit harsh.

"Enjoy," said Aideen. "We'll be praying for your souls," and she laughed.

The next day, Aideen made good on her promise and had Mr. Tommy drop us at the abandoned school. It was beside a highway overpass so that the passing cars and trucks made loud swooshing noises. It was encompassed by a chain link fence and had the appearance of a sad, old person, dripping with dead vines, the few hollow windows not boarded looking like eyes and the entry a gigantic black maw. The front was graced by huge white columns whose tops were weathered and grey. The old brick of the walls was blackened in places, red still in others, in some places nearer the earth painted with graffiti, some pornographic.

An old man sat on a crumbling step. He was thin and shriveled and wore a baseball cap and long pants and long sleeves though it was ninety degrees. "Death tryna' come out of this here place," he said, wagging a finger at Aideen. How would he have known she was the ringleader? "But death, he ain't never getting' out. That's 'cause death, he locked up in there."

"We're going to summon a spirit," said Aideen.

The old man just looked at us as if we were barely visible to him. "You ladies, I'm Alfred, but I can't be helpin' you none."

"I'm not sure I want to go in," said Shannon, predictably. I didn't want to either, truth be told, but I wasn't going to say anything. I could always count on Shannon to say exactly what she was feeling.

"Here, hold my hand," said Mandy. And Mandy grabbed her hand but waited for someone else to take the lead.

Aideen and Chanlina went first, walking past the old man on the steps, followed by Julie and Heather and Courtney, Mandy and Shannon, then me and Rachel.

Our feet fell on a disintegrating wood floor once we were past the peeling threshold. It was dark in the entry even though it was bright outside. We turned on the flashlights we brought from the house.

"This way," said Aideen and we crossed through a hallway where the sun shown in through huge gaping spaces where windows once were. Tendrils of vines pushed in the openings like fingers. Plaster had fallen away from the walls, exposing brick underneath. Trash and debris lay at the bottom of the walls and in the corners. And on all the walls were scribbled layer upon layer of graffiti, up to the ceiling in some spots.

"The whole building feels like it's crying," I said.

"It's practically shouting," said Julie.

"It looks like homeless people have been here," Mandy said. There were piles of tins and broken bottles.

At the end of the hallway was a concrete stairwell that looped back on itself. "The bathroom's up here," said Aideen and began to climb.

"Wait!" said Courtney. "I think I hear screams! Shh!" and she put a finger to her lips. We stood still. Nothing. Then she began to laugh. "Just kidding!" she said.

But Shannon wasn't so sure. "Shouldn't we call Mr. Tommy on the walkie talkie?" she said.

"Shannon!" scolded Aideen.

When we got to the top of the stairs, Aideen disappeared into a pink door frame, though the paint had worn off in places. The girls' bathroom. Leaves had fallen in through the smashed windows and filled the sinks and floor. The once white walls were gray with mildew and in places the plaster had come off, revealing the brick beneath. The stalls teetered on their hinges and a couple of stalls didn't have doors. We stood in a little entry area, all eight of us packed in and not wanting to go into the space between the line of sinks facing the toilet stalls.

"I don't even think a ghost would want to hang out here," said Courtney.

"Spirits are everywhere," said Chanlina. "But they won't speak unless we speak to them."

"Rachel," said Aideen, "Since you don't believe in all of this, why don't you call on Hanako-san?"

"This is so stupid, but ok," she said, shuffling through the leaves. Wind blew through the palms outside the window and we could hear the clacking of the long fronds and also the mournful sounds of cars whooshing past on the highway.

"Don't forget," said Aideen, "third stall."

Rachel turned to us and put a flashlight under her face, rolled her eyes and stuck out her tongue. We all laughed of course, though a bit quieter than when we laughed at Courtney's prank on the stairs. Well, everyone laughed except Shannon who was by now frozen. Mandy was quiet too, probably out of respect for Shannon.

"You have to turn out your light," said Aideen.

She turned her light off and Aideen motioned us to turn our lights off. Sunlight filtered through the broken panes of the window.

Slowly Rachel knocked on the stall door. Knock, knock, knock. Then she sang: "Hanako-san, Hanako-san, would you like to play today?"

We all stood there for what felt like an hour but it was probably a few seconds. No sound, no slowly creaking stall door, no ghoul in a red skirt. Rachel did not get dragged down into the toilet and to hell. Rachel shrugged her shoulders and shuffled back through the leaves.

Then there was a loud pop. We screamed. The door from the third-floor stall opened and smashed into the sink, breaking the porcelain.

Shannon wailed and shook. Mandy put her arms around her. The rest of us silently quaked in fear, huddled together tightly.

"Should we get Mr. Tommy" I said, my teeth chattering with the words.

"No fucking way, Lisa" Aideen lashed out, but I felt something desperate in her words.

We waited again.

Nothing.

"This place is falling to pieces," said Julie, breaking the silence. "What a shithole."

Heather chuckled.

"Yeah, and not a thing to worry about," said Rachel even though she didn't sound as confident as before. She broke away from the huddle to stand closer to the door frame where placed a foot on the tile wall and stretched her leg, affecting nonchalance.

Our exit from School Number Four was more somber than our entry had been, though we were mostly relieved the ordeal was finished and there was probably nothing to worry about.

Still, something had happened.

"Do you think that door was bound to fall off like that?" said Courtney, "Or do you think...." She didn't finish her thought.

"I was actually hoping to meet her," said Heather. "Personally, I think the door crashing scared her."

No one laughed, not even Rachel and Julie.

"Well, thanks for the memories, Devil School," said Aideen, spreading her arms out as if she was making a speech. She began to sing: "We love you Hanako-san, oh yes we do. We love you Hanako-san, and we'll be true. When you're not with us, we're blue. Oh Hanako-san, we love you." And her song reverberated off the disintegrated, graffiti walls, a faint echo returning to us.

At the bright threshold, the old man in the baseball cap sat on the stairs. "I done told you now, chillrun. You done seen death. I can tell. You scairt!"

We let his chiding follow us out past the chain fence where Mr. Tommy waited for us in the van. None of us spoke then or later that night as we quietly put on our pajamas and crawled up into our beds so strangely nestled into the wall.

In the dead of night when the only sound was the surf lapping up on the shore in little claps, there was the loud crash of the bathroom door against the wall. A dark figure, Chanlina, stumbled out and stood in the middle of the room weeping.

"Chanlina, what is it?" said Mandy, emerging from her bed, trying to put her arms around her to comfort her. But she jerked away.

"I want to go home!" Chanlina screamed. "Take me home! Mr. Tommy take me home!"

No one could figure out what had happened, only that something had happened in the bathroom. We all asked her questions and tried to get her to calm down but she kept getting more frantic.

Aideen went upstairs to wake Esmerelda and Mr. Tommy. We fetched Chanlina and stood in the kitchen and told our caretakers what had happened that day, about the story Chanlina had told us and what we had done at the Devil's School. Chanlina sat at the table, inconsolable. Esmerelda brought her milk and buttered bread, but she would have none of it.

Chanlina went home to her mother.

As the days and weeks past, the beauty of the beach and monotony of the waves took away the strangeness of our summer's beginning, like a water's current softening a sharp rock. Although I felt guilty for putting Chanlina out of my mind, it wasn't long before the eight of us were back to the way we used to be before a stranger was in our midst. And since we left off pursuing ghosts, the last time we would ever do this, I thought more about my mom and actually felt compelled to read from the little Bible she gave me and say a prayer for her. According to Dad, she was doing better.

When we got home in the fall, we received word: Chanlina was dead. She had fallen into a coma and doctors could not find the reason. One night, she slipped away.

MEG SEFTON

Meg Sefton's work has appeared in Best New Writing, Asylum Ink, Bizarro Central, Danse Macabre, and other publications. She received an MFA from Seattle Pacific University. Her favorite quote to live and write by was penned by Jorge Luis Borges: "Reality is not always probable, or likely." She lives in Winter Springs with her little white dog Annie and sometimes has the privilege of feeding her son when he is home from college.

Blog: https://brokenwriterblog.wordpress.com/ -- Within a Forest Dark
(I don't have a website or an Amazon Author Page - yet! I hope to remedy that very soon!)
Facebook: https://www.facebook.com/meg.sefton
Twitter: @margaretsefton
Instagram: margaretsefton

High Rise Dilemma

By Jon Park

Liquidizer

Addiction is the devils curse. No two ways about it. When you are an addict, like me, and can't afford that next hit, then you are liable to do anything. I mean seriously, anything, to get that next high.

Some people rob, steal or borrow. Others turn to prostitution to feed their habit. If I had kids, I would have sold them and right now I would have been so high, I would be suffering from altitude sickness.

But I didn't have kids. Pawned everything of any value. I couldn't rob and I didn't fancy my chances on the game. I mean, a body like mine is a temple and I didn't want just anyone entering it. I had my standards.

So, instead, I killed Colin, my dealer. His rapidly cooling body lay on the floor of my apartment, a dark pool spreading from it. I'm no forensics expert, but I believe the cause of death was the bread knife protruding from his neck. That combined with massive blood loss.

Now, to be honest, Colin has to take some responsibility for his current predicament. He's been around junkies long enough to know that they do not like to hear these words leave their dealers mouth.

"Listen, you prick. You know the rules. If you don't have the cash, you don't get your stash."

High Rise Dilemma

Who would have thought that Colin's last words would have been so, poetic. The world had not only lost a drug dealer, but a potential poet laureate, to boot. This made me feel pretty remorseful. That was until I helped myself to some of his goodies and chased the dragon for a while.

Now, I had a massive problem. How do I get rid of Colin's corpse? I mean, my apartments' situated on the eleventh floor of this tower block, bang in the centre of Newcastle. Challenging. You think?

So I took another hit, helps with the creative juices. Give the old grey matter a good stir, seeking inspiration.

Right, let's get down to the job in hand. Problem is, the disposal of one dead dealer. Whilst avoiding detection, thus avoiding spending the rest of my miserable life in prison. But ever the optimist, I had heard that it was easier to get your fix in prison than on the street. So every cloud and all that.

Now come on. Concentrate, Focus. Back to operation, "Get rid of Colin." I decided I could roll him up in the only rug I had. Carry him downstairs, put him in the boot of my car and drive him out to a land fill I knew in Blaydon, some ten miles away. Piece of piss.

I rolled him up in the rug, his size ten feet poking out the bottom like some nightmare canapé. Lifted him up on my shoulder and then realised I didn't have a car. I considered carrying him onto the number seventy three bus, but then decided that wouldn't work for a number of reasons. The passengers of the number seventy three bus, would surely be observant enough to see his feet sticking out of the rug, and I'm pretty sure would not tolerate travelling with a corpse. And I don't think the number seventy three bus even goes to Blaydon. So I quickly ruled that plan out.

It was then I regretted pawning my Mac. I could have googled it. Acid in the bath, ruled out. The bath was made of plastic. Bury the body under the patio, too much of a technical challenge on the eleventh floor and no doubt would attract unwanted attention from the tenants below.

Eureka! I had it. The hatch to the garbage chute was only metres from my apartment door. I could carry him to that, sling him down the chute into the communal bins, and then it becomes the refuse department's problem. Nobody would know where he had come from. Problem solved. Genius.

I dragged the body down the hallway of my apartment. Lay it against the wall while I opened the door and checked the corridor. Clear. I hoisted the body over my shoulder and staggered to the chute.

Opening the hatch to the chute, I discovered the flaw in this plan. The body was too big to fit through the hatch. So I had to quickly stagger back into my flat and deposit the body back on the floor.

I took another hit. Freeing my mind. That's when it hit me. Smaller pieces. Smaller pieces would fit through the hatch. In a previous life, I had worked construction and although all my best tools had long been sold or pawned, I still retained a couple in a sports bag in my bed room.

Retrieving the bag I dumped the contents onto the floor and selected a rusty hacksaw. Took another hit and cranked up the radio, for some old rock and roll and got to work.

I was surprised how easy the body came to bits. Even with a rusty hacksaw. Some of the bone and cartilage took some effort to saw through, but within half an hour, covered in blood, gristle and sweat, I had a grotesque soup of body parts bobbing in the bath.

I gathered the various parts into a collection of garbage bags and bags for live. Took a quick wash in the sink and changed into fresh clothes.

Next, I chose the first bag. Checked the hallway once more and set off for the chute. I was just placing the first load into the hatch, a leg hacked off just below the knee, with the foot still attached, wrapped in a Tesco bag for life, when I heard the ping of the lift down the corridor and the doors whispering open. I froze.

Out stepped my neighbour, an old Scottish guy. Frank I think was his name, made his way down the corridor towards me, preceded by the stench of stale booze. I could hear the carrier bags he held, rattling as he moved. I knew they would be filled with more bottles of the cheap whisky he favoured. He drank so much of it, the stench of it seeped through the walls. I had my back to him, so he would be unable to see what I was holding.

"Alright, wee man," he slurred. "Watch what you sending doon that there chute mind. I just seen the polis raking through the bins again. Looking for a mudder weapon, I've heard. So don't be throwing doon anything incriminating, eh?" Followed by a coughing laugh.

"Thanks for the heads up, mate. I was just about to dispose of this body!" I replied, cool as fuck.

"Nay bother son, you fill ya boots," he replied, as he finally reached his apartment door, fiddling with his keys. I stood there, the recently amputated leg, hovering above the black, inviting mouth of the chute. From below I could hear the echo of steel bins being moved about. He could have been right about the police. Eventually he found a key that fitted and disappeared into his apartment. And I was alone once more, just me and my extra leg.

I slammed the apartment door with some force and slumped to the floor, the leg still in my hand. Defeated. Wondering what to do next. So I took another hit. That's when my eyes alighted upon the liquidiser, sat on the kitchen shelves. I'd tried to pawn it, but they said for hygienic purposes they couldn't take white goods like this. I mean this baby was some serious bit of kit. I had bought it when I was into fitness big time. This thing could liquidiser anything. So I plugged it in, and set to work.

Several hits and several hours later, every container I could find was filled with thick pink sludge. The fridge and freezer had never been so full.

I discovered that adding some of my strawberry protein powder to the sludge, helped me keep it down. It was quite an acquired taste, but I soon got used to it.

Two weeks passed and the strangest thing had happened. I felt energised, my bowel movements for the first time in an age where back to normal. And all that remained of Colin was a solitary container. I fell terrific. No drug had made me feel so alive. I was sleeping like a babe and had so much energy I was even back exercising.

I had never felt so good. But now, I was down to my last Tupperware container. I had found the ultimate high. And I needed more.

That's when I heard the Scottish voice next door, break into a drunken ballad about the highlands. I collected the kitchen knife and made for the door, wondering if he would taste of whiskey.

Jon Park

J on Park from Gateshead in the North East of England. Encouraged by my daughters Emily and Charlotte and partner Tracey, I have been writing for just over a year. Some of my work has appeared in the Yellow Mama edited by the brilliant Cindy Rosmus and Near to the knuckle.

The Grave Little Toaster

By Jeremy Rodden

Toaster

"Why do you call?" cried the disembodied and hollow voice in the darkness.

"Oh my god, Janet, the spell is working! What have we done?" a male voice called.

"Shut up, Brad," Janet snapped. "Get the vessel."

A swirling vortex of red and purple smoke began forming in the air. The pitch-blackness of the unlit room highlighted the oddity of smoke that emanated its own light. The red portion of the smoke became centralized and formed something approximate to eyes on the shapeless purple form.

"Brad!" Janet cried. "We need the vessel!"

The smoke's 'eyes' narrowed as it scanned the room. Even though it cast its own minute light, there was nothing to see in the dark. It tilted the top of its plume to the side, as though it were listening.

"I form!" the smoke-creature bellowed. "I shall feast on your souls, amateurs," it added with a snicker. "You know not with what you meddle. Do you know who I am?"

"I got it," Brad called.

"Are you sure?" Janet asked.

Brad sighed. "Must you question everything I do, Janet? This is carving the turkey on Thanksgiving all over again. I'm not an idiot, darling."

"You absolutely destroyed that turkey, honey," she replied.

"Are you two done?" the creature asked. The vortex slowed and was beginning to form the shape of something almost human. Judging by the amount of smoke left, the creature would tower over eight-feet tall when it was done amalgamating itself.

"Put it in the circle," Janet commanded.

"Yes, dear," Brad complied.

"I hunger for your souls!" the summoned smoke demon mocked. "Please enter the circle, Brad."

There was a rustling of sound to the smoke monster's left and its red eyes scanned the darkness for what it presumed to be the male human responsible for its summoning. A clanging sound rung out below the smoke and the demon looked down. A metallic object had been tossed into the circle. These humans were smarter than they looked. They had a vessel prepared to contain him. Hopefully they won't know the way to bind—

"I command you, Mephistocrates the Hungerer, to enter this vessel until I release you from your prison or you complete my request," Janet said in a cadence that suggested she was reciting a memorized line.

Mephistocrates felt itself bound the second she used its name. How did this obviously weak practitioner know the name of such an ancient and powerful demon? The demon bounced around the circle and felt no weaknesses in the implementation of the power. It was flawless.

"Do you hear me, demon?" Janet beckoned.

It stopped struggling. Mephistocrates was bound and knew it. Best to just get this over with. The demon allowed itself to be sucked into the vessel that was thrown into the circle and stopped fighting. "What do you request?" it asked.

"I told you it would work, Brad," Janet mocked.

"I didn't say it wouldn't, honey. I just was a little worried that summoning a demon based on instructions from a Reddit forum would be disappointing or dangerous."

The Grave Little Toaster

"Well, my great-great-great-great grandmother was burned as a witch in Salem, you know. It's in my blood."

"What do you request?" Mephistocrates repeated. It was hoping to get this over with so it no longer had to listen to Brad and Janet bickering.

Janet took a breath in the darkness and commanded, "I wish for you to end the lives of Chris and Karen Smythe, our neighbors across the street."

"I shall do as you command," the demon answered. "What slight have these Smythes borne upon you that they require such a final judgment?"

Brad sighed.

"There have been many and sundry slights," Janet began in her best formal voice to match the demon's. "The time Karen bought the same bathing suit as me after she definitely saw me buying it at the mall. The way Chris mows his lawn at seven o'clock in the morning on Saturdays."

"He still has my hedge clippers," Brad added.

"Yes, that too. But the final straw was when they clearly cheated to win the homeowner's association's annual gardening competition that Brad and I have won every year for the last twelve years. Bribing the judge with brownies. Who does that?"

There was silence as Mephistocrates processed the information given to it by the couple that summoned it. "Are these grievances so egregious as to justify death?" the demon ventured.

"Absolutely," Janet said with a scoff. "Now do as I command, demon!"

The shrill pitch of Janet's voice hurt Mephistocrates. There was power in her words but the demon couldn't tell if it was the supposed witch's blood in her veins or the underlying expectation that this woman would clearly get what she wanted via persistence even without it.

"I accept your charge, m'lady," the demon answered. "I shall be bound to you until such time as you release me or I complete your request. You may return light to the world and break my circle. You have my word that I shall commit you no harm."

A flicked switch turned on overhead lighting and the basement of a house came into view. Mephistocrates looked around from its vessel on the concrete floor of the building. A space had been cleared in the center of the room and, as the demon realized, a perfectly executed circle of power was drawn on the stone in chalk. It looked up at the two humans that had summoned it and saw nothing special. They had yellow hair and appeared fairly average in practically all things humans used to measure one another.

"Jesus, Brad, what did you do?" Janet asked.

117

"I thought it was the vessel. It was dark!" Brad answered, terrified of the woman's calm tone. "Can't we just transfer it to the right one?"

"It's not a damn MP3, you idiot! There were no instructions other than letting it complete its task from within the vessel. Anything short of that is opening us up to letting Mephistocrates take control of the situation. That is why they said to put him into something with limbs it can control!" Janet slapped Brad across the back of his head and muttered to herself. She walked away from him and picked up a small metal soldier, which about a foot tall and wielding serious, if tiny, weapons. "How did you confuse that—" She pointed to the demon at the center of the circle. "—With this?" she held up the soldier.

"They're both metal?" Brad asked.

"If I could intrude," Mephistocrates said politely from the floor, "could I ask what vessel I have been contained in?"

Janet threw the soldier at Brad, who cowered and received the blow. "Let me show you what this moron did," she said to the demon. She retrieved a small circular mirror and placed it in front of Mephistocrates and let the demon gaze into it.

In the reflective surface, Mephistocrates observed a rectangular metal object. It was approximately the size of the soldier but had no arms or legs. The demon hopped around to get a look at the side of its vessel and saw a few knobs and a lever. A long tail protruded from one end and the demon swung it around to see two small metal prongs poking out from a molded plastic. "What is this device?" it asked.

"It's a toaster. You're in a damn toaster," Janet sighed.

"That was a lovely service," she said.

"Still hard to believe they're dead," he replied. "I still have Brad's hedge clippers you know. How does that work? Are they mine now?"

"That's terrible, Chris. You shouldn't joke about things like that."

Mephistocrates, from its perch on the kitchen counter where he had been resting, watched Chris and Karen Smythe enter the room in their best funeral clothes. It had been stewing and biding its time since the "toaster" was gifted to the Smythes as a good will gesture several weeks ago. Or had it been months? For an eternal being, human constructs of time were hard to follow. The demon was banking on simply not completing the request in the hopes that it could convince Janet to release it eventually. It wasn't that Mephistocrates had a problem with killing humans who didn't really seem to deserve it. He just didn't really feel like it.

But now he had to.

When it heard that Janet and Brad had died in a car crash, the demon's plan for getting released fell through. Now Mephistocrates had only once course of action: complete the dead woman's command and thus be free from the bindings of the ritual spell that kept it on this plane of existence.

"If you want my opinion," Chris continued, "Brad drove off that bridge on purpose. I bet he felt death was better than listening to Janet call him an idiot or talk about how everything he did was always wrong." Chris mimicked driving a car and sharply turned the imaginary wheel to the right, making screeching sounds. "Game over."

"I didn't ask for your opinion, dear," Karen said through a smile. "It doesn't change the fact that two people are dead right now. I still think it's wrong to make fun of the dead. What if they haunt us?" She sad down at the table next to her husband and took his hand. "I know you don't believe in those things, but I do. We weren't on great terms in life. I'd hate to have them as enemies in the afterlife too."

Chris squeezed Karen's hand. "I'm sorry. You're right. Would now be a bad time to ask about that?" He pointed to the toaster on the counter.

"The toaster? Why?"

Chris rose from the table and ran fingers through his dark hair. "Isn't it a little weird to keep it now? I know the Hendersons gave it to us as a 'sorry we got angry about the gardening contests' gift but why would they give us an old toaster as a gift? It's just kind of . . . weird," he repeated.

"What would you suggest we do with it?"

"Throw it in the trash? We don't even use it." Chris pointed to the superior toaster oven in black and chrome that sat to the left of the demonically possessed toaster. "It's only out there because you were afraid Janet would ask why we weren't using it if they stopped by."

"But…"

Chris held up his hand. "I know, I know. Ghosts. What's the statute of limitations on keeping a useless gift from a dead person? A month? Two?"

Mephistocrates listened to the conversation in earnest. Many a demon has been in this situation before. Getting trapped in some sort of vessel for an indeterminate time is one of the most infamous ways for a demon to go missing from their plane for millennia. It would be damn sure to not add its name to the tales of warning told to freshly spawned demonic entities. Toaster limitations aside, it was time to act.

That evening while the Smythes slept, Mephistocrates began its plan. The first step would require an elimination of the demon's shelfmate and competition for bread-warming option. The demon used its tail that the humans hadn't even bothered to plug in to slowly sever the tail of the fancier toaster oven beside it on the counter. "And now," it thought, "we wait."

"What on earth did this?" Karen asked the next morning. She was holding the severed cord of the shiny toaster oven in the air so Chris could see.

Chris looked behind the oven and saw the cleanly cut cord still plugged into the wall. "It looks like it was cut with a knife. That is so strange." He reached to unplug the remaining cord from the wall.

Mephistocrates grinned, to the extent that it could grin without a mouth.

"Wait," Karen called.

Chris pulled his hand away from the cord. "I don't know what I was thinking. Thanks. I'll shut the breaker first." He exited the kitchen into an adjacent room. After a few moments, he returned, unplugged the cut end of the cord, and removed the now-broken toaster oven from the shelf. "Guess we'll have to get a new one," he mused as he exited the room again.

"I still need to toast this bagel," Karen said. "Flip the breaker back on and I'll just use this one," she called to Chris in the other room. The female human slide the less fancy toaster over and plugged it into the vacated socket.

Mephistocrates felt the surge in power as the circuit was opened and electricity flowed into its vessel. The demon was not put off by the lack of success in the male human not electrocuting himself stupidly. It was a simple tactic but was worth a try. "Now to test the female," it mused.

Karen dropped two circular pieces of bread into the open slots on the toaster and pressed down on the lever.

As she moved around the kitchen, making coffee and obtaining some sort of cheese from the refrigerator, Mephistocrates watched and waited. It could feel the electricity convert into heat within its metal coils and the bagel slowly cooked. When the internal mechanism that served for a timer, the demon allowed the heat to stop but held firm onto the bagel halves with its walls.

"This thing should be done by now," Karen said as she returned to the counter. She looked down inside the toaster and sighed. "Oh great, it's stuck." She pushed up on the lever in an attempt to release the toasted bagel but it didn't budge.

"What's wrong?" Chris asked.

"The stupid bagel is stuck. Of course Janet would give me a busted toaster as an apology gift."

"Can I throw it out yet?" The silence as Karen fiddled with the lever more lingered and Chris didn't pursue the line of questioning any further.

Karen opened a nearby drawer and shuffled around with utensils. She obtained one and slammed the door shut. "I'm already late for work and if I don't eat I will not be happy," she said more to the toaster than Chris.

Mephistocrates sat patiently waiting. All she had to do was use that utensil to try to get the bagel out and the demon could send a jolt of electricity through her to stop her heart. Crude but effective. It felt the utensil make contact with its metal coils and released the stored electricity.

And nothing happened.

Karen cried triumphantly as she released first one half of the bagel and then the other with a plastic fork. "I'll order a new toaster oven today," she told Chris while smearing butter on her bagel. "You can throw it out when we have the new one."

The demon fumed inside its useless vessel and plotted its next move. It could no longer think like a being with infinite time. It had a deadline now: kill the humans before its 'replacement' arrived or be doomed to potential eons in this vessel.

While Karen and Chris left the house unattended to do whatever it is humans do all day, Mephistocrates prepared for its next move. It used its control over the object to hop off the counter and explore the domicile, a two-story building far larger than the two of them needed for just themselves. The demon considered the irony of its massive form being trapped inside such a small vessel while they moved around freely in this structure. Even if they didn't deserve death for their supposed affronts to Janet and Brad, Mephistocrates felt this injustice alone was worthy of the sentence.

The possessed toaster slowly made its way upstairs to the second floor and there the demon set in motion its next plan. In its observation, a good fall from such a height was more than enough to eliminate a human. They were a fragile bunch.

Mephistocrates sat at the top of the stairs and plotted. It whipped its tail around the uppermost railing and pulled it taut across the landing. Once again, crude, but the demon had no other choices with its limited vessel. It didn't even have limbs. It disconnected the cord and found a closet near the stairs in which to wait until morning.

CRASH! BANG! CRUNCH!

"Oh my God, Chris, are you okay?" Karen screamed from atop the stairs.

Chris lay in a heap at the bottom of the stairs. The door to the coat closet was broken in two pieces on top of him. There was no movement.

"Chris?" Karen quested again. She stepped gingerly over the electrical cord slung across the top stair and ran to the bottom. As she got there, the pile of wood that used to be a door moved and Chris emerged from the debris.

"I'm okay," he said. He was bleeding from a few places but was otherwise steady on his feet. "What did I trip over?"

The two humans both looked up at the toaster sitting on the side of the top step with its cord tied across to the railing and shivered.

Karen spoke first. "Who would have put that there?"

Chris brushed off some splinters of wood from his pajama pants and winced. He rotated his shoulder suggesting some sort of injury. "Well, if it wasn't you with some elaborate prank, I certainly wouldn't have tripped myself with it!"

Karen walked back up the stairs and untied the cord. Picking up the toaster, she said, "I think it's time we get rid of this thing. I am totally freaked out by it now."

"If I had known falling down some stairs would have gotten you to see my side of this, I would have done it days ago," Chris said with a laugh.

"Wait!" the disembodied voice inside the toaster shouted.

Karen dropped the toaster and it rolled down the stairs and directly into Chris's crotch.

"Ugh!" he called, doubling over in additional pain.

"I'm so sorry!" she said, running back down the stairs. "It talked!"

Chris lifted the toaster and looked it over. "It talked?"

"Yes," the voice said again.

Chris avoided dropping it but held it a little further away from his body. He stepped out of the broken door pieces and walked to the living room, placing the toaster down on the coffee table along the way.

Karen followed. "Is it the ghost of the Hendersons?"

"Like one shared ghost or both of them in the toaster?" Chris asked. He sat down with a groan and wiped some blood from his forehead.

"I don't know. But what the hell?" she asked.

"Good question." Chris turned his attention to the toaster. "So what the hell?"

"I am not a ghost. Or several ghosts," Mephistocrates explained from within his vessel. "I am a demon summoned by your Hendersons to dispatch with you due to their jealousy over losing some type of contest."

Karen let out a breath of air covered in anger. "That bitch summoned a demon over an HOA gardening competition with a fifty dollar gift card to Applebee's?"

"So it would seem," the demon added.

"What the hell is wrong with her?" Karen asked rhetorically.

"Aside from being dead?" the toaster asked.

Chris laughed. "I like this guy. Hey, did you kill our toaster oven?"

"I had to try to complete my objective," the demon explained. "I am bound by my charge to kill you in order to be released back to my plane of existence. As the Hendersons are now dead, there is no other way for me to escape this vessel."

"Man, that sucks," Chris said.

"I can't believe you are sympathizing with the demon that is trying to kill us," Karen cried. "And also broke our toaster oven," she added after a thought. She drew her attention to the mess of broken door at the bottom of the stairs and pointed emphatically to it. "Also that."

"Oh come on," Chris said. "He didn't ask to be summoned here. You shouldn't be mad at him. Janet and Brad are to blame. And I don't even blame Brad that much. I still think he crashed on purpose to get away from her."

"I surmise you are correct, Chris," Mephistocrates said. "It is his fault I am stuck in this inadequate vessel but she was the one that summoned me."

"That guy really couldn't do anything right," Karen said.

"Don't start," Chris said.

There was an awkward moment of silence as the three of them sat staring at one another. Mephistocrates broke the silence with a question, "So now what?" it asked.

"How come you're allowed to talk to us?" Chris asked. "Like shouldn't your presence be a secret or something?"

"Not a rule, per se," the demon answered. "Usually better to have the element of surprise but I had to change my plan when I realized you would simply discard me to exist in this vessel alone for demons know how long. Originally, I attempted to reason with the one you call Janet."

"You cannot reason with that woman," Karen said.

"So I discovered," Mephistocrates said. "Then I attempted, feebly I may add, to still complete her command. And now, I attempt to reason with you."

Chris rubbed his shoulder. "You couldn't have tried that before tripping me down the stairs?"

"It's generally far easier to kill someone than it is to reason with them," it said.

"Hard to argue with that logic," Chris assented.

"What exactly are we discussing here?" Karen asked.

"Just trying to figure out the rules and limitations. What harm could there be?" Chris turned his attention back to the toaster. "So you're like a demon and not a genie or anything, right?"

Mephistocrates pondered the question. "That depends on perspective, really. I am of a different plane of existence than you, much like all spirit beings. I do not grant wishes, however, so don't bother asking."

"So what's your deal, then? You harvest souls for Satan?"

The laughter was tinny coming from the toaster but it rang out heartily. "Of course not. That fool. I feast on souls." Mephistocrates paused as the humans, especially the female one, shivered. It debated whether or not to continue but figured there were worse options. "I am called Mephistocrates the Hungerer."

"I think I'll call you Mitchell," Chris said.

"What?" both Karen and Mephistocrates said at the same time.

Karen stared incredulously at her husband. "You can't be seriously thinking about keeping him around? He may try to kill us again."

"Maybe," Chris said. "But what if we come up with a new deal, Mitch."

The toaster turned to the side as though it were thinking. "I'm listening."

"You're stuck there until we die, right?"

"Until I kill you," the demon corrected.

The Grave Little Toaster

"Okay, fine," Chris accepted. "Until you kill us. But you're like an eternal demon, right? We've only got a good fifty to sixty years left in the tank. That's nothing to someone like you, isn't it?"

"I suppose."

"So you stay with us. Make sure we stay protected and alive and, when the time comes, we'll make sure you get credit for our deaths. It's either that or we can toss you in the trash and you end up on the bottom of a landfill forever."

Karen's mouth dropped open. She stared back and forth from her husband to the toaster. She didn't say anything, however.

Mephistocrates thought about the offer. This human was beyond reasonable. In fact, he was pretty smart. He found a way to benefit himself within the initial parameters of the summoner's charge and the demon would only need to wait a single human lifespan. This deal was too good to pass up. And, if an opportunity arrived, Mephistocrates could always just kill them along the way when their guard was down.

"You have yourself a deal," the toaster said.

"Welcome to the family, Mitch! I think we're gonna be good friends," Chris said with a smile.

JEREMY RODDEN

J eremy Rodden considers himself a dad first and an author second. He is the author of the middle grade/young adult cartoon fantasy *Toonopolis* series as well as numerous fantasy and science fiction stories in several anthologies. He can be found on his author/book review blog at www.toonopolis.com or active on Facebook (facebook.com/toonopolisfiles) and Twitter (@toonopolis).

Amazon page - https://www.amazon.com/default/e/B00515J2LC/

THE LUCKY DEVLINS

BY TERESA EDMOND-SARGEANT

BOOK

When I learned that the cause of Dad's death was a brain aneurysm (in spite of him being healthy, according to his doctors), the news shocked me and my family. Yet there was hollowness in my heart. I couldn't shed a tear. No emotional connection to my father.

If I did cry, it was only for show. Even the wake and the funeral were awkward because I was an emotional desert while wearing the mask of a bereaved daughter consoling her mother and sister.

You don't have to be physically absent to be considered an absentee parent.

My relationship with Dad is dead, and he got buried (metaphorically speaking) right in the middle of his home library.

"How much should we mark this for?" I asked Mom a week after his wake and funeral, holding up a blue hardcover book with the frayed pages and yellow-tinted pages. Of all the possessions surrounding me – furniture, clothes, odds-and-ends – for some reason, this book was what I held up as I adjusted my black horned glasses.

I was sitting at my father's desk when I set "The Lucky Devlins" on it. Dad had commissioned a woodworker friend to create the desk, the library's cherry-oak centerpiece with author quotes painted in black cursive on the sides. These words wrap around a painting of a tree, with separate pictures of me and my sister Charlotte at the trunk as well as our names and birthdates. Branching upward in the tree were pictures of my father and mother with their names and birthdates; going through my ancestors back to my great-great grandfather on Dad's side.

Mom was standing on the other side of Dad's massive library in his lakefront house, surrounded by stacks of hardcover books and paperbacks. They were organized into different stacks on the couch, floor and book-shelves lining all four walls. To think that my Dad spent decades collecting these books, reading them, re-reading them, and penciling notes all over the margins.

Dad liked to read. His stacks of books with caramel-yellowed aged pages prove that. Why shouldn't he have this hobby? He was a *New York Times* bestselling novelist in the mystery genre.

I glimpsed at that blue-covered, worn-out book. "The Lucky Devlins" was the title, spelled out in black blocks of letters. I imagined how Dad had opened and closed that book, opened and closed that book, opened and closed that book.

Devlin. Our family name. What a coincidence. Except it wasn't.

When I was seven and Daddy was on one of his many hour-long flip-pant drivels, he revealed that "The Lucky Devlins" inspired him to choose that surname as his pen name, long before he married and had children. The book inspired him to dare himself to write the first draft of his debut novel in two weeks, thanks in one-part determination and one-part copious amounts of coffee. He was a convenience store clerk at the time, sometimes working double shifts, with a freelancing journalism gig here and there. He polished up his manuscript, submitted it to a few agents, and found one who saw enough potential in Dad to go pitbull on his behalf. Dad's first novel, "Between the Covers" sold a few thousand copies its first week of release and received local media interest. From there, he scaled the best-sellers list with each novel he wrote.

"The Lucky Devlins" is about a girl and her dead father, I learned from Dad.

"You should read the book – compelling stuff," he once said during another one of his blatherings. A book about a relationship so dysfunctional Shakespeare should have written a play about it, Dad added.

The Lucky Devlins

As I thought about this, a pang hit my stomach, that feeling I get whenever something must be amiss. I couldn't put my finger to it, but I sensed it'd come.

"Your father was such a hoarder. He never could let anything go," Mom said, interrupting my train of thought. "All these books, these notebooks. That's why we divorced after 20 years of bliss. If Chester knew we were having an estate sale, we'd never hear the end of it." She dropped her voice a few octaves to mimic Dad. "'Tracy, you're doing this as payback for all the years I wouldn't throw my golf clubs away.' We both knew well he hardly used them anyway. 'Tracy, as my final wish, I want my house converted into a historical landmark and a foundation established in my honor, one that'd take in writers and stay here as a place of residence.'" With the Sharpie, Mom scribbled on a small pink Post-It memo and stuck it on a stack of encyclopedias.

"Anyway," she continued, "now that he's resting in peace, he has no say in this. When we decided to divorce, there was no use in pretending everything was fine between me and your father. Yet we were so concerned that the divorce would impact you and Charlotte. Well, at least neither of you wound up in therapy as a result. I'd be so disappointed if either of you were sitting on some therapist's couch."

Disappointed. Dad often used that word to describe me, a word that served as jettison in the middle of an ocean of words he'd used in his lectures about "the real world" and "how life worked." Disappointed. That word triggered me, but no worries; that was what my weekly therapy sessions for the last four years have been for. I hadn't done much with myself – sure, I got good grades in school, went to college (a no-name community college, not one of those high-flying public institutions Dad was enamored enough to donate his royalties to), and became a receptionist for a non-profit. Nothing that would make me stand out in history. But between my job and volunteer work with the community garden club, I'm fine. Dad believed I should "live more" like he did – engage in culture, hobnob with the elite, and exchange thoughtful, cerebral philosophies *du jour* that, to me, had no basis in reality whatsoever but to puff up those snobs' egos.

"Uh, Mom ..." Hesitation blocked my thoughts, but I steamrolled over them and went ahead with what I had to say. Who cares about Mom's opinion on my mental stability? "I've had arguments with Dad wherever I go," I said.

"Is that so?" Mom asked without moving her eyes from skimming an encyclopedia – the letter 'A.' "Same with me – that's why we divorced."

"No, I mean, I've been having conversations with him nowadays, like, after he died."

Mom set down the encyclopedia. "But, he's dead, dear."

I scowled. "I know – I just said that. That's what makes it weird."

Mom pursed her lips in deep contemplation and rolled her eyes. "Maybe you *should* see a therapist after all."

I continued. "We argued at the supermarket, in my car – one time, in a library. Dad was schooling me, giving me a hard time about my life choices. I got kicked out of the library because our conversation got too loud, though we were in the most secluded section of the library. I might as well get kicked out of society if I go on like this. What is 'normal society,' anyway? Do you know?"

"Honey, even insanity would be normal if everyone has it." By now, Mom was thumbing through another encyclopedia – the letter "Z" this time.

Judging from Mom's tone, I understood she wasn't interested in this conversation.

Harold, my black terrier mix, stopped at the library door and shook his fur. He lifted a paw, lowered it, and moved back. He winced. Moved back. Winced. All this while Mom and I watched.

"What is wrong with that dog?" Mom cried out.

I snapped my head toward her direction. "Shhh!" I waved my hand at her, motioning her to shut up.

Harold dashed toward the oak desk. From where I sat, I couldn't see Harold, but the next sound hinted that he as clawing at the wood.

I got up, rushed to Harold, and snatched him up. He squirmed in my arms, struggling to escape my hold. I kissed him on his head, the way good "dog mommies" do to comfort their "fur babies." He shivered.

"What's gotten into you?" I asked him.

"I told you to leave that dog at home," Mom said. "We have lots to sort through. He'll just be in the way."

My strength gave way to Harold's restlessness. He leaped out of my arms and landed, paws first on the floor, and shot straight for the closed door. I followed him, reached out for the brass doorknob, and opened the door.

"Much gratitude to you, Catherine," Harold said.

The Lucky Devlins

I screamed, stepped backwards, and stumbled before catching myself from falling over. Harold trotted out into the hallway and toward the living room.

I slammed the door and pressed my back against it.

"Harold did not just talk," I muttered.

"Are you taking up ventriloquism again?" Mom asked. "Because that was a fine job you did with Harold. I thought you could only do it with puppets, but to do that with animals is advanced work."

"I've never done ventriloquism, and I'm not doing it now." I staggered toward her. "I could have sworn I ..."

My heartbeat escalated, but Mom continued to organize Dad's stuff.

"Oh look," she said while studying a hardcover book, "a first edition of 'The Turn of the Screw.' What do you think – sell this through an auction or keep it as part of that whole residency/museum project your father never shut up about?"

I heard her question, but I was too immersed with Harold to give full attention. "I could have sworn that Harold talked. He sounded exactly like Dad."

"Honestly, I don't know why you are a secretary for some non-profit. You should be doing something bigger with your life, like be in the entertainment industry – like your sister in New York." Mom read the clock on the library wall, above a table where a potted plant sat. "Oh, how time flies. I must be off."

For some reason – I didn't know why – I grabbed "The Lucky Devlins." I absorbed its energy. I never read the book, but from holding this one item, out of all the items and books in that library, there was a realization that I knew the story cover to cover. That I *am* the story.

"You certainly are off," I said out loud. You know how sometimes you believe you're thinking a thought, but instead you made it clear to the universe what's on your mind? That happened here. Even though *I* said it, the sound of my voice wasn't mine. It belonged to my father.

"Wow, and you're doing it again," Mom said. "If I didn't know any better, I'd think you're your father."

Mom grabbed her scarf off the recliner next to the door and wrapped it around her head.

"I'm sleeping here tonight," I said in my normal voice. "No use driving back to Atlanta. That's, like, a 12-hour drive."

What the – why did I say that?

"You want to know what it's like to drive for 12 hours? Do that with your father," Mom said. "That was a challenge. My quality of life would drop every time I listen to him rattle on, and on, and on. Sometimes he made sense about world politics and the prominent figures he'd be friends with – name dropping and all that – but many times, I'd get lost in his labyrinth of words. For all the interesting things about your father, he could be so boring."

To Mom, Dad was boring. To me, I'd use a different word that started with a "b" to describe him. Boisterous. You thought I was going to say some other "b" word, huh? What kind of daughter would I be to disrespect her dead father?

As Mom chattered about my father, a drive within me compelled me to throw "The Lucky Devlins" at her. Just then, it ... hovered.

It hovered!

The book floated a foot above the other stacks of books on the desk. No air swirled around me, nothing in my environment or the living room that made me suspect that was making this book float. The book floated for a few seconds, then ...

WOOSH!

As if it flew out of a cannon, the book hurled straight for Mom's head. At the speed it was going – perhaps at 100 mph –I feared it would have knocked her out.

If only.

Mom jumped out of the book's path, lost her balance, and crashed into the bookshelves behind her. Books that were stored on the shelves rained upon her.

The book slammed into the shelf and fell onto the floor. Opening up, the book's pages fluttered for two seconds before becoming still. I rushed to Mom's side and helped her up, asking if she were okay. She said she was fine as she rubbed her upper arm, relieving it from its collision with the bookshelf.

"Like I said before, I'm sleeping here tonight," I said, unsure whether I should back out of my statement though what I witnessed my mother go through did nothing to change my mind.

"No, don't," Mom mumbled, her tone losing her characteristic overbearing tone.

My eyes drew toward the blue book on the floor next to her feet.

"Mom, Dad is dead. What is he going to do? Come back and haunt me?"

The Lucky Devlins

I was engulfed in sorting through Dad's stacks of books in his library, when one glance outside the window and I discovered that night had snuck upon me. Mom left the house a few hours ago. I adjusted my glasses as I looked at the clock that had struck 9 p.m.

By then, I had created three stacks of books in the room, on the floor in front of the bookshelves that lined the eastern side of the library. To my left were books that would be given away to charity – the charity that employs me. Next to this stack was one of books that sparked my interest enough to read them. The third "pile," the one that stood next to the books of interest, consisted of one book: "The Lucky Devlins." Though I had seen the book fly and nearly hit my mother earlier today, for some reason, I was not afraid of it when I picked it up after mom had gone and began sorting my way through the books.

"The Lucky Devlins" trembled again. I stepped away from it and cowered into the corner, shaken. Yards away from me, in the center of the room, light shot out from the open pages. The book glowed white, as if the sun exploded. I covered my eyes.

Some seconds later, a voice called out to me from the direction of the book: "Catherine!"

By now – I sensed – the light had died down, so I uncovered my eyes and looked up. There, a distance away from me where the book was, was a shadowy figure, translucent – I could see the furniture and bookshelves behind it. This figure wore a suit and tie – a well-tailored one, at that – and was clean-shaven. His eyes had no expression; I suspected he was watching me, but then again, it was as if he didn't see me.

My jaw dropped. Sweat pooled at my glasses' rims. "Dad?"

Oh, why can't the dead *stay* dead?

Dad ... this ghost ... cocked his head to one side, but somewhat longer that it would take for a person to do this action. "Did you gain weight?"

It was Dad all right.

I rose from my spot, removed my glasses and wiped them down with the edge of my top. I put them back on and stared at this ghost in my father's library.

"Are you going to stand there, or are you going to hug me?" the ghost asked.

I paced myself toward him –it?—and opened my arms, though the muscles all over my body stiffed with fright. I wrapped my arms around this apparition, but due to its transparency – you know how ghosts are! – my arms swept through him.

"Wh-what are you doing here? I mean, besides the fact that this is your house?" I asked.

"I wanted to make sure everything was squared away once I'm gone. I could trust that your mother is taking care of affairs, but seeing you help her, well ..."

I turned my back on him. "Just saying 'Good to see you again' would have been a nice ice-breaker."

"There you go again, running away from the discussion instead of engaging –"

I looked at him. "It's not running away when your own father won't shut up about his crap!"

To say that out loud – what a relief!

Dad scrunched up his face and pouted. Can ghosts make expressions? I assume they can, from what I'm seeing.

"Let's get to the point of me appearing to you, shall we?" he asked. With a raise of a finger, he pointed at the open book on the floor. "The Lucky Devlins. As you must have found out by now, that book is about us, this family."

"I know that. What you mean by that is, the book is relatable to us because when you read it, you see us in these characters."

"No, I *mean*, we are actual characters in this book. Without this book, we don't exist."

"What?"

Suspicion weighed down on my expression as I snatched up "The Lucky Devlins" and flipped to the first page. There it was, my name – Catherine Devlin. I read about my life growing up as the daughter of a famous, eccentric father, his long-suffering wife, and as the sister of the "perfect child." The 'surprises' Daddy bought for me every day like a candy bar or some $2 plastic toy, his constant ramblings about "the real world," his gradual slip into fantasy and away from reality. The fights my parents had.

I flipped to the copyright page, to see what year the book was published. I thought it was written some time in the early 20 century. Instead, the year was 1980 – 40 years ago, five years before my birth.

The Lucky Devlins

It was all in that book, a book that reflected my reality, a book that I believed was fiction all along, but was a manifestation of my reality.

"You said this book inspired you to become an author," I said. "How you adopted "Devlin" as your last name – as our name – and then went on a novel-writing blitz like some time after."

Dad shrugged. "I lied. When I first discovered that book at a garage sale at a neighbor's house, I read that the book hit close to home—too close. About my family life growing up in as one of six, the moving around because my father was in the Navy, my dreams of becoming a writer. The truth was just too fantastical to believe, and so I made up the one about how the book inspired my life, instead of my life directly inspiring it. Then as my life went on, the book added on details about *our* family. This was the one book that illustrated my past and my future, and also and what I expected from you most of all. That was the reason for all my talks with you, but you responded to me as if I'm looking for an argument, and I wasn't."

"Yeah, because what's more frustrating than arguing with a Dad who's alive is one who's dead."

I stopped my thoughts from spinning out of control, before I said something I might regret later. I'm not sure how this ghost would display its wrath if I angered him.

"So why are you here?" I continued. "To repeat for the billionth time how disappointed you are in me? Because I've had more than my fair share from the turd you call lectures plopped onto me when you walked this earth."

"I'm your legacy, one that you will never escape." Silence. Then, from him: "You are going to finish that book for me."

I glanced at the book. "Finish it? What's that supposed to mean? It's a published book, not a manuscript. Do you want me to write a sequel?"

"You *will* be me. Not just a mere carrier of my DNA – sad as it is to admit that – but you will be *me*! Let's face it: You're a disappointment."

At first, my mind shut down at his comment. I wanted to shrink back, to get away from his ghost, to escape that library and out the house. But I couldn't. My feet were like lead, weighed down to the rug-lined floor.

"Dad, for a successful writer, you could really benefit from a thesaurus," I said. "If I've been such a disappointment, to use your word, why not just give up on me? Why pursue me from beyond the grave."

Without hesitation, he said, "Because I love you."

Loves me, he says. Though he's sad to acknowledge that I'm a "carrier" of his DNA.

As hard as I tried in searching through my memory, I have no recollection of him uttering "I love you" to me.

"Besides, if you're a means for me to preserve my legacy, you can establish my house into a non-profit and a residency for writers," Dad said, shrugged.

I gulped. "What about Charlotte? Why not haunt her?"

I knew that I'd walk into that one by mentioning my sister, but hey, when you don't have much in your arsenal, right?

"She's appearing on Broadway right now and she's been on reality show competitions. She's already doing something with her life. You, on the other hand – what do you do? Work as a secretary for a non-profit? If you're going to do that, why not at least consider doing something more ... worthwhile? Like being a spokeswoman and talking to people, convince them to part with their checks for a good cause."

Across the library, on the floor, "The Lucky Devlins" glowed. Light shot out from its pages. Once again I covered my eyes from the brilliance. Still shielding my eyes, I cast them downward, but the light still illuminated my feet. Then, the light disappeared, and I returned my attention to the book. A hush fell throughout the room.

Then tips of what seemed like tree branches reached out from the pages. They stretched out, and out until they towered over me, forming its crown and twigs sprouting outward. A trunk much wider than if there were two of me emerged not long after, with the tree's crown continuing to grow until barely scraping the ceiling. By the time this phenomenon finished, the tree towered over me at maybe 15 feet tall

I gawked at this presence, then glanced at Dad's oak desk, where the family tree was carved onto its surface. This 15-foot-tall tree before me resembled the one on that furniture piece.

The tree before me reached out its spindly branches and seized me by my arms. I screamed.

"You should take more pride in where you come from," my father's ghost said as the tree dragged me toward it. I squatted, hoping that my weight on the floor would give the tree a larger obstacle in dragging me to wherever it's from in that book.

Disappointment.

The Lucky Devlins

That word rattled inside my head like an errant pinball in a globe. The only word my father ever said to me, despite his gifts and "surprises" that were alleged tokens of his love for me.

Dad's ghost stepped in front of me, observing me in capture of this monstrous tree.

"My legacy is one that must be preserved," he said. "great-grandfather was also an important man in the community, with him being a senator. It's a shame about what I'm seem." He shook his head and tsked tsked.

Dad placed his hand on my shoulders, all the while my fear chilling my skin enough to form goosebumps on it.

"Even though I'm snuffing you out of your existence by possessing you, I'm doing this for your own good," the ghost said. "And I have relished in our conversations these last few weeks – in the grocery store, in the library. But there was no need for you to be so argumentative."

I snapped my shoulder away from his hand. "I don't know, Dad, maybe it's because being called a 'disappointment' is what gets under my skin."

"As I told you time and again: Learn to take criticism. You'll be a better person for it." The ghost reconsidered his statement; I could tell in his expression. "On second thought, in your case, left to your own devices, you haven't benefited much from all the advice I'd given you."

The tree tightened its grip around me. I writhed to break free, but when you're dealing with Dad, it's like a losing battle.

"If you really wanted to torture me, why not just give me one of your infamous hour-long, useless lectures?!" I said.

The tree branches stabbed me in my eyes. My glasses broke. Shards of it, combined with the unspeakable hurt my nerves felt, stung my eyes. What I realized to be blood, trickled down my cheeks and chin. Though pain stung me, it was numbed by a greater one: my father's words to me all those years I grew up in his house.

"No more working for that charity, no more fritting your life away, no more of this you call your life!" I heard Dad say. "Much gratitude to you, Catherine, for letting me do this."

Dad's ghost entered me, and my body absorbed his spirit. My flesh sucked in his ghost without warning. My nerves felt as if I were zapped by lightning, and my consciousness short circuited. With that, my life as myself ended.

TERESA EDMOND-SARGEANT

Teresa Edmond-Sargeant is an author, poet, freelance editor and writer, and journalist who lives in Orlando, Fla., with her family.

She has received three awards from state press associations for her work at New Jersey and Central Florida newspapers.

Among her contributions to print and new media, Edmond-Sargeant's short stories have been published in the horror-humor anthology "Demonic Wildlife," and the online literary magazines Short Fiction Break and 121 Words. She is the author of the poetry book "How Fate's Confusion Connects," as well as several short story ebooks available on Amazon Kindle.

Her favorite writers are Emily Bronte, Edgar Allan Poe, and Rod Serling.

When she is not writing, she enjoys spending time with family and friends, reading, working out, shopping, traveling, photography, volunteering, and daydreaming.

Author Facebook URL: www.facebook.com/teresasedmondsargeant
Author Twitter URL: www.twitter.com/teresaesargeant
Amazon Author Page: www.amazon.com/teresasedmondsargeant
Goodreads: www.goodreads.com/teresaesargeant

JUST DESSERT

BY ARIELLE HAUGHEE

OVEN

Edith bumped the oven door shut with her wide hip, wrinkling her nose at the bubbly chicken casserole. The smell. The stink of meat cooking always repulsed her. She hadn't made it for herself of course. Her tofu scramble sat cold on the stove. Fifty years of preparing two dinners every night and she always made sure Mortimer's food was hot and ready when he came home.

She set the casserole down and scratched her orange tabby cat Hermia. "Now how did you turn it off again?"

Edith had Morty install this latest catch from his secondhand shop just yesterday. Gold trim lined the outside, encasing the creamy white interior, and a row of gold knobs winked at her from the upper panel. Even the door handle was gold. It definitely didn't fit in with the cow butter dish and rooster cookie jar on the counter next to it but that was the way of their house—a little bit of everything mixed in. Something special about this beautiful oven hidden in the back caught Edith's attention and Morty had been surprisingly quick to bring it home. Maybe he thought of all the dinners she would make for him with such a stunning appliance.

Hermia pawed at the oven door, then hissed with bared teeth.

"Stay back, little one. I don't want you to get hurt. Let's see...here's the off knob." Edith switched it off and carried her sweet girl away from the oven. She scratched behind the cat's ears and was rewarded with a soft purr. Edith smiled. That cat always saw the best in her, unlike some people.

Tires crunched gravel in the driveway. Edith took a deep breath, steeling herself for whatever mood her husband would be in this evening. The side door opened to reveal Morty in his overalls holding that scuffed up old apple crate. He glared at Edith and set it on the table, daring her to say something about the load of junk inside. Every day he came home with another batch of crap she'd have to figure out what to do with. Two days ago he left a particularly obnoxious bit on her counter when he knew she needed space to prep for the baking contest. Some sort of wooden box with a bunch of metal doohickeys inside. Well, she didn't waste her breath asking Morty about it. She threw it straight out, just in time for the garbage truck to roll by and toss it in the back. By the way her husband's lip curled as he looked at her, he must still be steaming about it. She assumed he'd gotten over it when he installed the new oven yesterday.

"Your dinner's ready." Edith scooped out the chicken muck and plopped it into a floral-patterned bowl. She pinched some freshly chopped parsley and sprinkled it on top. The least she could do was dress up the disgusting concoction that was his favorite.

He grabbed the bowl with a grunt and stalked out of the room toward his throne—the decades-old brown La-Z-Boy. The throne room held much of the king's accumulated wealth. VHS tapes surrounded the three antenna TVs hooked together on a walnut-colored entertainment center where the remaining shelves groaned under hundreds of NFL knicknacks. Four separate beer logo signs hung on the wall above it. A foosball table with a busted leg leaned in one corner although it was barely visible underneath the stacks of books. Edith had stuck a silk geranium on top to at least add something attractive to that corner. The kitchen was her refuge, the only room she adamantly refused to have any clutter. The largest of the TVs turned on and Morty harrumphed in the other room.

No matter. He'd be over it by the time final Jeopardy came on.

Edith glanced in the apple crate, her left eye twitching. A hand-crank egg beater, scuffed bowling shoes, a splattered chicken cookbook...she didn't bother rooting around to see the rest. Garbage. All of it. Like every day for decades. Morty would eat his dinner, then dump everything out on the counter in the laundry room, and spend the rest of the evening finding homes for all the junk. The next day when he went to the store, she'd figure out where he squirreled away all his prizes and throw them out, most of them anyway. She couldn't bring herself to thoughts of the stack of broken picture frames that put her over the edge last week. All she wanted was a tidy house. Her stomach grumbled.

Edith left the junk and went to the stove to heat her dinner.

"We need to eat quick so we have enough time to get in a round of practice. The bake-off is next week," she said to Hermia who sat big-eyed on the kitchen rug hoping for some tofu.

The Hillcrest Bake-Off was the biggest community baking event of the year. Nancy Kettermeyer beat her every single time with her stupid cream puffs. Weren't the judges sick of those things yet? This would be Edith's year. She had her cousin's wife's sister's grandmother's secret recipe for butter brickle bread. That first place plaque *would* be hanging in her kitchen this year.

Movement in the backyard brought Edith's attention to the window over the sink. Red waves of sunset alighted the garden. In the back corner, the fence slats popped inward, once, twice, a third time. That dog again. Her neighbor Steve had an obnoxious mutt who was always getting into trouble. Roxy also wasn't the brightest animal on the block, earning her the nickname Box-of-Roxy. The dog's head smacked into the fence again and three boards wrenched loose, nails popping into the grass.

"Morty!"

The volume on the TV went up. Edith gritted her teeth. She always had to choose her battles carefully with that man, another thing that exasperated her.

Box-of-Roxy rammed her head one more time, snapping the fence slats in half and revealing her brown head. She shimmied through the opening and trotted over the busted wood and into Edith's back yard.

"She's going to stomp all over the petunias. Nevermind getting any help," she yelled over the TV. "Stay on the rug, Hermia."

Tossing her apron onto the counter, Edith grabbed her broom and stormed outside. "Get, get!" she yelled, waving her sword of justice.

The dog hopped over the flower pots and into the camellias. She squatted down, arching her back.

"Oh, no you don't!" Edith raised her broom.

"Roxy!" Steve called over the fence. "Come here, girl."

Box-of-Roxy dropped her present among Edith's carefully tended camellias then pranced over to the opening in the fence and disappeared.

Heat flared in Edith's ears. She stomped to the fence and smacked it three times with her broom. "Look what your dumb mutt did to my fence!"

Steve grunted as he moved his rotund body toward her, sweat beading on his upper lip. "Sorry, Ethel."

"Edith."

He stopped behind the fence and assessed the damage. "Looks like we could just nail these back." He tapped the busted boards still attached to the fence. The rest of one slat fell to the ground, revealing his greasy T-shirt and surprised expression.

"We will not be putting these damaged boards back. I'm going to have a fence company out tomorrow to put up a new panel and I'll send you the bill."

"Do you really need to do that?" He tapped the remaining boards again. "This is good wood."

"Your dog broke my fence and you need to pay for it." Edith turned on her heel, refusing to give that lazy slob another second to think of an excuse.

Jeopardy blasted from the TV when she got back inside. She pulled the phonebook out of the closet from between a stack of old blankets and National Geographics that were "going to be worth something one day." One of these fence companies had to have someone who could come out tomorrow. She looked at the clock. 6:30 PM. With cell phones these days, people answered after hours. And if they didn't at first, she knew how to hit redial until somebody did.

Sweet steam escaped the warm slice of bread Edith lifted to her nose. Vanilla and butter swirled together in perfect harmony. This batch turned out much better than yesterday's. Using real vanilla instead of that artificial junk made all the difference. She bit into her second helping, letting the moist sponginess crumble apart in her mouth. The judges would never be the same again. They'd all beg for the recipe and Edith would turn them away with a smile, telling them to buy her forthcoming cookbook featuring the world-famous Butter Brickle Bread. She'd be rich. Maybe even get one of those fancy electric scooters to drive off to wherever she pleased.

Just Dessert

The little apple timer on the counter dinged, letting her know the oven should be ready at the higher temperature for Morty's dinner.

"Might as well make it now while we're already bustling about the kitchen, right Hermia?" The cat's tail flicked from her sunny perch by the window.

Edith opened the oven door and slid in the shepard's pie. While she arranged the dish on the shelf, the oven door snapped back. Edith wrenched her hands away.

"Phew! A half second slower and that would've been a serious burn." She made a mental note to have Mortimer look at the door when he got home.

Running her hand down Hermia's back, she peeked out at the fence repairman taking down the rest of the ruined panel in her backyard. He tossed two boards on the ground, right on top of her petunias.

Edith flew into the backyard with Hermia hot on her heels. "What the heck do you think you're doing?"

The middle-aged man pushed up his scrubby baseball cap. "Fixing the fence you told my boss *needed* fixing today."

"That doesn't mean you get to ruin my flowers!"

He glanced down at the ground, rolled his eyes, then kicked the boards to the side. "Better?"

The flowers were all snapped in half, lying flattened on the ground. Edith clenched her teeth. "You kill one more flower and I'm calling the cops," she ground out.

The man sighed then grabbed his hammer and ripped off the next board, setting it carefully on top of the other two. Edith watched for another minute, satisfied he'd learned his lesson, before heading back inside.

Her ears pricked at a curious sound coming from the kitchen. The oven made a low hiss that almost sounded like a growl.

"Air must be whooshing out." she said to the cat. "Gotta be a leak in it." Edith held her hand over the stove, feeling for escaped heat. Nothing. "Hmmm...be sure and stay back from this thing, girly."

A loud rap made them both jump.

The fence man stood at her window with an annoyed expression. Edith lifted the pane and he leaned in. "Your neighbor's sprinkler has been facing the next panel, probably for years. The whole thing is rotted at the bottom. You're going to need that one replaced, too."

Of course there was something extra. There was always something extra that "needed" to be done with these kinds of people.

"I'm going to get my camera."

She'd show Morty the "damage" and see what he thought, even though she already knew. For some reason, workmen accepted a *no* better if it came from the husband. Edith walked to the back bedroom, picking up the Polaroid.

A metallic bang echoed through the house followed by a grinding screech.

"Hermia!"

She dropped the Polaroid and raced to the kitchen, searching for the cat. Padded footsteps came up behind her accompanied by a weak meow. "Oh, thank the lord. What was that noise?" The kitchen sat undisturbed— farm plates lined neatly on the walls, baking canisters in nice rows, cabinets polished to perfection. "Let's check out back." They stepped outside. Nothing was out of place, just a toolbox next to her feet. She pushed it with her toe but it didn't make that strange sound.

"Must have been a car backfiring." Edith glanced around one more time. The repairman wasn't in the backyard either.

"Probably went to his truck for something...bet it's to call his boss and tell him he's got another sucker lined up to pay extra for something they didn't need." Edith waited, tapping her foot. Hermia wandered to the birdbath to sneak a drink.

Several minutes passed. Sweat trickled down the back of Edith's neck.

"Temperature's spiked in the last hour, don't you think?"

Hermia swatted at a butterfly, nearly falling into the water. Edith picked her up and walked out front, checking the truck for the fence man. It sat empty.

"Isn't it just like those people to up and take a lunch break without even saying anything? Most likely walked to the gas station down the street."

Edith went back inside.

"I don't have time for his shenanigans." She set Hermia down on the couch. "I need to stop in Morty's store and help him tidy up. Haven't been there in a few days and Lord only knows the disaster he's..."

A bizarre smell cut off her thought, the usual stink of meat but with a foreign umami mixed in. She put on her red oven mitt and carefully opened the little door. A wave of heat blasted out, sending her hair flying back. Edith winced then peered into the oven. The shepherd's pie mounded out of the pan and the mashed potato topping had splatted all over the bottom burner. Strange red goo dripped from the pan and added to the mess. Edith pulled out what had been the shepherd's pie. The meat jiggled when she set it on the stove. Edith held back the bile climbing up her throat.

She glanced over at Hermia. "Must have bought some rancid meat at the supermarket. Morty's gonna have to make do with take out tonight. Why don't you watch for the fence man out front while I clean this up?"

Edith pulled out a pair of yellow gloves and snapped them on. She couldn't help but notice the outside of the oven remained a pristine white. Not a spec of the mess within showed on the surface.

The bell jingled when Edith opened the door to Mortimer's Miscellany. The scent of worn wood and dusty clothing triggered her organizing itch. Laundry baskets overflowing with dishes, shoes, books, and random bits towered behind the register. Edith rolled her eyes. Morty couldn't have sorted inventory for a full week to be this backed up.

"Morty!" she shouted up to the second floor. Edith made her way around two antique bookcases to get behind the counter. Knotted Christmas lights and other odds and ends littered the floor. She shook her head and scooped up an armful, dumping it on the counter.

"Don't touch anything!" The steps groaned under Morty's weight.

"You can barely walk back here. What have you been doing all week? Watching that darn fishing channel?" Edith slid a set of teacups to one side then picked up a rusty wrench. "Why the heck did you get this thing? You've got ten better ones already on the shelf. This is junk."

Morty snatched the wrench from her hand. His eyes blazed. "I said, don't touch anything."

"You're never going to get that boat buying crap like this, Morty." She lifted yet another cracked picture frame. "Get rid of this thing."

His nostrils flared. Quite a mood he was in today. This happened at least once a month. Morty would get backed up at the store, Edith would try and help, he'd blow up at her, then he'd eventually submit to her assistance when he had no other options. Mortimer's Miscellany would be a rusted, stinking heap of garbage if it wasn't for her.

She set the picture frame down, knowing she'd be back tomorrow, and walked out from behind the counter. "You'll need to grab some dinner on your way home. That oven has some kind of weird leak. You should look at it later."

The bell rang again as Edith left with a grin. He'd come around. He had to.

Edith pulled into her driveway and scowled at the truck still sitting outside her house. What to do about it?

"That repairman must have gotten drunk on his lunch break and forgotten to come back to work," she said to Hermia as she walked inside. Edith pulled out the phonebook again. "Time to get another fence company, but first we'll call a tow truck. That bum will have to explain what happened to his boss, probably pay the towing bill. Serves him right." Hermia yawned and rolled over on her bed.

After a brief call, she smiled to herself. Only forty-five minutes and that fence truck would be gone. Her stomach rumbled. The beans and rice in the fridge would make a great dinner, especially if she added some fresh cilantro. Edith made her way into the kitchen, almost tripping over a croquet set. Now was the perfect time to get rid of it. She reached down, stopping when she saw brown flash through her backyard.

Bits of dirt flew through the air in quick bursts. "Roxy!" she yelled.

Steve appeared at the gap in the fence and called the dog's name. Box-of-Roxy continued to fling dirt from a giant hole she dug next to the camellias. Steve stepped through the gap and his giant stomach caught on the remaining boards.

"Roxy!" he called out, yanking his body once, twice, three times before he made it through the opening, ripping the bottom two buttons off his green plaid shirt. Roxy hopped back when she saw him, her front half lowered to the ground with her paws out and her back end up high, tail wagging. He stepped towards her and she jumped to the side, tail wagging even faster. He reached out and she hopped away again, her tongue hanging out the side of her mouth. The pair darted back and forth all over her garden, knocking over the trash cans on the side. All the junk Edith managed to get out of the house the last three days toppled out.

The tops of Edith's ears flamed hot as a supernova. Time for the big guns. She was going to get the hose.

Pulling on her galoshes, she whipped open the back door and headed for the spigot. The metallic bang echoed again behind her. Edith dropped the nozzle and ran to the back. Roxy tilted her head to the side as she stared at the back of the house. Then she turned and trotted back through the opening in the fence. Steve had disappeared.

Smoke misted out the bottom of the kitchen window.

"What in the world?"

Edith hustled back into the kitchen and walked right into a gray cloud. A fierce beep. Then another. The smoke alarm wailed. She opened the window and waved her arms back and forth before realizing the plumes billowed from the oven.

"I didn't even turn that thing on!"

Edith pulled open the oven door and a shockwave of heat pulsed out, singeing her eyebrows. Something was in there but she couldn't see around all the smoke. Grabbing a potholder, she coughed and fanned it back and forth trying to clear the air. Meat had exploded all over the inside of the oven. Blood pooled at the bottom and lumps of fat hung from the oven racks in goopy blobs. She pulled out a wooden spoon and nudged the closest mass, revealing a hint of green. Was that a button?

She slammed the door closed.

"I don't know what happened, Hermia." The cat meowed from the threshold of the living room. Her mind raced for an explanation. "That shepherd's pie must have exploded all through this thing yesterday."

Edith flipped on the fan, clearing out most of the smoke. As soon as it cooled down, she'd clean it all out before Morty got home. He needed to look at this thing. Tonight.

Headlights beamed through the front curtains at half past nine. About damn time. She'd been waiting hours for him to come home and deal with that oven. Edith quickly tossed another handful of broken laundry clips into the trash. Why did he save those things?

"I'm sick and tired of my whole life revolving around Morty and his junk," she said to Hermia. "You know I deserve better, right sweetie?" The cat rubbed her head against Edith's leg.

Morty flung open the door then kicked it closed with his foot.

"What took you so long?" she asked.

"You told me to stop and get dinner." He dropped another apple crate on the table. It brimmed with even more garbage. Was that the broken picture frame in there? Another cracked frame in her home. She knew last week with all the other busted frames it would never end. A flame lit in Edith's chest, rolled through her whole body, and set every nerve ablaze.

"I've had enough of your crap!" she yelled. She snatched the crate and flung open the backdoor, heading for the trash cans.

Morty stormed up behind her and grabbed her elbow. "My crap has paid for your whole life! You throw everything out, too stupid to realize how much things are worth. Do you have any idea what you got rid of a few days ago?"

Morty stepped closer, tightening his grip. A metal groan sounded from the wall behind them.

"That box thing with all the metal inside? I know exactly what it was — another waste of money taking up space in my house!"

He leaned in, his face inches away from hers, his eyes narrowed to thin slits. "That was an antique sextant. I had it appraised." His voice dropped to a seething whisper. "You threw away $2,000."

Edith swallowed and gripped the crate.

"How do you like that new oven?" he asked with a smirk. "Looked pretty special. The appraiser finally sent back his estimate. After hours of research, do you know what he said about the oven you nagged me about incessantly? $50."

She backed into the garbage cans, trapped between the wall and Morty's seething face. The metal groaning grew louder.

"You cost me my boat," he growled.

The warm wind blew through the backyard. It rustled the oak leaves and twisted around the two of them, pushing Edith's hair back and resetting the power between them.

"You're never going to have a boat." She shoved the box of junk into Morty's chest. He stumbled to the side and dropped the crate.

"And about the oven..."

With a grinding roar, the back of the house split open behind Morty.

"It really is something special. I'd been watching it every week for quite a while, seeing some of the more interesting things it can make. Turn around. I've been wanting you to take a look at it."

Morty turned and blanched. Metallic tentacles whipped out with a blast of heat.

148

Just Dessert

"I told you I'm done with your crap," Edith said with a smile.

The tentacles curled around his legs. Morty screamed and reached for Edith. She smiled. Rows of blades set in double lines of teeth clacked together from the opening.

"Goodbye, Morty."

Morty's scream halted mid-shriek as he was flung inside. The bricks of the house closed behind him. Edith picked up the apple crate, opened the garbage can, and tossed it inside—the broken frame rested on top. All she wanted was a tidy house after all.

Edith relaxed in her clean kitchen with the cat, enjoying a warm cup of tea. A slice of pie sat on a plate in front of her. A burnt spot marred the outside crust. She turned the brown part away from Hermia. That cat always did get to see the best in her, unlike some people.

She took a bite, chewing the unfamiliar bits and rolling them around in her mouth. Maybe she could get over the smell.

Perhaps she could enter this dish into the contest. After all, there was plenty of it. Of course she would need a new name....maybe, Just Dessert? She glanced at her freshly cleaned oven. She was going to beat Nancy Kettermeyer, one way or another.

ARIELLE HAUGHEE

Arielle Haughee is an Orlando based writer with short stories and memoir published in a variety of print and web publications including *Havok* magazine, *The Hunted* anthology series, and FWA *Collections*. Her micro-memoir "Learning to Kick" published in the *Lost Dreams* anthology won a Royal Palm Literary Award in 2017 for published creative nonfiction. As well as being the Contest Coordinator for Writer's Atelier, she is also a judge for the Florida Writer's Association RPLA awards. Arielle is a multi-genre author and writes fantasy, science fiction, horror, romance, mainstream fiction, and children's picture books. She is an active member in several writing organizations including FWA, SCBWI, IBPA, and the Seminole County Writer's Group. Arielle is also the owner of Orange Blossom Publishing which features the anthology series *How I Met My Other* as well as other upcoming titles. Learn more about Arielle at www. ariellehaughee.com and Orange Blossom Publishing at www.orangeblossombooks.com.

www.ariellehaughee.com
www.orangeblossombooks.com
https://www.facebook.com/AuthorArielleHaughee/
https://www.facebook.com/OrangeBlossomPublishing/
https://www.amazon.com/Arielle-Haughee/e/B074V9Y9H2/
ref=dp_byline_cont_pop_ebooks_5
Instagram: @how_i_met_my_other

THE RITUAL ROOM

BY LARRY GRIFFIN

STORAGE CLOSET

Krista and Mike's new apartment was bigger than their previous place, with a nice old-Southern ambiance Krista said reminded her of her grandma's house. There were kitchen tiles that alternated red and white and black, creating a sort of retro-diner feel, which Krista said was very 1950s. There was a big living room space, and Mike was picturing where they'd put the TV and his prized record player and vinyl collection, cultivated over the years, all rare cuts and copies and old classics. Krista wandered through the kitchen and the bathroom, and then she was calling his name from one of the other rooms.

"This could be the bedroom," she said as he came and joined her. And it *was* just about the right space for a bedroom.

Not like there were any hard criteria, though. It just had the right *feel* of a bedroom. Mike couldn't explain it.

There was one more room. Mike pushed the door open and felt a small but definite change in the temperature. It was a small room likely used for storage, and the heating and water heating system, a big gray tank with tubes connecting to the bathroom, separated by the wall, lay at the far end. It was dark and had a musty smell to it. Krista came up behind him and wrinkled her nose. "Ew," she said. "What's that?"

"Looks like a storage room of some kind," Mike said, shrugging.

"Place smells like something died in there," Krista said, walking away and back down the hall. She had always had an acute sense of smell.

"Something probably did," Mike said.

She was unpacking their plates and bowls in the kitchen. "When did that lady say was the last time someone lived here?"

Mike said, "Like, 10 years, I think?"

Krista shrugged, wrinkled her nose and said, "I guess it's good it was cheap."

The two of them put the plates away and the sounds of ceramic on ceramic created a rhythm that filled the apartment and they figured they'd grow to love. Mike could already feel the place as a kind of home.

Over the next month, they settled in until their bodies were like imprints on everything, the air and the beds and the couches, and the house had surrounded them in its servitude to them, rather than appearing to be oppressive and ominous. They went to work, Mike at his engineer job downtown and Krista as the social media director for a local energy drink shop. When they came home, the apartment was like a sanctuary inside which they could retreat from the world. It was perfect in its solitude. The both of them enjoyed cooking, so they took turns; he with his beef stew and corn-on-the-cob and she with elaborate Shepherd's Pie or chicken pasta dishes passed on by her mother. Things went along smoothly. Though their relationship had had its ups and downs, the move to the apartment had smoothed them over, sanded off the rough edges for the time being. They were both focused primarily on the move, the practical things.

The only point of contention became the room. The one used for storage. They'd loaded their boxes inside, wanting to keep them in the case of another move, broken down now and stacked neatly against the wall. And when Mike had gone inside to put them there, he'd felt a kind of coldness that wasn't natural. The rest of the house was warm; it was a Floridian summer day and the A/C wasn't on. But in the storage room it was cold.

The first sign of trouble was a little over a month in. Krista was having trouble sleeping as she was wont to do at times. Brief bouts of insomnia had riddled her since her youth. She was standing in the kitchen drinking a glass of milk and leaning against the counter. The stillness seemed complete, and in these moments she felt like the only person awake.

The Ritual Room

Then, through the open window in the living room, diagonally adjacent to where she stood, she caught a glimpse of a figure in black passing by the outside of the house.

Her blood ran cold. She'd once lived in a college dorm and there was a stalker who had prowled at night peering into rooms and even entering a few times, going through underwear drawers, filling the entire populace of girls with a fear. But they had been a team then. And there had been so many of them that they'd formed a kind of network of information, always passing around hushed words of where he'd been rumored to be stalking and protecting themselves. Finally, after several weeks, the pervert was caught; just some disgruntled mama's boy from the town nearby, a creep who had never had any social interaction.

Out here, it was just her and Mike, and Mike was dead asleep and would remain so through a firestorm. And they were in a desolate area, with houses on the other side of the street, but a whole lot of woods, deep and winding and full of twisted branches and patches of utter blackness, on the other sides of them.

She thought about waking Mike up.

No, she thought then. No, it would take too much time.

She got her phone from the bedside table and went to the door, went outside. The pavement was cold on her bare feet. She just needed to check if anyone was outside. And if she saw anyone, anyone at all not supposed to be there, she'd call the cops. Of course there was the concern about profiling. But wasn't safety more important?

She was on the grass, then. The night was chilly for Florida. She inched her way around the apartment building and she was alone outside.

But she was *sure* she'd seen someone, passing by the window outside.

"It was probably just that you were tired," Mike would say the next day over the phone, the first time they'd been able to talk about what happened, the both of them at work and speaking on a brief break.

"No," she said. "I know what I saw."

"I'll check it out tonight," he said.

"How?" she asked.

She could hear his irritation, his deep sigh, and she felt a twinge of irritation of her own. Like *well if it's that much of a problem...*

"I'll check outside," he said. "I'll look and make sure no one's out there, doing any weird shit."

He said he had to go. They hung up and she felt vaguely discontented.

They had applied air freshener to the storage room, and it had done well until that point, to keep the odor away. It now smelled vaguely like strawberry-banana when they passed by the room, but in the rest of the house, it had been expunged, now just smelling like themselves, the human scent of general life.

Until that day. When Mike got home that day, the smell hit him full force, something deep and rotten, as if soaked into the very fabric of the house. It had not been there that morning. Immediately he knew where it was coming from. He walked down the hall to the storage room and the smell was *strongest* there, like an aura.

When he opened the door, the smell exploded and what he saw was enough to send him to the bathroom, vomit rising up.

"A crow," the cop with the notepad was saying, writing down what they had told him. "A crow, crucified and burned, somehow got into your extra room."

"Yeah," Mike said. Krista was behind him, arms crossed, looking pallid and sullen. The pervasive feeling was one of violation.

"The cross was made from Popsicle sticks," the cop murmured to himself, writing this down as if it were something totally normal.

He would leave saying he'd be in touch if they found anything. Krista doubted somehow that he'd find a suitable amount of clues leading to the crucifier of dead crows. But at least he was a cop who seemed to be doing something, she thought. That had not always been her experience.

Mike was wiping his mouth with the back of his hand. "I goddamn hate throwing up," he said.

"I know," she said.

"Let's go clean out the room, then," he said. They got their gloves and mops from the kitchen.

While cleaning, Mike said, "A fucking crow. Crucified. I wonder what fucking sicko would do such a thing."

Krista shrugged. "One with a lot of imagination, I guess." She had always fallen back on darker humor as a vehicle for coping.

"Yeah, but *why* would they do this?"

Krista shrugged again. "What else are you gonna do with a dead crow, I guess?"

"Babe, that's pretty morbid," he said. Mike had never understood her tendency toward sick humor. It made for an interesting dynamic, a bit of a challenge, to dance around his sensibilities.

The Ritual Room

They cleaned up mostly in silence. She took out the trash. After she threw the bag into the dumpster, she stood there in the small space surrounded by trees and saw something behind one of the trees. A figure in black stood there, hooded, face obscured. He seemed to be bare-foot, and his feet were white and pale.

Krista felt something in her clench up again, like a valve shut off. But then she blinked and the figure was gone.

Then she went from scared to annoyed. She walked out to the wooded area and looked around in the trees. "Anyone out here?" she asked, raising her voice. "I saw you!"

But nothing. It was now silent. She wondered if she was losing her mind. When she turned, there was a man with a track suit walking a dog, stopped now, staring at her as if she were insane. And maybe she was. She was certainly not making a strong argument for sanity; this woman in shorts and a dirty T-shirt, bare-foot, standing and shouting at the trees.

She grinned nervously and walked forward, past him. He told her to have a nice day, in a voice that suggested he was afraid she'd stab him.

At the dinner table that night, Krista told Mike she wanted to go talk to someone.

"Like, a therapist?" Mike asked, furrowing his brow.

"No," she said. "About the house. There's something *wrong* here. You feel it too. The bird on the cross? And I told you what I saw."

"Yeah, but what are we going to say?" he asked. "That we think the place is haunted? C'mon, babe. What are we gonna do? Call an exorcist?"

Krista didn't answer, shrugging and looking at Mike with the power of suggestion. He rolled his eyes.

"I know it's fucking weird," Mike said. "But I don't know what to do. And I got no explanations."

"I know that's hard for you to say," Krista said.

"Shut up, babe," he said, but he was smiling.

The moment of peace did not last. For at that moment, a great racket arose, howling and banging, loud enough to wake the devil. The walls seemed to shake. The whole house was full up with a booming like a mortar shell had gone off. It lasted only a few minutes, but Krista was covering her ears and Mike was shouting but his voice was dwarfed by the cacophony of sound...

Then it was gone. Their ears were both ringing and the silence seemed to be oppressive in the wake of the chaos.

"Jesus Christ," Mike said.

They went to look in the storage room, the both of them knowing intuitively to check there. The room was empty save for the boxes they'd had piled there. No more crow carcasses, crucified and rotting, had been placed there; nor had anything else. But there was a kind of stillness in the air that made them want to be quiet. It reminded Krista of being in church as a little girl with only the pastor talking, only this felt wrong in a much more pronounced way than the boredom and, when she was older, the social implications of the many scandals of the church.

There was something fundamentally *different* in the little storage room and they couldn't put a word as to why. They closed the door and left it that way.

The next day, they went to the office that had gotten them the apartment in the first place. It was a small, cool air conditioned office in a beige-colored strip mall, surrounded by a dentist's apartment and a tax firm. They waited in the lobby and then were seen by Laura, the skittish, mousy woman with thin straw-blonde hair and rectangular spectacles who'd sold them the apartment a little over a month prior. They told her they'd been experiencing strange things in the apartment.

"Hm," she said, furrowing her brow. She clicked around on the computer for a few moments. Then her eyes widened and she said, "Oh, my..."

"What?" Mike asked.

"It seems that, apparently, someone else has had a key to your apartment," she said. "How did we not see this before?"

"Jesus," Krista said. "Well, who is it?"

"Can you change the locks?" Mike asked.

Laura told them the information they needed, and then promised to get someone over to change the locks. They left, feeling a growing irritation toward the process of renting an apartment. They vowed to buy next time. Next time, they'd be ready, they were telling each other as they walked out of that cool air-conditioned building, into the summer heat.

Krista and Mike found themselves at the library researching the case of the previous tenant, Wilbur Rosenstein, and the group called The Midnight Club, who had requested that they been given a key to the apartment. The Midnight Club, apparently, was a donor to various fundraisers and charities in the city, and several big names counted themselves amongst its members.

But precious little information was available as to what the Midnight Club was *about*. Its odd name seemed to indicate sinister intentions, they agreed, even though they were both trying not to stereotype so much. There was so much of the world they didn't understand, and they had both vowed to try to be open minded.

Taking a break, standing outside and smoking, Mike asked Krista why they were at the library when they had perfectly good working internet at home.

"Well, I always see this in movies," Krista said. "When people need to concentrate, they go to the library. It's just a good vibe."

Then she added: "Plus, I'm just afraid as fuck to go back home."

To that, Mike said he could relate.

They went back inside and sat down again, scrolling through Google pages. "Holy shit," she said a few moments later.

"What?" Mike asked, leaning over to her screen.

"Looks like our apartment was built on the site of this old burial ground," she said. "This old place where they found the bodies of pilgrims, back in the 20s. It was like, a whole thing."

Mike looked at her screen. He said, "Shit. That's pretty gross."

Wilbur Rosenstein, it turned out, was recently deceased. He had passed away the previous summer, of a heart attack, in the small house he'd bought with his wife Georgette out in the country. Krista looked it up and it was a 45-minute drive, way out of town and into the deep country, the fly-over state area, which Krista and her friends used to refer to as the 'horror movie slasher' area. With its deep orange groves and the piercing silence, punctuated only by the buzzing of flies, the area was certainly formidable. But now she would have Mike with her, and they would have a purpose.

The drive was long and they alternated music playlists. It made for a schizophrenic drive, as he played Pantera and 80s Metallica and she played Amy Winehouse, The Decemberists and a smidgen of Nick Drake, and the drive adopted a sort of oddball soundtrack. They both laughed. It felt good to laugh again.

Eventually, after the GPS told them they were close but they could not see a turn, Mike pointed out the little road through the tall groves, abandoned seemingly by time and the rest of civilization. Krista asked if they were seriously going to drive through there. Mike said it was obviously the place they were searching for, and it would be stupid not to. They'd already driven this far, after all.

Krista rolled her eyes and made the turn, marveling over his ability to make her feel so small.

Then the little house sat before them in a clearing invisible from the road. It was made of wood and looked as if it could fall at any moment. And outside, the little old woman sat there, eyes unblinking and on them.

Georgette Rosenstein offered them tea, and they accepted. She went inside the house and came back out with a small metal tray and two cups upon it, balancing them perfectly. Krista and Mike took them and sipped. The air was cleaner out in the country, Krista thought, and the quiet felt more natural, less like someone was around every corner.

"How can I help you two?" Georgette asked.

"Well, we live in the apartment your husband, Wilbur, had lived in last," Krista said. "He lived there in about 2005, we found out."

Georgette was nodding. "Yes," she said. "That was before we moved here. It was a troubled time."

"Troubled?" Mike asked. "Ma'am, would you mind telling us how?"

Now she was looking down. "It was a bad time. He wasn't in his right mind. He had moved out of our house and I couldn't track him down for months... and when I did, he was making that pact. That awful pact. He wanted to be young again, and he had made some deal with some awful devil to do it."

Krista and Mike listened to her words in silence. Krista felt a chill, thinking of the two sightings of the black-cloaked men with their pale, bare feet...

"And we intervened," Georgette said. "We saved him, my friends and I. We got him out of there before he could go through with it. He was just going a little bit senile. It ran in both our families, see. He was just scared."

"Well, something's still there," Krista said. "We've been experiencing... things."

She nodded her head. There was something bright and jubilant about her, almost unaware. She said, "I know how to help you."

"You do?" Mike asked.

She was nodding more. "Yes," she said. "I have the remedy. What you have to do is find the afflicted room. You want to take some roses and scatter them all around the area, and then have a priest bless it. Then you just say the words... oh, darn, what were they?"

She got up, the rocking chair creaking as she did, and went inside. She came back out several minutes later with a wrinkled piece of paper, with three lines of incantations in a language she hadn't seen before, in a messy black pen scrawl.

The Ritual Room

"It's Arabic," Georgette said. "It's the family sacred pact. It kills the evil. I have faith that you two can do it. That you can banish the evil."

They would leave after that, with the paper in Krista's pocket. After they had gone, a second car pulled up to the house. A registered home nurse assistant, portly and bespectacled and of kindly demeanor, sat with Georgette on the porch and said, "Who were those people who just left?"

Georgette now had a confused look about her. "I don't know, actually," she said.

"Are you telling people stories again?" the nurse asked, shaking her head. "So creative. I'll give you that."

On the ride home, Mike raised the possibility that the old woman was crazy. "I mean, the whole thing just felt real... I dunno, weird. Like it wasn't real. And she *did* say that thing about maybe being senile."

Krista, hands on the wheel and eyes on the road, didn't say anything to this. She was mulling over it all in her head. She could not stop thinking of the room, of its strange and bizarre power.

Mike was saying, "It ain't too late just to *go*, babe. We could run."

Krista was biting her lip as she'd been told was a bad habit since she was young. But she'd never been able to quit. She was thinking now of another memory of childhood, when she was working on a school project all night, until her mother, going to bed herself, peeked into her room and asked if she was okay. Krista, feeling sleep coming fast, that irritable childlike exhaustion all about her, was forced to tell her mother that she didn't know if she could finish the project. An admission of defeat! Her mother, seeing the rings around her eyes, and the amount of time put into the work, took her daughter's side. The next day her mother wrote a note to the school, explaining that the work had been too much, that there was no way her daughter could have sufficiently completed the project.

Krista had gone on to graduate just fine. The scar of the failure had stuck with her, though. It was the nexus of a common insecurity for her, that she couldn't finish anything, couldn't commit.

But that would not be the case this time.

"No," she told Mike. "No, I want to see if this works. We said we'd stick with this place. I don't want to go back to living in some cramped studio thing downtown."

Mike sighed. "Okay," he said. "I guess we'll try it."

The priest they found was Father Eric Hanrahan, who said he'd be glad to come over and deliver a blessing. Mike was deliberately vague.

Krista pored over the paper they'd been given and tried to make sense of it. It didn't look overtly fake, but then, it wasn't like she had majored in other languages. They had to try everything. She didn't want to just give the place up. With its semi-rural surroundings, the quiet could be so nice. If only they could just do away with all of the creepy stuff, she thought. Then it would be perfect.

And all the while, there were wails and banging sounds from the room. It was always from the room, and they always knew it was coming from there even when the sound was untraceable. Even after only a few days, it had settled into their bones, the essence of the room.

"I can't believe we're about to do this," Mike said. Krista told him that it was their best shot.

The priest, Father Hanrahan, portly and egg-shaped and bespectacled in his black robes, walked around the little storage room, sprinkling holy water around the border. The roses were in the middle of the room. Hanrahan's face was contorted in an unpleasant expression.

"There's definitely something off here," Hanrahan was saying. Krista nudged Mike. *See?* she was saying. He shrugged. He wanted badly for it to be over, so he could go to the bar, watch basketball, drink a beer or five. All of this was too stressful.

He pulled Krista aside and told her so. "There's a huge chance this isn't gonna work, babe," he said. "That lady, I just think she was crazy. She didn't know who she was talking to, or what she was giving us."

"Well, we gotta try," she said.

"Do we?" he asked.

"I want to," Krista said. She was thinking again of the times in her life when she'd let things go and given up. Some days, it seemed Mike himself was a part of that.

He rolled his eyes and that was that, they were doing it.

The priest read his rites, a low-murmured set of words, and then Krista stepped up and read the rites, those incomprehensible pages, which if she had to be honest, seemed like gibberish even to her now. She didn't know what she was doing. It was hot in here now – had it always been so hot? Her hands were slick and sweaty and the paper was harder to hold. Father Hanrahan was tugging at his collar. Mike fanned himself with the priest's bible. Beads of sweat were forming on his forehead. The room seemed smaller now, the walls closing in. But surely that could not be true. It was impossible. And what was the high, barely perceptible ringing she was hearing now? Was it growing louder?

"Does anyone else live here?" Hanrahan asked, his voice thin and uncertain.

"No," Mike said, sounding congested. "Why?"

Hanrahan was closest to the door, and was silent for a moment. Then he said: "Because I hear footsteps."

The room was definitely hotter now. It felt like someone had left the heat on all day. The air had the texture of a fuzzy blanket on a summer evening. Krista could feel sweat running down her arms and legs now, down her neck. "Jesus," she said. "Do you..."

But the thought vanished as if like vapor. There were footsteps now, yes. They were louder and louder and then they stopped at the door. Mike was saying, "I think we got it wrong. I think the lady was wrong."

Hanrahan had grabbed the paper they'd been reading from. He said, "Yeah, this isn't anything I've ever seen. It's a bunch of gibberish."

"Must've been senile after all... goddammit..." Krista mustered, before the heat took them.

They were tied up when they woke, arms behind them, ankles bound, and sitting up against the wall in the tiny storage room. There were three men with cloaks standing above them and they all had bare, pale feet, skeletal and bony. The tallest one was the leader, apparently, as he stepped forward and began to talk.

"This is the gateway," the man said, his voice surprisingly banal; nasal and weak like a guy you'd hear in an office building, just any random sap. "You have tread upon these grounds and now you must bear witness to its ritual opening."

"The gateway," Krista said. "It's just a fucking storage room."

"And behind these walls, a doorway to the next dimension," the cloaked man said. "Surely you've noticed all the strange noises and things happening. I mean, if you hadn't, that would really be something. The crow should've been warning enough to leave. But you stayed, and you woke the monster. So we had to act."

Krista said, "Figured you were behind all that."

The man in the cloak chuckled – a low, humorless sound, making them wonder if this man had ever actually felt human emotions, felt warmth of any kind. "No," he was saying. "We are mere curators. And you, today, are the food."

Krista felt her stomach drop. "Any chance this thing's vegetarian?"

The cloaked men did not respond, for they did not consider her worthy of conversation. They all murmured a grocery list of more incomprehensible words. The ground began to shake and there was a great tremor from beneath the Earth and all around them. Krista could envision the world outside being decimated. She had a small iota of hope that the commotion was as audible outside as it was in the room. But no one was coming.

Then the thing they could not describe or explain happened, which drove them insane, turning their minds to putty. In the interest of the completion of this tale, I will chronicle the onset of the gate's opening the best I can:

It looked to them as if the wall was opening. Then it was like a window to another world had opened there. It was all red and fire and hard, jagged rocks in this other world, like a desert cast in the shade of blood, and it seemed to go on forever. Then there was the shape, lumbering slow, across that vast plain, and the closer it got they could see its details and contours. It was covered in thick fur and there were long, twisted horns protruding from its horse-like head. The eyes were shrouded by fur, but as it got closer, they could see the eyes, burning little slices of coal, yellow and black and full of fury.

It reached the door and did not pause, coming through like a dog in from the outside, and it filled the room. It opened its mouth and the thing had rows and rows of teeth, sharp and white, and so many of them, seeming to stretch on for all eternity...

LARRY GRIFFIN

Larry grew up in Orlando, Florida on a steady diet of dark movies, books and music, which have influenced all his work since then. After graduating college, he immediately moved out to North Dakota to work as a journalist during an oil boom, and he's also written about countless crimes and stories of political intrigue since then, including reporting on the 2016 presidential election. All of this has influenced his fiction. In his free time, you can find him at the beach, pool or at the movie theater.

PREVIOUS STORIES CAN BE FOUND HERE:

http://www.close2thebone.co.uk/wp/?cat=736
Guest in the Storm

http://www.bodypartsmagazine.com/primal---larry-griffin.html
Primal

http://www.freedomfiction.com/2015/11/faces-by-larry-griffin/
Faces

http://pagespineficshowcase.com/larry-griffin.html
New House

And his story "Blood and Sand: A Cult Love Story" will be out in Bards and Sages' Society of Misfit Stories in the fall.

It's Just a Little Mouse

By Marya Miller

Computer Mouse

Jason stared at the object in the battered box, the musty odor of damp gift wrap making his nose itch. "Thanks, Nanna Mossman. It's, uh, just what I wanted."

He had asked her for a SteelSeries Sensei 310 gaming mouse, taking great care to make his request as simple as possible — the exact model name, the best price, the link. He hadn't held out much hope that she would get it right, but this... He shook his head, not even aware that he was doing so.

"You don't like it? Wasn't it the right one?" His great-grandmother sounded as disappointed as a child.

Jason swallowed back his disgust. He managed a smile. "It's wicked, Nanna! I've never seen a mouse like it!" He stared down at the fat, pink oval, painted like a cartoon mouse. A cute little creature, with big black eyes that stared up at him from entirely the wrong angle, like that crazy Escher puzzle his sister had got him last Christmas.

It s Just a Little Mouse

A kiddie mouse.

"Oh good." The old lady's face relaxed into a gentle glow. She gave him one of her sweet, vague smiles. "Run along and play with it, dear. Your mother's bringing in the tea, and I know you don't like tea."

Jason waved his birthday present at her, swallowed again, and left, bolting straight out the front door and holding his breath till he had left behind the sharp miasma of dried cat pee that always emanated from the east corner of the dark front hall. Nanna Mossman's oversized cat, Dandy, stared down at him from the roof of the porch, hissing as he leapt the three steps to the front path. It let out a hiss, and recoiled, surprising him. Dandy was usually friendly.

Jason sat down on the bottom step, lifting the mouse out from its second-hand box (which had once apparently held Parma Biscuits, whatever they were). He wondered if he should give the pink childish monstrosity to his little cousin, Miranda. Surprisingly, the musty mouse seemed to be wireless, though there was no nub, no tiny Nano receiver to shove into any USB ports. He wasn't surprised if it was actually Nanna who had lost the Nano receiver, who didn't even know it needed one. She had probably picked it up at a church jumble sale. He sighed as he put the thing back in its box.

It was only when he had done this that he noticed it had left his hand with an oily feeling. He flexed his fingers, gave a little shudder and wiped his left hand on his jeans.

When Jason got home, he shoved the box with the mouse in his bottom desk drawer and promptly forgot about it until three weeks later, when the mouse he was using – the one that cut in and out and went through batteries the way his little cousin went through cookie dough – died, once and for all. He hauled out the pink-painted mouse with the crazy twisted eyes and flipped the rocker switch underneath it.

The little light glowed blue. Jason almost fell off his chair. He really hadn't expected it to work with his old mouse's Nano receiver. They weren't even made by the same manufacturer. But it was alive.

He tried it out. The thing worked perfectly. It still made him want to cringe whenever he touched it, as if it had absorbed dirt, oil, sweat and cat pee from its past eight lives, but soon he found himself immersed in Age of Eternity III, and forgot all about the mouse's creepy feel.

Everything was fine with it until he told a lie. "Mum, that mouse Nanna gave me is garbage. I need a new one."

"What happened to your birthday savings?"

"I spent them all on Age of Eternity III." He hadn't really wanted to admit that, but it was the truth.

His mother sighed. "What were you using last night, then? You were playing for hours, and don't try to tell me you weren't. You didn't even notice me when I brought your clean laundry in and put it on your bench."

Caught out already. "Okay, I was using Nanna's mouse. But it feels disgusting, it's oily and it smells of cat pee."

"Mow the lawn for me, and I'll buy you a new one."

Jason went back to playing his game, feeling as if a mountain had been lifted off his shoulders. He longed to put the pink abomination in the dustbin.

The next day, he met up with Piers Martin. The two boys lived four doors apart. Both loved gaming, and there was always plenty to talk about on the way to school.

Piers nudged him. "So, what do you think of Age of Eternity III?"

"Faster game play than Age II, but those zombies are a nuisance."

"What zombies?"

Jason looked up, and saw that Piers wasn't teasing him. He genuinely seemed bemused.

"Piers, what level are you up to?"

"Level nine. Don't tell me you've passed that already?"

"No, I'm only on level four."

"There aren't any zombies in the game. Are you sure you got the right game?"

"They turned up in Level Three. I kept getting killed. I don't know what the designers were thinking, putting zombies in Age III."

"You're shitting me! Zombies?"

"Come over after dinner. You can see them for yourself."

Too late, Jason remembered that he only had the pink mouse. He hoped to hell his mother would buy him a new one while she was shopping in Nottingham that day.

She hadn't bought a new mouse. Piers laughed his ass off at the pink cartoon mouse.

Jason took his teasing with his usual resigned gloom. "You finished yet?"

"Yeah, I guess so. I want to see those zombies."

It s Just a Little Mouse

But there were no zombies that night. Not in Level Four; nor Five, nor Six. Jason even went back to Level Three, in case you had to play through it to make them appear.

"You're dreaming, Jase."

"I'm telling you, there were zombies! I could hardly keep up with them."

His mother stuck her head round the bedroom door. "You boys, stop fighting and keep it down. I can't hear the telly for all the shouting."

Jason set his teeth. "Piers is just leaving anyway, mum. We're done for the night."

A few moments later, he heard the front door close below him. Piers set off into the night, whistling.

And the first zombie appeared on Jason's screen.

"Shit! Where were you when I wanted to see you, you little sucker?"

Ten minutes later, Jason shut down the computer, tired of zombies who kept appearing and swarming his screen, thicker than ants. He wiped his hands on his jeans, and started getting ready for bed, but the zombies invaded his dreams.

Jason knew he was dreaming. For one thing, no one went to school in the dark and zombies didn't really exist. He tried to wake up, but the dream went on all night. When he woke up in the morning, he felt shivery, as if he was coming down with flu. And he was clutching the pink mouse in his hand.

Jason yelped, and hurled it across the room.

Piers didn't turn up at school. At half-past-ten, the headmaster interrupted the class, right in the middle of algebra. Mister Harkins held a murmured conversation with Mister Batty. Before Jason could even begin to wonder what it was about, he turned to the class.

"Boys, I have some sad news. Your classmate Piers Martin was apparently the victim of thugs last night. He is in intensive care at Saint Margaret's." He turned to Jason. "Mister Keller, will you accompany me to the office? His mother tells me you were the last person to see him."

Jason scrambled out of his seat, feeling sick and frozen. Four doors down. Piers lived four doors down. They had found him a mile way, down by the railroad tracks, unconscious.

He answered the policewoman's questions in a daze. Apparently satisfied, they sent him back to class. As he walked back up the corridor, he was sure he heard the policewoman say, "The lad was badly chewed by rats."

That couldn't be right.

That night, a musty smell like old wrapping paper penetrated Jason's sleep and made him open his eyes. His mother stood over him in the gloom, staring down with eyes like a blind person's, filmy-white. Her skin shone green in the light coming through his thin curtains.

Jason shot up to a sitting position. "Jeez, mum! Don't do that. You scared me to death."

She opened her mouth, and hissed, like Dandy the cat. A stink like rotten meat hit Jason, making his supper rise up in his throat. She turned and shuffled out of the room, trailing the meat stink behind her.

As soon as his bedroom door shut, Jason leapt out of bed, heart hammering.

"It's a dream, it's a dream. I'm dreaming again. It's just a dream."

But the floor tiles felt cold and solid. He could feel his heart bounding in his chest, every nerve in his body tingling like an electric current. He switched on his bedside lamp, and with the flood of warm golden light, the world suddenly became normal again.

I must have been asleep.

His mother woke him up again the next morning, only this time, she looked perfectly normal. She yelped when he jumped out of bed and hugged her.

"What's that for?"

"I love you, mum."

"Well, I haven't heard you say that since you were ten! But don't think you're staying off school."

He held onto his mother, sniffing to make sure she smelled alive: That clean scent with a chalky hint of floral talcum powder.

"Why would I stay off school?"

"Well, poor Piers, you know. You can't help him if you miss classes."

"Is there any news?"

"No, love. I'm sure Glenda will call us if there's any change." Glenda was Piers' mother.

"Mum, please let me stay home…"

Jason won the argument, as he had known he would. After she left for work, he ate a quick breakfast, and took a second bowl of cereal back up to his room, balancing it carefully – he had filled it too full of milk. He booted up his PC and switched on the repulsive pink mouse.

The screen lit up. Jason stared at it, not able to comprehend what he was seeing.

Zombies swarming all over the monitor desktop screen. *The desktop!*

He hadn't even booted up the game yet.

Involuntarily, he glanced down at the mouse.

It blinked. Those big, black, painted cartoon eyes blinked at him. Then it stretched back lips he didn't realize it had, over painted, pointed teeth.

Jason never knew how he managed not to hurl it across the room. But this was real. This was no dream, and he was alone.

Show no fear.

"What are you?"

It grinned and wriggled out from underneath his palm, skittering across his desk. It turned and faced him, still grinning.

If I move, it will launch itself up in the air and fly at me. It will fasten onto my face and eat it.

He wished it would speak, but it sat there grinning. It skittered and jumped after a few moments, as if urging him to move.

Words danced across his screen.

Hungry.

Jason pushed a napkin carefully toward it. That napkin had been sitting on his desk since the weekend, when his mother had brought him a sandwich.

The painted mouth suddenly opened. The thing lunged toward the napkin, and tore it into shreds, chewing and swallowing in a guttural, snuffling frenzy. It went still for a moment and then skittered again, that odd little dance.

Hungry.

Jason shoved a pencil at it, even more carefully than he had offered the paper. There was a noise like a miniature sawmill, and the pencil disappeared in a spray of sawdust and splinters. The mouse licked its lips with a pointed, red tongue that made Jason think of a stepped-on worm.

"Did you have anything to do with my friend, Piers, getting attacked the other night?"

The mouse blinked at him. The air around it shimmered and wavered, and for a horrible instant, it transformed itself into a huge, grey rat; a real, live one. Jason watched as fleas hopped up from its back as if they had been scalded.

The mouse shimmered again, and went back to its normal, pink, plastic self. The fleas hopped drunkenly away.

"Did you turn my mom into a zombie? Or was that just a nightmare?"

The mouse suddenly looked innocent. The painted eyes darkened and enlarged, like a cartoon child's.

That was the worst moment of all.

Jason dropped his forehead into his hand. He let out a huge sigh. "Alright. Answer me this. What are you?"

The skittering dance began again. Jason glanced at the screen and saw one word.

Demon.

Jason made a fist and banged it several times against his own mouth, trying to think. He was pretty certain that if he showed the least fear, the thing would fly at him. Maybe turn into a rat and chew him like it had chewed Piers.

You don't ask a demon why it wants to hurt people. That's like an invitation.

"Want to play zombies?"

The mouse danced up and down. That nightmare grin appeared again, but it seemed to be doing its best to seem cute and innocent.

Jason booted up the game. The mouse let him pick it up. It seemed to quiver, as if it was excited.

He dropped it into his bowl of cereal.

The mouse squealed, and there was a strange fizzling sound. The paint on the thing suddenly wavered and disappeared, leaving a flat, grey mouse. No pink. No eyes. No whiskers.

No teeth.

Jason got up. The last thing he wanted to do was touch the bowl, but he was damned if he'd leave it there for his mom to clean up. Knowing her, she'd try to dry out the mouse. He picked it up, and walked carefully down the stairs, straight out into the street.

He took it to Saint Hilda's, two blocks away, ignoring the stares from startled housewives out doing errands. He kicked on the side door, the one he knew would be unlocked, until someone opened it. A church volunteer stared at him in disapproval, which turned to shock as she saw the bowl of cereal with the computer mouse floating in it.

"Excuse me, please." He really wanted to barge past her, but visions of the mouse and bowl going flying – of the mouse reviving – gave him iron control.

Politeness worked. She stood aside, apparently stupefied.

Jason carried the bowl down the side aisle all the way to the main double doors. He tipped the contents of the bowl into the font of holy water, dropped the bowl, and kept on going, waiting for the sound of skittering, which did not come.

That day, Jason Keller disappeared. The police and his doctor speculated he had suffered a breakdown because of his best friend's attack.

Piers Martin pulled through but would never talk about what had happened to him. A rumour went around the school that Jason Keller had actually been his attacker. After all, why else would his former best friend disappear? And why wouldn't Piers talk?

After more than two years of police searches and a media blitz, even Jason's parents gave him up for dead. Seven years and multiple articles later, journalists started to make TV shows about him. ("Whatever Happened to Jason Keller?") A famous ancient-alien theorist even produced a documentary proving that Jason had been sucked through a Black Hole into another dimension, and his sister eventually wrote a best-selling book.

Nobody believed old Nanna Mossman when she announced, quite soon after his initial disappearance, that Jason had merely joined a Luddite commune in nearby Derbyshire, where people shun technology and live the way their ancestors had done in the eighteen-hundreds. She produced a letter, but the doctor told Jason's parents the old woman had written the letter herself: A desperate bit of make-believe to explain her grandson's tragic disappearance.

After all, nobody hand-writes letters these days in real ink on slightly musty paper that smells, ever so faintly, of cat pee.

MARYA MILLER

Marya Miller is a former magazine editor and busy ghostwriter who loves bringing elements of fantasy and horror into her own fiction. She has one book out on Amazon, "Tales of Mist and Magic", and is working on the Dragonish series. Fittingly, her first published short story back in the 1980s, "Deus ex Machina", was inspired by her Smith Corona Coronamatic 2200 electric typewriter. You can find her at MaryaMiller.ca.

WEBSITE: http://www.maryamiller.ca
BLOG: http://www.maryamiller.ca/blog
FB: https://www.facebook.com/maryamillerwriter/
TWITTER: https://twitter.com/Marya_Miller

"MIRROR, MIRROR, ON THE WALL..."

BY K. WALKER

MIRROR

Ashley flung herself down on the bed and sighed. "College is going to be the death of me," she groaned. Mariana rolled her eyes at her roommate of three months and shook her head. "You've been saying that since we met, and you're still fine," she replied.

"Yeah, but who knew plants could be so hard? I thought it would be an easy major."

"You only have seven classes. They aren't so bad; I have ten, so stop complaining," Mariana replied. She shifted in the desk chair before continuing her Spanish report. The small room on the top floor of an off campus, two-story house they were renting from an elderly couple was usually peaceful, but sometimes it wasn't easy to study when Ashley was home. "You know you have a report due, don't you?"

Ashley frowned, thinking. "What report? I don't think so..."

"Yes, you do. You know the one for Spanish class? Remember? The only class we share?" Sometimes she regretted meeting Ashley. She was a good friend, and fun most of the time, but she wasn't the best at focusing on her classes. *That's what I get for trying to help*, she thought, remembering the day they'd met. It had been the first day of Spanish class. Since it was her easiest class, she'd decided to help the girl sitting next to her, a blonde beauty with too much make-up. She'd looked lost and confused, and entirely out of place.

She was the complete opposite of dark-haired Mariana, who had little time for friends and even less for make-up. *I'm surprised she even spoke to me*. Most rich white girls were so full of themselves. But thankfully, Ashley wasn't, and they'd become really good friends in the short time they'd known each other. It wasn't until after Mariana had invited her to move in to help pay rent, that she'd finally realized why Ashley had been so confused.

"I don't know why I'm even *IN* that class. It was supposed to be Russian. I want to be able to speak Russian like my grandmother," Ashley complained.

Aggravated, Mariana finished her paper and put it away. "I don't know either, but since they wouldn't let you switch, you should just accept it and try again next year."

Ashley pouted unhappily. "But my parents weren't even happy paying for the *one* language class. I don't think they'll be too pleased if I switch."

Nodding, Mariana replied. "They likely wouldn't be. Personally, if I were you, I'd be happy that my parents were willing to pay for all my classes and leave it at that. They even pay your rent."

"Your parents at least *care* about your future. Mine just paid for my classes to get me out of their hair. That's why they sent me all the way to West Virginia. They thought it sounded like a good college, and it was far away from California."

"They may care, but I had to get in on scholarship. There's no way they could have paid for any of my classes. I didn't even get to go out of state. You should at least try and keep your grades up," Mariana admonished.

"I do keep up. With the agriculture classes," Ashley replied with a careless shrug.

"You know you're really lazy, right?" Ashely just laughed. "I'm not lazy. I'm just naturally a very relaxed person."

"Okay well, fine," Mariana replied with a smile. "If you aren't going to work on your paper, do you want to go for a jog before dark?"

Ashley considered the offer. "Hmm… nah. I think I'm going to try meditating! A girl from my Astronomy class said it might be fun," she said, clapping her hands like a child. When Mariana frowned, she continued. "Well I'm tired, and it beats sitting around doing nothing." Mariana turned to stare at her in disbelief. "What?" Ashley asked when she noticed the stare.

Try as she might, Mariana couldn't keep a straight face. Smiling, she replied, "Sometimes I worry about you." Shaking her head, Mariana got up and started getting ready for bed. If she wasn't going to get to jog, she might as well sleep. She had an early class in the morning. When Ashley didn't reply, Mariana glanced over at her friend and noted with amusement she'd already fallen asleep. Knowing it would be pointless to try and wake her back up again, Mariana reached over and covered her with a blanket before seeking her own bed.

The day dawned bright and glorious, a beautiful sunrise spanning the horizon as Mariana got ready for class. Equine Production and Management wasn't exactly exciting, but at least she was able to work with horses part of the time. It was also more exciting than the medical classes she was taking. Glancing at the schedule they'd written on a marker board, Mariana saw Ashley also had a class in an hour. With a groan, Mariana went over to her friend.

"Ashley! Ashley, get up. You've got a class. Hurry up, or we'll both be late." When she only got a grumpy moan, Mariana scowled. "If you don't get up and get ready, I'm going to dump water on you again," she threatened.

With a gasp, Ashley shot up in bed. "I'm up, I'm up… geez, you're so mean. Ugh," she replied, glancing at her rumpled clothes. "I'm yucky. Give me time for my teeth and a shower."

Well used to this by now, Mariana sighed and sat on the bed. "Well hurry up or I'll leave you behind. Then you'll have to try and catch the bus and you WILL be late."

Ashley made a face. "I hate that bus. I swear it runs twice as fast when I'm trying to catch up to it than it does when I'm actually on it," she said as she hurried to the bathroom.

That's probably because you're late so often the driver thinks it's funny making you run, Mariana thought dryly. A quick 20 minutes later and she returned, toweling her hair dry. She got dressed quickly and they headed out, Mariana grabbing her car keys on the way.

Mariana pulled up to the agriculture building, puzzled when she saw students already leaving. She could see Ashley talking with some other girls and honked the horn, then felt sheepish when several kids jumped and gave her annoyed looks. Thankfully Ashley spotted her and ran over to open the passenger door. "Did you even say goodbye to your friends?" Mariana asked in surprise, and then regretted it a moment later.

A blank look crossed Ashley's face, before she straightened and shouted at the top of her lungs. "BYE GUYS!!!" waving madly as Mariana winced. Her friends waved back, trying not to laugh.

When Ashley got into the car, smiling happily, Mariana asked. "So why are you getting out early? Don't you have another half hour or so?"

Ashley giggled. "We-ell… I kinda tripped over some bags of dirt."

"Uh oh… that doesn't sound good," Mariana returned.

"Well it wouldn't have been so bad, but then I fell into the seed cabinets. They fell over. I'm ok, but the professor wasn't too happy. She needs to get new cabinets now."

Mariana tried and failed to keep a straight face. "Oh no…"

Ashley nodded. "So, everyone got to help pick up seeds, then she dismissed us so she could call to get the remains taken away." She frowned. "But why are you here so early anyway?"

Mariana sighed, before replying. "I got a phone call from our landlady. A water pipe burst in the house. Water is everywhere, and we need to go get our stuff."

Ashley was silent for a moment after Mariana had finished explaining. Finally, she replied. "I guess you should have moved into the dorms with me instead."

Mariana rolled her eyes and started the car, but she couldn't quite hide a smile. *I should have known she'd take it lightly,* she thought, shaking her head.

When they got to the house, they saw the landlady had been right. It looked like a disaster area, with debris strewn all over the lawn. Workers were there, trying to fix the pipe, but no one even glanced in their direction when they went inside. Trying to avoid the puddles, they headed upstairs. The room matched the outside of the house. Somehow a window had broken, and water was everywhere. The dresser holding Mariana's clothes had fallen over and was also soaked.

Ashley saw it and said cheerfully. "Hey, now we BOTH need to do laundry!"

Mariana laughed in spite of herself. "Right.... So, I guess we aren't sleeping here for a while."

Looking around again, Ashley spotted the beds. "Yeah, you'll drown if you sleep on that now; it's a lake. Looks like the water came from somewhere in the attic."

Mariana just shook her head and started throwing the clothes into the laundry basket holding Ashley's dirty clothes that had piled up again.

After a moment, Ashley started gathering things too, sighing unhappily. "I guess we can try looking in the dorms to see if anyone will let us crash there," Ashley said, completely unconcerned about the turn of events.

The desk and books were ruined, so Mariana left those alone after a mournful sigh. Hearing her, Ashley looked over. "Looks like you shouldn't have bothered with your Spanish report either. The universe must be telling you that you're working too hard."

After giving her a half-hearted glare, Mariana gathered the rest of what little stuff she'd brought from home into a duffle bag. Once they were done, they headed out to see if they could salvage anything that had gotten washed outside. After that, they dumped the wet things into the trunk of the car, then headed to the campus.

There were several dorm buildings they could choose from. Mariana drove to the nearest one first, hoping to find one quickly. Once inside, they stopped in the common room, looking for someone to ask, but they everyone was listening to a story told by a hippie-looking boy with long hair. Hoping he'd be done soon, they stopped to listen.

"....So after we got the acid, we went and headed to the woods. Less likely to run into any authority figures, yeah? But we ran into a bear. That was even more of a buzz kill. I look over. Dwayne was standing there, right hand raised, swearing to help prevent forest fires." He paused as laughter filled the room. "So then we get him away from the bear, and he puts his arm around my shoulder. Says man… Smokey is waaaay more intense in person!"

Mariana and Ashley shared a look, then turned and left, not wanting to stay with anyone in this dorm. Before leaving the building, they stopped at the bulletin board, hoping someone had posted about available rooms.

Ashley grabbed a flier. "Hey, how about this? This sounds good."

Looking over, Mariana read the flier doubtfully. "I don't know. You've never cleaned anything before," she said uncertainly.

"Pfft. How hard can it be?" Ashley replied, taking out her cell phone.

Wanted: House sitter

Required: Light cleaning- Sweeping, Mopping, Polishing, and Some dusting

Must be responsible adult and willing to sleep at the residence.

Absolutely NO parties allowed

If interested, call.… 555-5238

Surprisingly, the number was answered immediately. Ashley set up an interview and said they'd be right over before hanging up.

"Ashley!" Mariana scolded, looking at the time on her phone.

"What? He wanted to meet us right away. He said he was starting to wonder if anyone was interested."

"Yeah, but I have to go to class," Mariana complained.

"Oh.… Well, it isn't too far. You can drop me off, and go to class after that."

"Oh, not far, huh? Where exactly is 'not far'?" Mariana asked.

Ashley seemed to hesitate for the first time. "Well, he said Cemetery Road."

Mirror, Mirror, On the Wall

"*Cemetery* Road? Because THAT isn't creepy or anything! I don't like going over there, Ashley. Bird Street was already closer than I liked. I'm not so sure this is a good idea," Mariana said apprehensively.

"Oh, it'll be fine! Come on, or you'll be late to class," Ashley replied, leaving. Mariana muttered unhappily, wishing she could go back to their room on Bird Street, before reluctantly following her. Getting into the car, Ashley carelessly threw the flier onto the dash. They drove in silence until they got to the road.

"So where is it?" Mariana asked warily, eying the thick trees passing by on either side.

"Uh, he said at the end of the road, just before it turns back onto Armstrong Street."

"Ugh! Why didn't you tell me that *before* I turned onto Limestone Road? We could have avoided driving past the cemetery!" Mariana complained.

Ashley glared at her. "Well how was I supposed to know? I've never been over here!" Mariana returned the glare but didn't say anything as the trees opened up on the left. Ashley's eyes widened at the sight. "Wow, that's a *really* big cemetery!"

"Yeah, I know…that's why I avoid this road," Mariana replied, a chill going down her spine. After passing the cemetery, gloom returned as the trees closed in once more. "I'm not seeing it," Mariana said uneasily.

"He should be standing outside…yes! That must be him!" she said, pointing at an older man in a suit, standing by the roadside, who waved at them. Mariana slowed, pulling alongside him.

"Good day. Are you here about the house-sitting job?" the man asked.

"Yes," Ashley replied. "My friend and I are both applying, but she needs to go to class now," she continued, pointing at Mariana.

"Well, 2 applicants weren't expected, but it should be fine. If you want, the young Miss can either get out here, or you can pull into the drive," he said, indicating the drive to the left of him.

Both girls looked over in confusion. "But… I don't see a mansion," Mariana pointed out, puzzled.

"Look closely," the old man replied with a smile. "It's a bit hard to see in the gloom." Squinting, they tried and failed to see anything like a building.

"There's nothing there…" Ashley said uncertainly.

The old man just smiled. "Would you be so kind as to wait here a moment?" he asked, turning to walk down the driveway without waiting for a reply.

The girls shared a puzzled glance before turning back to watch the old man. Both frowned when he stopped at what looked like a cluster of trees, only to appear to open one of the trees. "Is that it?" Mariana asked in disbelief.

Still puzzled, she pulled into the drive, stopping when an image of the car appeared next to the old man. The girls got out and walked up to him, startled when their images also appeared. Mariana reached out to touch the wall next to what was obviously a door. Her eyes widened in surprise when she felt the cool surface. "It's a mirror!" she said in wonder, looking closer.

"Yes. In the gloom from the trees, the house is very well hidden," the man explained.

"Why are the walls covered in mirrors?" Ashley asked.

"The master seems fond of them," he replied, laughing. "You'll find a great many more once you're inside. That's why parties are absolutely forbidden. You wouldn't wish to break one, would you?"

When the girls seemed to be at a loss for words, he continued. "Now, why doesn't young miss..." looking at Ashley.

"Ashley...and that's Mariana," she responded.

"Miss Ashley, come inside so we might discuss things in a more comfortable setting? And Miss Mariana may go to her class. When should we expect your return?"

Looking uncertainly at Ashley, Mariana replied. "My class lets out at 6:00pm. I should be back by 6:30pm at the latest..." her voice trailing away.

"Very well, I'll have a meal prepared for the both of you at that time. After the interviews, you'll have the house to yourselves. There will be food for your meals in the pantry, but you'll need to cook them yourselves."

Mariana nodded, clearly reluctant to leave Ashley behind. "Ok... well... see you then," she said returning to the car and backing out. She made certain to turn away from the cemetery, and quickly disappeared behind the trees.

Alone now, Ashley smiled nervously as the old man, clearly a butler, gestured her inside. She hesitated, then complied, stopping just inside, her mouth dropping in shock. Mirrors lined the walls from floor to ceiling. There were even tables with mirrors on stands. Everywhere she looked, she saw a different type of mirror.

"Is the entire mansion like this?" she asked, shivering.

"Indeed, it is, Miss Ashley," the butler replied, sounding suspiciously cheerful. The door creaked loudly as he shut it, making Ashley jump. "If you'll follow me, the sitting room is this way," heading left as he spoke.

Having no other choice, Ashley started to follow, when she froze and turned to one of the mirrors. "Did you see…?" The butler paused, waiting. "See what, Miss?" Ashley hesitated, uncertain how to describe what she'd seen. "Uh… it's nothing… sorry."

Another smile crossed the butler's face, as if he could read her mind. "It's alright, Miss. The mirrors tend to play tricks on you. You'll get used to it," he said, continuing.

Now I know he's laughing at me, Ashley thought crossly. She held on to the anger, hoping to ease the chill she felt. *It had to have been my imagination. No way does faces show up out of nowhere, only to vanish when you look at them,* she scolded herself. Behind her, in a different mirror, a pair of red eyes with an evil grin watched them, before fading away.

The sitting room had 3 couches surrounding a small coffee table. Trying to ignore the mirrors lining the walls, Ashley chose the nearest couch and sat down. "Would you like something to drink?"

Ashley considered. "Do you have orange juice?" "Yes. I'll bring you a luncheon to tide you over until dinner."

"Thank you," Ashley responded uncomfortably. *It feels really strange in this place.* As she waited, she felt eyes on her and glanced around nervously. *I wish I hadn't seen that flier. This place is creepy.* Sighing in relief when the butler returned, Ashley smiled at him. Returning the smile, he sat the tray down on the coffee table, before sitting across from her.

"Now, the master has left already, so I am in charge of the interview. He's waiting for me to join him, so the interview will be rather short. You will be able to take the job, won't you? All that is needed is to keep the mirrors polished and do some sweeping and mopping. There really isn't much else to be done."

"Well… the place we were staying had a pipe burst, so we don't have much of a choice. We need a place to stay," Ashley confided.

Nodding, he continued. "Well, that's enough for me. Do you have any questions? Would you like to see where you'll be staying?"

"That's it?" Ashley asked, surprised. "That's the entire interview? Don't you need to… I don't know… check my I.D. or something?" *It really isn't that easy, is it?*

"No. As I said, I'm in a bit of a hurry. And you need a place to sleep, so it works out, don't you think?" Not sure what to say, Ashley nodded. "Splendid. Now then," he said, standing. "If you'll follow me, I'll show you to your room."

"Oh… but the sandwiches…" Ashley protested. "They'll still be there when you return. And there's more juice in the fridge too. Come now," he said, opening a door she hadn't seen.

After some hesitation, Ashley obeyed. *This is going way too fast… something doesn't feel right…* she thought, stepping into a hallway.

He stopped sooner than she expected, only having gone a couple doors down the hallway. "The first door is the kitchen. The 2nd door is the pantry, and has a connecting door to the kitchen." Before she could reply, he opened the 3rd door. "This will be your room. There's also another bed where your friend can sleep," he said as he led the way inside. There were a lot fewer mirrors lining the walls of this room, and Ashley sighed in relief, ignoring the butler's knowing grin.

"Okay, now I will leave you in the kitchen. The cook has already left," he continued, heading back.

"What? Wait, already? Don't you even wanna interview Mariana?"

"No, I trust you. We'll be back in about a month. Keys to lock the door are hanging in the kitchen, though I doubt you'll need them. Most can't even see the door," he said, smirking. Ashley blushed in embarrassment, just as they reached the kitchen.

As he entered, he pointed to a side door. "That's the pantry. If you want to leave, use the front door. All the other doors leading outside are locked. Oh, would you look at the time," he said, glancing at his arm.

"There's nowhere within the mansion you're forbidden to go; feel free to explore, but don't neglect to clean! Have a good stay!" he said as he rushed out the door they'd entered, leaving Ashley staring dumbfounded. *What just happened?*

After she got over her shock, she tried to catch him, but by the time she reached the front door, he was gone. *Where did he go? He couldn't have just vanished…* But no matter where she looked, there was no sign of him.

A wolf howled, sounding fairly close, and Ashley closed the door with a shudder, turning the lock. *Okay… I'll just… I'll go eat the sandwiches and wait for Mariana. She'll know what to do,* she thought, trying to ignore the goosebumps creeping up her spine.

Mirror, Mirror, On the Wall

As she headed for the sitting room, she caught a glimpse of the face again, but this time she didn't stop to look. Increasing her pace, she practically ran into the sitting room, followed by laughter.

I did NOT just hear laughter. Nope. No laughter, creepy or otherwise. What time is it? She thought, checking her phone. *Only 5:30pm? That's it? I thought it was later than that,* she thought despairingly.

Ok uh... cleaning... I should clean. Cleaning stuff... maybe in the pantry? She went to check, completely forgetting about the food. She found the cleaning supplies without a problem and decided to try mopping first. She filled a bucket with water before dipping the mop in.

Oh I need soap... uh... this? She thought, picking up a bottle of floor polish. She shrugged, pouring some into the water and mixing it in. She mopped as best she could, trying to ignore the reflective surfaces. The fridge and the toaster were especially hard to ignore.

She shifted her feet, focusing more on the mirrors than her footing and yelped as her feet flew out from under her and she landed hard, the mop falling beside her. *Ow...That's gonna bruise. Yeah, cleaning... 'How hard can it be,'* she thought, mocking herself.

"Ugh... just my luck." She muttered, starting to get up. Only to be thrown into darkness as the lights went out.

Letting out a scream, Ashley fell back to the floor, panicking. Unable to see, she ended up hitting her head on the kitchen island.

*Ow, ow, ow...*she cried, holding her head. Unaware of how much time she'd been wasting, she screamed again as her cell phone rang. Seeing the light, she fished it out of her pocket, answering automatically. "Hello?" she asked desperately.

"Ashley? What's wrong?" Mariana's voice sounded.

"Oh thank God! Are you on your way here? This place is creepy; the lights just went out, I can't see a thing!" Ashley complained.

"What? Where's the butler? Did he go to turn the lights back on?"

"No, he's gone. He practically ran out of here and disappeared. I tried to find him, but he wasn't anywhere. I didn't even see a car!" Ashley bemoaned.

"Okay... calm down. I'm just going to my car now. Why don't you try meditating? It might help you stay calm," Mariana suggested.

"Can you stay on the line?" Ashley asked.

"Sorry, but you know I can't talk and drive. I'll be there as fast as I can, I promise."

"Okay..." Ashley replied, trying not to cry as she hung up the phone.

Mariana ran to her car. *I knew I shouldn't have left her there. Maybe I'll get lucky if I call that number from the flier. He could tell me where the circuit breaker is...* But when she glanced at the dash, the flier had vanished, and a search of the floor revealed nothing. Goosebumps ran across her arms and she shuddered, starting the car.

Trying to calm down, Ashley took a deep breath. *Ok...meditation... Cindy said it might be hard... hopefully not...* Crossing her legs and breathing slowly, she closed her eyes and began counting. *....1... 2..3, 1...2...* CRACK!

"Ow! What the..?" Cradling her head, she squinted in the dim light, making out the mop handle. *How... it was on the floor... how could it hit me? I need to get out of here...*

She began crawling towards the door, using her phone as a light.

She made it to the door, freezing when she heard skittering. *Oh, please, please, not rats...* She prayed, inching into the sitting room, trying not to hit anything else.

Shrieking when something brushed her leg, she shot to her feet and ran, hitting the opposite wall and knocking into a mirror. She paled when she heard more laughter. She quickly aimed her phone, looking for the door. *Where is it? Where is the door?*

"Ashley? Where are you?" Mariana called, making Ashley jump.

Relieved, Ashley called back. "Here. I'm in the sitting room. Something touched my leg..." she moaned.

"And where is that? I've never been inside, remember?"

"It's the first door on the left after you get inside. It's too dark to find it," Ashley complained. The beam of a flashlight appeared a moment later. Seeing Mariana, Ashley ran over and hugged her.

"Let's get out of here! Please let's just leave," Ashley begged.

"Okay, come on. We can go sit in the car and regroup," Mariana soothed, leading the way, Ashley close on her heels.

They found the door closed when they got near it. "That's odd... I left it open..."

Looking at her with dread, Ashley whispered. "How did you even get in here? I thought I had the door locked..."

"No, it was open when I got here..." Mariana shuddered. They shared a look, before trying to force the door open, but it wouldn't budge.

"It won't open... why won't it open?" Ashley asked hysterically. Mariana, just as scared but trying to hide it, grabbed Ashley's shoulders. "Calm down, we'll think of something. It's ok... let's go somewhere we can think."

"We can try the kitchen... I guess... but I heard something. I think it might be rats!" Ashley wailed.

Gulping loudly, Mariana took a deep breath. "Ok... well... those are small. We can handle those. We can," she encouraged. With the flashlight, they easily made it to the kitchen, thankfully without any rats appearing.

Mariana immediately spotted the mop and bucket on the floor. Distracted, she stared at them. "You were cleaning?" she asked doubtfully.

"Yeah... I was hearing things....and... seeing things. It was creepy, so I thought it would be a good idea. But then I slipped, and the lights went out... Oh! And then the mop hit me in the head, I swear! It fell next to me, but it still hit me! How can it do that?" Ashley whined, nearly panicking. Before Mariana could reply, the lights flashed back on. Blinded, both girls shut their eyes as they watered, rubbing at them furiously.

"What in the world?" Mariana complained as they waited for their eyes to adjust.

"I don't know, it's been weird from the start," Ashley replied.

"Ok... well... let's try and find another way out while the lights are on. Did the butler mention anything about another exit?" Mariana asked.

"Um... yeah, he said there were other doors, but they're all locked!" Ashley answered.

"Locked, huh?" Hmm... Looking around the kitchen, Mariana spotted a board on the wall, with several keys hanging on hooks. Another mirror was attached to the board as well, and Mariana frowned. "The guy wasn't kidding when he said there were a lot of mirrors in here, was he?" she asked heading over to the keys, handing the flashlight to Ashley.

"No! They're everywhere. The place we're supposed to sleep doesn't have as many, but they're in there too." Ashley replied with a shudder.

"Well hopefully they won't make it too hard to find another door." Mariana grabbed keys as she spoke, choosing the ones labeled 'door key,' with various locations. "Come on; let's try the front door again first, since it looks to be the closest. Hopefully one of these will work."

Making their way back to the front door, they quickly tried the first key.

"Trying to leave so soon? But the fun has just begun," an eerie voice said as the floor beneath the girls disappeared. They screamed as they fell onto a kind of slide, coming to a stop without injury.

The flashlight fell next to them, illuminating countless bones.

The girls screamed in terror as the source of the voice appeared in a mirror, which seemed to hover above the bones. It was the face Ashley had glimpsed earlier, only more detailed.

With the blood-red eyes and evil smile was a face made out of smoke, outlined in green flames. A pair of horns arched prominently over the translucent, green-tinged face. "Why don't you stay a while? We have alllll month to play!" it cackled gleefully.

K. WALKER

K. Walker has always wanted to be a writer. She has a huge imagination, helped along by her love of reading and the written word. With the dictionary she carries around in her head, she also makes a good editor. K. has always wanted to spread her love of reading by writing her own stories for others to enjoy. She'll write about anything that catches her interest. Her favorite genre to write is fantasy and anything that makes her imagination soar, because there's no telling what will pop into her head. She loves to read Sci-Fi, Fantasy, Paranormal Romance, and even a bit of Mystery and Horror, but Non-Fiction books have been known to put her to sleep. Her imagination gets pulled in so many directions, her mind is pure chaos, so this is the first story she's managed to finish, though she hopes to one day finish the other stories bouncing around inside her head. She also enjoys spending time on games and will most often be seen playing League of Angels with her friends when she isn't reading, editing, researching, or trying to write down all the ideas clamoring for her attention.

Night-time with Nettle

By Rita Sotolongo

Bed

The woodland critters scuttled away from the parade villagers blundering through the brambles and their fire-lit torches. The mother owl flew as fast as she could toward a log cabin nestled between the arms of two ancient live oaks. Perching herself on the branch draped in front of a yellow window flickering with candlelight, she hooted three times.

Inside, Agatha Nettle knew even before she heard the call that her time was up. She'd failed to save the little boy from his imminent death and in return the villagers had accused this old medicine woman of being a "Witch!"

"Never-mind all the lives I have saved," she thought just before she lay down on her straw-stuffed mattress and pulled the covers over her head. "If I wanted to kill them, I could've. I ought to have killed them all."

When the townspeople burst through the door, all they found was an empty room and a messy bed. Agatha Nettle was gone.

188

Night-time with Nettle

And they say, a witch's last thought before she removes herself from this plane to another will determine the legacy she leaves behind. For the vengeful villagers of this small town, their accusation would turn prophecy and the legacy of the little old hedgewitch they'd tried to burn at the stake is said to have lived on inside the walls of her old log cabin so that anyone who visits the place never stays more than one night. Whether this is fear or the fact that to this day the townspeople don't welcome visitors staying in Agatha Nettle's old home, no one knows for sure.

Erica finished reading the story online and considered her plans. She wanted to escape all modern living for a place with a history and, most importantly, be inspired out of her writing slump. This place was just right. She wasn't one for ghost stories, but the surrounding oaks with arms stretched wide like a mom ready to comfort a crying child were calling to her.

Well, now I know why it's so cheap. Even for an Airbnb, you can't beat $10 a night.

She clicked the button to request a booking and felt her pulse quicken. She was going to spend two weeks in the woods alone with no distractions! No phone. No email. No Facebook. No stupid boyfriends who don't take the hint that it's time to piss or get off the pot.

This is what you wanted, Erica reminded herself over and over as she sat on the floor of a sparsely furnished one-room cabin with her back propped against the ancient dustbag the owner considered a mattress. The thing looked like it literally had been here since the night Agatha Nettle is said to have disappeared under the covers.

No one had held a gun to her head and forced her on this vacation-slash-writing-retreat. She'd given it all her effort not to build the suspiciously cheap cabin up in her head. But it'd been impossible. She couldn't help imagining herself as a modern-day Paula Bunyan in her hiking boots, ax in-hand as she chopped her own firewood, caught her own fish for dinner and lived off the land. She'd thought she'd return after the two weeks with caramel tinted skin, looser jeans and the tough demeanor of a roughneck.

Instead, she was sweltering in the humidity of the unairconditioned room with the window swung open and no breeze. The buzzing bugs brought a hum to her ears as they swirled around her head and everywhere else. The dust from the mattress where her duffle bag had landed was now settled onto the already grimy floor where she could see footprints from everywhere she'd stepped since arriving. And she could've sworn that when she'd weight of the bag send a *swoosh* of dust into the air, she'd also heard the faintest hint of a cackle.

A cackle Erica, really? You're letting that story get into your head. I mean even if Agatha Nettle was a witch, the whole cackling thing is a creation of the people who made The Wizard of Oz.

Still, the goosebumps rose again across every inch of her skin. Determined not be scared by some silly marketing ploy to attract visitors looking for a spooky vacation story, she got up and started to unpack.

As part of her whole "escape modern living" plan, she'd packed lightly, and two minutes later she was done.

Okay, now what?

She had brought two weeks worth of food easy to warm up using a single burner gas stove, and though she wasn't hungry yet, she was bored. It wasn't until the Ramen noodles were in the bowl burning her hands she realized there was nowhere to sit but on the floor or on the bed.

She put the bowl down and went to lift the mattress.

I'm going to take it out and beat it with a stick.

Just as she thought it, a gust of wind blew hard against the nearest open window and in flew a branch broken off from the tree outside. It smacked her cheek and she was knocked onto the bed. And there it was again. Mixed in with the wind rustling the branches, a soft but distinct cackle.

The small boy was crying in front of her. "What's wrong?" She wanted to ask, but she was busy stirring a pot of something boiling on the stove. Every time she went to ask the boy if she could help him or she tried to stop stirring, her muscles tensed and she lost all control of what her body was doing.

As if she were a marionette controlled by strings, she grabbed the herbs in a bowl next to her and tossed a pinch into the concoction. The pot let out a loud snake-like hiss and somehow she knew it was time to turn the heat off and give the boy his drink.

Night-time with Nettle

"Now drink up little one." The spoke the words, but they hadn't come from her.

The light beamed through the window and pried open her eyes. She was drenched in sweat and the bed was trembling under her. No, it wasn't the bed shaking, it was her quivering so violently the bed was moving with her. She shot straight up and scanned the room. There was no little boy, no steaming pot, and it the morning sun was shining bright outside.

Boom-boom-boom-boom-boom-boom!

Her beating heart matched the vehemence of whoever was pounding on the door. Afraid to answer, she sat on the bed and waited for them to go away.

"Open up! This is Sheriff Dalloway!"

Oh, this can't be good, she thought and as she jumped from the bed the image of the crying boy swam across her mind.

"Hello officer, is something wrong?" she asked the raised fist caught in mid-knock now hovering in front of her face.

Lowering his hand, he sized her up from head to toe and said, "Yes, I'd say there is. A little boy in town went missing last night, something that seems to happen every time one of you city folk think you'll have a getaway here to Nettle's Cabin."

"That's horrible! I assure you, though, I had nothing to do with it. I've been asleep all night. I haven't gone anywhere."

"That's what they all say."

"No, seriously, if you'll come inside, I'll show you. There was a branch that flew in through the window and knocked me unconscious. I've literally been passed out all night."

"Yeah, that's what they all say when I tell them that's what all the rest of them say."

"No, no. You're really not understanding me. I haven't even gone into town yet..." but he didn't let her finish.

"Let me guess, you're going to tell me you came in last night, unpacked, made yourself something to eat and as you went to sit down with it on the bed you were knocked unconscious somehow and only woke up a minute before I got here," he paused to watch her open her mouth about to say something but when she couldn't think of a response he continued, "Listen,

I grew up in this town and I know there's something off about this place, but if you don't leave town now I have no other option than to arrest you."

This can't be happening. The story on the internet didn't say anything about crazy law enforcement chasing people out of town. Then she remembered that it had mentioned people never staying longer than one night. *This must be why.*

"Well Sheriff, with all due respect, I paid for two weeks. I'm a writer and I'm here for inspiration, and I'm not leaving until my stay is up."

"Well ma'am, in that case, I'm going to need to take you down to the station."

"On what charges?"

"Kidnapping."

"But you have no proof!"

"I'd say that pair of Billy's Spiderman shoes sitting on top of the bed is all the proof I need."

In the holding cell Erica could barely concentrate on the situation she found herself in. As soon as the shock of her arrest had worn off, the itching had kicked in.

Ugh that nasty old mattress must be full of bed bugs.

"Sheriff? Sheriff Dalloway? Damnit sheriff, answer me!"

"What can I do for you city slicker?

"I need to ask you, if you were going to let me go home then why are you holding me now. Something tells me you don't believe I did this, you believe in that ghost story, don't you."

"Ma'am, if you were born and raised here, and you grew up to be Sheriff, and you'd seen it happen enough times, you'd know it was a true story, not one to be told around campfires."

"Okay, then if it's true and it was the curse that actually took that boy, let me go and I'll help you stop her!"

"And how do you suppose we're gonna do that?

"Come back with me to the cabin. Stay tonight. If another child goes missing you'll be there to see what happens."

He didn't like the idea of staying the night at the cabin, she could see that written all over his face, but she could also see the internal conflict of wanting to know for himself what was really going on inside the old place. He nodded and crossed the room to release her.

Out of the corner of her eye, Erica saw Sheriff Dalloway lying stiff as a board on the floor next to the bed. He looked like he was fighting against restraints though there were none. His eyes bugged and his face turned red from the effort to escape. He made muffled shouts as if gagged, but again, Erica saw no binds.

She wanted to look closer at him, see what had him upset, but again she was at her stove stirring a pot of boiling liquid and couldn't turn her head from side to side. Again she reached for the bowl of herbs and grabbed a pinch to add to the potion, and just like it had the night before it emitted a hiss.

Ladling a helping into a clean bowl, she turned and with the heavy footedness of a zombie headed to its second death, she shuffled towards the little girl sitting on the floor staring daggers at her.

"I won't drink it!" the little girl spat at her.

"Now, now. Drink up my little one. It won't hurt you, I promise. It will only make you all better." Staring straight into the child's eyes as she spoke these words, the girl's eyes glassed over and she held out her hands.

Horrified and helpless to stop it, Erica handed her the drink and then let out a high-pitched cackle.

When Erica jolted upright, the sun was shining again. She was gasping for breath, certain she'd just choked mid-cackle and was now having a coughing fit.

"Sheriff! Did you see that? That little girl... what did she drink?! We have to find her. Now! Sheriff? Sheriff?"

Looking around, Erica saw she was the only one in the room.

Oh no! He must've gotten spooked and ran. Or maybe he's searching for the little girl. Maybe he knows who she is.

And as if she was caught in a horrifying version of the movie *Groundhog Day*, someone began pounding on the door, just like two days before.

"Open up! I'm Deputy Smith and I know you're in there."

Erica practically flew across the room to swing open the door.

"Thank God you're here! There's a little girl gone missing and Sheriff Dalloway disappeared on me this morning. We have to find them!"

"Yes ma'am, I know all about the missing girl and our missing Sheriff. And that's exactly why I'm here. To take you in."

"What? No! You don't understand. Sheriff Dalloway and I were working together. It wasn't me! It's Agatha Nettle!"

"Yeah and Sasquatch came to me last night and told me where I could find the Easter Bunny and Santa Claus. Turns out their having an affair and they took off to Aruba."

Oh shit! I thought everyone in this town believed this story.

"You don't believe me? Sheriff Dalloway did?!" The panic was rising in her voice and the bile was rising in her throat. The room was spinning as fast as her head now.

Where is he? What the hell is going on here?

"Sheriff Dalloway is a small-town country-bumpkin who was raised on this bullshit story and so of course he'd believe your crap about being haunted by a ghost. I grew up in the real world. I don't believe in fairy-tales. What I do believe in is evidence and what I see right before me are a pair of pink glitter slippers that belong to the missing girl and a pair of department issue boots I'll bet belong to the Sheriff sitting right there on top of your bed. So, like I said before, you're coming with me."

Erica found being arrested easier to believe the second time around. She gave up pleading her innocence. Didn't try to explain or argue, she just sat quiet and waited for her inevitable doom.

How could I have let this happen? I should've just left town.

She heard the arrogant deputy on the phone.

"Yep, he's missing and we got two kids unaccounted for… Nope there's no priors… Yep, she's sitting right here… Now, how would I know? I'm not a medical professional. If she's insane we'll have to get someone in to look at her… Alright, see you soon." He hung up the phone and turned to her. "That's the public defender. She's on her way in. Until then, you just sit tight and keep quiet."

What the hell do you think I've been doing here, asshole?

After what felt like days but was probably only a few hours, a harried-looking woman rushed in. Digging through her oversized bag she spoke rapidly to Deputy Smith, "Okay Dean, I'm here, now where's the loony?"

Night-time with Nettle

Erica felt her jaw clench with the anger and she her stomach fall out the bottom of her feet with dread. *Well, I can see I'm gonna get a lot of help from this woman.*

"She's just over there. Why don't you get set up and I'll have her brought to interrogation room 1 when you're ready."

"Sure, sure," she nodded still while digging around for something in her bag and hurried off away from the Deputy.

Fifteen minutes later Erica was being introduced to Samantha Swells, public attorney, and according to her, Erica's best hope if she wanted to get out of this alive.

"Alive? Are they asking for the death penalty?"

"No, don't be silly girl. Agatha Nettle. Once you're no use to her, she'll kill you too. Now, Smith out there says she's already used you to kill off two kids and dear Anthony?"

"Anthony? Who's... oh you mean Sheriff Dalloway? No! I didn't kill anyone. Listen here, I came to take a vacation and find some inspiration for a story and instead I got nightmares and locked up! You have to believe me, I'm innocent!"

"Well, you got quite a story, didn't you? Listen, I do believe you. The problem is our new Deputy doesn't. He's not from around here, so he just doesn't know any better. But those of us who grew up in this town, we know. And me and Anthony, we *know* what Agatha Nettle is capable of. We both had siblings go missing when visitors came calling at that cabin back when we were kids."

"If that's true then why don't you stop letting people rent it?"

"That's the thing. We don't know who owns it. We don't know who keeps putting it available for rent. And without being able to prove these crimes are tied to the house, no judge is going to court order it be removed from the web."

"Why don't you just burn the damn thing to the ground."

"If you believe Agatha Nettle has been carrying out a curse on the town for over three hundred years, let me ask you, are you willing to risk pissing her off more than she clearly already is?"

"No, I suppose not."

"For now, I'm going to make bail for you. You're going to go gather your things and you're going to get out of this town and never come back."

Erica wasn't going to argue with that. After Samantha handled the paperwork and much to the displeasure of Deputy Smith, Erica piled into the passenger seat of Samantha's Jeep and they were off.

Once inside the cabin, Erica threw her duffle bag onto the bed and went to grab her clothing from the dresser. When she turned around, her arms full with almost every belonging she'd brought, the bed was bare.

"Samantha, did you move my bag?"

"No, of course not. Hurry up!"

Erica dropped her things on top of the bed and got down on her hands and knees to look underneath to see if her duffel had fallen, but nothing was there. When she stood back up, the bed was bare again.

"Samantha, did you take my clothes and stuff?"

"No! What are you on about? We haven't got time for this!"

Just at that moment, the wind blew open the window with a bang so hard the glass shattered. Prepared this time, Erica ducked and fell forward onto the bed, but rather than land on the mattress, she sank right through. And sank. And sank. And sank some more. Into a dark abyss. Until she landed again on the floor of the cabin, only it wasn't the same cabin. Nothing here was dusty. There was more furniture. Candles were alight around the room and the gas stove was now a wood-fired stove. And it was dark outside, no longer day time.

What the...

Before she could wonder what was happening, the door from the outside pushed open and a little old lady, slightly hunched, walked in.

"There you are my little one," she said to Erica. "It's going to be all right now. Mama Nettle is going to brew you up a tea that will make you feel all better."

"Like hell you will!"

And Erica tried to bolt out the still-open front door.

"Now just where do you think you're going?" Agatha Nettle's voice was suddenly deep and demonic and with a boom Erica was thrown back by a force she couldn't see and landed on top of the bed.

"You're not going anywhere until you've had your medicine." And then Erica heard it clear as day, the bone-chilling cackle coming from Agatha Nettle and the snake-like hiss of a magical herb hitting the boiling liquid atop the stove.

Erica recognized the marionette-like feeling of having her body controlled and as the little old witch handed her a large mug full of steaming liquid Erica couldn't stop herself from drinking it. It burned going down her throat and by the time she was finished the room around her had grown to be sized for a giant. Everything was huge. Or maybe she was tiny.

Either way, Agatha Nettle hovered over her with a giant magnifying glass making one of her eyes even larger than it already was. Her voice booming, she said, "There you are my little one. Now you're all safe and sound, snug as a bug in a rug. Or snug as a bed bug, should I say." Then she cackled again, and the ground underneath Erica shook. Only it wasn't ground, it was mattress and it stretched out for miles in front of her. And across it were thousands of life-size brown bugs scurrying around.

"See, I could've killed them all and I ought to have killed them all, but my curse got a little muffled by the mattress as I was sinking through. As I was thinking about murdering the whole lot of them, the bed bugs were biting me and somehow I ended up cursing anyone who dared to try and sleep in my bed to a fate worse than death–an eternity munching on the buns of any future uninvited guests."

RITA SOTOLONGO

Rita Sotolongo is a poet with publications in Black Fox Literary Magazine and Petite Hound Press and has been nominated by the latter for a Pushcart Prize. She has a short story published in the 2017 Florida Writer's Association Annual Collection and works by day as a copywriter and blogger.

http://www.zenmamamantras.blog/

Entering Hell: Loading... Please Wait

By Clint Doyle

Game Console

Lightning flashed outside the window. "F you newb!" Matt screamed into the mic of his headset. He grabbed a few cheetos from the bag next to his monitor while he waited for the respawn counter to tick down. The rain pummeled the window, the storm had been going all night. He sat in his dark room fuming.

"You mad bro?" taunted the voice on the other end of the console. He had been sparring verbally with some dick who clearly had to be hacking. Nobody was that fast or accurate. "If you don't shut up dickhead I will find you and ram that controller up your ass." Thunder crashed outside as his character loaded up again to hunt down the insurgents. Duty Calls was the latest first person shooter from Mark of the Beast Studios. Everyone was playing it at school. Matt spent time with his phone comparing stats with other players and showing off his customs skins that he won. He just hated dealing the kind of assholes these kinds of games attracted. They made his blood boil. They just drove him crazy.

A cat yowled next to him and he missed his shot, his enemy turned and killed him again, and once more he watched the respawn countdown appear on his screen. "Damnit cat!" he kicked at the little monster. He hated his sister's cat. The black feline dodged nimbly and yowled again as it darted for the door. As the countdown continued, the light from his screen illuminated his room. It was the only window full of light on the whole block.

Guzbrak powered on his machine and picked up his headset. He was just about to start his shift when Overseer Targreshi approached his cube. The supervisor demon was a special kind of take on middle management hell. Maybe there was something to that comparison, Guzbrak didn't think on it too much. Targreshi cleared the phlegm from his throat and his whiny voice struggled successfully to escape, "Guzbrak, new numbers from last quarter are in. Looks like your KPI's are slipping. I see your Temptation metrics are down... again. You are crutching too hard on Suggestive Sin. If you want to achieve your next Performance Bracket you need to engage targets in direct requests, stop beating around the bush."

Guzbrak didn't give a damn about Performance Brackets. Trying to work your way out of the Direct Sin Generation Center was a fools game. It was a long eternity and really only the favored few ever really got out of here. No, Guzbrak was going to ride a wave of mediocrity until Judgement Day. Why sweat so self important nobody's like Targreshi can just take credit for your efforts?

"Are you even listening?" the management demon wheezed. "You are training the new guy. Get him up to speed and get those numbers up!"

Great, Targreshi was going to saddle him with some newbie and then gripe when his handle time dropped because he had to hold the new kids hand. See, this is exactly why no one got out of here without the kissing the ring.

Before he could get his coffee and sync his station, controller, and load up Duty Calls he was assaulted by the sound of someone stumbling down the aisle. He peered over his cube to see someone carrying a giant box full of what sounded like rocks. The younger demon set it down on the desk across from him and leaned over. "Hey man, I'm new. I guess you are like gonna train me or something?" He set out a hand and Guzbrak took it thinking, something like that.

"Yeah, I am doing the training. First things first though, let's get some coffee and I will give you rundown on how things get done here."

The kid started digging around in his box and fished out some sort of plastic toy. "Sure thing man, just let me get my desk set up real quick." He began setting up more toys and various knick knacks. Oh hell no, this wasn't happening. Not one of those guys.... "Um, what is that?"

"Oh, this? This is a collectors edition Daryl Dixon with detachable crossbow. It is the most possible figure on the market and has over 30 points of articulation." Beaming, the new guy start posing the toy on his desk. He hadn't even connected his computer yet.

"Right.... Daryl. See, Daryl there is shit and I don't care, let's get our coffee and get things going." This was going to be a long shift.

"Oh. Right. I read you. More of a GOT man?" he prompted.

"Yeah, that isn't a kind of car either. C'mon, coffee is this way. It is way too early to be getting into that sort of thing before caffeine. Guzbrak made his way out of his cube and down the row rookie in tow and said over his shoulder. "Hey, kid. I can't keep calling you kid. Makes me sound like some sort of out-of-touch uncle, or washed up coach helping someone find his true potential."

"Oh, you can call me Mike. You know, you are sort of like my coach, this being my first day and my doing training and all."

"Shut up Mikey."

"Man, you don't really run into a lot of girls on these things." the young man cleared his throat. "I mean, uh, you know shooters are typically a guy thing. I mean, uh, well I don't talk to many girls online." He fired as the enemy team began their assault.

The voice on the other end tinkled back, "Heh, I could guess that, but you are nice. Not like most of the other toxic assholes I am matched up with on here. At least you know what you are doing. Most people are just shouting orders and bitching when people just do whatever they want anyway. Especially when they suck and don't know it and are trying to push people around like they are pro." The pair quickly took down a group of three Special Forces. The last enemy was actually sort of skilled and used the cover of the warehouse pretty well. It took twice as long to bring him down as it did the two newbs he was with combined. "Hmm, well that guy knew what he was doing. Too bad his group didn't. Might have been a real problem if one of them did something other than just spray their ammo in the air straight away. Heh."

"Yeah, no doubt. I am glad I could get off early today. My rank has gone up like crazy since we started meeting up. Got to go in a bit though, girlfriend will notice if I don't come out soon enough when my shift was supposed to end."

"She seems really demanding. She doesn't play?" she asked with a hint of disdain.

"Ha! Her, no way. She thinks these games are lame and just encourage people to be dicks and dwell in their mom's basement."

" I obviously don't think that. It sucks she seems so controlling. I mean if you want to play a game on your free time, what's the big deal. I do all sorts of stuff when I am not online. I had two dates last week, and I didn't even set it up over Firestarter."

"Oh, um, you're not seeing anyone?" the question hung in the air like the stale air of the previously mentioned basement. Romeo, this one was not.

"Oh, well I see guys, but no one seriously if that is what you meant." you could hear the grin on the other side of the headset. "I spend a lot of time on my photography. Sort of my hobby you know?" They stormed a guard post the opposing team had taken in their initial rush. If they lost this the match was as good as done, they would have to walk in from the respawn taking fire the whole time.

"I didn't know you do photography. You should send me some of your pictures."

"Heh, I get paid for my pics. You want one for free? I dunno. Shit! They flanked left move over behind the elevator. Tell you what. You send some to my DM first and I will think about sending you something depending on what you send me."

The battle continued, but the game was over.

"So that is how to use the Gender Modulation System." sighed Guzbrak. He began updating his report and tallying the work he had put in on the poor sod he had been grouped with.

"Wait," objected his new protege, " your note shows he is likely to break faith with his girlfriend, how can you possibly expect him do anything?"

"Look Mikey" he drawled, "this is the internet and getting pics of any kind from some dude is the least risky proposition there is. *What* kind of pic you get is a different matter." His computers virtual console blipped to let him know one of his accounts received a new DM. He looked at Mikey and then slid his eyes away as his eyebrows climbed in the most 'I told you so' expression he could give.

The two go up to go to the coffee station. Mikey took a cup and asked, " So... that's it? Getting some people to fight or break up, someone shouting some racial slurs, or a man to scream at his wife?"

Guzbrak slurped at his coffee. It was hot, extra cream, just right. He sighed and prepared to let the kid down. It always came to this. Some new greenhorn came in here thinking they were going to go down in history as a some awesome force of temptation and destruction. This was hell, and that applied doubly here in the network center. "Look kid, everyone thinks they are going to be this awesome force of sin generation. They are going to inspire true acts of villainy and have their name recorded in history. Maybe even get moved up to Possessions if they can really nail a truly hateful sin. Things don't work that way." He patted the kid on the arm. "You are going to spend your days generating piles of small sins. That is the real way to make it down here. Don't extend yourself. You put a lot of time in on building up these big sins and temptations, but most folks have a stronger conscious than you think. They back out when the time comes to make good on all that work you put in, and then you are left with nothing. Your metrics are shit, and pretty soon you are back down in the Lake of Fire tormenting souls."

"But what about the guys at platinum tier? They are earning all sort of perks and things. Hell, I was talking Targeff yesterday in the break room and he was telling me.."

Guzbrak cut in, "Targeff is just fucking with you. Sure, you could hit platinum tier, but ask yourself, how many entities they got working this gig? Why are there only a handful of platinum guys? Can it be done, sure. Are *you* going to be one of them, no way. There are politics involved you haven't even begun to wrap your brain around. Trust me man, if you don't want to go back to swimming in the fire, just focus on putting up steady numbers. Small things, easy to get mortals to execute on. Forget the flashy stuff because if it doesn't come through, boom you are on probation, next cycle you are out. Stick to the strategy kid, you got a long run ahead of you. Don't try to win the race on the first day."

"Those assholes won't leave me alone." The kid was hot, and good with his gun too. A terrorist went down in a hail of bullets and he reloaded. "They keep pushing and they are going to be sorry."

"I hear you dude." Came back his teammate over his headset. "You should put a brick or something in your backpack and when they aren't looking, Pow! You could probably really fuck'em up that way. Shit. They got me, respawning. Move back and grab me and we can push into the room."

The kid fumed, "That won't work. He has a whole group of friends. If I went after him, they would all just kick my ass after." You could hear him growl at the thought, you could hear is teeth grind. A terrorist appeared on the catwalk and fired a shot killing the kid. "Fuck!" he screamed. Over team chat an asian voice taunted the kid. He shouted back some obscenities. "I hate those assholes. They can play all day, they got no fucking life. Then want act like they are so fucking awesome."

"I hear you man." came back the other voice. "So, you still planning your victory dance?"

"Yeah man, you know it. Don't worry though, I will give you a heads up so you can be sick that day. The rest of those fuckers though, they get to pay."

"Watch out behind you." The game boomed a shots flew off screen. "See I got you covered. Yeah. That day is going to be extreme, so you don't know when?"

"I had a day but not sure I can make it." the kids replied. "Not sure I can get the supplies you know? Maybe I can do something in a few months." the kid trailed off, maybe he was reconsidering?

"Dude, I told you. Just get a bus ticket and head to the show over the river. You won't have to wait that way or anything. No one is going to give you any grief, you can get whatever you want probably. I heard someone else did that." the voice prompted.

"Really?" the kids sounded genuinely curious.

"Oh yeah, I can maybe send you a link or something." The two defused the bomb and the end of the scenario's countdown began.

"Yeah… Yeah! You're right. Those fuckers are going to get wants coming. Oh, man this is going to be great, then everything will be over. Those assholes will never know what hit them."

Guzbrak drug his feet heading to the conference room. He noted the cake on the long table with 'Congratulations' written in blue icing. Damn, he hated icing, tastes like cheap plastic. Why can't anyone use cream anymore?

All around him people were stopping to shake hands with Michael. Targeff stood right next to him with his hand on his shoulder like he was to credit for everything. Guzbrak stopped to fill his mug from the coffee pot facilities had set up. It sputtered and died at the halfway mark. Great. He was going to have to suffer this essentially sober.

Targreshi cleared the phlegm from his throat. It took an impressively long time. He then managed to speak above the assembled team of demons. "Folks, today we want to recognized the efforts of our newest team member!" He coughed, then sounding like he swallowed bubbling sludge continued, "He has managed to racked up an impressive feat in his first few weeks with us. His engineering of a mass murder has boosted numbers for my team to the highest levels, probably in half a decade. Targeff here is going to start mentoring his excellent talent, and who knows what is next for my young star." The group politely clapped at this declaration and began to break up to find the snacks that had been prepared or to get a cup with whatever they found for punch this time. It all tasted like someone had dropped a pack of Kool-Aid in tub of lemon juice. Guzbrak knew time was short and began to make his way past the groups of his coworkers who were taking this time to not do anything productive, and get away before anyone could rope him into conversation. He nearly made it to the door when a hand landed on his shoulder and a wheeze and gasp announced the presence of this supervisor.

"Hey, glad I could catch you." he moved rapidly beyond the expected platitude. "I need to speak to you about your TPS reports later, so don't leave. Also, I need to speak to you about this weekend. With Michael training, we need some team players to cover our bases. I need you to cover some of the gaps in the night shift."

CLINT DOYLE

Recently moved to the Portland, OR area for new work. I am an IT guy, a cancer survivor and a father. Between my wife, kids, and pets there are seven females in my house. I live in constant chaos. I am a stereotypical nerd and never have enough time to dive into everything I am interested in to the extent I would like. As far as writing goes I am working on a steam punk novel and I expect to have my highly anticipated completely inappropriate blog up.... eventually.

My wife thinks I am brilliant and my mom says I am special.

You should read my stuff.

amazon.com/author/clintdoyle

Zapping Filth Away

By Ross Ellison

Bug Zapper

Tom prided himself on his cleanliness. He vacuumed his studio apartment every day at the same time. Then, he checked the food in the fridge to remove anything expired. Afterwards he would mop the floors following a pattern that ensured he would not muddy his own work with his messy feet.

He had been accused of suffering from Obsessive Compulsive disorder, but Tom could not fathom how wanting a consistently clean house made him ill. He checked the portrait of his dead mother, bless her heart. The man would not allow his memory of his wonderful parent to be tarnished by a crooked photo.

Next, he went into his bathroom. Germs could not be allowed to multiply in his house, but the man had to make use of the toilet. Once he finished, Tom cleaned the entire bathroom to avoid any risk of a breakout. His heart skipped a beat when he heard a sound most foul: A buzzing of a fly.

"Get out!" he yelled as he ran to get his flyswatter. He almost forgot to pull his pants up all the way before he exited the bathroom.

Once he had his handy pest remover in hand, Tom went on the hunt. He had mastered the art of killing insects with many tools. Carriers of filth would not be allowed to live in his house. Indeed, it was a shame that humans could not exterminate flies from the earth. His eyes flicked right and left looking for a single sign of corruption on his walls. Tom could almost see the filth the fly was spreading leaving a trail for him to kill it.

One well-placed attack turned the fly into paste. Quickly, Tom put what remained of the bug in the trash can and immediately tied the bag up so that none of the filth would ever threaten his home again. He washed his hands thoroughly and then got to work cleaning the wall where he had eliminated the pest. Finally, he took out the trash feeling confident that this would not be a recurring problem.

Tom went to bed that night content with his clean home. He felt safe knowing that all threats to his living space were gone and he could sleep soundly. The man woke up screaming in the middle of the night when he heard more buzzing.

Another threat eliminated and a sheer certainty that this was a freak occurrence were the only reasons Tom could fall back asleep that night. But he would soon find that his life was about to change profoundly. His little clean kingdom was about to be threatened in a much more profound way.

A couple weeks passed with Tom back into his cleaning routine and his job as an administrator was barely a blip in the lack of stress in his life. That changed when he walked in his door at the end of the week. He had barely taken his shoes off and began scouting his house looking for what to clean when he heard it again. That buzzing noise.

Worse he heard multiple instances of the sound. Only by spinning around did he come face to face with a serious problem. A swarm of flies was buzzing around his house! *Flamethrower! Kill! Destroy! Cleanse!* All these ideas flashed through Tom's head to stop the state of panic that was now flowing through his every muscle.

Instead he grabbed his cleaning spray knowing that with their wings covered in sticky substances, the creatures would be unable to fly. It was the most wonderful sight as he watched the swarm fall to the ground.

"DIE!!!" Tom screamed as he sprayed the ground that was now covered with filth. Once not a single insect stirred on the floor, he grabbed a paper towel and set to work cleaning up his now blighted floor.

The horror did not end once he had fully cleaned his house and went to bed. The middle of the night brought new nightmares into Tom's life. More buzzing! "Where the hell are they coming from!"

He spent a good part of the night cleaning his studio as well as going on a midnight shopping spree to get the best bug killer he could find. He also needed spray that would keep the insects from entering his house at all.

Tom checked his bank account after his purchases and groaned when he realized how little he had to work with until his next paycheck. Despite being a salaried employee, Tom was still new to his higher status in life and had spent a bit more money than he should have. Not to mention that he constantly had to clean his house. An expensive and needed cost of living.

Tom arrived home and spent the rest of the night spraying the studio to protect himself and his sanctuary from further invasions from filth with wings.

Stress was rising quickly in his life and he needed for his studio to remain clean so that he could return to normalcy. But despite his best efforts, Tom was forced awake again in the middle of the night by more buzzing. He used as much of the spray as he could afford to kill this newest infestation, but he was beginning to breath heavy and his anger continued to rise.

By the time the weekend was over, it was obvious from any who looked at Tom's red eyes that he had gone without much sleep. His work suffered as a result. Feeling defeated from a horrible weekend combating filth, the man entered his home ready to rest before he could even properly clean the house.

He stumbled in the middle of his studio and fell face first towards the ground. When he woke up, it was several hours later. Tom truly was more tired than he realized, but there was a house to clean and he could not let sleep stop him.

Instead he found himself defeated by more buzzing. The bugs were still getting in and persisting!

"I need to get a hotel room and call a professional!"

There were many hotels in the city that Tom lived in and it was quite simple for someone with his credit score to gain a quick room from which he could begin to recover his sanity. With packed bags, he found himself at an upscale hotel room that was clean to the point of perfection. No flies, and no other pests.

But there was work to do and Tom called the exterminators immediately. Then when he hit the answering machine and looked at the clock, realized they were closed.

"No! No! No!" Tom screamed. "I need to get rid of these insects now!"

There was a sudden knock on his door, and he feared that he was yelling too loud and disturbing other guests. Instead, when Tom opened the door, a well-dressed man was on the other end.

"Pardon my intrusion," the man in a suit said. "My name is Phil, and I could not help but overhear that you have an insect problem."

"Yep I do." Tom stated, "confused by this turn of events.

"I can help with that. For you see, I sell bug zappers of the highest quality. I can give you a card if you wish."

"Yes please." Tom could not mask his excitement! What incredible luck!

"You will find my prices to be very affordable and reviews that ensure that my products do their job well," Phil added. He handed Tom a business card which was of the exact quality that the man expected from a person as well dressed as this salesman.

The most remarkable thing on the business card, was the way the man's name was spelled. "P-H-Y-L" not "P-H-I-L" as Tom had assumed. But the most important part of this bug zapper company was their 24-hour customer service. He got to work and used his laptop to order the bug zapper immediately.

The payment process was much easier than expected, and much cheaper. But best of all was the shipment date. Within one business day he would have it. And all he had to do was be present when they arrived to let them in.

This simplicity was the sure sign of a strong and efficient business. The very kind that Tom had ambitions of running one day. All he had to do was continue cleaning his home, then move on to keeping order in bigger and better things as his life continued. This bug problem was only a minor interruption. A small matter.

Only a few days later, Tom let the mechanics in and despite the buzzing noise he heard from within, he was confident that this new accessory would end his problem once and for all. Stopping one of the mechanics on his way out, Tom asked him how long to wait before he could be confident that the infestation of flies was clear.

"Well, the Zapper kills them as they enter, not before." The man explained. "But as for the current problem, no need to wait more than thirty minutes before you can safely enter your home again."

Tom shook the man's hand probably more aggressively than he meant to. He could not contain his feelings of joy! Even if more of the damned bugs came into his house, the Zapper would deal with them as they deserved.

"Thank you so much!" He told the mechanic when he finally let the man's hand go.

"All in a day's work," the mechanic explained before speeding off to his truck with the rest of the crew. They seemed in a rush and it occurred to Tom that there were probably more customers waiting.

After setting a timer for thirty more minutes to be on the safe side, Tom impatiently paced near the door that led into his first-floor studio. He could think of nothing else but how much cleaning he would need to complete to finally purge the filth from his home. The insects had stolen his clean space for multiple days now. But the Zapper would punish them as they deserved. Now it was time for him to clean up the mess.

The beeping on his phone indicated that the timer was ended. Tom confidently walked into his messy house, and got to see as the final insect met its end by the blue glow of his new Bug Zapper.

But such a beautiful object could not be ignored. Staring at it even from the doorway commanded his attention. He could clean later he decided as he walked slowly towards the blue glow on his wall. Grasping outwards towards it, the beacon showed him where his hand was to go.

Zap! Tom reflexively pulled his hand back in confusion. *Why had he touched the Bug Zapper? What was he doing at all? He had a house to clean!* Tom turned away from the accessory and began his cleaning. Multiple days of neglect commanded his utmost attention.

However, eventually Tom turned to clean the wall near the Zapper and let the duster he was making use of fall to the floor. Transfixed on the beauty of the blue light, he reached towards it. *Zap!* He tried to look away. *Zap!* Again. *Zap!* He forgot about everything else. *Zap! Zap! Zap!*

It took the actual pain building in his right hand to remind Tom that he should not be feeling the Bug Zapper. Instead he turned away yet again, and decided not to look at it the rest of the day. Something odd must have happened to him after the bugs.

"Yes, just finish cleaning and then go to bed. You have had a rough week," He reminded himself.

His work to finish making his house perfect was complete without any other interruptions. Content that his safe space once again met his expectations, Tom shut off his phone and decided to sleep the rest of the day away.

His dreams were dominated by a blue light. The most amazing color he had ever borne witness to. He wanted to be one with its lovely embrace. The light was the perfection that he had strove for his entire life. Touching it was to gain its blessing. Having this blue light in his grasp was the quickest way for him to be the best and cleanest human being alive.

Tom awoke with a start and his eyes jumped right to the Bug Zapper. He ran towards it eagerly, ready to gain whatever he could from the blue light. *Zap! Zap! Zap!* When his right hand hurt too much, Tom switched to the one on his left. Why else had he been given two hands, if not to alternate becoming one with this perfect light?

However, he saw the time and realized he would be late for work soon. With great regret, he dragged himself away from the Bug Zapper. He would have to spend the night trying to learn the clean secrets of the blue light.

Phyl was very pleased with the results of his labor. The flies being added to Tom's house had driven the man right into his six arms. Not that the human needed to know what his fate would be from now on. More pressing to Phyl was the massive ratings he had already gained.

He stretched his wings with excitement. The idea for another Reality TV show using the human cattle was a gift that continued to give. This specific show gave entertainment to audiences everywhere. This was not limited to earth alone, but to the countless planets that their species had enslaved. Watching Tom, as well as other humans zap themselves with their new accessories would become the new trending thing on the extranet!

Phyl would be famous the galaxy over for this! And all it required was tapping into the new human phenomena of not reading the terms and conditions all the way through. This glorious idea had been instilled in humans thanks to the massive overhaul of their education system.

The masters never wanted their slaves to be too smart after all. Phyl was just a buisnessbug, so he did not know the more complex details of what had been changed. What he did understand was that the reading material in schools had been picked with care to be as boring as possible. That way, humans grew up not wanting to read. Indeed, not wanting to think for themselves was the best way to keep cattle in their pen.

This masquerade was great for business. The humans were such a foolish species so willing to believe that they understood the universe. The perfect race for reality tv shows in general. There was already one that played with human aggression to force men to think with their fists. Another interacted with women that were labeled as Third Wave by their own species. This second television show allowed viewers to see constant battle of the sexes.

The Reality TV show that Phyl hoped his own could compete with though, was called "Politics Now!" This lovely show existed on multiple worlds and involved watching species elect the most incompetent leaders to head their world governments. Both entertaining alongside giving his species the ability to control all their cattle across the galaxy, it was Phyl's hope that viewers desired a more simplistic TV Show over the complex ones that were dominating air waves right now.

Yes, one day his TV Show would be able to compete with such famous Earth Shows such as "American Exceptionalism", "How Dreams Turn into Terrorism" and Phyl's personal favorite. "Humans Debate at the UN: The Big Boys Table"

By handpicking those with the human condition known as Obsessive Compulsive Disorder, another condition that had been genetically added to humans to ensure they were too distracted with their personal lives to ever evolve in such an undesirable way, Phyl had found the perfect contestants.

Tom continued to zap himself as he found cleaning futile, and Phyl hoped his own laughter was reverberating around the entire galaxy by other viewers. Katherine continued to ignore the baby crying in her house as she zapped herself. The drama this was causing was sure to garner attention. Finally, his personal favorite. A man whose name he had never received because he was far too paranoid that he was being watched by the one world order, kept throwing money at his Bug Zapper. This foolish human never realized that the One World Order was his new appliance.

This show would make Phyl a household name! A brand that would be forever remembered in the Galaxy!

ROSS ELLISON

R oss Ellison is an Author, Entertainer, Video Game Streamer, and All Around Menace to Society. Living in Orlando, Florida he currently is working on the next two novels in his Search For Eden Series which the End of Utopia Anthology serves as an introduction for. He also is working on a Post Apocalyptic Series with the working title of "Earth Everafter"

University of Central Florida's Online Publication Imprint selected his work for publication . He works at an online publication called BentoByte where one can find reviews on Anime and Video Games as well as articles on pop culture. Ross pesters society at large with his political commentary.

Writers of Central Florida or Thereabouts selected Ross as a featured Speaker. He is known as "the writer who always goes first" at the many open mics hosted by the organization. Odyssey Orlando has also published multiple pieces of work by Ross.

Whether through his Dark Fantasy Fiction, or commentary on issues that strike his fancy, Ross strives to entertain and educate audiences. Though his writing may deal with difficult issues, these are the ideas which drive society forward. Braving through his work will reward readers with high entertainment value as well as the potential for learning.

He is always looking for collaborators to aid in his endeavors of bringing his work to life. If you are interested in working with him, or have an idea to pitch, do not hesitate to visit the Collaborations Page

Sofa King
Tired of This

By Kim Plasket

Sofa

"**H**ow did I the sofa king end up here" he thought to himself. "This is such a small place, someone like me should at least be in a mansion if a castle is not available"

"I am the sofa King, there is nobody like me" he began to speak out loud, scaring the poor old cat who was sitting nearby cleaning his whiskers.

He thought about the last place he really liked. It was the first place he became aware of who he was, what he was capable of. It was a jail, he could smell the ocean, there were other smells such a feces and vomit, but the smell of the ocean was the best. He could recall one human who would bring others into where he was. The human would beat on the others until they told him what he wanted to hear. It was there he began to see how low the humans were, he knew he had to get rid of every last one of them.

"I showed those last humans who thought they could dump food on me. It was so funny, there I was covered in cheetos and blood. The police showed up, the silly canine who witnessed the whole thing was telling the police what happened but as usual they ignored him. The cat jumped on me, little did he know I was still hungry, With one gulp he was gone." the police merely thought he fell under the cushions and would come out when they left.

"No bodies only blood" they decided it was simply a house invasion gone horribly wrong. To the sofa king it was quite funny after all whoever would suspect a piece of furniture to fight back.

Each time he moved to a new home he made sure the humans paid for their sins against him. One time he was in a store which was filled with old things. He hated it there the only thing he had to eat was rats and anyone who has ever eaten a rat knows they do not taste anything like humans.

"I will show them all" he muttered as the old cat simply looked at him.

"You feline, the sofa King is your master" he really enjoyed the sound of his own voice. "You need to respect me, or I will figure it is time to eat again." he laughed to himself as the cat hissed at him and moved away.

He felt himself being moved, knew he was being loaded onto some truck. He wondered where he was going to next, maybe they finally realized how wonderful he was. He knew his leather was pristine, he could never lose the shine he had when he was first created.

Some time passed before he was moved again, this time he knew it was someplace worse than before. He could smell the unwashed bodies, tobacco with a hint of gun oil. He at first thought maybe they loaded him onto some kind of ship.

"How could anyone think I would prefer to be on a ship?" he muttered to himself.

"Hey Nathaniel, get a load of the couch the pigs put in here" he heard a rough male voice say.

"Yea, they think it's a treat for us cons" the other male voice said with a laugh.

"A beat-up piece of shit eh?" a different voice said, and the sofa king felt someone sit on him.

"Hey, we could see how much abuse this thing could take" there was a hint of something in the voice which made sofa king cringe.

He had no idea where he was but had a feeling he was going to get hungry very quickly. There was evil in the air and someone like the sofa king couldn't handle evil without wanting some for himself.

"Go ahead boys and see what could happen to you," he muttered not really expecting anyone to understand him. Everyone knew the humans were undeniably stupid.

"You boys are making me angry and this is not something you want to do" he muttered his anger growing.

"You need to stop–"

"W- Wait" he heard a different voice say. This one sounded timid and shy as if the person wasn't used to talking.

"Come on Jinx, you can't stop us from sitting on the damn thing"

"Patterson, its evil. You should hear what it's saying. It is going to make y-you pay," the timid voice became stronger.

"Jinx, go peddle your insanity someplace else. Me and the boys don't want to hear it" the sofa king felt something like feet on his cushion.

" the one called Jinx tried again.

"If you don't want us to take your ass next you will just go" the sofa king heard a male scream then felt something dripping onto his surface then laughter and grunts.

"I- I need to go just know it was not nice knowing you lot" the sofa king waited until the ones who were still in the room were discussing how to get rid of the one they called Jinx.

The sofa King decided it was time to make them pay. He quickly made them all vanish. There wasn't even a trace of blood simply four more gone. He wanted to laugh when the other humans walked into the room.

"Where did they go?" the sofa king heard someone calling out. Made him think of the ocean, he knew the name of where he was Alcatraz. He wondered why such a name made everyone cringe in fear. He enjoyed his time there, so many good things to eat, he was never hungry here.

He recalled when his secret was figured out, instead of reacting in fear the man would regularly give him those certain prisoners who misbehaved. He would tell the others they tried to get away but couldn't.

The sofa King was very sorry to see him go, he sat there for the longest time before someone took him. From that moment on he was not happy. There were sometimes he was okay, there was a while he was simply sitting in some alley. There were plenty of bodies who would sit on him and they would just disappear.

"The sofa king would prefer carnage to simply making them disappear but sometimes the blood wouldn't go away" he muttered waiting for the chaos to end.

"Jinx, you need to stay out until we figure what happened" the sofa king heard the one called Jinx tell them he was fine.

"I know you can hear me, but how?" the sofa king said as Jinx sat on the floor next to him.

"They say I am insane so I guess this is why" Jinx said hesitantly.

"Well I guess now there will be someone I can talk to in this place. It has been a long time since the sofa king had a minion to talk to." his voice to Jinx's ears was grating but he knew he had to listen.

"My name is Jinx, not minion" after all it was not because he was timid he was there.

"Why are you here? I imagine it is some sort of prison unless the smell of unwashed bodies and filth is in every home now."

"No this is a maximum security facility for those who will never be able to function in normal society" from the way he spoke the sofa king he heard it before.

"So why are you here?" again he asked the man.

"Not something I like to discuss" even as timid as he sounded, the sofa king knew when something was closed. He did not get as far as he was by being stupid.

"There will be time, you will learn to trust me" he was so sure of himself. "I am after all perfect. The sofa king is the supreme being"

Yet, they call me insane" Jinx couldn't help himself after all he wondered if the sofa king knew just where he was.

"I am the sofa King, I am beyond mere mortals as you have seen I have ways of getting rid of those who annoy me. Do you want to be one of them?" his tone was haughty.

"No, but really you can stop the act now" all timid behavior was gone from Jinx. His normally grey eyes flashed red as he stared at the beat up sofa which was acting as if it was the one in charge.

"It is not an act" the sofa King could not believe a mere mortal was defying him. "Come sit on my ultra soft cushions and you will feel my power"

"I am not going to be seduced by a piece of furniture, not what turns me on. Maybe you should try such an act with the inmates, most of them have rather perverted tastes." Jinx scoffed as his true nature took over.

"You will obey me" the sofa king had a feeling this particular human could not only feed his hunger but add to his power. He had to get him in a position where he was powerless, where the sofa King had all the power.

"So you want me to sit on your what cushion or face?" Jinx knew he was baiting a live shark but he was actually enjoying himself for once.

"Neither just come a little bit closer. You and I will make a good team" The sofa King used his voice, it no longer sounded grating to Jinx, it had a melodic quality to it which seemed to draw him in. As if he were a simple moth being drawn to a flame.

"Wh-what are you doing?" Jinx felt as if something was crawling across his mind slowly taking it over. For once he knew it wasn't his insanity. He felt a power taking over him, he took a step closer to the sofa, unable and unwilling to stop his feet.

"Come closer, I promise it will not hurt" the sofa King knew he could get the power for himself he just had to have the man willingly give it to him.

"You want to take me over, do you think they will not realize what you want to do?" Jinx somehow willed his feet to stop moving. He faced the sofa king, feeling the evil emanating off of him.

"They won't care, one more gone." The sofa king was growing tired of the games he wanted the power he knew this mortal possessed.

"I am sure you are correct but you cannot get me to willingly go to my death. Why do you think I am in here?" Jinx stood tall, his insanity became very clear as he told the sofa king all he had done to land there.

"You really killed an entire hospital staff simply because they ran out of red jello?" the sofa king was shocked.

"Have you ever eaten the green jello? It makes me think of boogers and to be honest it's disgusting" for a moment the sofa king wondered if the power he wanted was too much for him but he hungered for it in a way he never felt before.

There was a red light starting to glow from beneath him, it felt as if he were burning. "Do you feel it ?" his voice quivered as if he were excited.

"So you feel the fire from hell. Do you think I haven't felt it before?" Jinx knew what was going on, instead of being scared he felt drawn to the fire.

"So this is what it feels like to know pure evil." Jinx thought to himself as the fire consumed him. He knew the sofa king wanted his soul but what the sofa king failed to realize was Jinx never had a soul in the first place.

The only thing the sofa king would feel was the fires of hell as they consumed them both. "What have you done?" the sofa King was enraged.

"You did it on your own. Your majesty. You are the sofa king after all am I correct?" Jinx used his last remaining ounce of life to mock him.

"I am sofa King tired of this" were the last words the sofa king uttered as he was consumed as he had consumed so many in the past.

Kim Plasket

K im Plasket is a Jersey girl at heart relocated to sunny Florida. She enjoys writing mainly horror and paranormal stories and lives with her husband and 2 kids. When she is not slaving away at her day job, she can be found drinking coffee with fellow author Valerie Willis and planning the demise of some poor character. Currently she has several short stories featured in anthologies such as 'Demonic Wildlife' and 'The Hunted', also has a story in an Anthology Titled Fireflies and Fairy dust she also has had a story featured in Shades of Santa. Also, the newly released DrabbleDark Anthology, with more to come.

She also has several short stories and a post for Women in Horror Month on the website The Horror Tree.

https://www.amazon.com/-/e/B074YCLRCF

The Overstuffed Chair

By Mark McWaters

Chair

The overstuffed chair sat on the curb like indignant royalty. Its floral pattern of bright red blooms and swirling greens refused to go quietly, even after a long life—*several* long lives—of service.

So, its classic padded shape had seen better days...So, that tear on the left arm leaked a puff of white tufting. Was that any reason to discard something so magnificent with so much yet to offer?

In a final insult the previous owner, who shall go unnamed, unceremoniously tossed its seat cushion to lean cavalierly against the chair back. Not bothering even the barest dignity of seating it in place.

The nerve. The shame.

To occupy a spot on the street like so much common refuse.

To bake in the sun like some lawn toy for squirrels to chase and scamper over.

To sit idly by while scruffy neighborhood curs sidled up to sniff and lift their—but, hey? What is this?

"Dude, check it out."

"What?" Grafton, lost in the thump and crump of Jay Z's latest, drummed his thumbs on the steering wheel. He thought for like the tenth time today how awesome his new Alpine with Kicker amp and speakers sounded, filling his little Toyota truck with righteous sound.

"STOP, MAN!" Pearly, his roommate and all around best friend punched him on the shoulder. "YOU DEAF OR *WHAT?*"

Grafton glanced over at his passenger, saw him swiveled backward in his seat. "What'd I miss? Chick? I didn't see her." He hit his brakes. "She hot?"

Pearly—some kid back in high school gave him the nickname because of the boy's shockingly bad teeth—turned around and smiled. Grafton didn't even see the gnarly browns and yellows anymore.

"Jackpot," Pearly said.

Grafton looked in his rearview, scanning the street on Pearly's side for a babe. He saw nothing. Nothing hot on two legs anyway. He grabbed the rearview and swiveled it around to be sure. "Nobody there, man. Unless, you got a hard-on for dog all of a sudden. There's a mangy mutt with a nice ass sniffing at some poor evicted fucker's stuff on the curb."

"One man's garbage..." Pearly said.

"Is *another* man's garbage. Come on. We just *washed* Bumblee." Grafton had named his yellow short-bed the day he drove her home. "No way I'm piling a bunch of crap back there."

Pearly didn't hear it. Impatient fuck had already bailed and scampered back toward the discard pile on the curb, waving his arms and yelling at the dog to go piss on someone else's furniture.

Grafton cranked the wheel and spun the tires as he backed up, narrowly avoiding Pearly who jumped nimbly out of the way at the last second. His friend kept running and yelling while Grafton followed in reverse. The dog tucked its tail and skulked off as Grafton screeched to a halt by the curb.

Pearly sat proudly on his find when Grafton got out and walked around the tailgate.

His friend bounced a few times in place before sitting back and resting both skinny arms on the stuffed chair's much fatter ones. Grafton remembered a kid's story about some vagabond king re-claiming his throne.

The Overstuffed Chair

"I like it," Pearly pronounced.

"That is one double-ugly chair," Grafted countered. "Tell me you don't smell that." He sniffed once. Long and loud, like hitting a line of coke.

Urine, gym locker funk, old lady's perfume — and a faint whiff of something rotten. *Nice.* Grafton walked to the upwind side. "You're not riding in Bumblee after sitting on that thing. No fucking way."

Right.

Grafton breathed through his mouth the entire ride home.

Stupid chair barely fit in the truck bed.

Pearly watched his prize through the back window and winced at every bump in the road. "Easy, dude. She's fragile."

"My ass. Roll your window down at least. You stink like that friggin' chair. Which I *told* you would happen."

"Isn't she beautiful?" Pearly stared backwards while he obliged with the window crank. "I never owned furniture before."

Ownership decided, after Pearly spent that day and the next scrubbing the odiferous addition to their apartment with Ajax, dish soap, Pine Sol. Pretty much every household cleaner Grafton's mom had set them up with got used for the first time on that stupid chair.

Pearly dried it with his bath towel, leaning in hard with both hands.

"Smooth move, brains. That's your one towel."

Pearly stopped his up-and-back on a chair arm, glanced under his armpit and said, "So?"

Grafton pinched his nose.

"I'll wash it, man. Jeez." Pearly shifted his attention to the other chair arm. "I wish everyone would quit dissin' on my chair."

Everyone, so far, included Grafton, and two neighbors in the complex who'd waited at the top of the stairs, only too happy to comment as he and Pearly wrestled Pearly's find up the steps.

Unwilling to wait any longer, the two neighbors had started down when the boys were only half way.

"Hey, geniuses. Since when did the dump hold a yard sale?" said Neighbor One.

"Smells like someone *took* a dump *on* it," said Neighbor Two.

The neighbors chortled and high-fived one another as they squeezed by. A nail sticking out of Pearly's chair chose that exact instant to snag the shirt of the second guy and rip a hole in his sleeve.

Grafton didn't help matters when he squinted at the new scratch in Neighbor Two's arm and inquired about the dude's tetanus status. He'd thought it pretty damned clever at the time. Neither the neighbor nor Pearly saw the humor....

"I'm not dissin' your baby. Try a half bottle of that Febreze my mom gave us and I'll loan you my hair dryer. I'm sure it'll be fine."

"Thanks, man. You'll see," Pearly said. "I can't describe it, you know?" He sat down and wiped his forehead on the towel. "It's the craziest thing. Like this chair speaks to me." He sat back and ran his hands along the chair arms.

"What's the chair saying to you right now, Mr. Psychic?"

Pearly knit his brows together, concentrating hard.

"Ah, well, she says, *Thank you*, first off. She's happy to have a home again."

"First off?"

Pearly squirmed a little.

"Come on. Out with it."

"It's probably nothing."

"What?"

"She's kinda pissed at you."

"Serious? After I hauled her fat ass off the curb *in my clean truck* and up those friggin' steps outside?" Grafton chuckled and headed down the hall for his hair dryer. "That's gratitude for you."

"Hey, dude?" Pearly said quietly.

Grafton stopped and turned around.

"I wouldn't laugh. She says she doesn't like your *cheeky* attitude. Whatever cheeky is...."

Their place smelled like Febreze for a month. After that, it either faded or he got used to it. Probably, door number two. His mom and dad visited last weekend and they smelled it.

"Honey? I'm really proud of how you and Pearly are keeping up with things." His mom sniffed and looked around. "I give you a B+ for clean. I can tell you are really trying."

His dad said, "Smells like you spilled a whole bottle of that crap your mom likes."

"Dan!" she said.

"Well, it does." His dad looked at Pearly sitting back in his chair, a place Pearly hadn't left for their entire visit. Even to eat. "And where the hell did you guys score that monstrosity of a chair? *Goodwill* has classier inventory."

Pearly scowled and scooted forward quickly, ready to defend his baby.

Grafton deflected with, "You know, Dad. Two guys, first apartment. You do what you can, right? Bet you had some *monstrosities* in your first place."

His mom laughed at that. "If you only knew, son," she said. She grabbed her husband's elbow on the way out. Good thing, too. His dad tripped on the threshold as they were leaving and almost pitched headfirst over the stair rail outside.

"Walk much? *Sir?*" Pearly said through a tight smile.

His dad had turned around, frowning, ready to reply when Grafton stepped in again. "That first step is a killer, hey Dad? I'll call maintenance to have a look. Maybe have 'em tack it down better."

The parents left without further incident.

But when Grafton shut the door, he turned on Pearly.

"Nice, asshole. After all they've helped us?"

"Lighten up, Grafton." Pearly rubbed his arms along the chair's. "Having a bit of fun, is all. Don't get your knickers in a twist."

"Knickers? What the fuck?"

Pearly waved a hand. "Language, Grafton, language.

"Don't tell me—you're reading Charles Dickens now?"

Pearly *had* been reading a lot lately. He discovered libraries over a week ago and out of the blue, came home with a *library card*.

"Grafton. You know these things are *free?*" He'd held up his new laminated treasure. "You should get one."

Book after book after book he read. Real books, too. Nothing digital. Snuggled back in that big, fat chair with a book light strapped to his forehead. No TV. No X-Box. No *laptop*, for God's sakes. Pearly never could go an hour without making the rounds of his favorite porn sites. Now he buried his nose in moth-eaten stories from yesteryear.

"Charles Dickens rocked, man," Pearly said. "Taking up for the lower classes and all. Right now, we're working our way through *Jane Eyre*. Charlotte Bronte rocks."

"Who. The fuck. Are you?"

Pearly reached for his latest book on the side table he'd actually *bought* from IKEA. "Ah, ah." He waggled a finger. "Coarse language reveals a coarse intellect, Grafton."

Grafton walked over to the chair and kicked the corner of it. One good, hard *thwack*.

"I want my friend back you overstuffed piece of shit, right now. Give him to me or, I swear I'll put you right back where we found you. Don't think I won't!"

The tingle started up his leg immediately. Like hitting your funny bone, but this felt funny as cancer and doubled him over. "Oww! *Shit*."

Pearly pulled his lips back in a snarl and said, "Try it, Grafton. And we'll put *you* in hospital."

That had been two weeks ago.

Doctors said the cast on his leg would have to stay on for a few more months at least.

Funny how life progresses, is it not?

First, one is *kicked to the curb* as they say. A decidedly vulgar expression. Yet, so horribly descriptive. You are put on display, powerless, for the whole world to gawk at and cluck their tongues. As if you did anything wrong.

But then, life takes a twist and a kind young man comes along. A knight errant with his trusty, if intellectually challenged sidekick, who swoops you up in his arms and rescues you. Takes you to his castle, bathes you in scented soaps and water.

'Twas absolute heaven on earth. Plus, the dear boy completely misses or, has the supreme good manners not to mention, the bloodstains.

But, why stop to question?

Why indeed? When the noble young man who positively *could* be of royal lineage, turns his youthful energies to pampering you in befitting style?

Oh, the young gentleman has rough edges. What young man doesn't? But those are easily addressed, over time. We will see that he blossoms to the full potential of his noble heart. Doing so will only improve our lot and insure that which is most important above all.

Our very survival.

The Overstuffed Chair

No one must be allowed to stand in our way. Nor, cause harm to befall us.

To even *threaten* such a thing cannot and will not be tolerated.

Even though the threat should come from someone as close and beloved as say, a tactless and rather dimwitted sidekick.

Over the next few months the changes in Pearly came fast. Too many and too quick for Grafton to keep track of them all.

His friend changed his diet to fresh fruits and vegetables for one thing— *That which you call fast food must be so named because those who consume it will most assuredly die fast.*

He started dressing better. Wearing shirts with buttons and pants without holes. Shoes that could actually take a shine. *One must look the part if one is to reflect one's true station in life.*

Then, Pearly got a job. A real job, with regular hours and a regular paycheck. It may have been bagging groceries at the local grocery store but as Pearly put it the first night he came home with a tie and his store apron— *It is a first step on a long journey. But at least I am on it. Which, I might say if I were to harbor a wish to be cruel, is more than I can say for some.*

But, the night he came home humming to himself—it sounded like the brass section of some stuffy classical piece of garbage—topped them all.

Pearly slid grocery bags onto the counter and, still humming, removed cottage cheese, yogurt, oatmeal, hummus, and bricks of tofu.

Grafton stared, open-mouthed. "You sick?"

"Hm?" Pearly answered.

"Life in the fast lane giving you an ulcer? What's going on?"

That's when Pearly smiled.

He opened his mouth and like a light switched on, bright white choppers grinned back at Grafton. The most beautiful set of teeth he had ever seen. Whiter than J. Lo's. More perfect than Brad Pitt's.

Pearly tapped his front tooth with a fingernail and winced. "Still tender," he said.

"Holy fucking shit."

"Nothing nearly so profane," Pearly said. "And I do wish you'd try harder with your language, Grafton. No, my man," he ran his tongue over his front teeth, "benefits. *Dental* benefits."

"Jesus, Pearly. Good for you, man. They look great."

"Why, thank you Grafton. And please call me Richard. It *is* my name after all and *Pearly* is so from another time. Don't you think?"

Then *Richard* made a bowl of oatmeal, sprinkled a few blueberries on top and retired to his chair. He fairly wriggled in delight at being there, like a dog overcome with joy at seeing its master.

He sat back, placed the bowl in his lap and ate. His spoon held at a perfect horizontal, traveled in a precise arc to his mouth and down again. He never missed. Never spilled a drop. That stupid shit-eating—now oatmeal-eating—grin plastered on his face. Happened every time Pearly sat in that goddamn chair. Like he and that fucking fat-ass piece of upholstery were on the same wavelength, mind melding or something.

Grafton didn't like it.

Not one bit.

New teeth be damned, Grafton decided right then to do something about it.

He wanted his best friend back and this thing oatmeal-swilling *thing* was not the Pearly he'd known since fifth grade.

Stupid as it sounded, he blamed the chair. Clearly, the damn thing had to go.

One good thing about having a roommate with a steady job? It got Pearly out of the apartment for predictable stretches of time.

Grafton wouldn't need long.

Not an hour, even.

The plan seemed simple enough. Trade that overstuffed *monstrosity* for a recliner his dad didn't want anymore. Get rid of that rotten pile of stink in their apartment and get a *way* more comfortable chair in the bargain... Pearly would be down with that...Eventually....

Grafton snapped his fingers and did a little shuffle step as he went to the kitchen to filch some of Pearly—*Richard's*—yogurt.

Woohoo. He had a plan.

He couldn't wait for the right time to put it in motion....

As it happens, Grafton didn't have to wait long. A couple days later Pearly—*he can blow me if he thinks I'm calling him Richard*—had a full eight-hour shift at the market. Plus, Grafton's dad gave him an ultimatum—*Come get that recliner out of my garage or I'm calling Goodwill.*

Thank you Universe. Today was the day.

The Overstuffed Chair

Knowing he could use some help with the move, recliners are a bitch, Grafton knocked on their neighbor's apartment a few doors down. After the shit they gave him and Pearly on the stairs that first day, he figured they owed him.

The door squeaked open and an eyeball peered out of the crack. "What do *you* want?" When the neighbor saw Grafton he opened the door wide. The sweet reek of burning weed wafted out and Grafton peeked in to see Neighbor Two on a couch inside, sparking a bong. "Speak."

"Want to make a quick twenty-ten bucks?"

Neighbor One narrowed his eyes. "Doing what?"

"I just need you guys' help with something." Grafton shrugged. "Take a half hour, tops."

Neighbor Two came to the door and stood behind One. Tight-lipped, chest puffed full with a bong hit. "Buzz off," he squeaked. Two smoky puffs leaked out with the words. He squinted through fiery red eyes.

"Fifty bucks," said Neighbor One.

Neighbor Two leaned forward and exhaled. *Whoosh.*

Grafton closed his eyes against the smoke and smelled high-grade marijuana and chilidogs.

"Yeah. Fifty. *Cash.*" Two punctuated his demand with a cough.

"I can't afford that much."

Neighbor Two stuck his lower lip out. "So sad. Too bad." He flicked his roommate in the back of the head. "C'mon man. Tell the little dude to get lost." He turned back for the couch and his bong.

That's when Grafton noticed Two's arm in a sling. "What happened to your arm?"

"Fuck you," Two said over his back.

"What we gotta do?" Neighbor One still dangled on the hook.

"Probably just *you*, now."

"Ah, he's all right. He's just being an asshole."

"No, I mean," Grafton flapped his arm like a chicken wing, "I need some help moving something."

"Like?"

"You remember our chair from that day?"

Neighbor One recoiled backward like Grafton had suddenly developed leprosy.

Neighbor Two froze in mid-bong reach and straightened.

"I think you better leave." Neighbor One whispered. He tried to slam the door, but his roommate stood beside him in a flash and yanked it open.

"Still have that fucking chair?" He breathed heavy, his squinty red eyes gone squintier. "You know what's good for you, you'll burn that piece of shit. Fact, how 'bout I come down there right now and help you."

He tried to shove past his roommate, but Neighbor One grabbed his shoulder and pulled him back. The shoulder on the bad arm.

"Oww! God *dammit!*"

Neighbor One cringed. "God, dude. I'm sorry."

"That chair of yours gave me this." Two waved his sling at Grafton and winced. "*Fuck.* I already called my lawyer. We're suing your ass, *asshole.*"

Grafton peeked inside the end of the guy's sling and saw a wad of white gauze and tape.

"Flesh-eating bacteria," said Number One quietly. "They had to cut off a lot to save his arm."

"From your FUCKING CHAIR!" Two screamed. He had tears in his eyes. "I'm telling you, burn that thing or YOU MAY BE NEXT."

Neighbor One slammed the door in Grafton's face.

Good. Saves me from thinking of something to say.

He headed back to his apartment, walking slow and thinking fast.

He'd heard about that bacteria shit on TV. Very bad news. They say it's everywhere. Anyone can get it. From a little scratch on anything. But if any*thing* spread flesh-eating bacteria, Pearly's overstuffed piece of curb crap seemed a more-than-likely candidate.

When he got back in their apartment the chair sat in its corner, innocent as a bloody knife, daring him to try and move it.

"Think you're so clever you piece of shit? Your days are numbered."

Grafton walked over and looked Pearly's Pride over carefully. Up and down, both sides, looking for nails, anything sticking out. He did what he could without touching the chair. Why take chances?

Ratty old piece of crap.

A flower pattern from the turn of the century—probably a huge hit with old ladies and blind people. Scuffed wood feet peeked out under the corners, round and fat like the chair. Left front one had a split up the middle.

Stupid chair definitely wasn't *all that.*

He bent closer and examined the fabric. Rip in the arm barely showed anymore. Looked like Pearly could add seamstress to his new list of skills.

Stitches were hardly visible. The cushion had a deep sag in the middle. He wondered how many asses over the decades had sat there.

He leaned close and sniffed. What did he expect? His mom's famous Febreze, certainly. Pearly's eye-watering new cologne—*It's French, Grafton.* Some leftover smells from the curb life.

But nose-clearing *eau de dead body*? Jeez. Smelled like someone stuffed the chair with body parts ripening to a fine bouquet of decay.

The stink stood him straight up and he backed away, blowing out of his nose, trying to rid himself of the memory. That's when he saw the stain. *Why hadn't he noticed that before?* Dead center in the chair back, a dark, brownish-red stain hid itself in the red flower pattern. The free-form shape fit in perfectly with the shapes of the flower petals, like it had been planned.

Pretty damn cunning. If you didn't look for it, you'd never see it.

Now it's all he saw.

"Someone died in that chair, didn't they? You overstuffed evil shit."

The chair sat silent, implacable.

"Sure as hell that's a bloodstain. Let me guess. Shot? Stabbed? *Both*?"

The chair, squatting like a caged predator, didn't deny a thing. How could it with the telltale evidence soaked right into it?

"You may have Pearly wrapped around your coiled springs but I got you figured. He's mine. Not yours."

Grafton grabbed his wallet and keys and headed for the door. "Don't go anywhere, fucker."

This shouldn't take too long. Gas station around the corner's three minutes away.

Why, oh *why* was it so difficult to locate even a modicum of civility in this contentious and crass world? Try as one may, it does seem as though the universe is constantly having a laugh at our expense.

So, what is left for us to do? Clearly, we must protect ourselves. Elude the coarse grasp of hands that would do us harm.

Is it our fault? At the risk of unseemly hubris, we give the universe fair warning by asking a most simple and pointed question—*Is there nothing to be said for justice?*

For justice is coming.

Stupid boy, ineffectual skin bag. Flailing about in its self-righteous little human pique. Its limited faculties truly sense nothing of its immediate future.

What a shame. 'Twould be much more entertaining otherwise.

To watch it twist and turn on a gibbet of its own devising.

Pierced by a sharp awareness of its pitiful and woefully inadequate shortcomings.

How delicious to contemplate such fancies. But, that is for later, for much more opportune times.

Right now, we must make ready.

Grafton returned to their apartment and stepped inside. He placed the sloshing can of gasoline by the door and balanced a small box of wooden matches on its cap.

"Miss me?" he said.

No answer. He didn't expect one. But *something* felt different. The chair sat in its same place, poised in its corner. Was it the room? The apartment trying to tell him something?

The atmosphere in the room crackled and the hairs on his neck tickled. He took three steps toward the chair and static electricity in the carpet sparked underfoot.

Too weird. Must be a storm coming.

He pulled a pair of gray leather welder's gloves from his back pocket and pulled them on. No sense taking any chances with nails and other pricky things.

"Wanna go for a ride, hm?" He said it like his mom talked to her Yorkie. "Big fat fuck want to go on a trip? Hm?"

He propped the front door of the apartment open with the gas can and slipped off a glove to slide the matches into his jeans pocket. He rattled them at the chair.

"Can't forget these, hey?"

Gloved up once again, he clapped his hands and felt nothing through the padding. Excellent. He approached the chair, grabbed both its arms and leaned back, tugging hard.

The chair scooted forward an inch, if that. Like the friggin' thing dug in its heels. *Jesus.* It definitely wasn't that heavy on the way up.

232

"Ah, don't want to leave? How sweet. I'll be sure and tell Pearly. Now, *move*."

He dragged it forward a bit over a foot, enough so he could get behind the thing and push.

"Come *on*. Christ Jesus and Joseph. MOVE. YOUR. FAT. *ASS!*

The last syllable did it and the chair slid across the floor and banged into the doorway.

"Whew, man. You sure know how to drag out the inevitable." Grafton rested both hands on the chair back to catch his breath.

That's when he felt it. A slight vibration. Either the chair had begun *humming* or someone in the apartment below had an out-of-whack washing machine about to go tilt. He bet on the washing machine.

"Let's go, fatso."

He wrestled and shoved and stood the chair at all angles to fit it through the door. Not so easy with one person. But, then again, he didn't give a shit whether he scratched the crap out of the thing.

One last push and the chair fell through the open door. He heard a slight crack as it crashed onto its feet.

"Oops," Grafton couldn't help but smile. *Yeah, boy. He'd done it.* Damn thing evicted from the old abode.

Grafton pushed some more, scraping ten feet down the cement walkway to the top of the stairs and made ready. He leaned over the railing to be sure the coast was clear. No sense pretending any longer.

"This is for stealing my best friend."

Grafton squatted, got his hands under the chair back, tipped the chair forward and shoved. He watched the chair cartwheel down the staircase and crash to the cement walk at the bottom. He resisted the urge to jump and clap. That would have been gay. But he did whistle a happy little tune as he went back to the apartment to retrieve the gas can.

Halfway there, Graft old man. One more step and the monstrosity *is history.*

He put the can on the seat and pushed and shoved the chair along the walk, back to the parking lot behind the apartments. They hid their garbage area there and today was garbage day. With any luck, they'd come and go before Pearly got anywhere *near* home from work.

Grafton shoved the chair up against a dented, lime green dumpster.

"Welcome to your new home, asshole. Though, not for long." He checked the sign on the dumpster—*Pickups Monday and Thursday at 4:00 P.M.*—and then his watch.

"You got about an hour."

He snatched the gas can off the cushioned seat and contemplated his next move. A little risky, yes. But the poor dude with the bacteria arm had decided it for him. No sense inflicting this disease-spreading, overstuffed evil on anyone else.

He unscrewed the gas can's cap. The petroleum smell of gas hit him and he breathed deep. He always loved the smell of gasoline. He took in another deep breath.

Whoa, dude.

The smell made him light-headed all of a sudden and he shook his head to clear it.

Whew. Must have taken more out of me than I thought moving that damn thing.

The world tilted slightly and before he busted his ass, he twisted and sat down hard on the edge of the chair. The gas can slipped unnoticed from his hand and fell over, gurgling its contents onto the asphalt.

What the hell, man?

Grafton placed both his arms on the chair arms to steady himself. The world continued to spin without letup and he shoved himself back into the chair to get a better anchor.

Just as the spinning began to abate and he started to get his wits about him, he felt the same vibration he'd felt upstairs in his apartment. If he didn't know better, he'd think the fucking chair had a massage feature, like those recliners at the mall.

Well, someone sure as hell turned up the vibes on this one.

He closed his eyes to enjoy the moment.

Felt the thrumming sink into his bones. It felt good, really.

Kinda buzzy.

Kinda tickly.

Kinda—.

The Overstuffed Chair

The fireman unbuttoned his yellow, Nomex jacket and took off his helmet as Rescue wheeled the kid into the back of the wagon. No need to hurry. They'd already put in a call to the Coroner.

Lieutenant Ramsey ran a hand through his graying crew cut and chuckled without a trace of humor. Damnedest thing he'd seen in 15 years on the job.

A perfectly healthy kid, impaled through the heart on a coiled upholstery spring.

He'd been the one to cut the body free, leaning it forward, back of the shirt soaked in blood. He'd yelled for tin snips when he saw he couldn't pull the spring free. One good *snik* and the rest of the spring recoiled into the chair back as if nothing had happened. A tiny rip and a spreading bloodstain were the only evidence that anything untoward had even happened.

One day, he'd have to write a book about all the weird stuff he'd seen on the job. Today might make Chapter One.

Ramsey put his helmet back on, hopped into the truck and pounded on the seat in front of him. "Let's go."

As the fire engine pulled away, he glanced out the window at a stray dog that'd come up to check the chair out. It sniffed...sidled closer...started to lift a leg....

He laughed when the dog suddenly yelped, tucked its tail and ran.

MARK McWATERS

Mark McWaters--called Mark THOMAS McWaters by his mother when he did something stupid, which he often did--came into the world in 1952. Mark was born in Cuba, NY and in his early years "Cuba" got raised eyebrows until he remembered to add "New York" to it. Mark carried a pad and pencil around from age nine on, finally parlaying his love of writing into a career as an advertising copywriter with a slew of national, regional and local advertising agencies. His ultimate career move lasted 17 years as a partner/copywriter/creative director at his own agency.

Mark has the ubiquitous MFA in Creative Writing—from the University of North Carolina at Greensboro. (He owes a great debt to Mr. Fred Chappell there.) He is a member of the Florida Writers Association and a multiple winner of that esteemed organization's literary awards—the Royal Palm Literary Award in flash fiction, short story, and novel.

He currently lives in Longwood, Florida with his editor, a learned and highly opinionated West Highland Terrier named Bentley. Personal literary tastes run to the bizarre, the macabre and to the downright strange and those sensibilities are dominant themes in Mark's rapidly expanding portfolio of work.

www.amazon.com/default/e/B01MSB7OXP

236

Frozen Freud in Three Part Harmony

By J. P. Dildine

Refrigerator

Cassi Stirn had stopped complaining to herself about the incessant humming noise that had been vibrating through her head as she stood at the back of the school cafeteria covered in sweat. There were more tangible things that were annoying her right now. The Texas heat was merciless and her car's AC had decided to quit the day before and she was livid that her husband Abel, motherfucker, had not taken care of it that morning. Instead, he had spent his day cleaning out that old broken beer fridge for the garage and getting his old junker ready for the trip to see his deadbeat mother all the way out in Nowheresville, Utah for Spring Break. She'd told him she wanted the garage to be a goddamn garage, not a man cave. Where was she gonna park now? Who does he think he is? Now she couldn't park in the garage and the cracked faux leather seats in her ancient BMW had sat in the sun all morning and had scorched her skin when she'd jumped in to race to the PTA meeting. Between her son, Adrian, demanding more microwavable chicken tenders and her keeping a firm

237

eye on newly acquired kid she had at home, it felt endless. The humming sound was getting louder. fuck!

The cafeteria was packed, and she was late. Goddamned Abel. Goddamned kids. She zeroed in on an empty seat and began the journey between pulled in knees and the backs of too tiny chairs, but before she could get there, Lorraine, one of the yoga wearing Candy Cunts with an oversized wedding ring, let her know by her stink eye and a wave of her hand that it was a saved seat. Cassi reversed her trajectory as a drop of sweat fell between her eyes and off the end of her nose. It landed on Lorraine's husband's knee. She was so embarrassed. Maybe Frank hadn't noticed the tiny drop of moisture through the nice fabric of his pant leg, but she was sure he had. You're a goddamn sweaty mess and everyone can hear your cheap heels clicking on the cafeteria floor, she shamed herself. Eventually, she found a spot at the back of the room with the other latecomers.

Anastasia Bourdain yammered on and on from the multifunctional stage. Her hair was perfectly coiffed and dyed blonde, and her nails so lacquered that they occasionally caught light and brought attention to themselves. It had been months since Cassi had gotten a manicure. My nails are so defective, she thought, and suddenly she remembered her mother's disgust one night before she'd dropped her off at her 8th grade dance. "It's too bad you have your father's nails and thighs, Cassi."

Frank turned to look at his wife, Lorraine, sitting beside him. Then Cassi caught his eye for a brief moment. Yeah, he's bored. She wondered if he hated his wife as much as she did. She imagined what his curled up mustache would feel like against her. Then there was Corbin who was standing off to the side of the neatly placed seats looking bored while his Candy Cunt wife went on about fundraising for new teachers. Why does this school need money? We live in the wealthiest neighborhood in the area and have these fundraisers just about every six weeks. Did she just say something about bassoon instructors? Who needs that? Maybe if Mary, her new responsibility, played bassoon it would be helpful, but that ungrateful child had chosen to learn the flute. What was she going to do with that? Join Jethro Tull? Cassi was not pleased to have her niece living there, but she had a gameplan to solve that. Corbin and Anastasia's daughter was a cheerleader. God that kid was beautiful. That's how you get noticed. Become a cheerleader! Corbin turned his beautiful baby blue eyes downward to look at his watch. He's bored. Yeah, his wife was boring, she was sure that wasn't all she bored him with. She'd blow his mind! Cassi smiled. She looked at her own watch, but it had stopped again. Fuck! She'd asked Abel to take it in. Of course, he forgot. Forgetting was his thing.

Cassi thought about the money they'd be getting soon and lost herself in the idea of moving into the Cherry Downs subdivision, not far from hers. They had moved into what the locals referred to as the "Last Hippie Stronghold in Austin." These were the houses off of Cuernavaca. Back in the seventies, hippies had moved into the hill country areas next to the lake where there were no HOA's and lots of cheap land. The area was over-loaded with all kinds of structures that made for shelter for these hippies including mobile, manufactured, and oddly built, DIY homes. Abel had felt the area had character, but Cassi thought the two-story place they lived in was falling apart and lacked curb appeal, but still, it did get her closer to Cherry Downs the community on the other side of Cuernavaca. Over the decades the whole area had become more gentrified. Most of the hippies sold out and huge mansions went up, but no matter how hard people like Anastasia tried, she could not create a unified HOA. Abel and Cassi did agree on one thing - the neighborhoods provided the best schools, and now she was here. However, with her administrative job and the small amount Abel made from writing and his two warehouse jobs, they still couldn't afford to move into Cherry Downs. So they lived a on the other side, back in the "Cuernyhood". She loved it at first. It was great being so close to the lake and rent was very affordable. Bernie, their landlord, had moved so that he could be closer to the hospital due to his aging heart, but he refused to sell off his property. He fucking hated Anastasia and their kind. The hatred went both ways.

Cassi glanced at the back of Frank's head. He was a Captain in the police department and always got personally involved in anything remotely questionable in Cherry Downs or Cuernavaca. He'd actually recovered her son's bike from some ruffians down the street one time. She remembered when he'd walked the bike up to her house. As he'd reached out to return the bike, the side of their hands had touched… it was electric. The smile on his face accentuated the manly 'stache… She wondered what it would feel like.

Frank leaned over to give his wife a peck on the cheek. She barely acknowledged his sweet gesture. Candy Cunt.

Cassi's cell phone rang. Shit, shit, shit! People turned around and looked for the perpetrator with the offensive phone. Anastasia stopped talking. Cassi dug in her purse frantically. As she dug around, Anastasia announced in the most condescending tone possible, "Please everyone! Just a reminder to turn down your volume until the meeting is over, please… we're here for the kids, not to hear from the kids." People chuckled. Cassi muted the call because she was sure it was just another attempt from a debt collector. Although the phone was muted now, she was worried to look up. She brushed at her red bangs as she avoided eye contact and lifted her head. The meeting had moved on. She noticed Bob was looking at her. He stood by the water fountain near his very plump wife. Bob was smiling at her. He jutted his chin toward the blonde on stage, then raised his middle finger only so Cassi could see him and and silently said, "Fuck her." Cassi giggled. Bob is so funny. I am so much hotter than his wife. I'm a downright supermodel compared to her.

Cassi's phone vibrated in her hand. It was her son, Adrian. The text read "Hell a cometh swiftly." She didn't have time for anagrams today. She wished sometimes that she hadn't introduced anagrams to him. She felt an unusual tug of guilt. "What kind of mother are you?" the voice echoed. She texted back she'd work on it later. Why was she even there? She left.

Goddamn this heat. Damn, why can't they get shit done around the house? Why did she have to do everything? They made her late, and if the dishes had been done then she would have gotten a decent parking space and an actual decent seat. Now her feet hurt from her cheap shoes, and the walk back to her car seemed endless. The car. "Fuck, fuck, fuck!"

She had pulled up on the side street behind a Mercedes, and now a Porsche not only was behind her but entirely too close. She wouldn't be able to get out. The humming sound in her head was intense again. She looked at the power lines by the school. Must be it. Sounded like that fucking old beer fridge humming. She gently backed her BMW with blue faded paint into the Porsche and gave it a nudge. It gave way slightly, but when she tried to turn she realized she wasn't going to be able to do it without causing serious damage to her car and the Porsche.

She screamed, "Fuck, fuck, fuck! Goddamnit!" She began to cry. Even her sobbing didn't drown out the vibrating noise in her skull. She gasped for air between sobs. Her head was throbbing. She slammed her balled up fists onto the dash and then slapped at the radio volume knob causing the the sound to explode from the little speakers. "Black Hole Sun" roared inside the cabin as she forced the car into reverse and mashed her foot onto the accelerator. "Fuck it all!"

Frozen Freud in Three Part Harmony

When she got home, she walked in feeling refreshed. Even the sycamore tree Abel had planted and let get out of control hadn't bothered her when she pulled up. She was alive. As she walked into the kitchen, she saw Mary playing on her phone. It was that app that superimposed funny wigs and hats on pictures.

"Hey," Cassi said half heartedly to her as she reached into the fridge for a diet cola. Mary responded by extending her overly thin arm out to show Cassi the latest wig. "Aunt Cassi, do you think when I get my haircut they could die my hair purple?" Cassi turned her back to the girl and fumbled for something in a kitchen drawer. She did not want to have this conversation with her niece.

"No they don't do that. I told you it's just gonna be a cut, nothing fancy. We're not made of money, and also..." she stopped fumbling and popped the top of the diet cola, "like I said fifty times before just call me Cassi, cut the 'Aunt'."

Mary bit her lip sheepishly and uncurled her leg from underneath herself. Her long unkempt hair fell forward creating a safe cave for her eyes and her phone.

Three weeks ago Cassi had received the call. Her estranged meth addicted sister had been arrested, and when the cops found out her pimp boyfriend was not the biological father, they had taken the child into protective custody. The boyfriend mentioned Cassi's name. What a nice guy. At first Cassi revelled in the excitement of it all. Everyone was so grateful she'd saved the little girl from such a bleak fate. The CPS officer, the neighbors, her husband and even the Candy Cunts at the community park made her feel like a hero. Mary buried her frail and undernourished eleven year old frame into her aunt's and everyone looked on in pure awe. Cassi would tell them, "We did the right thing. It's not a bother. This is what family does. We protect each other." But that faded. Eventually, Mary's constant need for reassurance and physical touch became a burden and made Cassi nauseous every time Mary gave her a hug. The fanfare faded, and the child eventually gravitated towards Abel. Always Abel. Everyone always loved Abel. He would have nothing if it weren't for Cassi. Did people even know he didn't fix her AC today? No one understood what she went through. If only they did.

Cassi heard Abel laughing. She guessed he was probably on the phone with his literary agent. He'd gotten one crummy book deal after years of self-publishing, but where was the fucking money? She had plans. Abel wanted to pay down debts and put money into savings. Fuck that. She'd been supporting his dream for years. She wanted that house over in Cherry Downs, and she wanted that fucking three car garage. She deserved it. She's a better writer than him anyway. She just never had time. Abel was so needy and Adrian too. Now they had Mary on top of everything, and Cassi wondered if Mary still had lice. Her head ached and buzzed. She thought she'd caught a whiff of the medicated shampoo. Thankless kid was taking even more time from her and her own dreams. She wished Mary could just stay in a motel for a while until they knew for sure the bed bugs and lice were gone, but Abel said it was fine. What about her son? What about his needs? He gets lice and then people at school find out, he'll be the laughing stock. What then?

Her phone vibrated, and she looked down to read a text. She looked up to see if anyone was around and then quickly responded. Hastily, she deleted the electronic correspondence. Goddamned kid. She had to go. Cassi wasn't going to burden herself much longer. The internal humming stopped for just a moment. A branch rubbed against the living room window. Goddamned Sycamore tree. It irritated her that he never bothered to trim the damn thing. She bet Bob, or Frank, or Corbin would have trimmed her tree. She giggled to herself at the double entendre. Those Candy Cunts didn't deserve men like that. They'd give her everything and she'd give them all of her.

Adrian stared at the anagram. He should have taken longer to solve that very first one. When she'd introduced the game, she was so fragile. She explained that it took a while to learn to problem solve and then showed him his first anagram. It was "The best things in life are free," and it took him less than a minute to come up with "The end of the world is nigh." He didn't have the heart to tell her he had found three others in that time. He knew she needed to feel like she was teaching him something, but he was having so much fun, he'd forgotten about her. For an eleven-year-old he had amazing, analytical mind, or at least that's what his mother would tell people. He got it from her, she said. It was confusing how much she praised him to other people because when they were alone, she always got angry and then sad. He knew people had been cruel to her. She lost that scholarship at MIT because her mother forgot to mail off her application in time. Then when she was training to be an opera singer, she was in that car accident that damaged her vocal chords. Worst was losing her opportunity to dance at Julliard which she couldn't do because she'd gotten pregnant with him. She still got letters begging her to come to Oxford. Adrian had never seen them, but she liked to talk about them. He looked up from the notebook and the doorless entry to his room. He'd gotten a B in PE. He hated not having a door. He would have to participate more and get an A if wanted his privacy back.

Abel Culp hung up the phone and couldn't have been happier. Tomorrow the advance would hit the account, and more importantly, they were all packing up and driving to see his mother in Utah. She hadn't spoken to him in years, and he was finally going to introduce his family. He was so proud of the family he'd inherited. He had been a bachelor most his life, and marriage never seemed to be in the cards for him until three years ago when he met Cassi. Never before had he been out with such a beautiful (younger) woman. He was a mess when they'd started dating staying up late, going out with friends regularly, playing dungeons and dragons, watching an irresponsible amount of anime and cooking compulsively. Cassi cured him of all of that. Well everything except the cooking. He got an extra job, moved her and her son into a nicer neighborhood and began to write again. While she wasn't a huge fan of his work, she did tell him that if he was serious about writing, then he would make time to write. But not before working his jobs, doing chores around the house, and spending quality family time together which consisted mostly of validating Cassi's feelings. He knew it was important. Women like her needed that. She'd had a rough life. Her mother was so judgmental, and her father who was a professor at MIT had killed himself when she was only six. He was a genius, and according to Cassi, "very, very good looking." Women were profoundly jealous of Cassi's good looks too, but he didn't notice. Observation was not his strong suit though as Cassi liked to remind him. He knew she was above his pay grade, but he won her over with his undying loyalty. Sure, sometimes he blew up. He had even screamed at her before, but that was because he was a piece of unlovable shit and couldn't take all the "loving truth" she unloaded on him. She was only critical because he was so irresponsible. Recently though, he'd drawn a line in the sand after she blew up when he got that old beer fridge, she wanted to keep "a proper garage for her car." He wasn't sure what had gotten into him lately. Cassi believed he had gotten a big head. Maybe he had, but if not for his writer's group encouraging him, he would not have met his agent and wouldn't have a publishing deal. And that would mean no advance. He knew she was disappointed he'd told her no. He knew she was frustrated that his beer fridge caused her to park in the driveway. He knew she was insecure about the way it might look to the neighbors, but he also knew that once the money hit the bank tomorrow, she would be right as rain. He had already packed the car, cleaned the house from top to bottom, arranged for his friend Jeff to work on her vehicle while they were gone, and had bought Cassi a new watch which he was going to present to her at his Mom's place. He couldn't wait.

Cassi couldn't sleep. All she could think about was Abel and that skinny little kid cuddling while watching that stupid movie earlier. He'd been hurt when she told him before bed that she wasn't going to his mother's with them. "Well, I'm hurt too," she said. He was being affectionate with that girl and not her. Abel argued that she never wanted to cuddle, but that wasn't her fault. He was always so sweaty. She clenched her fist and imagined punching his fat, pathetic face as he explained how emotionally neglected and abused the dumb girl had been. He wasn't a man. He was a man child. That was it. She was not going to go if that girl went. "She is not family!"

Abel's eyebrow shot up. "She is literally your blood relative." That was not the point. How many times had she said to him over the last week that family is about relationship. She didn't know this kid. She'd been avoiding her drug addicted sister for years. "She can go to her biological father," she said and then suffered the dramatic reaction from Abel. He whined about how the kid's father was a felon and that every time his name came up Mary withdrew. Whatever, he is her father. As she laid in her bed, the noises clanging in her head were becoming unbearable. That goddamned tree made her want to, well, she didn't know what. It felt as though the branches were scratching the inside of her skull. "Fuck this."

She sat up and grabbed her phone and went downstairs. She texted furiously and set a date to meet in a public place where there would be plenty of people. She wanted to be safe. Abel would be at work, she could hand-off the kid and be done with all of this drama. If anyone asked her what happened, she would claim he kidnapped her. It would be her word against a felon's. Abel will get over it. She looked up from the phone screen and saw the moonlit shadow of the tree. Abel had wanted to plant a tree as a symbol of this new family he wanted. She thought a vacation to Vegas would be better. Pictures to last a lifetime. She told him he planted it too close to the house. Too fucking close to the house. She was going to do something about that.

Frozen Freud in Three Part Harmony

Cassi marched into the garage and hit the opener. As the door lifted, intense moonlight filled the garage. She found the ax on top of the stupid beer fridge. Maybe she would take the ax to the old metal later, but now she slammed the blade against the base of the tree repeatedly while an old tune played in the recesses of her mind," By the Light of the Silvery Moon", and quieted the humming for a little while. She was going to teach Abel a lesson. There must be consequences and she was going to give them to him.

Her vision blurred, and when she could see clearly again, she found herself lying in the cool grass. She was drenched and it felt good against her wet skin. The tree leaned trepidatiously against the house. She'd almost cut all the way through, but not quite. She got to her feet. That will teach him. Maybe he can think about while he's driving across God's country to see his useless mother. Maybe they all can. She stumbled back into the garage and then stopped. That humming fridge. The handle of the ax slid through her loosened grip until the metalhead met the concrete with a clang. The old refrigerator proudly displayed its brand in the typical 1950s style font emblazoned at the top. It was hideous with patches of rust and dents like polka dots all over it. She tightened her grip on the handle then moved swiftly toward the eye sore to strike but just as the ax head descended toward its target, she stopped short. A familiar tune could be heard coming ever so slightly from the annoying appliance. She lowered the ax and put her ear against the freezer door. What she heard from inside made her jump back in surprise. She tightened her grip on the ax handle and stared dumbfounded at the ugly box. Was that a man humming... inside the freezer? She examined it more closely and found that the fridge wasn't even plugged in. What the fuck? She reached out with trembling fingers, grasped the handle, and pulled the freezer door open slowly.

"Nice to see you," the disembodied, mustached head said to her, quite calmly. Cassi's mouth hung open in complete shock. Why was Lorraine's husband in Abel's freezer? "I know these are strange circumstances," Frank said, "and unfortunately, I have no arms to hold you with." Cassi smiled nervously at him and whispered, "How?"

"Oh, my sweet girl, you know how," Frank replied. "You've always known."

"Abel did this to you?"

"Doesn't really matter as far as I'm concerned. I'm just glad I'm finally able to be alone with you." Frank's eyes danced with desire. She nodded slowly and her buzzing brain tried to make sense of it all. "Of course, course he did," she agreed. "I always knew he was jealous. He always tried to hide it, but I knew. I knew it bothered him. Bastard is a killer."

"And a killer of dreams...your dreams, Cassi." Frank sympathized with her. He may actually understand her better than she thought he did. "Well you're the cop. What should we do?" Cassi didn't give him time to answer. "I know. I'll wait until after they leave for their trip in the morning. Then I'll call."

"Brilliant idea." Frank gushed. "You are so intelligent. I've always known that about you." Cassi knew Abel wouldn't hurt the kids. Cassi continued fleshing out her plan with Frank. "He loves Adrian even though the kid thinks he's a dumbass, and Mary... well, we know how he really feels." Frank winked at Cassi. "Yes, we know exactly how he feels about the Mary situation." Cassi felt her cheeks warm. He really appreciated her. "Ok, that's what I'll do. It's the safest thing. Wait till he's gone."

Frank cleared his throat. "Will you tell me about that marketing idea you had? You know the one you shared with that snotty agent your husband has? I thought it was brilliant." Cassi welcomed the new topic of conversation. There wasn't any reason to waste any more time thinking about Abel and his offspring. Cassi smiled, "I'd love to!"

Cassi woke up groggy - wrapped up in her sheets and alone. She was still in that in between state of consciousness and dream, and she vaguely remembered goodbyes and did she hear the muffled sound of children crying? Leaning on one elbow, she rubbed her face. Her body ached, especially her hands. She smiled at the idea of Abel seeing the tree in the state she left it in. That's why he didn't say anything before he left. That's what he always did... he pouted. Well, he had many miles to think about what he'd done to her. As she made her way to the stairs, she glanced into her son's room. It was a mess which was very unlike him. Abel never helped discipline. She always had to be both father and mother to Adrian. Boys need structure and consequences, but Abel had no spine. She stood over the boy's disheveled bed and looked at his open notebook. He had such nice penmanship. She'd taught him that. "Hell a cometh swiftly" was written at the top of the page and underneath were the words "All of Them Witches."

"I knew that one," she announced to nobody. She would text him the answer later. She looked at the unmade bed again. Adrian knew the rules. A messy bed meant no video games. There must be consequences and she was going to give it to him. She gathered his games and went to put them in the attic, but when she turned the knob, the door was locked. Damn Abel. She told him they needed to rekey the door, but of course, he'd done nothing about it. She pulled harder, but her hands ached. She gave up quickly. Goddamn him. She went to get a screwdriver to pry it open.

As she moved through the grimy kitchen she thought of Abel in jail and wondered how he would handle it. Didn't men in prison violate each other? She was sure he would be on the receiving end, and it made her laugh. What would she wear at the trial? What if reporters wanted to interview her? She had time to figure it out. She didn't have to call the cops until she was ready. It's not like Frank was going anywhere. He was hers for now, and she was happy to finally have a man in her life that was attentive and listened to her. She found the screw driver. She was sure Frank missed her, but she needed to hold that boy responsible first and then freshen up before she saw him again. She went upstairs to the attic and then went to shower. Quickly, she made her way to the garage, her hair still wet. She opened the freezer door, full of anticipation.

"Good morning, beautiful!" The blue-eyed man winked at her, and Cassi gasped. Corbin's head sat next to Frank's, and her eyes darted between the two men she'd seen only days before at the PTA meeting. She looked at Frank for answers, but he said "I'm just as surprised as you are. Dumbfounded even." Cassi didn't know what to say except to ask Corbin how he was.

"Well, I'm much better now that the hypnotic and bodacious Cassi is here. Your skin is glowing, and you smell like peaches. Yum." Cassi's pale face blushed "Yes, it's my shampoo." Corbin continued to flirt. "Delightful." He winked at her again.

"I'm so sorry Abel got you too." Corbin was quick to ease her mind. "Cassi, don't you apologize for anything. We are all Abel's victims here. Those magnificent full lips should never apologize for anything. They are meant for other things."

She suddenly looked worried. What was he implying? "For kissing, darling. Lingering, wet, sensuous kissing. I know you had that jaw injury, and I don't care for that filthy stuff anyway. Anastasia is always trying to do obscene things with me. It makes me uncomfortable."

Cassi was relieved. "Yeah, Abel is so gross. The things he wants to do in the bedroom make my stomach flip." Corbin curled his lip in disgust then added, "Did you know Anastasia's breasts are fake?"

Cassi clapped her hands together. "I knew it!" she exclaimed.

"If you don't mind me saying so, I adore your all natural figure," Corbin said with a gleam in his eyes. Cassi blushed again.

"Looks and intelligence," Frank inserted, "a tremendous combination." Cassi giggled. Finally, men who really cared. Men who appreciated her mind and her body.

She slept especially hard that night and had vivid dreams. The kind a good girl doesn't talk about. A weeping penetrated her dreams, but it was peaceful. A gentle childlike sobbing she heard mixed with the humming, and she could only think it must be from the utter ecstasy she felt in her body after her racy fantasy.

She rolled over and looked at her phone. Mary's bio-dad let her know that he and Mary would be staying with some friends of his up in the mountains. No one would find them there. He assured she would be safe and sound. She texted back a thumbs up emoji.

Cassi spent the next few hours cleaning and ignoring the constant ringing of both the landline and her cell. She'd checked the phone, and it was CPS. She didn't need them anymore. They were useless anyway. They hadn't sent her the documents she needed to enroll Mary in school yet, and she wondered what kind of people worked for the government. Lazy people, obviously. She muted her phone.

The landline rang again. Abel always called the landline because he's a technological caveman. She pulled the plug out of the wall. Fucking coward. She was going to leave him. She'd contemplated it for a while now and told anyone within earshot how much she endured, but she stayed because Adrian needed a father. She knew she'd been slumming, but she was done. Now she had two men who adored her. She wondered what would happen if she didn't call the police about the murders, but she had to. How else would Abel be punished? People must suffer consequences for their actions.

Maybe she could keep Frank and Corbin after Abel was locked up for life. She delighted in the thought of finally having time to write her book. Maybe then she'd do a book tour and a television appearance or two with her heads sitting beside her. They would be so proud. And wouldn't her mother be jealous? She'd always wanted to be a writer, but she wasn't willing to do the work. Lazy mother. People are inherently lazy.

Hours later, Cassi was proud of her hard work. The house smelled of bleach and Lysol. Maybe she would actually get to keep a clean house for more than 5 minutes since the kid was leaving and Abel would be locked up soon. Moving the kitchen table to the garage was difficult, and she wasn't much of a cook, so she had food delivered. Cassi was happy she was able to find the only heirloom her grandmother had left her - a white linen tablecloth with beautiful embroidered butterflies along the edge. She'd had to use the screwdriver to unlock the attic again to get to it, but it was worth the trouble. She'd also found Mary's dead cell phone that Abel had bought the kid just a few weeks ago laying on the attic floor. The ungrateful child had left it behind. There must be consequences and she'd given them to her.

She looked down at her lingerie, the ornate bustier and garters Abel had gotten her for Valentine's a couple of years ago. Earlier, she had to cut off the tags, but after the struggle to get it on, she admired her reflection. "Maybe black is a good color on me." She powdered her breasts and remembered she needed to light the new candles. A muffled voice called out from the freezer.

"Cassi, what are you doing?" asked Frank. Corbin echoed after him, "Cassi, we miss you and that spectacular figure!"

"I know, I know," she said, adjusting a placement. "I've got a surprise for you!"

"Well, we have one for you too!" Frank shouted. She clapped her hands excitedly. She wondered again what his mustache would feel like. Like heaven. A tickly heaven. That would be a nice surprise. She grabbed a lighter from the drawer, and lit the candles hastily. As she opened the freezer door, in the most sultry voice she could manage she began to say, "Surpr-" then she saw a new noggin in the freezer!

"Cassi!" said Bob, "Wow! You look amazing!"

Frank noticed how much effort she'd put into her presentation. "Your ensemble is from the French collection that Haute Tension created and designed for maximized sensual appearance and durability. Well done, Cassi."

"Thank you, Frank." Her attention turned to Bob. "Bob, how did you get here?"

"I know it's crazy!" Bob exclaimed. "Can you believe Abel could get all of us in here? The guy can barely tie his shoes, but he managed to figure out how to kill us, behead us, and stick us in the freezer without you knowing. Remember how he made reservations for the wrong day for your anniversary last year? I'm amazed, and to be honest, a little embarrassed for him."

Cassi laughed continuously all throughout the magical dinner. The wine she had purchased earlier, a damn fine pinot, helped loosen a few morals, and as the candles melted to their base, the conversation became more personal and intimate. When Corbin asked to kiss her, she didn't mind. She didn't even mind the garlic she tasted as she gently flicked her toungue into his mouth. She would help him with that later. Then the others each asked for a kiss of their own. She was caught up in the naughty moment. In an act of unusual passion, she ripped the tablecloth away and the carefully arranged plates crashed to the ground as she crawled onto the table, writhing in passion. She was lost in physical bliss so she didn't notice the daylight crashing in as the garage door lifted and exposed the freaky scene.

"Get on the ground and put your hands up!" She was in a compromising position. Later she would think about the demanding voice. It sounded a lot like Frank's. Did he have a mustache like him? She liked kissing a man with one. She froze. The only thing she said was, "Abel did it."

Cassi Stirn explained everything as best she could at the police station. They were all shocked at the way Abel treated her. Must be disturbing to have something like that happen in our neighborhood, she acknowledged. She appreciated all the visitors hanging on her every word but thought the cuffs were unnecessary. She had trouble focusing sometimes, she kept catching glimpses of herself in the mirror. She looked amazing. She was sure she caught several of her visitors enjoying her buxom womanliness.

She was disappointed that there was no paparazzi waiting to take her picture. No press waiting to interview her. She wore the blush chiffon blouse for the hearing anyway. She told them everything. She explained how Abel must have finally grown a backbone after years of denying his jealousy because of all the men who stared at her. She told them about the time he proposed but he didn't do it right so she made him do it again, but he still failed. There was also the incident when he didn't defend her when that slut waitress was so dismissive and ultimately, how he had planned to get rid of Mary by giving her to that child molester father of hers. He was a bad seed, and he deserved to be punished. Throw away the key she told the judge. It was good to get it off her chest and have these esteemed men listen so patiently. She felt the weight lift. Now if only the Candy Cunt court reporter would stop staring at her. Jealous. Jealousy will eat you up lady, just like Abel. The pictures that were presented were disturbing. Why Abel would finger paint all over the walls? What had gotten into him? He was dramatic, but this was extreme. In red, "All of Them Witches" was scrawled everywhere. Did his jealousy reach beyond the men's attraction to her and make him jealous of even her and her son's game? He must have done it while she was having the time of her life in the garage. He did always manage to ruin her good time.

For twenty years Frank had seen some of the most disturbed souls in the great state of Texas, but he had never experienced a woman so dissociative and delusional as Cassi. It was weird for him to think about the fact that her kid had gone to school with his. The only case he'd heard of that bothered him this much was the case against the Houston lady that drowned all five of her children in the tub claiming that God had told her to. Frank and his partner walked Cassi down the corridor to her new living space while she hummed an eerie tune. Somehow what the lady in Houston had done seemed more tragic. This was just pure evil.

Cassi appreciated that the police had put her somewhere that would keep her safe from Abel. She didn't like being locked in, but as the moon shown through the window in the stark white room, she was comforted by a familiar song. She turned her head to find her gentleman callers singing deeply and richly, "By the Light of the Silvery Moon," in three part harmony. A sick, sweet smile crept across her face. "You know me so well." Bob was slightly off pitch, but that's ok. They would work on that later.

J. P. DILDINE

J.P. Dildine used to skip school so he could go read. His writing has been forever shaped by the first 4 books he read one fall while sitting under a county road bridge next to the Brazos River. "The Hitchhiker's Guide to the Galaxy," "Jaws,""Silence of the Lambs," and "The Stand." Throw in the influence of the hordes of film and television he consumed and you have the hot mess that he is today. A new novelist, his debut "Toby Finkelstein and The Dandies of the Underworld" will be out in Fall of 2018. J.P. lives in Austin,TX with his badass wife who edits his crazy writing and three creative kids. When he's not turning tricks, he likes to write music, ramble about brain science, and drink far too much beer.

https://www.facebook.com/jpdildine/

UPGRADED

By Christina Bergling

ROUTER

Dave drummed his fingers impatiently on his standing desk. He stood in baggy pajama bottoms, crossing and uncrossing his ankles. The network icon mocked him from his taskbar, tragically branded with a tiny red x. He tried to ignore his lack of Wi-Fi, but the indicator was so inconveniently close to the clock.

Two full hours had passed since the Comcast technician was supposed to replace his wireless router. To "upgrade" his router to their new standard model.

"Fucking stupid Comcast," Dave muttered. "Never on time. Forcing me into this stupid router upgrade. Can't even show up to take over my damn network. When is Google fiber going to make it to this hellhole?"

Dave's voice echoed in his home office. Anxiety teemed on the fringe of his skin, that crawling disconnected feeling. His phone buzzed on the desktop, and he knew another email waited for him. The idea of them accumulating stacked heavily on his brain. He could not bear to open the queue, so neutered by his lack of connectivity. The small phone screen was not enough; the cell 4G LTE network was not enough.

Instead, Dave found the customer service number in his call history and dialed again.

"Good morning. Thank you for calling Comcast customer service. My name is Dante. For quality assurance, this call may be recorded. How can I help you today?" the voice said when he finally reached a human.

"Hi Dante," Dave said. "A technician was supposed to arrive here over two hours ago to replace my router. No one has showed."

"I'm so sorry, sir. Rest assured, Milton will be there today to get you taken care of."

"What is the point of the two-hour window if he can't even show during it?" Dave growled.

"Often times, our technicians encounter unexpected obstacles at the previous appointment. He will call the number on your account when he is en route to your location."

"I don't even want this new router. You should not force your customers to use mandated equipment. I have a great router now."

"I'm sorry, sir. Updating to these standard routers is the only way to ensure the best service for our customers."

"That doesn't even make any sense!" Dave yelled.

"I'm sorry you feel that way, sir. If you would like to lodge a complaint, I can transfer you to our Customer Relations department. If you are at all unsatisfied with your internet coverage, we invite you to research additional providers."

"There are no other providers!"

"Yes, we know. Is there anything else I can help you with today?" Dante's voice thickened in Dave's ear, turning his stomach.

"You didn't help me at all."

"Thank you for being a loyal customer, Derrick."

"It's Dave."

"Have a wonderful day."

Dante disconnected the call. Dave flexed his fingers around the phone case and willed himself not to chuck it into the wall. The cascade of meticulously arranged model starships it would cause served as a stronger deterrent than the price tag of replacing the device.

Dave paced over the area rug swirled in black and green. His footsteps drew ragged lines on the fibers, stomped in obscure patterns. He would log onto a gaming console, but all of his games were online. He palmed his phone briefly, scrolling through reddit and checking his chat threads, but his mind refused to accept the distraction. He scanned through his inflating inbox queue but felt the choking anxiety at not being able to connect to the corporate VPN and all the associated tools as his task list only swelled.

Dave heaved up his oversized Starfleet Academy mug and gulped down his third cup coffee. The doorbell finally chimed.

Milton casually lumbered into Dave's home, arrogant and detached. Dave glared at him from the sides of his eyes as he scrawled his signature on the work order. Then he paced anxiously in the hallway outside the office as Milton "upgraded" his router.

When Milton had finished violating Dave's network and left him to his restored connectivity, Dave returned to his computer to see a pleasantly enabled Wi-Fi symbol. He picked up the network information Milton had dropped in his hand on his way out.

"What in the hell?" Dave breathed. "That motherfucker renamed my network. You don't rename another man's network! Kobal? Who the hell names a network Kobal?"

The rage prickled along Dave's neck, causing his throat to constrict and his pulse to throb in his temples. His legs become twitchy beneath him, causing him to cross and uncross his ankles. Dave had always named his network Federation, so that it could properly connect his gaming laptop (Enterprise), his work computer (Voyager), his neglected spare laptop (Kelvin) and his servers (DSK7, DS5, and DS9). Such a fleet could not exist on a network named Kobal.

Comcast, in its infinite customer service, had stopped providing configuration access to the router or network. Dave would have to hack through all of that but another time. He had to submit to Kobal, get all his devices back online, and get some work done.

Frustration continued to roll over Dave in waves. He felt the heat swell in his belly, bubble up under his ribs, and wash over his face. Selecting Kobal on each device made him nauseous. Each email he read was another he could have answered three hours ago. He could feel the weight of all the wasted seconds, minutes, hours. All the seconds, minutes, hours, he would have to recoup that night instead of gaming.

"Comcast communist bullshit," Dave said to himself.

As soon as Dave's status turned green, his boss pinged him.

Bill: Hey, Dave. You missed the SCRUM.

Dave: Yeah, I've been offline all day. Comcast just left. I sent an email a few hours ago.

Bill: Didn't see it.

"Of course you didn't see it, asshole," Dave said to the screen. "That would require you to actually do your damn job."

Bill: Where are we with those new automation scripts?

"Why they're right where I left them when you told me to develop a script for a product I don't even know. Firmly up your tight ass, Bill."

Dave: I will get them uploaded after I deliver the regression plan to Bob.

Bill: COB?

"COB is four fucking hours from now, you incompetent dick. Guess you can't count that high."

Dave: Before SCRUM tomorrow.

Bill: Fine.

An uncomfortable pause.

Bill: Thanks for your hard work.

"Yeah, screw you, Bill. You antagonizing moron."

As Dave typed, he noticed the sweat accumulating on his palms. He absentmindedly wiped his hands on his pajama pants and continued typing. Yet the sweat secreted again almost immediately, accompanied by a sliding moisture trickling along his forehead.

"It's hotter than Hell in here."

Dave placed his fingertip on the power button of his phone until the screen twitched to life. He swiped over the pages to locate his home management app.

"100 degrees? How did this get set to 100 degrees?"

Tapping furiously on the screen, Dave reduced the setting and wiped at his forehead again. He placed the phone on the stand of his center monitor and closed the irritating chat with his tech lead.

"Tech lead, my ass," he mumbled. "How am I supposed to account for the scope for a customer environment I've never spec-ed or seen?"

Dave shook the rant loose and rolled his neck in preparation to draft an avalanche of conjecture, duplication of previous projects, and straight bullshit. He opened the document he started last week and squinted at the screen. As he typed, a shadow seemed to pass over the monitors, almost like something moved behind him. Yet the monitors were the light source in the room, so a shadow could not get cast upon them. And Dave did not purchase these models out of his own money to deal with glare.

Dave looked behind him anyway, instinctively. Only a fleet of model spaceships silently pointed back at him. The usual silence felt altered, inhabited somehow. As if the vexing presence of Milton destroying the network Federation had never left.

Dave's phone hummed and scooted below his monitor. Relieved at the distraction, he gathered it up in his hands. His Tinder app boasted multiple messages. A slight flutter stirred at the back of his brain at the increased notification count.

Regan: Hi sexy! What are you up to?

Emily: Hey handsome. How are you?

Dave usually did not enjoy this much interest on the hook up app. He had been steadily chatting with Beverly for a couple weeks now. He had yet to meet her, so it couldn't hurt to evaluate other prospects.

When Dave turned his attention back to his document, it was blank, fresh and untouched as a new draft. He felt the panic run cold along his arms as his mind spun as empty as the document. Frantically, he tabbed, scouring all open applications. He pecked at CTRL+Z until the computer binged agitated at him. Nothing restored the hours of work.

"Shit," he breathed.

At least twenty hours of his best fabrication evaporated. No trace lingered on his local drive. Nothing appeared on the cloud backup, which he had specifically checked Friday night before signing off. Anger seized his throat, a strangle hold on his breathing, making his hands feel tingly and far away.

He groaned heavily and threw his head back. His fingertips resisted the very idea. He did not want to reduce himself to the query, but he also could not stand the idea of telling Bob he lost the plan. Gritting his teeth, he forced his hands to the keys. He drafted the email to Roy and Maurice in IT.

Dave felt the sweat squeezing out of him again, trickling maddeningly from his pores. He did not know if it was from the temperature or his own frustration.

"Come on, boys," Dave said. "Give me a miracle since I'm too retarded to even keep a regression plan."

Just saying the words make him writhe again.

"You guys know everything down there. Maybe you can find the magically vanishing file and save my ass."

Dave snatched up his vacant coffee mug and stomped out of the office. As he walked down the hall, he heard a whoosh swell from the living room. He felt the air displacement against his face. His bare feet stuttered along the hardwood, and he pivoted to chase the sound.

The electric, Wi-Fi-enabled fireplace roared to life in his living room. The flames danced and licked over the fake logs at a feverish setting Dave did not know the fireplace achieved. Before his feet even transitioned to the carpet, he could feel the extra heat in the already stifling and humid house press against him.

Dave thundered back up the stairs to retrieve his phone. He punched at his home management app. The thermostat had climbed back to 100 degrees. The fireplace was set on high. Dave scrolled the settings down again.

"I'm going to have to call these guys."

He moved to press the contact button when he heard the notification on his computer, followed by the vibration and a flurry of chimes on his phone. He side-stepped before his monitors. His inbox has inflated by 30 in just the time he had failed to fill his coffee. He squinted, perplexed to see the timestamps reached back over an hour and that some of the subjects were prefixed by "Re:".

"What in the hell is going on here?"

As he shifted his mouse across the screen, a new chat from Bill popped up.

Bill: DAVE, WHERE THE HELL ARE YOU?

Bill: WHY AREN'T YOU ANSWERING YOUR EMAIL?

Bill: WHY AREN'T YOU ANSWERING YOUR PHONE?

"My phone didn't ring." He confirmed in his call history. Nothing.

Dave: What's wrong?

Bill: WHAT'S WRONG??

Bill: The automatic scripts. WHAT HAVE YOU DONE?

"What is he talking about? I didn't do anything."

Dave frantically clicked through the latest emails.

You assured us this script was properly vetted. Running in our environment leaked our test customer credit data to an undisclosed location. Had this been in our production environment rather than QA, it would have put the real identities of all of our customers at risk, and we would have pursued legal action.

"Holy shit!" Dave yelled.

He jerked away from the keyboard in horror. His elbow collided with his empty mug, and it tumbled from the elevated plane and shattered on the floor. Dave did not even look at it.

"I didn't send any scripts. Hell, I didn't even write any scripts."

Dave combed through his sent emails. The first few entries were entirely foreign yet stamped with his name at times he had not sent anything.

"I never sent this."

And the next.

"I never sent this."

And the next.

"I didn't write this!"

And the last.

"I did not send these scripts!"

Panic constricted Dave's heart. The pressure seemed to stifle the beating, and Dave felt the throbbing lack of blood flow in his ears. Every follicle along his skin arched and bristled.

"What is going on here? Did I send these scripts? Maybe I'm fucking losing it. No. No, no, no. I didn't write or send these damn scripts."

Bill: We need you in the office for damage control. When can you be here?

Dave: Maybe an hour.

Bill: Get here now.

"Shit. Shit shit SHIT! I'm so fucked. I'm so completely screwed. I don't even know what happened!" Dave screamed to the empty room.

His phone chirped in answer to him.

"What in the hell can it be now?"

Tinder boasted more direct messages from both Regan and Emily. Dave did not have the time to indulge them, but he could not leave that red notification indicator glaring at him from the screen. When he opened the first thread, his mouth gaped, and the phone nearly toppled from his fingers.

At the bottom of the chat, the last message from his account, a picture of an erect yet unimpressive penis loomed. The bearer's face did not appear in the frame, but based on skin tone and body hair color, it certainly could be misconstrued as Dave.

"That's not my dick! I didn't send any picture of a dick."

Regan did not seem offended by the image. Oddly, she reacted enticed. She rattled off a blur of messages that made Dave cringe.

Regan: What time can I come over? Give me your address.

"Gross. I am not that guy! I don't send dick pics."

Dave squeezed his fingers around the edge of his phone and tapped it firmly against his forehead, groaning.

"I don't have time for this. I have to get to the office."

He turned to hurry to the shower when his phone erupted in a fury of chimes and vibrations.

"What now?"

Dave's text messaging notification counter numbered 10 then climbed to 11 then 12. The buzzing continued uninterrupted. His inbox flooded with messages from his mother, his sister, his aunts and uncles, his buddies. As they continued to rack up, it looked like everyone in his contact list.

He tapped the message from his mother. The same small penis greeted him at attention.

"Oh fuck, no."

Mom: David, how could you send this to me? Why would you send this to me? What's going on? Are you OK?

Dave paged back to the inbox and checked every message. All the same raging erection. All angry and confused replies. Dave wobbled backward on unsteady legs. His consciousness swam in the frothing sea of his panic and dismay. His heart dropped into the empty pit of his stomach. He lost his hands all together.

Through the numbness, he tapped at the screen. He returned to his mother's message and pressed his finger in the text field. The keyboard did not appear. He pressed the phone button to call her. The phone did not respond. Instead, he watched foreign words appear in the field then leap into the conversation.

Dave: Because you cursed me with a baby dick, Mom!

The anger exploded in Dave's head, the charges causing his skull to rattle. He gripped the possessed device tightly and hurled it with all his might toward the floor. The gesture itself felt like a sin after so much careful juggling to never drop the coveted technology. Yet he whipped it toward the ground with a desperate yowl.

Dave could not bear to watch the impact. Despite his rage, he flinched away. The ominous thud edged with a telling crack. He stormed out of the room, panting and stomping. Then he heard a text alert ring out behind him and froze. He hurried back and stared down at the floor where he had chucked the foul device. It was not there.

It chimed again from below Dave's center monitor.

Dave lost his breath. He stood bewildered, somewhere between terror and insanity. His jaw bobbed in unconsummated words. The heat thickened the air around him, cradled him in his shock. It pressed down around him on all sides. Sweat began matting his ragged hair and soaking through his shirt.

The computer chirped again. Not corporate collaboration, not email. Dave did not even bother with an outburst. Instead, he moved mechanically, detached to the screen—his body's default position. The task bar icon for his instant messaging client flashed orange at him. His online gaming thread had been raging on without him as his phone was distributing pornographic images to his entire virtual address book.

C4ptPriiiiiC3: L0Qtus, what the fuck are you doing?

Gh0st_1987: I did not sign in for a day game for this bullshit, man.

McT@v!$h: You are ruining our entire fucking campaign. We are never going to recover from this bullshit.

B4hlsD33p: Fuck you. You're out. Don't message us again

System: You have been removed from this conversation.

Dave fled the office again. He stumbled sloppily down the stairs, wet hands skidding down the handrails. In the living room, the fire blazed even more ravenous, leaving black scorch patterns along the glass. His enormous, flat smart TV had turned itself on to show his avatar dancing on the battlefield, pumping rounds into friendlies.

He stared at the screen, watching his once proud character utterly humiliate him. His heart could not sink any lower into the heavy pit opening inside him, yet it managed to seize up as the crashing sound sent a startle ripping over his nerves.

Dave's brain felt raw, overstimulated. He moved from the TV on sheer instinct, some damning blend of curiosity and fear. He hurried around the corner into his kitchen to witness his Wi-Fi-enabled refrigerator steadily spitting ice cubes out over the floor. Each glinting chunk careened to the hardwood then skidded across the grain, immediately beginning to melt in the sweltering climate. Already, puddles spread and comingled into a growing pool on his floor.

Then the doorbell rang.

"What in the HELL is going on?" Dave's voice exited his lips foreign and ragged with unnerving desperation. "Who in the HELL could that possibly be now?"

He was losing the ability to form coherent thoughts. His mind managed the question but did not reach into the possibilities. Or the consequences. His dumber, baser instincts simply marched him to the front door.

A ghastly creature greeted him on his small stoop. His jaw dropped heavy and unmitigated.

"Oh my GOD, Dave!" the thing screeched. "You look even better than your Tinder pic!"

She pushed past him without invitation. He could taste, even chew, the odor of stale cigarettes wafting up from her cracked skin. Her frame was so sickly and skeletal that she seemed to click when she swung her hips past him. Once she had fully penetrated his home, she spun around to face him. Her eyes bulged terrifyingly wide, and her mouth hovered agape to reveal yellowed teeth clinging to receding gums. Raw and agitated sores speckled and festered on her face.

"Who are you?" Dave managed to stutter through his gag reflex.

"Duh! I'm Regan. You sent me a picture of your cock like half hour ago."

"What are you doing here?"

"You told me to come, dummy. I'm here to work you out. So let's get working."

Her horrendously spaced teeth grinned wider. The way she tilted her head made him think it might spin around backward. She threw up her arms with limp wrists and dove at him. Dave shrieked in a startled and disgusted octave and darted under her intended embrace. He sprinted through his own hallway and rounded back into the kitchen, racing around the corner.

His feet slipped into the deepening puddle of disintegrated ice cubes on the floor. He heard the splash of his footsteps before he felt the traction vanish beneath. He flailed his arms desperately, groping against his balance or toward any surface or handhold. He only caught handfuls of thick and hot air. The floor came up fast. He saw it coming in slow motion yet felt the impact of its speed. The pain exploded across his forehead as his senses receded into the haze.

"Where did you go, baby? What game are we playing?" Dave heard the grating voice somewhere at the edge of his hearing.

Dave pulled his head from the water in time to see Regan break into the kitchen. She had shed her shirt at some point, exposing the blue map of track marks along her arms and the crisscrossed paths of scars and stretch marks across her sickly thin abdomen.

"Oh, a slip and slide. You know I'm slippery when wet, lover," she rasped. As she spoke, the movement of her cheek split one sore, and it leaked down her face slowly.

Upgraded

Regan launched herself into the air. Dave saw her incoming shadow eclipse the light, blot out the world. Dave's face contorted as his sad, electronic life flashed before his eyes. He scrambled backward, almost swimming through the water. Regan collided with the floor in his wake. Her head bounced on the hardwood then fell still. As Dave clawed further away, he could still hear her heavy respirations rippling the water.

Dave fumbled across the carpet soaked through with the melting ice. The fridge continued to spit cubes angrily. They splashed mockingly behind him. He choked on the hot air as the sweat poured from his face. He could feel his heartbeat in every inch of his flesh, his skin painfully sensitive drenched in adrenaline. The nausea from the smell of Regan's sores lingered at the back of his throat.

He strangled the doorknob. He had to get out of there. He had to get out of this cursed house. The knob near burned his hand, but the door did not budge. He looked down at the deadbolt, controlled by his home management app. It blinked red at him.

Locked.

He had not locked it behind Regan. He did not even remember shutting the door after she barged past him. He wrenched the deadbolt over only to hear the mechanism engage and roll it locked again.

"Fuck!" Dave screamed, hopelessly.

He dreaded returning to the office. He did not think the phone would allow him to affect the app anyway, but he did not know what else to try.

He ascended the stairs gingerly, fearfully. His pulse rattled on his fraying nerves. His eyes burned from being held so wide. The office seemed quiet enough, normal enough. He crossed side steps as he eased cautiously toward his desk. He reached toward the demon phone when the monitor above flickered.

A draft email opened itself on the desktop. Dave looked down to see the keys depress themselves in patterns his fingertips recognized.

To: corporate-all-mailinglist

The enlivened computer attached an unknown video file but provided no content above Dave's clear and identifying signature block, which included all his contact information. The Send button twitched, and the draft window disappeared.

Almost to answer his question, the computer launched the video file it had just provided to every single inbox in the corporate directory.

In the video player, Dave saw himself from the view of his computer's webcam, below his right monitor and used for the SCRUM meetings he loathed every day. Video Dave's smug mug donned an irritated curl. He stared between the screens as he clicked away on the keyboard.

"Of course you didn't see it, asshole. That would require you to actually do your damn job."

Video Dave shook his head back and forth and rolled his shoulders.

"Why they're right where I left them when you told me to develop a script for a product I don't even know. Firmly up your tight ass, Bill."

Video Dave typed at the keyboard.

"COB is four fucking hours from now, you incompetent dick. Guess you can't count that high."

Video Dave stared at the computer with his eyes wide and unmoving in agitation through the uncomfortable pause.

"Yeah, screw you, Bill. You antagonizing moron."

The clip ended, and the black screen mirrored the blackness closing around Dave's mind.

"No," he mumbled. "No no no no NO!"

He backed away from the demon computer until his back gently collided with his shelves of starships. The models rattled on their perches then settled back into silence. In the distance, he saw the message pop up on the screen.

Bill: You fucking asshole, Dave. Don't bother coming in today. YOUR FIRED!

Bill: HR will ship you a box to return your equipment. Your passwords will be disabled immediately.

"NO!" Dave shrieked again.

He dove at the laptop cradled in the docking station. He intended to throw the accursed tech right out the window. He seized in both hands and went to rip it free of its connections.

The pain froze him. He felt hot and cold in every cell of his body simultaneously. The sensation surged the most intense at his contact with the laptop, yet he felt it vibrating down through his bones, charging them. His entire brain, every fiber of thought that remained, shrieked to release the laptop. Yet he could not. He was a prisoner of the pain.

When it finally relented, he collapsed to the floor, feeling like he was sizzling. The computer perched on the desktop completely unaffected.

Notifications began to pepper the screen. His passwords were relinquished; his accounts were revoked.

Dave scrambled across the floor and pulled himself into a ball against the wall under his fleets of starships. He dropped his head into his hands and went to pull his hair, but his hands were too sensitive.

"The router," he said to himself. The realization broke so clean and clear upon his fractured mind, the answer he should have known all along. "It has to be the router. Fucking Comcast."

Dave crawled across the area rug, weary of the computer, trying not to attract its attention. As if he could hide from the Wi-Fi anywhere in this house. He moved toward his server closet, where Kobal cohabitated with DS9.

The lights on the router should have blinked green to indicate a healthy connection; however, they blazed an eerie red instead. Each flash seemed to make a sound that Dave felt inside his head more than he heard. He sneakily wrapped his hand around his full replica Bat'leth propped in the corner and drew the weapon close to him.

As he raised the blade to strike, the router emitted a strange popping sound. Subtle, almost hidden in the darkness behind it. Dave cautiously and foolishly leaned toward the device, feeling the undulation of the indicator lights throb in his brain. He could almost feel the vibration hum off it through the air.

The router spat a single spark at his face. The tiny light arched toward Dave before diving to the carpet to ignite the synthetic fibers. The flames flared unnaturally, raging up as a wall between Dave and Kobal. Dave felt the heat singe his nerves. He flailed back as the fire followed him faster than he could move. He drew his legs up and launched himself backward. As he dragged himself past the doorframe of the office, he slammed the office door hard behind him.

Dave leaned against the hallway wall panting, singed, near tears, when the doorbell rang again.

Dave did not know what to do but answer it. It could not get any worse. Defeated, he dropped himself down the stairs. He grasped the knob tentatively but found the door unlocked. He opened to reveal a looming, dark shadow obscuring the sunlight.

"Hello, sir," the man said cheerily. "My name is Damien."

Damien smiled down at Dave with viciously straight, white teeth. His bright red eyes pulsated in the same sickening rhythm as the lights on the router. They matched the red Comcast logo on the breast of his shirt.

"I understand you are having some trouble upgrading to your new router. Let me come in and help you," Damien said.

As Damien crossed the threshold, the flames in the fireplace burst through the glass and crawled rapidly across the carpet, climbing toward the ceiling. The paint began to melt off the walls, and the water beneath Regan started to writhe and bubble. The door swung closed behind Damien gently, muffling Dave's desperate screams.

CHRISTINA BERGLING

Colorado-bred writer, Christina Bergling knew she wanted to be an author in fourth grade. In college, she pursued a professional writing degree and started publishing small scale. It all began with "How to Kill Yourself Slowly."

With the realities of paying bills, she started working as a technical writer and document manager, traveling to Iraq as a contractor and eventually becoming a trainer and software developer. She avidly hosted multiple blogs on Iraq, bipolar, pregnancy, running. She continues to write on Fiery Pen: The Horror Writing of Christina Bergling and Z0mbie Turtle.

Limitless Publishing released her novel *The Rest Will Come*. HellBound Books Publishing published her two novellas, *Savages* and *The Waning*. She is also feature in ten horror anthologies, including *Collected Christmas Horror Shorts, Graveyard Girlz, Carnival of Nightmares*, and *Demonic Wildlife*.

Bergling is a mother of two young children and lives with her family in Colorado Springs. She spends her non-writing time running, doing yoga and barre, belly dancing, taking pictures, traveling, and sucking all the marrow out of life.

christinabergling.com
facebook.com/chrstnabergling
@ChrstnaBergling
chrstnaberglingfierypen.wordpress.com
goodreads.com/author/show/11032481.Christina_Bergling
pinterest.com/chrstnabergling
instagram.com/fierypen/
amazon.com/author/christinabergling

Knit One, Pearl One

By Maxine Grey

Beryl rubbed the sleep out of her eyes. Squinting in the bright sunlight that seeped through the vertical blinds that she had forgotten to close the night before. Beryl swung her legs around to sit on the edge of the bed, bracing herself for the pain she knew would come with standing up. She cursed the arthritis that had plagued her, even after the hip replacement that was supposed to help the pain. Wincing, she moved gently to not aggravate things further.

A stickler for tidiness and routine, Beryl made the bed and plumped up the pillows on either side. Her eyes wandered to a large framed photo on her bedside table, her wedding photo taken almost 50 years ago. She looked so happy in the picture, glowing with hope and excitement for the future. Her husband, Arthur, looked so handsome, he was a real head-turner and she had felt like the luckiest woman on the planet to have snaffled him up to be her own.

A sadness washed over her, she missed Arthur, he had been her rock and her best friend for so many wonderful years. He was taken under duress and rapidly by lung cancer. Arthur had never smoked a cigarette in his life and kept himself fit and well. It was a huge injustice and Beryl had nursed him right to the bitter end. Watching him suffer was traumatic, seeing him evaporate and shrink as cancer ate him up from the inside. Having to watch this big, strong man become dependent, weakened, and suffering in such horrendous pain was so harrowing and difficult. His dignity stolen as his bowels and bladder stopped working on their own. He was a stubborn man and refused to go to a Hospice, instead kind home Nurses had helped him in his final few months.

Arthur had begged her to end his life early and she had been ripped apart at the time. He told her to just snuff his life out with a pillow, his eyes beseeching hers to help him. She understood he just wanted the pain to end but how could she *murder* her beloved? When animals were suffering and can no longer be helped they get euthanized. Humans, however, were not afforded that same option, which in her mind was wrong and unfair.

Feeling soft, warm fur brush up against her leg, Beryl looked at Riley, one of her beloved cats that had become her companions in later life. She didn't care that she was known as a crazy cat lady, she knew that the love they gave her was unconditional and it kept her going on the darkest of days. Riley head-butted her leg making Beryl smile. It was breakfast time and he wasn't going to let her forget it. Beryl put her slippers on, shrugged on her warm bathrobe, and shuffled to the kitchen to prepare breakfast for her five cats and herself. She sat down for a moment to pet each one of her five feline babies one by one. You would think they were starving by the purring and meowing that was going on.

Five bowls were laid out on the kitchen bench and Beryl dished out their food whilst talking to her little cat family. She knew she sounded a bit silly but really didn't care. When you live by yourself, even the sound of your own voice can be a comfort.

"Where are my little pussy-cats then? My babies, my bubbas. Look what Mummy has got for you! Salmon wet food and chicken dry biscuits for breakfast!"

"It's knitting group today, my fluffy-bums, so I expect best behaviour from you all. Do you hear me? That means you, Riley and Toddy, and you, Sultan and Dharma, and especially you, Tiddly-Weeny! No nibbling at toes or begging for food! Do Mummy proud."

With five cats happily eating, she popped the kettle on for her much-loved morning cup of Earl Grey tea and put two slices of wholemeal bread in the toaster. The same breakfast every single day for as many years as she could remember. She sighed as she looked out of her kitchen window at the grey concrete of her backyard. She remembered the day that Arthur had told her he had found a nice two-bedroom terraced house in the little village of Pity Me, only a few miles from Durham City Centre. Over the years they had decorated and modernised the house as different home trends came and went. The last bit of work to be done was a bathroom renovation. They had felt very posh having both a walk-in shower and a bathtub in the bathroom.

The kettle boiled just as the toaster popped and Beryl sat at the kitchen table, spreading salted butter and marmalade on her toast. Riley jumped up on the kitchen table, sniffing out the butter. "Oh, you are naughty, Riley! I know you love butter but on the table is not good manners is it?" Riley moved closer to Beryl and rubbed his head on her shoulder, purring for England as he did. "Oh, go on then, just a little bit." Beryl got a little bit of butter on her finger and watched as Riley licked it all off. Nothing wrong with spoiling her babies once in a while she figured.

The shrill tone of her phone ringing nearly had Beryl having an accident on the kitchen chair, incontinence issues becoming more and more obvious as the years went by. She had resorted to wearing incontinence or pee-pads as she called them for "oopsies" moments just like this one.

"Hello?"

"Oh hi, Beryl, it's Gladys here, Gladys Porter?"

"Gladys! How are you? You are up bright and early this morning."

"I know, I have so many chores to do today. I am just calling to check that knitting group is on this afternoon as planned?"

"Yes, absolutely. I am expecting yourself, Norma, Joyce, and Edna around at 2:00 p.m. Everybody is bringing a little plate of something yummy to share and of course, don't forget your knitting kit."

"Great, Beryl, I will see you this afternoon I'm looking forward to us all getting together for a knit and a natter. Bye now."

"Bye Gladys, see you then."

Beryl hung up the phone, turned to her little feline family, and said, "Make sure you all wash your gorgeous faces, you lot." She headed to the shower pondering just how grumpy these ladies had become and what she could do to help.

Freshly showered, a touch of face powder and peach lipstick applied, Beryl was dressed in her favourite pair of elasticated waist trousers (not sexy but ever-so practical) and a new cream blouse. She believed that no matter what, a lady needed to be presentable to keep good impressions up. Nobody would find her stuck in her bath robe in the afternoon. Shameful that would be indeed. She fluffed up all the cushions on the two large floral sofas, gave the sitting room furniture a quick polish.

Plonking her more -than ample bottom in her favourite armchair, Beryl sat with her Apple MacBook (a birthday gift from her eldest son, Terry) and opened up web browser and started her research. Preparation was the key to everything, in Beryl's way of thinking.

Toddy and Sultan both tried to get on her lap and sleep on the warm keyboard. *They were such funny buggers,* thought Beryl chuckling to herself, what would she do without them to cheer her up? She pushed them to either side of her on the chair where they settled down to sleep, purring in her presence.

The hours sped by as Beryl finished her the research project that she had been working on for weeks now. She put her laptop away and went to the kitchen to get the mugs ready for the ladies arriving and put some chocolate digestive biscuits on a plate along with some lemon drizzle cake that she had bought the day before (she might say she made it, nobody would ever know).

The doorbell sounded and Beryl opened the front door to find Gladys, Norma, and Edna all on the doorstep.

"Come in! Come on in and make yourselves comfortable, you know where the sitting room is."

As the three ladies got settled, the doorbell chimed once more and Maureen arrived to join the group of Natty Knitters as they liked to call themselves. Maureen was always late; it was like she operated in a different time zone to the rest of the world. Beryl noticed it had become worse over recent weeks.

With coffee and tea orders prepared and the spread of cakes and biscuits out on display, the ladies settled in for their weekly knit and natter. Beryl prepared herself to put on her "listening ears" and to fight the temptation to over-advise her friends and sound too opinionated.

The click-clacking of knitting needles was quite a musical sound but before long it was drowned out by the chatter of the bunch.

"Did you watch the Royal Wedding on Saturday ladies?" Edna said through a mouthful of biscuit. "I thought Meghan's dress was so elegant and really suited her".

"Elegant?" moaned Maureen with a sharp tone in her voice.

Oh crap, here we go, thought Beryl. Bring on the moaning that *always came*

"It was plain, didn't suit her one bit. both Diana and Kate outshone her on *their* wedding days!" Maureen added. "The Queen must have been cringing inside. Mind you, she looked a bit ridiculous in lime green. At her age there is nothing dignified about lime green," Maureen whinged.

I know what I'd like to do with a lime and your moaning mouth, Beryl thought with a hint of a smile.

Edna was focused on her knitting, looking up at Maureen now and then. Edna was suffering from anxiety after a horrible break-in at her home a few months ago. She had been in her bedroom as she heard the thugs ransacking her home. Edna thought that her time had come and she was going to die. The police never caught the burglars and Edna was constantly in fear of them coming back. Beryl had spent many hours comforting and reassuring her friend that thing would be okay. Listening and offering never ending cups of strong, sugary tea.

"I thought they looked so much in love," Edna ventured in a timid voice in comparison to her opinionated friend. "I was thinking of how proud Diana would be of her son."

"Don't be ridiculous, Edna" Maureen shouted, making Edna jump. "The whole thing was a bloody shamble

The sound of loud laughter from Gladys and Norma made Maureen glare at them. The two ladies were always known to bring cheer to any catch-up and Beryl was glad that someone had broken the horrible atmosphere in the room.

"Look" exclaimed Norma. "Sultan and Toddy are all tangled up in my wool, the little monkeys" Gladys was crying with laughter as she untangled the cats and Beryl could not help but smile at Maureen's sour face.

The rest of the hour rolled on, each lady immersed in their knitting.

Looking at Edna, Beryl said "Um? Would you like to pop over tomorrow afternoon for lunch and a chat with me?"

"Oh, that would be lovely, Beryl, you are so very kind. What time would you like me to come?"

"Twelve-noon would be perfect, Edna, I will prepare us something nice to eat."

Watching Edna's face, Beryl felt like a good friend and was glad she was going through with her plans to help her.

"Huh, some people do get a lot of favouritism, don't they?" Maureen said with jealousy and no regard for Edna's feelings. "When do I get my special invite then, Beryl?"

Knit One, Pearl One

"Actually, Maureen, I was going to ask you over on Friday if you are not busy?" Beryl smugly responded, eyebrows raised at the look on Maureen's face.

"Um, oh, right then, that's very nice of you, Beryl. Shall I come around at noon also?"

"Perfect," said Beryl.

After the ladies had left, Beryl tidied up and washed the dishes then settled down to watch her favourite true-crime TV show "'Cops In Action" surrounded by her purring feline babies.

Beryl got up early the next morning. As always she made the bed and sat and looked at the photograph of herself and Arthur.

"Arthur, my love, you taught me that suffering is an awful thing, please be with me today to help me as I help my friend."

The photograph was silent.

Beryl got through her morning routine with the cats and herself fed, watered, and washed (well, she didn't wash the cats, she had tried grooming them once but it left too much fur in her mouth).

She had everything ready for Edna and eagerly awaited the arrival of her friend. She was feeling a buzz of excitement as well as a touch of nerves, Edna hoped her pee-pads help up today and did their job if required. Busying herself in the kitchen, Beryl made some tuna and cucumber sandwiches, regretting her choice of filling as the cats did a chorus of meowing, vocalising their wants as they did best – loudly.

"Oh, you lot. It's a good job Mummy got extra tins." She put a little bit of tuna in each bowl then moved her chopping board and items to the kitchen table.. With the sandwiches made she covered them in cling-wrap and popped them in the fridge. She also had a nice carrot cake as a special treat for them both.

Nerves were getting to her now and a quick toilet dash was necessary. As she sat there, Beryl looked at her lovely curved bath tub with it's extra depth for a good soak and planned on a nice bath tonight when all was done for the day.

Pulling up her trousers, Beryl flushed the toilet and washed her hands with super-antiseptic soap, one could not be having germs spoil the day today. After all – cleanliness was next to Godliness, her mother had always told her. Beryl was pretty sure even if you didn't wash your hands, God still liked you but today the hand washing mattered. Just then, she heard the doorbell and walked downstairs to the front door with three cats getting under her feet on the way, she opened the door to see Edna.

"Edna, hello, dear. Come on in and go through to the kitchen."

Edna took a seat in the kitchen and ended up with Sultan on her lap. He was a lover of lap cuddles and attention and loved a good stroke under his chin. Edna was happy to oblige.

"How are you, have you had a good morning?" Edna asked.

Beryl was standing in the kitchen staring at the tomato sitting on the chopping board.

"Beryl? Are you okay?"

Beryl's mind was racing, she knew she did not get that tomato out of the fridge as Edna didn't like them. So how did it get there? Was she having early onset dementia? Something just felt strange and her stomach turned over.

"What? Oh, yes I am fine. Sorry, I was miles away with the fairies! Will you have tea or coffee love?"

"Tea please, no sugar and just a dash of milk."

After putting the kettle on, Beryl picked up the tomato and went to the fridge, opening the vegetable crisper she counted the tomatoes. She knew she had bought four off-the-vine tomatoes from the fruit and vegetable shop two days ago. There were three in the fridge and one in her hand. Something really weird was going on, Beryl was sure of it. Putting the rogue tomato back in the crisper Beryl grabbed the milk and focused back on making tea for them both and putting out the sandwiches and cake.

"How are you doing, Has the counselling helped very much with your nerves and bad dreams?"

Edna looked despondent. "Not really, I just find I talk over and over what happened, the counsellor says very little, and I leave feeling like it has just all been dragged up again. I am sure the counsellor means well and wants to help but I have given up on ever feeling whole again after such a fright."

"Have you thought about any alternative therapies? Something other than the counselling?" Beryl watched Edna's face and body language as she asked.

"I am honestly in a place where I trust nobody. A friend suggested acupuncture to release the bad cheese or something?"

"Chi, Edna. Chi, not cheese. It's like the life flow in the body."

"I can't do anything like that, I don't trust strangers anymore. Other than coming to knitting group and seeing you, that's as far as my people contact goes – oh, apart from my counsellor once a week. The social butterfly I once was has well and truly gone back into the cocoon, probably never to come out again."

Sultan looked up at Edna. Cats just *knew* things. He stood and arched his back and raised his head to give her a head-butt cat kiss under her chin. Edna started to cry and Beryl knew that the time was right now, or never. *Thank you, Sultan!*

"I can help you, Edna. I have been learning a new healing and relaxation technique that can help with anxiety and nightmares, as well as lots of other things. I know that you are scared to put yourself in the hands of strangers, but you and I have known each other since school. Would you trust me to help?"

Beryl anxiously waited for her response, giving up a silent message to Arthur, wherever he was, to give this a nudge in the right direction.

"What does it involve?"

"It's really just relaxation with some essential oils and guided meditation, helping your mind clear and focus on positive things. It is a bit like having your brain cleansed, washing away all the bad memories."

Edna was nibbling at a small piece of carrot cake. "Okay, if you really think it will help, I trust you."

"Edna, honestly, this will make life so much calmer and better for you." As she spoke, she caught a dark shape moving out of the corner of her eye and the three cats that were in the kitchen all started hissing and acting strangely. Sultan jumped off Edna's lap and ran out of the cat door, followed by the other two. Putting it out of her mind, she led Edna to the spare bedroom, ready to help her friend.

She had filled the room with candles. An aromatherapy burner was diffusing a combination of soothing lavender and uplifting bergamot oils. A massage table stood in the middle of the room with a soft blanket and pillow. She had also covered the windows with blackout curtains to give the room a real sense of escaping from the outside world.

"Ooh? This is lovely, it reminds me of the spa place I used to go to for facials back before my awful event."

"Hop up on the table for me, there is a little step to help you get on easily. Put your head on the pillow, and just relax " As Edna got settled on the massage table, Beryl pressed play on her portable CD player and soothing rainforest sounds (annoying bloody birds) streamed through the speakers.

Beryl gave Edna two small tablets with a glass of water. "These are herbal tablets, part of the process to help you relax and get the stress out of your muscles that are holding the anxiety in."

Beryl expected Edna to question the tablets but to her surprise, she took them and swallowed them with the water. Lying her head back down on the pillow, Beryl told Edna to close her eyes and drift away with the sound of bird-song for a while. Beryl sat on a chair in the corner and set a timer on her phone for thirty minutes.

Beryl poked at Edna with a sharp, very thin knitting needle, checking that she was in a deep sleep from the strong sleeping tablets she had given her. There was no response to the needle and Beryl felt confident she was in a deep place.

She pulled out a tray from inside a cabinet in the corner of the room. Everything was prepared and ready to go. Beryl was already thinking that if this was a success that Maureen would be a great candidate for the treatment on Friday also. Perhaps she could make a new career of it? On the quiet, of course.

Beryl had to improvise and used a sewing needle to pin back her eyelids eyelids so that her eyes were now wide open. She stared down into Edna's eyes to check she was not really looking back at her. So far, so good. Beryl now turned on the overhead light,. Beryl had sterilised the thin knitting needles that morning and they lay on the tray by her side.

Picking up the knitting needle, Beryl brought it closer to Edna's left eyeball and started to insert it slowly into the corner of the eye. She picked up a small toffee hammer in her right hand from the tray as she talked to Edna, telling her what a wonderful thing was happening to her.

"Edna, I am performing a lobotomy on you. I have been studying the technique on the internet for months. They don't do them very often these days but I am a believer that they gave up on a very effective treatment for all sorts of mental conditions and mood disorders. After this, you should feel much calmer in your nerves and have no anxiety."

Tap, tap, tap – Beryl tapped the end of the knitting needle, watching it descend further into the corner of the eye. "I am now severing the connections that the frontal lobes, or prefrontal cortex, has with the rest of your brain. The tapping and wiggling around I am doing is to break the bone very gently, now I am twirling the needle to cut the fibres in the brain. This severs the white from the grey matter if you like"

Beryl removed the knitting needle from Edna's left eye and sat back on the chair exhaling a big breath. Success. She had done it. She leaned over Edna, double checking that she was still out of it then waited the required ten minutes before getting a new knitting needle and readying it for the right eye. Both needed to be done for the lobotomy to be successful. In the past, hundreds of these procedures had been performed and Beryl was baffled as to why they ever stopped at all. She knew they were still used in extreme cases, but should be available to everyone. Doctors and GP's should be trained up to perform it in their surgeries and rooms. The whole procedure only took thirty minutes.

Beryl poised the new knitting needle in the corner of Edna's eye, readied with the metal hammer in her right hand again. She gently tapped on the end of the needle, taking great care not to tap too hard. Suddenly Beryl felt like someone had pushed her from behind, forcing her to put enormous pressure on the needle. She screamed as she realised that the needle was now embedded in Edna's brain.

A meowing at her feet exposed Riley sitting there. He jumped up on the table and settled down on Edna's chest, which was no longer moving up and down. "You stupid, silly cat! What a time to get under my feet! What am I supposed to do now? We have killed her good and proper. Oh, my days, I am going to go to hell for what I have done."

Riley just looked at Beryl and purred.

Beryl sat with Edna's body for hours until the sun started setting. The shock of what she had done had frozen her in place. Riley had gotten bored ages ago and she could hear the cats in the kitchen howling to be fed.

"Oh, Arthur, help me, you always knew what to do in a crisis," she sobbed. "Please do something, say something."

A creepy whisper whooshed past her left ear at the same time as the temperature in the room dropped considerably. Beryl had a strong, uneasy feeling.

A voice that seemed to come from nowhere made her jump. "Beryl, you have well and truly gone and stuffed this up good and proper."

What the...? She could have sworn that sounded like Arthur's voice. She was delirious and still in shock obviously from killing her closest friend. There were no such thing as ghosts or voices from the other side. Death was death...right?

"Beryl, look at me, in the corner of the room. Look at me, my darling wife."

Beryl didn't want to look, she knew now it was Arthur's voice but what if he looked like a zombie, all flesh peeling off him like a ripe tomato, eyes sucked out of their sockets, bones poking out. It reminded her of the tomato in the kitchen, it now made sense, it was Arthur saying he was nearby. He had been an avid tomato grower in his greenhouse down his allotment for years when he was alive.

She braced herself and looked at the corner of the room. There was Arthur, well, half of him anyway. She could only see him from the waist up, just his torso and head. Beryl could also see right through him like he was transparent, like blurry glass. But he looked fine, no shredded skin or bones. Despite her terror and desire to just run as fast as she can she worked on calming her breathing and staying in the moment.

"Arthur, where is the rest of you?"

"I didn't bring all my bits, they get a bit much to squeeze through the portal from the other side, pet. My big bum doesn't do me any favours in the ghostly realm."

Beryl was speechless. She had a vision of Arthur squeezing himself through a hole that was too small, a bit like if he was trying to get through the cat flap and got stuck. She giggled. Not that anything was funny. Shit had just gotten real.

"Right, Beryl, this is what you are going to do. You are going to go to the garden shed and get out the extra tough hedge trimmer that I used to use to do the hedges and branches off the trees in the front garden. Bring it back to the house. Go back to the shed and in the back, right-hand corner is some tarpaulin from camping days, bring that to the house also and lay it around the room, on the floor and under Edna as best you can. Hurry up as rigour mortis sets in after twelve hours and six have gone by already."

Beryl wasted no time in going back and forth to the shed in the back yard, looking around to make sure none of her nosy neighbours were wondering what she was up to. She brought the hedge trimmer in and began to put the tarpaulin around the room. She managed to get it on the floor around and under the massage table, reaching to the walls and some of it pushed under Edna who felt very cold and waxy at this point. It made Beryl feel sick. She was terrified, her plans had gone horribly wrong.

"Right, now, with the hedge trimmer you are going to slice up Edna. First a leg at a time, then both arms then her head. This will leave you with 6 six body parts and you will be able to move them on your own. Keep your arms and hands steady or the damn hedge cutter will take on a life of its own, it's powerful." Arthur was advising her as if she was at a DIY course.

Beryl had seen this method on the countless TV shows, movies, and true crime stories. She could do this. She revved up the hedge cutter, pulling the cord to get it going and to her surprise, it roared to life. The whole moment was so surreal, Beryl felt like she was almost disconnected from her emotions and any reason at this stage. There was no turning back. She had to sort this mess.

Taking Arthur's advice, she put the trimmer on the top of Edna's thigh and it began to slice through bone, muscle, nerves. It was gruesome, Beryl was getting splattered with blood and bits of tissue and it was harder than she thought it would be. Systematically, she took off the rest of Edna's body parts. The head gave a bit resistance and rolled off the massage table with a loud plop. Edna had always talked of a face-lift, now she had one.

"Okay, pet, you are doing really well. Now you need to get soil from the front garden and potting mix from the shed, go upstairs with it and fill the bathtub a layer just on the bottom," Arthur whispered.

He seemed to be fading in and out, like a radio station that was slightly off-air. By now, Beryl's hip was agony and she had a limp. There was no way she could do this alone.

The stench of copper was strong in the air, that unmistakeable smell of blood. Beryl took stock of herself, covered in thick blood, pieces of flesh and sinew. She felt sick, feeling the bile rise up and burn the back of her throat. She had to get cleaned up. Glancing at Edna's head which had rolled sideways Beryl felt like Edna's eyes were accusing her of this awful event that went so wrong.

Stepping into the shower, Beryl watched her white tiles turn red, then pink as the blood and bits of flesh circled around the drain then disappeared with a gurgle. She scrubbed herself raw, washing her hair until the water ran clear again. ~The hot tears flowed with the water as Beryl finally gave in to her emotions. Turning off the shower she quickly dried herself and put on some old clothes that she used for gardening. She had to go and get help. Shoving her bloody, dirty clothes at the back of the wardrobe, Beryl headed downstairs and out her front door.

She went out to the front garden and walked down the little pathway and round to her neighbour's house. Andrew Chapman had lived next door for about ten years and had been a help to Beryl before.

Andrew answered the door. "Hello, Beryl, how are you love?" Beryl remembered that Chris worked as a bouncer in a nightclub and his muscles were bulging through his t-shirt. If she was just 30 years younger she would...*Stop it, woman! You can't get distracted, there is a friend cut up in the spare room!*

"Um. Actually, Andrew, I could do with some help if you have time? I am making a bespoke flower arrangement in my bathroom. An idea I saw in a Homes & Garden magazine but at my age, with my dodgy hip I can't carry any soil upstairs."

"No worries, I will hop over right now. Just let me get my trolley I use for moving heavy things also."

Andrew went to get his metal trolley, putting it near the front door and brought some big buckets and metal tubs of his own. He dug into the soil and started to fill everything up whilst Beryl watched on anxiously. Did dead bodies start to smell after six hours? God, she hoped not.

With six containers filled, Andrew carried them, one by one, backwards on the trolley upstairs to the bathroom and put them on the floor. He lifted them as if they were pillows for the bed. "Now what, Beryl?" Andrew asked as they stood at the bathroom door looking at the soil. "Can you put it all in the bathtub please, and pat it down a bit?"

"In the bathtub?" Andrew rubbed his head with a look of confusion on his face.

"Yes, I am making a flower garden in my bathtub, wonderful new concept. I have a shower so no need for the bath"

Andrew looked at her like she had gone slightly mad, which wasn't far off the truth, and did as she asked. She asked him to bring in the bags of potting mix from the shed in the yard also. Beryl carefully watched him head to the kitchen and out to the yard and upstairs, panicking in case he ventured down the hallway to the spare room.

Once everything was done, she said a quick goodbye to Andrew telling him a cup of tea and cake was on offer another time. She slammed the door and raced back to the spare room. Unfortunately, Edna was still in pieces but Arthur was nowhere in sight.

"Arthur, Arthur, where the hell are you, don't leave now, you silly sod!"

She watched a silvery grey glimmer in the corner of the room and to her surprise, saw Arthur's copious backside coming into the room! This was followed by his hips, legs and feet.

"Sorry, Beryl, I can't get the hang of this haunting thing, I have come in arse-end up."

"You most certainly have, Arthur. I did always say you talked through your arse sometimes."

"Haha, no time for jokes, Beryl. This mess is not cleaned up yet. Now, take the body parts, one by one, up to the bathroom and lay them out like that Tetris game you like so much. It doesn't matter if they are not in order, just get them in that bathtub."

Beryl picked up Edna's left leg, grunting as she carried it towards the stairs. "Bloody hell, Edna, shame you had not started that diet," she puffed. She could not carry the heavy body parts; this was just too much for her, they were slippery and hard to manage. Beryl decided to put each part in a big black bin bag so she could drag the pieces up the stairs. The torso was the hardest to shift.

Eventually, Beryl had everything in the bathtub and started the slow process of adding the potting mix over the body parts using a small trowel, there was no way she could lift the potting mix bags up. Once the bags were emptier she could tip it in. Finally all the parts of Edna were covered up.

She turned to go downstairs and found her head going up Arthur's arse, well not so much going in but through. Talk about having your head up your arse. Or up Arthur's arse. The things you did when married!

"Right, Beryl, try to get some rest, the first thing in the morning go to the garden centre in town and get lots of bedding plants and flowers, If I am not here when you get back, plant the flowers on top, okay?"

"I won't be found out, will I? I mean nobody visiting will tell?"

"No, I don't think so, but make sure you get rid of the tarpaulin in the room and clean everything with super strong bleach!"

Beryl has a fitful nights sleep, her head filled with nightmares and visions of murder, gore and death.

She rose early, skipped breakfast for herself, dressed and fed the cats, Beryl grabbed her car keys, got into her little red hatchback, and sped off towards the middle of town.

Hours later, after getting back from town and ensuring everything was cleaned up she stepped back to take stock. Beryl had managed to bleach parts of the dark carpet but could do nothing until she could get the carpet fitter around to sort it. She was totally exhausted, there was no sign of Arthur or his backside, sadly she realised she missed him so much. He had been there for her, just like he always had. Nothing like a good ghostly visit from your husband to cheer you up when your day has gone to shit.

Beryl fed the cats, and went to bed early, curled up under the covers on the edge of the bed, whilst the cats took up the rest of it and fell into a deep sleep.

The next morning seemed to come around too quick and Beryl could tell by the light it was earlier than usual. Checking the clock, it glared back at her with big red number 5:34 a.m. Beryl didn't know what had awakened her but she needed to pee really badly. Putting on her bathrobe and slippers, Beryl went to the bathroom trying not to notice the flowers and soil and potting mix in her bathtub. If she didn't look at it, then it wasn't there.

She pulled up her knickers as Toddy and Tiddly-Weeny wandered through the half-closed door. They both jumped up on the soil and to her horror, Toddy started to defecate, finished, then was flicking soil everywhere in his hurry to cover it up!

"No, Toddy, no!" she yelled at the surprised cat. "Get out, out!"

Both cats raced from the bathroom, not used to being yelled at.

Heading to the kitchen to sort breakfasts, Beryl stood in shock as she surveyed her kitchen, or what was left of it. Cupboards were flung open, drawers were pulled out, the table was tipped over, and as she stood there with shivers running up her spine, she watched the taps turn on with nobody there.

"Arthur, what the hell do you think you are playing at, sunshine?" she yelled. "Now, this is just not funny!"

"Hello, Beryl, I thought I would pop by and pay you another visit. I was feeling a bit angry so my apologies for the mess in the kitchen."

Beryl went cold. Freezing cold. She knew that voice, she had heard it for years. Edna was back. This just could not be happening. One day her life was peaceful and normal now she was a killer and being visited by people that are dead. Beryl felt sick to her stomach as she realised that Edna had not fully left her house.

"Hi Edna" Beryl ventured feeling fearful of what was happening to her."Um. So how are you?"

"How am I, Beryl? I am a bit cut up to be honest. I don't feel quite myself, you know?" Edna responded with a deep, demonic voice that terrified Beryl.

"Right, yes, I imagine you are not feeling your best, love. I am so very sorry for the accident yesterday. Please understand, it was nothing personal, I really wanted to help calm your anxiety and be a good friend." Beryl hoped she sounded sufficiently sorry.

"Well, it was an epic fail, you silly old bat. Poking me in the eye with a knitting needle was not one of the brightest ideas you have ever had. As a new Poltergeist, I get to wreak havoc on you for the rest of your miserable life. I am going to make you suffer for what you have done to me!"

As if to show off her new skills, Edna tipped up the cat litter boxes onto the floor, scattering poop and litter and urine clumps everywhere. "There, see how your cats cope with that, you crazy old best-friend-killing-cat-lady!"

The doorbell rang and Beryl nearly jumped. At the same time, she saw Edna vanish. Looking around at the mess that was her kitchen, she went to the front door. Nervously opening it, to see two stern faces at the front door. A male in a sharp suit was showing her his ID and a female in police uniform stood beside him. She had been hoping it was the Jehovah's witnesses for once.

"Good morning, Mrs. Tate – I am Detective Inspector Alan Nicholson and this is Police Constable Hannah Millar. We are making enquiries as to the whereabouts of Edna Mooney, may we come in please?"

Beryl was panicking inside, she was thinking of her crime shows and trying to remember if they needed a warrant or not. *Best not to be obstructive*, she decided, *they were just asking questions. Just be calm and they will be gone* quickly, she hoped.

DI Nicholson and PC Millar perched themselves on opposite ends of her sofa as she sat in her armchair. She had noticed the cats had not been in sight all morning and hoped they would not make an appearance now. PC Millar had a black notebook and pen and was peering at her with her blue eyes. Beryl felt like the woman knew what she had done already. DI Nicholson smiled at Beryl, not that this made her feel at ease, but she was sure that was his intent.

"Mrs. Tate," DI Nicholson began. "We have had a report that Edna Mooney has been missing since early evening the night before last. She was due to meet with her counsellor for a late appointment at 6:00 p.m. and did not show. This being unusual for Ms. Mooney, her counsellor contacted us. Her counsellor also told us your name and that you and she were good friends. Apparently, Ms. Mooney had mentioned you often in therapy but that's as much as we were told."

Beryl glanced at the policewoman and took a deep breath before responding."Oh yes, Edna was here for lunch the day before yesterday, but left by 4:30 p.m. I did not know she had an appointment. She must have walked to the bus stop, as she does not drive."

Her words settled in the air like bad smelling air-freshener and Beryl was sure that they could both sniff the scent of her lies. As she looked at them both she was horrified to see Arthur's bottom coming through the middle of the curtains behind PC Millar's head.

Following seconds after, to the left of Arthur's backside was Edna's head! It seemed the entire spiritual realm had decided to pay a visit at a very bad time! Beryl felt her bladder go and warm urine spread on to her super strong pee-pads and she hoped to God they did what the adverts said. She was fairly close to shitting herself too.

She could hear the detective speaking to her but her ears seemed to not be working. She was staring at the two spectres above their heads as they began to tussle with each other. "Mrs Tate!" the detective blurted, his face turning a rather unbecoming shade of pink. "I asked you if I can please use your bathroom, too much coffee on the road this morning, you see."

Beryl could not think straight as Edna was now a head and one arm and in that arm was the poker from the fireplace and it was about to go right up Arthur's arsehole as they fought in and out of her curtains!

"Yes, yes! That's fine," she said "Top of the stairs, the door that is shut."

DI Nicholson got up and made his way upstairs whilst PC Millar sat making notes in her little black book. Notes about her, no doubt. Did the UK still have the death penalty?

Arthur had managed to stop the impaling he had been subjected to and was now trying to suck Edna's arm up his backside, they were yelling to each other and Beryl was terrified that the PC was going to hear them, or worse, see them!

Just then she heard the cat flap bang and racing into the lounge room came Sultan and Tiddly-Weeny. They stopped short in the middle of the room, looking at Arthur's bum and Edna's head and arm (or what was left of her arm as half of it was up his bum), all their fur stood on end and they screeched as they raced upstairs together.

Suddenly there was a horrendous scream from upstairs. DI Nicholson was screaming like a banshee for PC Millar to "get her arse upstairs pronto". PC Millar raced up the stairs and Beryl got a sinking feeling in her stomach. She followed up the stairs.

DI Nicholson was standing near the toilet, PC Millar was staring at the bathtub, and on top of the bathtub, Sultan and Tiddly-Weeny had dug such a hole together that Edna's foot was sticking out of the bathtub. Slap bang in the middle, poking through the pretty flowers like a weed, unwanted, but unwilling to go away.

DI Nicholson shouted for PC Millar to handcuff Beryl, read her rights, and escort her to the car outside for questioning. It didn't take long for the forensic team to arrive after PC Millar called it in.

As she was being led downstairs, she noticed her two cats preening themselves, washing soil off their paws. Being a crazy cat lady had its downsides. She glanced near the curtains en route and saw that Arthur's bum and Edna's head and arm had vanished, a fat lot of help Arthur had been this time around, although he had put his arse on the line to help her.

One thing she knew. Once in prison, where she knew she was going Beryl would kill herself, but beforehand would write a will leaving everything she had to her loving cats and requesting they go to a local cat rehoming service. The other thing she knew for sure, was she was excited about haunting moaning Maureen and giving her a piece of her mind. Impressions counted, however, so Beryl would practice NOT coming through arse end first, she would never live it down. She sometimes dreamed of bathtubs and knitting needles.

MAXINE GREY

Maxine Grey is the pen name of Maxine Groves. When not busy writing stories with dark themes Maxine is a busy Book Publicist and a Top Ranked Book Reviewer. Also known as a cat lady and feline whisperer. Born in the North East of England, Maxine then lived in Australia for 30 years before England called her heart back again. She currently resides in County Durham with her husband, teenage son and two naughty Burmese cats.

Since being a young child, the world of books has been her escape and on average Maxine devours over 300 books a year. She was that girl in high school that read the whole book when asked to read chapter one to discuss in English class. Yes, it's an addiction. Her writing career kicked off in 2017 after being inspired by working with so many fantastic indie authors following their dreams of writing. Her advice to anyone who wants to write "Just do it!"

Maxine has been published in Demonic Wildlife Anthology - Volume 1 with a dark humour story featuring Koalas gone bad and gets a kick out of mixing horror with humour. In the pipeline is a non-fiction book expressing the voices of Women with Autism, a dark psychological thriller and the first book of a brand new crime series. Short stories will always be a passion, so expect to see more of those.

Maxine loves to connect with fans and book lovers and you can find her on social media here:

www.facebook.com/maxinegreybooks
www.twitter.com/maxinegreybooks

www.facebook.com/BookloverCatlady
www.twitter.com/promotethatbook

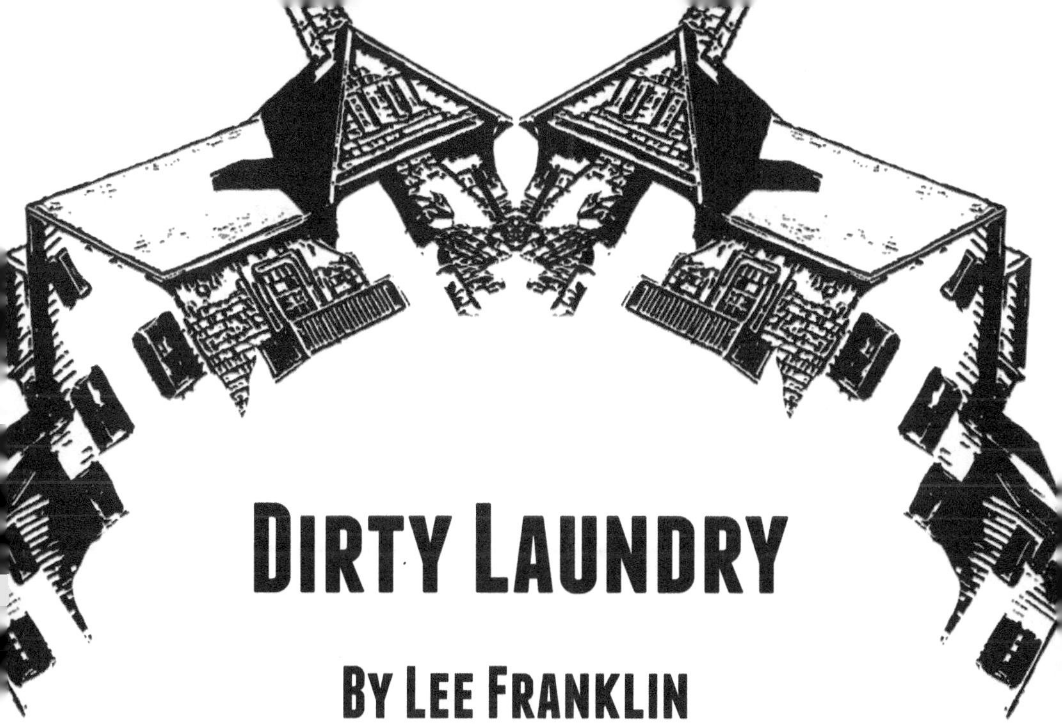

Dirty Laundry

By Lee Franklin

Washer

Emily Parker pushed her hair back into a greasy pony tail, her eyes felt like they were lined with salt. Not the regular table salt, serious Dead Sea rock salts with a squirt of lemon. With a small stir of pleasure, she gratefully swallowed the remnants of the now cold black bitter instant coffee. Bits of her husband's toast floated in it, but it was coffee, any coffee was good at this point even with incidental peanut butter croutons. Long gone were the hot frothy cappuccino's from a selection of her favorite cafés, long gone like her friends, her career, her dreams, sleep and any semblance of feeling remotely human.

Crossing the kitchen to rinse out her cup, she swore under her breath as she noticed her indoor herb garden descending into death and decay right in front of her eyes. Brown and lank parsley, brittle limp mint and the basil appeared to have lost a battle with a flame thrower.

"How the hell. I can't believe this. I do everything right for you guys. I'm not doing this again. Healthy home living, what a bunch of bollocks" as she upended the pots into the rubbish bin with disgust and frustration.

Goosebumps flushed over Emily's body and an ice-cold spike pricked at the base of her spine as she moved into the loungeroom. She would have to talk to Frank, there was a nasty draft coming from somewhere,

Emily sighed as she picked up the wash basket and headed to her new-found prison, the laundry room. Bright fluorescent lights flickered on as she navigated the metal staircase, that was more suited to a warehouse then a basement. For a large space it was decidedly toasty warm she thought as she trundled down her third pile of laundry for the morning. How could one baby create so much laundry? It was a constant circle she could never quite stay on top off. Rose, the baby was miraculously still asleep by the time she had finished loading the machine and Emily quickly pondered the likelihood of having a little nap herself. A mental snapshot of her house ruled out her bedroom, it was a disaster and the creaky floorboards always awoke Rose, the sofa too was out for the count as there were still bundles of clothes that needed sorting. Looking at the pile of warm towels taken from the dryer and it was an easy decision to plonk herself down in front of the washing machine onto her little nest. Desperate times she consoled herself.

Emily stared at the washing machine, it was a Bendix, one of the first washing machines ever sold back in the 1940's and had come with the house. It looked like a huge commercial machine one sees at the Laundry mat and was bolted to the floor and only ever washed in cold water. Emily and her husband Frank were not in a position to be picky, it worked, and they considered themselves lucky. Emily lay, rapidly fading off into sleep watching the swirl of the water and the froth of the bubbles turning to the steady rhythm boom, de boom boom, boom de boom boom.

"Emileeey, Emileey" a voice whispered

Emily sat up instantly like mothers of baby's do, in that half panic, half asleep mode and looked around gingerly wondering at what she heard, or if she was just imagining things or dreaming. Confused Emily started to stand back up.

"Emily, Emily please don't go" a bubbly woman's voice sung out. Emily stood up quickly.

Dirty Laundry

"Whose there? What do you want?" Emily demanded nervously, grasping the mop handle to her chest, all set to go kung-fu whilst trying to find the owner of the voice

"Oh Emily, it's me silly, back down here. You call me the 'Washing Machine' but my real name is Wendy."

Emily jumped back when she realized that was indeed where the voice was coming from, what else was in her husband's coffee, surely, she was losing her mind. Looking at the washing machine with her heart pounding in her ears and all she saw was the froth and bubbles as her underwear cart wheeled across the glass door in a contemporary dance Emily could only ever dream of performing. No way, this is one of those video prank things surely she thought as she gingerly poked the front of the washing machine with the mop handle.

"Yes, down here, look closer Emily, you will see me" the voice bubbled away. Emily looked closer, and there she eventually made out the face of a woman in her mid-thirties with her blonde hair in cut in a bob and curled with waves, she looked like a housewife straight out of the 1950's. Emily's jaw dropped in shock "Oh my God, what no way, is this some kind of joke, how did you get in there?"

"Oh, that is a long story" Wendy answered as she casually lit herself a cigarette. Is that why her clothes always smelt slightly of cigarette smoke, Emily wondered to herself.

"But suffice to say, I am really no more or less trapped then you, am I?" Wendy added looking at Emily with a smirk on her face. Emily thought of the piles of laundry that remained to be sorted, folded and ironed amidst the demands of a six-month-old baby and nodded in agreement.

"I guess not" she sighed, exhausted "Is it possible to be so tired, in your own dreams."

"You're not dreaming Sunshine" Wendy piped up.

"This simply isn't possible" Emily answered thinking it strange she was arguing with herself, pinching her arm trying to wake herself up.

"Well it is, what it is, this has been my life for nearly fifty years so don't talk to me about what is possible or not" Wendy answered sucking on her cigarette so hard, the end almost sparked.

"Fifty years!!!" Emily exclaimed "What have you been doing this entire time?"

"Oh a bit of drinking, sleeping, lots of sleeping and just watching the world come and go."

"Sleep?" Emily asked "Oh, I could kill for some sleep about now, real sleep"

Wendy raised her eyebrow as she threw the butt onto what could only be the ground, her body twisting as Emily imagined her stamping it out with her heel.

"Yes, I see you have a baby, a little girl" Wendy commented, pulling a little pink sock from the pile of clothes swirling around her.

"Yes, Rose. Beautiful baby but she will just not sleep, and I am just so, so tired" Emily answered her head feeling heavy with exhaustion.

"Why doesn't your Mother come around and watch her? Or a nanny? Surely if you live in this grand ol' house you can afford a decent nanny." Wendy asked curiously.

"Oh, my mum lives in another county a few hours drive away, plus she works fulltime herself still and a nanny? No, we definitely cannot afford a nanny, we can barely afford this grand old house as you say, we still can't figure out how we got it so cheap." Emily explained fatigue pulling at her eyes.

"Oh my, your poor woman. It's so hard being a mum, I remember it so well myself. I tell you what, why don't you let me help you? Wendy offered cheerily.

"Oh, I don't think that would be possible at all" Emily answered, "Your kind of stuck in there aren't you"

"Not really" Wendy smiled at her, her eyes full of mischief. "I can come out, but you would have to take my place in here. I can't stay out any longer than twelve hours, that's enough time for you to have a good sleep and rest. You can even bring in that book you have been dying to read. What is it "When Tomorrow Comes" "

"How do you know about that?" Emily asked

"I know a lot of things. I'm not just here you know, I'm in your pipes, in your shower.... I know your husband has been visiting Mrs. Palmer and her five daughters a lot in the shower lately" Wendy winked.

Emily's face burnt red "Is nothing private" she hissed "I've just been so tired and feel so horrible" Emily tried to explain.

Wendy put up her hand to dismiss her "No, need to explain to me. I've been there, done that I know exactly how you feel. Men are so selfishly demanding these days. They expect EVERYTHING!!! Wendy admonished, Emily shook her head in agreeance.

Dirty Laundry

"Well think about it, the offer is there" Wendy said. "You have to go Emily, Miss Rose demands your presence" as the sounds of a crying baby made their way down to them.

Emily rose to her feet. "Thanks Wendy, it's nice talking to you, please try not to pry on us in the showers anymore"

"Yeah sure thing Sister. Now I've met you it just wouldn't feel right." Wendy smiled, her eyes flickering red as she lit another cigarette. Emily paused momentarily, it must off just been a trick of the light, or reflection she mused. I must talk to her about the smoking but not just now. Wendy was the first woman she had a real conversation with in ages, let's not ruin it for now Emily thought to herself, all the while aware of how ridiculous she sounded.

Hours later Frank came home, threw his coat on the back of the door and the keys in the bowl with the door thudding shut behind him. Emily poked her head out of the kitchen and hissed at him.

"Rose is finally sleeping; can you please keep it down".

Putting up his hands in defense, he frowned as he walked over to give her a hug.

"Happy to see you too babe"

"I'm sorry" Emily sighed, resting her head on his shoulder "I'm just so tired and I have hardly been able to put Rose down all day. I haven't even had a shower yet and I've only just started dinner"

"Well, why don't I put this away for tomorrow night, order some pizza, open a bottle of wine while you go upstairs, have a shower, and relax, and get comfortable, and then maybe we can spend some time together" he suggested his blue eyes twinkling with mischief and his old panty melting smile on his lips. Emily sighed, oh a shower, pizza and wine sounded so good, she could finally shave her legs and then she might be able to make an effort for the rest.

"Ok it's a deal" Emily kissed him quickly on the cheek before darting away upstairs.

Half an hour later Frank went up looking to let her know the pizza was ready to find her passed out into a deep sleep. He smiled, kissing her softly before going back down stairs to enjoy the pizza on his own.

"Wow, your husband was in a foul mood with you last night" Wendy said after lighting a cigarette.

"What do you mean? Oh, because I fell asleep. I felt so bad, I didn't mean too, I just wanted to close my eyes for a minute." Emily explained, wondering again how to ask Wendy to stop smoking. Then considering further the ludicrous situation she was in, talking to a woman in her washing machine to begin with.

"Well he called somebody named B something, Bianca? and had a good moan about it before, well you know" Wendy continued blowing smoke rings. Emily's heart starting pounding in her chest, it couldn't be.

"He doesn't know a Bianca." She said quickly, her mind rapidly spinning with all the possible B named women they knew. Her heart sunk as her stomach turned over, Bronte, his secretary. It was always the secretary wasn't it.

"I don't catch her name properly, I just know it started with a B and he finished with an oh my God. Your husband has a big appetite and if you're going to keep falling asleep on him, well it's going to happen sooner or later. Got to keep the home fires burning." She smirked.

"Bronte? Could the name of been Bronte?" Emily asked, tears welling in her eyes as her face crumpled in heartbreak, thinking about the petite red head that had started a few months ago in Frank's office.

"Yes Bronte, that's it like the Bronte Sisters" She said tapping the ash off her cigarette as she watched Emily fall into a sobbing heap.

"Oh darling. Isn't no point to crying now" Wendy purred sympathetically as she looked at the red eyed young woman, her face streaked with tears and her nose running.

"I'm just so tired" Emily hiccupped. "I thought he understood. He said he doesn't mind, that he knows it's just a for a little while. How can he do this?"

"Because men are pigs. Of course, he doesn't mind if he is already getting something on the side. All men think about it sex, how and when they can get it. They don't give a damn about us women and what we have to go through, what we put our bodies through." Wendy said. "You girl have to wash off those tears and get back into bed with your man. So far, they are just on the phone it is up to you to bring your man home."

"But how?" Emily whimpered, exhaustion and stress making her mind foggy, everything so overwhelming, she just wanted to curl up in a ball and hide.

Dirty Laundry

"You need two things, help, sleep and, do something with your hair" Wendy said firmly.

"You come on in here and get a good day's rest, I can look after baby Rose and then come night time you are a new woman, ready to ravish your man." Wendy said, finally finished with her cigarette, she flicked it towards Emily where the butt landed at her feet.

Emily's eyes grew large as she stared at the smoking butt, burning just a few inches away from her feet. "But how, it's impossible isn't it."

"Nothing is impossible. But, remember I can only be out of this machine for 12 hours, not a moment longer. What you do, is we put our hands together through the glass like this" Wendy explained putting her hands against the glass, as Emily began leaning towards the machine.

"Then we push and we pass through. Simple really" she finished.

"That easily?" Emily asked edging even closer and raising her hands to the glass plated window, ignoring the churning of her husband's shirts in front of her.

"That easily." Wendy responded.

"Ok, and you swear you will come back in, you're not going to leave me in there are you?" Emily asked suddenly suspicious.

"Oh goodness, no. I can only leave for twelve hours at a time. Besides, what would your husband say if he came home and found a strange woman in his house. Trust me honey, my life is soo much easier in here, then yours out there."

"Ok, but one last thing." Emily agreed. But, please don't smoke around the baby. It's not healthy."

Wendy sighed "Alright, I won't smoke around the baby, but you better be ready swap, when I need a smoke, because all hell will break lose otherwise."

Emily nodded in agreement, a feeling of unease flickered in her belly but sheer exhaustion and the promise of sleep overwhelmed her instincts. Wendy smiled a wicked grin as she placed her hands up to the glass window of the washing machine. Emily took a deep breathe and pressed her hands against the glass also, gasping at the unexpected iciness. Pulling back, she thought she saw Wendy's eyes harden and flash red, but it got lost behind Frank's business shirt before she could be sure.

"C'mon girl, you haven't got all day" Wendy said, rolling her now very blue eyes.

I am definitely too tired, I don't even know what I'm seeing, I'm hallucinating. None of this can be real. Can it? Emily thought rubbing her crusty feeling eyes.

"Ok" Emily said and once again placing her hands up against the machine and gently pushed. A damp, foamy feeling ran over her wrists, but still she persisted until she was all the way up to her shoulders. Instinctively she took a deep breath and squeezed her eyes shut tightly before ducking her head into the grey foamy depths of the washing machine. Crawling all the way in, Emily finally opened her eyes, one at a time and released her breath still not quite believing what was happening.

Climbing into a standing position, she found she was in a massive bubble and everything frothing and swirling around her. The churn of the machine was a gentle rumble in the background, already lulling her to sleep. Peeking through the tumbling shirts, her jaw dropped, it wasn't Wendy standing her, but herself. Thumping on the glass, Emily felt a knuckle of fear curl in her belly.

'Wendy! Wendy!" she shouted. Wendy turned around to look at her,

"Oh, I didn't know this was going to happen. Maybe it's for the best, I won't scare the baby so much this way."

"Yeah, I guess so" said Emily feeling silly. After all the bizarre things that had just happened today, that at least made sense.

"You have a lovely sleep now and I will see you later." Wendy beamed "and, I will sort everything out for you". Emily just nodded the hum and the thrum of the machine, coupled with the gentle humid heat it took nothing for her to curl up on the floor, which seemed surprisingly soft, and fall into a deep, deep sleep.

Emily woke with a start, wow, she felt so human it was amazing. But, still something felt wrong, out of place, that knuckle of fear curled in her belly again. The machine had stopped its cycle and from deep within the pipes she heard noises, muted groans, soft giggles. Standing up quickly, Emily quickly searched around the bubble and found no way out. A moan of pleasure reverberated around the inside of machine, followed by a gasp and a cry of pleasure.

"Oh Emily" Frank purred "Oh God, I missed you so much"

A click of a lighter and a murmur filtered down to Emily's agonized ears before all she could hear was the thudding of her own heart in her ears.

"Since when did you start smoking?" said Frank with surprise

"When I decided to start shagging you again" Emily heard herself answer.

Dirty Laundry

"Oh, well I guess it's a small price" Frank mumbled.

"Good" came Emily's voice followed by the clink of glasses.

"Your drinking too!" exclaimed Frank.

"Oh, stop your whining, I've had a hard day too". Emily's voiced snapped back.

Emily saw red trapped in the washing machine. Pounding against the glass, furiously and shouting in rage, burning tears running down her face, the machine began to wobble violently.

"What is that noise?" Frank asked.

"Don't worry about it Franky boy. I'll go and sort it out" said Emily's voice with a chilling tone.

Emily was seething, beyond fury and started screaming in rage as soon Wendy stepped into the laundry.

"Oh, stop your crying, you weak pathetic blathering fool" snapped Wendy sitting down on the bench and calmly lighting a cigarette.

"If you were a half decent woman, I wouldn't have to do your job for you in the first place."

"I asked you to babysit my child, not fuck my husband. Oh my gosh, Rosy, where is my baby girl? Let me out of here you bitch." thundered Emily only slightly hurt at the truth in Wendy's words. Wendy pouted and looked at her watch pointedly

"Looks like I have at least thirty more minutes of playtime toots."

"Emily! Emily!" shrieked Frank's voice as his footsteps hammered through the house towards the laundry. The knuckle of fear in Emily's belly unfurled to a full cleaving fist, strangling and wrenching her insides with icy cold brutality. Wendy's face lit up with a malevolent smile and Emily was struck dumb when Wendy's eyes started pulsing a blood red as she brandished a pair of scissors from the laundry draw.

"Oh yes, I know exactly what I am going to do now"

Frank came flying into the laundry, almost tumbling down the steps, in his arms the tiny, lifeless body of their daughter Rose. At first Emily just thought it was strange that the blanket was covered in scarlet ribbons until she realized that they were rivers of her babies bright red blood. Then she saw Franks face, pale and locked in broken terror, his mouth gasping for words, bare chest heaving with his pajama pants pulled on. The look on his face told her everything she needed to know about their baby and she howled in her horror. But he never heard her grief, instead he stood face to face with the icy, cold face of Emily's indifference.

"What happened? What have you done to our baby?" he whispered barely recognizing the woman in front of him. Frank stretched out his arms showing Emily the broken and battered body of their baby, her chest sliced like open like a watermelon. His body was trembling violently, and a sheen of cold sweat broke out on his body. His eyes, flooded with tears as his face collapsed in on itself.

"Oh her" Wendy snorted, ignoring Emily's screams from the washing machine.

"She was holding us back babe. Me and you that's all we need"

"Our baby, what have you done to our baby" Frank cried. "I don't understand, what have you done to our baby?"

Wendy stifled a yawn "Well first I broke every bone in her body, like twigs really. Then I wanted to stop her from screaming, so I slit her throat. Her blood was so sweet, so pure like the finest wine. Then I got bored and just mucked around a bit."

Franks face flashed red, he carefully placed the body down on the bench top and charged over where Wendy was standing. Moving with remarkable speed Wendy ducked out of the way at the last moment. Frank hit the cupboard in surprise and started to turn around just as Wendy raked the scissors down his spine with super human strength. Blood splattered over her face, her jaw became disjointed and began to extend in rapture. Emily couldn't believe her eyes as Wendy's body morphed before her eyes.

Dirty Laundry

Her body cracked, snapped and contorted into the form a crippled old hag, her eyes glowed red and her bottom jaw was disjointed with a mix of blood and saliva dripping from gnarled and broken teeth. Grey, brown mottled skin covered her naked body pulsing with its own life. four large teats sagged against her body, nipples the colour of rotten fruit. Clacking her teeth together it smiled with its cracked weathered lips as it glanced at Emily in the washing machine, before shuffling its broken, decrepit body to straddle Frank's prone body, bony little knees sitting out like plucked chicken wings. it unfurled its pointer finger that housed a nail like kitchen knife and drew a long line of red blood down the center of his body.

"I thought it would be more fun if he died thinking you had slaughtered his baby" it wheezed and whistled with a deep husky voice, as it drew intricate patterns into Franks pallid flesh.

"Why? Why are you doing this?" Wailed Emily collapsing against the glass, numb with grief.

"I've been doing this since I climbed from the earths darkness. I wanted to be the protector of families, but the Great Mother shunned me and cast me back into the shadows." It mused. "I've been trapped in that damn machine long enough, that bitch Wendy did it. But I'm not getting trapped in a rubbish dump, oh yes, I can see that coming. I think I will be keeping your body, and your life Emily Parker" It grinned.

"You will go to jail for this!" Emily shouted, thumping against the glass door. It just smiled at her, and shrugged her shoulders, before leaning forward and slurping the blood pooling on Franks body. The sound of police sirens echoed through the house, as the flashing blue and red lights filtered into the basement window.

Frank must have called the police on his way down, Emily thought to herself with satisfaction. The creature didn't appear phased at all, yet slowly start to morph back into Emily's form again as she climbed off Frank's body and slumped her blood splattered body in the corner of the room and appeared to enter a trance, risking a wicked wink at Emily's rage.

The police came into the laundry, guns pointed.

"Jesus fucking Christ" one moaned in disgust taking in the scene around him. He directed one officer to check on Emily's body.

"She's alive, but totally zoned out, and I think we found our murder weapon." He said kicking the scissors away from where Emily sat.

"Looks like another domestic homicide, we will radio it in, we need forensics in here straight away.

"Oh hell, there is a baby here" vomited another officer.

"Cuff her and get her the hell out. I wonder if she even knows what's she's done. Looking like another one of those insanity pleas, she'll be out in a couple of years"

Emily thumped and walloped the inside of the washing machine, leaving a trail of blood on the glass door. But, nobody heard her screams and her tears, she was left all alone to sleep all she wanted.

LEE FRANKLIN

After ten years un the Australian Army, Lee Franklin has been a personal trainer, logistics officer and the mother of three boys. Recently moved from Western Australia to the Yorkshire countryside with her family, and with the full support and belief of her best friend, fan and critic; husband Marcelo, Lee is finally able to focus on her writing exploring across horror, action and speculative fiction genres. This is just the beginning.

More books from 4 Horsemen Publications

Anthologies & Collections

4HP Anthologies
Teen Angst: Mix Vol. 1
Teen Angst: Mix Vol. 2
My Wedding Date
The Offices of Supernatural Being
The Sentient Space

Demonic Anthologies
Demonic Wildlife
Demonic Household
Demonic Carnival
Demonic Classics
Demonic Vacations
Demonic Medicine
Demonic Workplace
& more to follow!

XXX- Holiday Collection
Unwrap Me
Stuffing My Stocking
Put a Little Irish in Me

CRIME, DETECTIVE, AND NOIR

JOE DAVISON
Journey to Hell

MARK ATLEY
Too Late to Say Goodbye
Trouble Weighs a Ton

HORROR, THRILLER, & SUSPENSE

ALAN BERKSHIRE
Jungle

AMANDA BYRD
Trapped

ERIKA LANCE
Jimmy
Illusions of Happiness
No Place for Happiness
I Hunt You

MARIA DeVIVO
Witch of the Black Circle
Witch of the Red Thorn

MARK TARRANT
The Death Riders
Howl of the Windigo
Guts and Garter Belts

LITERARY

CATHLEEN DAVIES
Cheeky, Bloody Articles

DISCOVER MORE AT 4HORSEMENPUBLICATIONS.COM